I0822287

THE LAST KNOWN SURVIVOR

THE LAST KNOWN SURVIVOR

Lou Ann Jasinski Book 1

By

Tanya Goodwin

This is a work of fiction. Names, characters, places, and incidents are the product of the author's imagination. Any resemblance to persons, events, or locales is entirely coincidental.

ISBN-13: 979-8-218-04538-8

Dedication

Because every thirty seconds a person becomes a victim of sex (human) trafficking, I wrote THE LAST KNOWN SURVIVOR to address the physical and psychological, and even death that victims horrendously experience during their captivity. Ninety-nine percent of victims are female, and the average age entering the world of trafficking is fifteen. One in six runaways are ultimately swept into human trafficking.

Most importantly, I dedicate The Last Known Survivor to all the victims of sex trafficking.

The graphic and violent parts of this novel are purely intended to address the reality of the seedy world of sex trafficking.

Secondly, I would like thank Faith Freewoman, my fabulous editor, and Rae Monet, my talented cover artist, A special thanks to Karen Duvall, who provided the cover flat for the print editions of THE LAST KNOWN SURVIVOR.

A final important part of this novel is the character of Dr. Gerald Newell, a gynecologist and the head of a sex trafficking ring. In no way am I disparaging male gynecologists. Gerald Newell is a fictions, and damaged individual. Having the character as a gynecologist only emphasizes that one never knows who is involved in sex trafficking.

If you know of anyone who is being trafficked, or if you are the victim of trafficking, you can call the following:

National Hotline 24/7

1-888-373-7888

Text 233733

Or dial 711 to access hotline

Runaway youth and homeless

1-800-RUNAWAY (786-2929)

Missing Children/Child Pornography

1-800-THE-LOST (843-5678)

Also by Tanya Goodwin

Suspense /Crime Fiction Novels

If Memory Serves- Dr. Tara Ross- Vol 1

The Embalmer- Dr. Tara Ross - Vol 2

Brush With Death- Dr. Tara Ross -Vol 3

Code Pink- Dr. Tara Ross-Vol 4

Cold Case- Dr. Tara Ross-Vol 5

Do Not Disturb

Hidden Obsession

Christmas Novellas

An Evergreen Christmas

An Evergreen Wedding

An Evergreen Baby

An Evergreen Holiday- Boxed Set

The First Star-Dr. Tara Ross Christmas Edition

Snowfall

Contemporary Medical Romance

Roxanne

Fang Hospital- Dr. Gabriella Van Court Book 1

Fang Baby- Dr. Gabriella Van Court Book 2

Fang Vacation- Dr. Gabriela Van Court Book 3

Fang Wedding- Dr. Gabriella Van Court Book 4

ABOUT THE AUTHOR

Tanya Goodwin writes suspense, police procedurals, and crime fiction. Her experiences as a physician are reflected in her characters and in her stories, and her life as a doctor allows her to switch from stethoscope to keyboard. A former New Yorker, she now resides in Florida. Tanya is a member of Sisters in Crime and Mystery Writers of America.

You can reach Tanya Goodwin at:

http://www.tanyagoodwin.com
www.facebook.com/tanyagoodwinauthor
Twitter: @TanyaGoodwinDoc
Instagram tanyagoodwinwrites

1

Dr. Gerald Newell glared at that cretin, Otto, who was lounging back on what remained of Gerald's mother's tattered green sofa. Otto sucked in a last drag of the squat cigarette hanging from his lips and blew the gray smoke in Gerald's face. He then smacked his lips and ground the stub into the sofa's armrest in a perfect line with the four other charred circles. That shitty sofa and Otto deserved each other. He hoped his mother could see it from her grave.

Usually Gerald wanted to throttle the bastard, but he still needed his long list of clients who'd pay handsomely for just the right girls—girls he'd procured—and girls that Otto refused to quit sampling.

But this time Otto and his grimy buddies fucked Joanna to death. Now Gerald had to clean up the mess and find another girl for that mega-millionaire Greek—fast. The Greek was one client Gerald couldn't afford to lose.

"I'm going to give you the opportunity to explain exactly what the hell happened," Gerald demanded.

"She couldn't get up anymore," Otto said with a shrug.

Otto dug his foot into the more-than-spent piles of stained avocado shag. "She looked pretty chipper to me just the other night. A least she was still warm inside."

Gerald ground his teeth.

Otto scooted forward and braced his hands on his wide-spread knees. "Okay, I may have fucked up. Perhaps things got a little out of hand, but I swear...you know... it was just like the usual. Like, when did this happen?" He inhaled through his nose and the sucked-in air whistled past his nostrils.

Gerald shook his head. "When I checked on her last night, her dinner tray was untouched and she was lying in the bed and mumbling. I touched her. She didn't flinch, but she was hot as hell. I rolled her over and took a rectal temperature. Not even a whimper. Registered 105. I started an IV. Took me three four tries–and you know I'm damn good– but her veins were flat. I gave her IV fluids and antibiotics. Then this morning she's dead."

"Fuck! They're gonna kill us."

"Ya think!? You have to quit sampling the merchandise."

"Yeah, I know. Can't help myself. You've done it too."

Newell shrugged. He did Joanna—once.

"We'll have to think of something fast. Perhaps a replacement."

"Not bad. All we have to do is find a five foot six, good tits and ass blonde in three days. Then we'll just make it." Otto stared at Newell. "Got anything like that handy?"

"Not anything I could farm out on short notice. But I have office hours tomorrow. I could scout around."

"Mmm. Not soon enough. We're in emergency mode. Huntin' time. But first we have to dump the dead body."

Gerald hated to admit it, but Otto was right.

2

Lou Ann Jasinski leaned her head back on the chaise lounge and wiggled her hips until she hit that sweet spot, all while balancing her beer bottle. She'd just banked two whole weeks off from her deputy sheriff duties and after last night's domestic call, she deserved a cold one. She'd hauled the SOB to the station, but the bruised and battered woman declined to press charges. It was all a misunderstanding, the woman claimed. She'd started the fight. But of course that SOB didn't have a scratch on him.

Some other deputy would be back there tonight, and Lou Ann prayed a call to the medical examiner wouldn't follow.

She took a long swig of her beer while looking at the yellow-flowered hibiscus standing full and tall against the picket fence that gave her privacy from neighbors—neighbors she had no desire to meet, despite having moved into the Clearwater house with Harry a year ago.

But the calls for him to leave for a case were unpredictable, and she worked rotating shifts, which left precious little time for them to sleep — mostly apart. And then Harry's roving eye proved to be the death knell of their already rocky relationship.

Kids' squeals echoed around the backyard fence. Lou Ann winced. Damn, they were loud. All she wanted to do was to relax on the patio, but raucous children combined with the oppressive Florida summer heat interfered with her plans. Thank God she and Harry never had any kids. They'd discussed it, but tabled it. With their unpredictably intersecting lives, they'd make lousy parents.

Isabelle, her chocolate Dachshund, clipped up next to her. Her tail wag melted Lou Ann's annoyed frown—that and a quick, cool breeze skirting her bare shoulders.

Lou Ann stroked Isabelle's silky, long back and tossed her an air-kiss.

Who needed kids?

Isabelle was the best. She wasn't the standard police canine, but miles better. She was more than brave.

Lou Ann had adopted Isabelle, a victim of animal cruelty. It took time and trust, but Isabelle grew to trust Lou Ann, and Lou Ann needed Isabelle as much as Isabelle needed her. They shared a traumatic past, and that bond deepened their understanding, affection, and loyalty to each other.

Yeah, who needed kids?

Lou Ann had everything she needed—without Harry.

Isabelle tip-toddled over to a bowl of water and eagerly lapped coolness.

Lou Ann grinned. Two best buds sharing a drink!

Her cell rang.

Shit! It was Harry. What the hell did he want now? Her search for tranquility had just gone bust. He knew every one of her triggers, and it pissed her off that he continued to deploy them. Maybe she should let his call go to voice mail. But then again, he resorted to calling her only because she refused to answer his persistent, hot-mess, multiple texts.

"Make it quick, Harry."

"Why haven't you responded to my texts?"

"I'm busy. I can't respond to your texts while I'm on the job. You know that."

That was a half-truth.

Isabelle barked.

"Isabelle riding with you?" Harry goaded her.

Hot air jetted from her nostrils.

"I've had a long night, and it's hot as hell. What is it that you want?"

"I've been looking for my gray NYU sweatshirt, and you must have it, along with my running shoes, electric razor, and my coconut shampoo. When can I come by and pick them up?"

Like never.

He was fucking coco-nuts! It was summer. He didn't need the sweatshirt, yet. And the running shoes were his old, worn ones. And she knew he had two new pairs. The electric shaver crapped out eons ago, and the shampoo bottle had a half inch left, barely enough to cover the bottom.

His texts had nothing to do with these moronic demands.

They were more like: *When can we get together "as friends"? I'll buy. How's the place? I'm always available to help with repairs.*

This from the guy she had to take to the emergency room for the nail-gun incident.

Really?

Lou Ann grimaced. No way was she going to give him the satisfaction of knowing he'd ticked her off from the get-go.

"Fine. I'll gather your belongings."

"Great! I'll stop by tonight and pick them up."

"Harry. Harry!"

Lou Ann shook her cell.

The ass hung up on her!

Grrrr!

Isabelle growled too.

"I knew you would agree."

Lou Ann finished her beer, and Isabelle emptied her water bowl.

"Shall we get this over with?"

Isabelle barked.

Lou Ann swung her legs over the lounge and pushed to her feet while holding the neck of her empty beer bottle.

Harry would use any lousy excuse to wheedle his way back into her life.

Special Agent Harold Boxer—the 007 of her life.

Lou Ann rummaged through the boxes she'd dumped in the spare bedroom. Six months, and she still hadn't fully unpacked.

Isabelle hovered in the doorway. Smart. She'd get lost in the maze of boxes.

Damn! Not an empty one.

She opened a box that contained an assortment of shorts, T-shirts, socks, and a bathing suit. Lou Ann picked up the bathing suit and remembered the day at Clearwater Beach. She hadn't been there since breaking up with Harry. She dropped the suit back into the box. Maybe she'd go again…alone.

Lou Ann had forgotten about most of these items—a hazard of moving.

She tossed the clothes, including the bathing suit, on the vacant side her bed, leaving her with an empty box for Harry's shit.

One less box haunting her house.

Lou Ann headed to the bedroom with Isabelle at her heels.

She wore Harry's sweatshirt almost as much as he did. It was soft and worn, and at better times, it carried his scent.

He hadn't claimed it until now, and truthfully, she didn't want to give it up. But returning it to Harry was one more reason he wouldn't return. Or pester her with phone calls. Or at least one could dream.

Lou Ann reached into the closet, grabbed his sweatshirt, and dropped it in the box.

"Bye-bye."

The next stop was the bathroom.

Lou Ann plunked the dead electric razor and the measly shampoo bottle into the box. The only thing left was Harry's worn pair of running shoes.

Hmm…? Did she toss them in the garbage?

She tackled the garage next.

The heel of the old shoe poked out from deep behind the lawn mower. Lou Ann pulled out the shoe and then unearthed the second one.

Running shoes?

Harry used to use them when cutting the lawn. And he'd abandoned the old, but reliable lawn mower, having moved to an apartment.

Lou Ann picked up the grass-stained "running shoes" and pitched them into the box.

Done.

She closed the box and returned into the house.

Lou Ann didn't seal the cardboard box because she couldn't wait to see the look on Harry's face when he discovered his half-assed belongings.

She carried the box to the front door and left it there.

Isabelle sniffed it and wrinkled her nose. Then she sneezed.

She was not a fan of either the coconut shampoo or the green-stained shoes—or both.

Lou Ann was ready for Harry. A speedy hand-off was the best approach. Then she and Isabelle could claim what remained of the evening.

Maybe they'd watch a movie before dozing off.

Isabelle and Lou Ann cuddled on the couch. It was just like Harry to show up on his own time. More buttons he loved to push.

Isabelle stood guard at the window while Lou Ann stretched out on the couch.

She blinked a few times before closing her eyes. The beer and the heat had made her sleepy.

Isabelle's barking roused her.

And then the doorbell rang.

Shit! Harry and his notoriously bad timing.

He hadn't changed.

She was type A, and he was type B at home and type A-minus at work, and type P for prowl, elsewhere.

Lou Ann got off the couch and took a deep breath.

This would be a sheriff versus an FBI agent, and worse, ex-lover versus ex-lover standoff.

Facing Harry wasn't what she'd planned…ever.

But avoiding him only complicated matters.

She'd stand her ground.

Unfortunately, standing ground was Harry's forte.

But she had the home advantage. This *was* her house now, and not his.

Harry leaned on the doorbell.

Lou Ann winced.

"Coming," she yelled.

Buttons.

Isabelle growled and barked her impatience, too.

"Okay. Let's not overdo it," Lou Ann told her dog.

Isabelle frowned but quieted.

Lou Ann balanced the box on her hip and grabbed the front door handle.

One. Two. Three.

She opened the door and shoved the box against Harry's abs.

They were still rock hard.

"Here!"

Then she slammed the door, right on his foot that he'd wedged in the doorway.

"Ow! Shit! Dammit you broke my ankle!"

"Fuck!"

Lou Ann swung the door wide open.

Harry grimaced while hopping around on one foot.

He'd dropped the box, scattering the contents.

"Oh, my God! I didn't mean to do it, but you stuck your foot right there."

Lou Ann wrapped her arm around Harry's waist, supporting and steadying him.

"I've got you."

Harry hobbled inside, and Lou Ann kicked the door shut.

"I'll get ice."

She set him on the couch and ran into the kitchen.

Lou Ann filled a plastic bag full of ice, grabbed a dish towel, and rushed to the living room to treat Harry's injured ankle…only to smack right into him.

What the hell?

"It's a bit sore, but it's feeling much better."

He was bearing full weight, and his ankle wasn't even swollen!

Lou Ann tossed the bag of ice into the sink and then walloped his arm with the dish towel.

"Hey! You're the one who slammed my foot in the door."

"Exactly where it didn't belong. So now that you're miraculously healed, gather your stuff, and get going."

"Is that any way to act after you shut the door on my foot and then towel-whipped me?"

"Hmmm? Yes."

"I'm trying to be decent with you," Harry said.

"A little late."

"I've told you, Lou Ann, nothing happened."

"It was more complicated than that. Harry, we're just not meant to be."

Harry stared at her with sad, puppy-dog eyes. Which used to work. Although, she was being a bit hard on him.

Then he shrugged.

Damn buttons!

Harry opened the fridge and pulled out a bottle of water.

Make yourself at home, why don't you?

"Harry."

"It's a scorcher. I'd appreciate a cold drink…for the road." He raised his brows and the water bottle. "May I?"

"Sure."

Anything to get him to move on. Preferably right now.

Isabelle toddled into the kitchen to inspect what was happening.

Harry bent over to pet her.

"Hey there, Isabelle."

Isabelle backed up two steps, but allowed Harry to touch her.

"Miss you," he cooed.

Isabelle returned a half-hearted tail wag and pattered away.

Loyalty!

"Well, I'll be on my way."

"Okay."

Harry headed to the front door, adding an ostentatious hobble for good measure.

Lou Ann opened the door.

The cardboard box lay upended on the concrete stoop. The sweatshirt clung to the edge, the dead razor had landed in the grass, and the shampoo bottle had rolled to the end of the driveway. The grass-stained shoes were the only items that must have stayed in the box.

Harry limped while gathering the items.

Oh, please!

Lou Ann walked to the end of the driveway and retrieved the near-empty shampoo bottle, walked up to Harry, and plunked the shampoo into the box.

"Thanks, and thanks for the cold water."

"Don't mention it."

"Take care."

Ooh, heart-string button.

"You too," Lou Ann replied.

She waved to him, smiling, then retreated into the house, and once again closed the door on her and Harry.

3

Kaylee smiled wide and bobbed her head while listening to her playlist. She glanced out her back seat window at the long-legged egrets along South Florida's Tamiami Trail's swampy roadside who appeared to march to the beat blasting through her earbuds.

Despite having her parents in tow, this Florida college road trip was better than she expected. But it was time to go home to Miami and wait for the acceptance letters. Although USF in Tampa was a good school, Gainesville's UF was her first choice, and the university tour nailed her decision. She had the grades, SAT score, and party spirit required for admission to UF in the fall.

Kaylee had finished listening to one of her many playlists when dark gray clouds rudely displaced the blue sky they left behind in Tampa four hours ago.

The less-traveled and often two-lane roadway that ran parallel to the heavier traffic of Alligator Alley soon became a dark cave, although they were better off here during the daily Florida summer thunderstorms rather than being stuck in traffic on Alligator Alley. And they probably would get home sooner.

A jagged lightning bolt lit up the car.

Oh, shit! That was a big one.

The accompanied thunderclap shook the car, and a brigade of raindrops assaulted the windshield leaving the windshield wipers helpless.

Kaylee pulled out her earbuds.

This was bad!

"Pull over, Lyle!" Kaylee's mother cried.

She had to agree with her mom.

"Melinda, just sit back. It's going to pass."

"You have the wipers on high, and I can't even see the road. Pull over, now!"

Dad slowed the car.

The next bolt crackled a warning.

Kaylee could see her dad's eyes in the rearview mirror, and right now they were huge.

"Dad, let's stop."

The storm and her and her mother's pleas outnumbered Lyle. He relented and pulled the car to the side of the road.

The rapid-fire of rain on the rooftop fed the waterfall cascading over the windshield.

The wipers went silent.

Kaylee watched Dad engage the emergency flashers.

She and her parents slouched in their seats, glad to be sheltered from the downpour.

Kaylee noted the time displayed on her cell.

This deluge could keep them stranded.

She sighed and lolled her head against the headrest. There was nothing to do but to wait it out.

Her mom sat up and turned toward the back seat.

"What did you think of Tampa?" she asked Kaylee.

"It was nice, but I really want to go to Gainesville."

"Wise choice," Lyle said.

"I liked the Tampa campus," Melinda said.

"So did I, but I've pretty much made up my mind."

"Tampa's not for her," Lyle insisted.

"I think she should weigh all her options."

"We visited all the Florida schools just to be complete. And now Kaylee's made her decision."

"To be fair, we rushed through the Tampa campus."

Dad shot Mom an exasperated look.

"You shouldn't let *things* color *your* judgement. Tampa is not Clearwater."

"Close enough. I acquiesced to the visit to Tampa because it was on the list."

"Acquiesced? USF was on Kaylee's list."

"Stop it, you guys!"

Kaylee knew about her aunt in Clearwater, who she couldn't probably pick out of a lineup. Mom once told her that her dad's sister was a sheriff, which was pretty cool. But Dad and his sister hadn't talked in years.

Kaylee was an only child, but if she had a sister, she would never allow so much time to elapse between visits or allow some stupid argument to fester.

She hadn't mentioned it to her parents, but she'd hoped to wander off and call her aunt, just to say hello. Kaylee had scored her aunt's cell number from a shoebox stashed in Mom and Dad's bedroom closet. She'd gone in there innocently to retrieve some family photos and mistakenly opened a box that contained no photos, but only slips of receipts. A folded piece of lined paper caught her eye, and when she opened it, she saw Lou Ann Jasinski's name written in faded blue ink with a cell phone number scrawled beneath it.

Kaylee took the note and hid it in her nightstand. Dad would never miss it. But every time Kaylee thought about calling the number while she was in Tampa—fantasizing that she could finally meet the aunt she'd last seen as a toddler—Dad approached, nixing her urge to call. Maybe her aunt Lou Ann didn't want anything to do with her. Or maybe she didn't have that same cell number anymore. It was Kaylee's mother who revealed that Aunt Lou Ann was now living in Clearwater, Florida, a stone's throw from Tampa. Perhaps she should reconsider Tampa.

The rain splattered to a manageable drip.

"See? It passed," Lyle said.

It was just like Dad to declare himself winner of any argument. What really went on between him and Aunt Lou Ann?

"Pulling over was the right thing to do," her mom countered.

Dad grunted loud enough for Kaylee and her mom to hear, turned off the flashers, and maneuvered the car back onto the shiny road.

The wet tires' squeal faded and the treads hissed while spewing road grime.

Kaylee stuck her earbuds back in and began another playlist, ignoring her dad's need to be in the right. Thank God she'd be finished with this playlist by the time they were home.

She couldn't wait to call her best friend, Shawna, and tell her all about the college road trip…in private.

The red taillights of the eighteen-wheeler ahead of them blurred closer and closer.

Dad slowed, tailgating the truck.

Good thing Mom taught Kaylee to drive, because Dad had no

patience on the road.

Her dad skirted into the left lane and gunned it to overtake the truck.

Mom dug her fingers into the dashboard.

Kaylee shook her head.

He's fucking crazy.

The loud honk blasted past Kaylee's music.

"Shit!" Mom screamed.

Dad swerved back into the right lane, just missing the oncoming truck.

The car hydroplaned and then spun 360 degrees. The steering wheel spun in Dad's hands while he frantically tried to regain control of the fishtailing car. Kaylee's head jerked back and forth and her earbuds fell out of her ears and her cell flew out of her hands.

And then she bounced along with her parents when the car careened farther down the swampy embankment. She smacked her head against the roof of the car while it plummeted into a death drop while tall blades of swamp grass obscured the windshield.

The seat belt squeezed her hips and she lurched forward and then the car crashed into something. Metal ground in her ears and the deployed air bags popped, pushing her against the back seat, and obscuring her view of her parents.

There was a delay before burning pain hit her face and then her knees popped. Kaylee swallowed the tinny blood rushing out of her nose and into her mouth, and her throbbing head convinced her that she was alive…for the moment.

No sounds came from her mom and dad.

She had to get to them. To call for help.

Kaylee wedged her hand down to her hip and released her seat belt buckle.

Her cell had to be somewhere. It probably fell under either her mom or her dad's seat.

Surely the trucker witnessed what happened and would call for help. They were in the middle of a long stretch, and emergency vehicles would take time to arrive. Time her parents didn't have.

Kaylee opened the back car door and the weight of the hanging door caused the car to slide, half hood first, into the green water, coming to rest at a teetering 90-degrees angle.

"Mom! Dad! Please wake up!"

Her pleas went unanswered.

Kaylee screamed at them again.

No reaction.

Her cell tumbled out from under her dad's seat, and Kaylee reached for it as far as her arm stretched, and she wiggled her fingers. This was doable. She'd call for help.

"Yes! Come. Come."

She coaxed the cell into her palm and tapped 911 with her thumb, but before her distress call was answered, swamp water rushed into the car displacing Kaylee and her cell.

"No! No!"

Hot tears ran down her cheeks.

The car lurched farther into the water.

Her distress call would be tracked. All she had to do was to stay with her parents. Surely they'd be rescued soon.

The car groaned and sank deeper into the water.

Kaylee gripped the seat belt but her hands slid across the soaked belt. She grasped the end buckle in a last attempt to hang on, but the metal anchor failed to stop her and she fell sideways into the water, submerged.

Kaylee opened her eyes under water, but only murky brown surrounded her.

She scissored her legs, failing to gain traction against the slimy rocks and sand under her feet. Kaylee curled into a ball and then thrust her legs out. That worked. She burst out of the dark green swamp dripping nasty water and worse, coughing up the putrid scum, But she was now standing only waist deep.

She needed to get out. Kaylee limped, favoring her right foot, her left ankle too painful for her to distribute her weight evenly.

Her cell was somewhere in this marsh pit. Her phone was supposed to be water-resistant, at least for the next thirty minutes. If only she could find it to make sure help was on the way, to communicate what had happened to them and get her parents to a hospital. Forget about her. She was going to be all right.

Kaylee tested her left ankle while balancing on her right foot. She winced at the twinge that zapped up from her left ankle, but she could move it so it wasn't broken. It must be a bad sprain, she thought. But she could work with it. She had no choice. She had to.

She hobbled in the water in tighter and tighter circles while tapping around for her cell, but it was a bust. By now the cell was probably waterlogged and useless anyway. She was wasting precious time.

She had to get to the roadside so she could flag down the emergency vehicles.

Kaylee floated on her belly and paddled her arms, snagging swamp weed to pull herself toward the shoreline. But some of the blades ripped away, leaving her with fistfuls of green.

She tried again, and this time grabbed onto bigger handfuls of swamp weeds to pull her up out of the water...only to slide down the slick, muddy bank and back into the water.

Two egrets stood by watching her intently as if they wanted to help her but couldn't. They croaked and squealed, as if cheering her on.

Kaylee clutched one sturdy plant and crawled out of the water, flopping onto the bank, and just lay there briefly until she could catch her breath.

She struggled to her hands and knees, determined to reach the road. But her soaked sneakers failed to gain traction along the slippery bank and she flopped face-first into the mud.

She got up and pressed on, again and again, sliding down the embankment only to get back up, even more determined.

Finally she slid up on her belly and pushed upright with her hands. Her left ankle throbbed. Drenched from head to toe in swamp water, she still managed to push up into the ditch on all fours.

Victorious, the first thing she did was look back to check on her parents.

But Mom and Dad remained lifeless and the windshield had huge spider cracks in it.

"Hold on! Please don't die! Help is on the way!" Kaylee yelled at them, her voice cracking.

But Mom and Dad lay limp and silent.

She estimated that the roadside was about twenty-five feet away.

Kaylee stood up with her weight on her right foot and looked down the deserted stretch of road, still shiny long after the rain had stopped.

She squinted, praying for flashing red lights. But there weren't any.

In the meantime, her head throbbed and her waterlogged ears crackled, especially when she moved her head.

She tried tilting her head from side to side, shaking it, and even pulling on her earlobes, but nothing she did dislodged the water.

She listened for sirens, but all she heard was her own breath echoing in her stuffed ears.

Help had to be on the way. She had dialed 911 before the swamp grabbed her cell so they could track it...track her...and most important, bring help for her parents.

She looked up and down the road. No ambulance. Not even a truck or passing car. *Shit!* What were the odds?

How much longer?

Gerald Newell suppressed a cough. Even with the car windows open Ottos's nauseating stogie still blew smoke in his face.

Gerald could only hope they would be able to dump Joanna's body deep in the swamp soon. Then all he needed to do was tolerate Otto's stifling smoke until they were back at the house, and where he could get his Benz and blessedly make his way back to his Miami condo. He had office hours early in the morning, and on top of that he had to zero in on at least two more candidates to make it worth his while.

He'd helped Otto stuff Joanna's body into the trunk, but that was as far as he was willing to go.

Gerald's stomach heaved while he thought about Joanna and his part in her gross death. He'd never meant for any of it to happen.

Yeah, he broke his own rules. He genuinely liked Joanna. Tried like hell to save her.

He'd originally made her acquaintance at a coffee shop. She was his waitress, sixteen, and barely old enough to work.

She'd left home, accusing her mother of not caring one iota about her, and according to Joanna, her mother constantly harassed her about being lazy and no good.

Joanna dropped out of high school and then left her small town in search of a job, money, and a new start, leaving her mother blessedly behind in a poverty-stricken hellhole. She'd even broken up with her abusive boyfriend.

But her new start didn't include any friends. The other coffee shop waitresses were older and according to Joanna, jealous of her youth and the customers' attention. She couldn't help it that every guy plunked down at her station. Joanna was also a loner and her circumstances checked every single box on Gerald's list. No one would miss her.

But he could offer her the life she craved. Money. Clothes. A rich man's undivided attention. He had her best interests in mind.

He pushed Otto to market Joanna to a lonely Greek tycoon. Plus, it would be a dream come true for Joanna, far better for her than that shitty diner job.

The Greek offered two million dollars, *to start.* If he found Joanna suitable, he promised a bonus.

In accordance with their contract the tycoon would care for her exclusively. Buy her everything she needed or could dream of. She could move about, of course only when he accompanied her. It was a for her safety the Greek insisted. Plus he had a courtyard where she could sun herself. Gerald had seen the photos. Lovely. It was a small trade-off.

Sure, she couldn't leave until he gave her permission. The men agreed to find a suitable replacement should that be the case. But Gerald was ninety-nine percent positive that the Greek would keep her long-term. Who knew? Perhaps they'd send another girl in time to give Joanna a well-deserved rest.

Gerald had done this all for her benefit.

It was Otto who screwed up, who wasn't satisfied until he broke her. To make sure she knew there was no way out. He even invited others come and do the same—for a price, paid to Otto, of course.

But Gerald could have brokered the whole deal without harming Joanna. Fuck Otto! She would have had a decent life. Now she was dead.

Gerald shook his head.

"What's up with you?" Otto asked.

"Nothing."

"Don't be so fucking glum. She was just another cunt. Don't worry. We'll get a nice blonde, and our Greek man won't know the difference. They all just want pussy anyway."

Kaylee swayed. She stumbled, then jerked upright. She needed to stay strong for her parents. She estimated that thirty minutes had passed, but she could be wrong. Why would an ambulance take that long? No, she had to be wrong. The Tamiami Trail wasn't in the middle of nowhere. It was Sunday, plus the rain must have kept most people off the road. Except for that trucker. Why didn't he stop to help? Was he pissed off because Dad gunned it to pass another of his own? That was no excuse. Maybe he didn't bother to call for help. She gave him the benefit of the doubt that he didn't see they'd crashed. But her 911 had to have hit.

Kaylee looked back at the crunched car that held her parents hostage.

Damn her selfish playlists! She hadn't paid attention to anything they passed on the roadside. Maybe there was a gas station, or one of those tourist stands offering airboat jaunts across the Everglades. Rain never stopped persistent tourists. Somebody running those rides was probably still there.

Yes! She'd backtrack down the road. She figured they were closer to Naples since she'd only gone through one playlist, and if she was moving toward Naples, a Collier County ambulance would be sure to see her, and she'd direct them to Mom and Dad.

She'd hobbled a few painful paces and halted, listening to a distant whir coming closer.

Kaylee turned around and squinted.

A car! A car! Her ears were right.

Kaylee waved her arms to flag down the oncoming car.

The black sedan slowed.

Thank God the driver saw her!

Otto tapped the steering wheel and grinned. "Look at that blonde, all alone. How lucky are we?"

Gerald squinted. "She's injured."

"So?" Otto sneered. "That's never stopped me before."

Gerald's stomach roiled at Otto's disgustingly candid statement.

"She needs our help," Gerald said.

"She sure does." Otto licked his lip.

If Otto hadn't previously given him generous cuts, Gerald would've popped him right in the head. He deserved to see stars. No. More like the whole fucking constellation.

Otto slowed the vehicle. Then he hit a pothole, and Joanna's body jostled in the trunk.

"So sorry about that, babe" Otto mocked dead Joanna.

He should've wrapped her tighter, Gerald thought. She at least earned that much dignity. It shouldn't have ended this way. But it was too late to change that now.

Otto shifted the car into park and Gerald climbed out.

"Hey! Hey!" Kaylee screamed. She pointed to the crumpled car sunk half into the swamp. "My parents! You have to help them. Please!"

Gerald rushed to her.

"It's all right. I'm a doctor. You're limping, and it looks like you have a heck of a sprained ankle."

"I'm okay. I need you to help my parents. My cell's gone, but I managed to tap in 911 before my phone sank into the swamp. I'm sure the ambulance will be here soon but meanwhile I need your help."

"Come on. I have a towel in the back seat. You're soaking wet, you have a sprained ankle, and you're shivering, no doubt because of what you've been through."

Gerald led Kaylee to the back seat of the car. He set her there and wrapped a towel around her, leaving the car door open to gain her confidence.

"You stay here. I'm going down to help your parents."

"Thank you, Dr…"

"Dr. Newell. And you're welcome. You'll be safer here."

"I'll keep an eye on the poor girl," Otto said.

Gerald tossed Otto a "don't you dare touch her" glare.

Kaylee strained upright in the back seat to follow Gerald's descent to the crashed vehicle.

"Lie back down and rest. Let the doctor do his thing," Otto said.

Kaylee tossed off the towel and reached for the door handle. "I'm going down there."

"No!"

Kaylee pulled away from Otto. His brusqe voice sent shivers down her spine. There was something wrong about him.

The back doors clicked on both sides.

He'd trapped her.

"Unlock this door, now!"

Kaylee banged on the window.

"Dr. Newell! Dr. Newell!"

"It's for your well-being. I couldn't let you go down there with your injury. You'll make it worse. All we can do is wait."

Despite his changed tone, she still didn't trust him.

When was Dr. Newell coming back? And more urgently, would he able to get her parents out and tend to them?

Kaylee jerked the door handle.

"Let go of the door handle…please."

Kaylee stared at Otto's eyes in the rearview mirror. His eyelids relaxed. She'd misjudged him.

Otto released the locks.

"I don't recommend it, but you can go."

Kaylee leaned forward, but the shot of electric pain from her ankle threw her back.

Otto cocked his head.

Kaylee drew a deep breath, readying for a second attempt. Dr.

Newell left a long time ago. What was going on? Was he rescuing her parents? Doing lifesaving CPR until the ambulance reached them? Had to be. She needed to help.

Kaylee grabbed the door handle and winced. She refused to allow the pain to keep her from helping her mom and dad.

She creaked open the door to find Dr. Newell on the other side.

Kaylee looked into his intense eyes.

Dr. Newell shook his head.

"No! No!" Kaylee screamed. "Let me out! Let me go to them!"

"I did what I could."

"No you didn't! The ambulance will be here any minute!"

Otto turned around to face the back seat and nodded.

Dr. Newell pushed her down on her back.

Kaylee kicked with her good foot and it landed with a direct hit to Dr. Newell's nose. He jerked and reared back, but still blocked her way out.

"Shit!" the doctor yelled, nasal from her smack. "Get the syringe out of my bag, now!"

Otto shot the pre-filled syringe to Newell. Newell grabbed it and popped the cap off with his teeth while pinning Kaylee.

"Get away from me!"

The needle torpedoed toward Kaylee and darted into her arm. The sting faded, and so did her vision. Newell's face blurred until it disappeared. Her head slumped back and her arms and legs went limp, leaving her completely vulnerable. Then everything went black.

4

"She's out," Gerald said.

"Good. We need to hurry."

Otto popped the trunk. "Let's take care of Joanna before anyone comes."

"Right."

Gerald and Otto exited the car.

"You sure she's out?" Otto asked.

"At least for an hour. I'll need to monitor her on the way back."

"We need to strip off the girl's clothes and put them on the dead one. We can't dump a naked body."

Gerald stomped his foot. He hadn't thought of that. But still, Kaylee appeared by happenstance on their way to rid themselves of Joanna. Funny how life and death could upend your plans.

Otto rounded the car while Gerald remained outside next to the open back seat door and at Kaylee's feet. He rubbed his nose. The girl could land one hell of a punch. That could be a problem.

Otto leaned into the back seat. "I'll get her arms. You get her feet."

Gerald and Otto stripped Kaylee.

"Man, she really is down for the count," Otto said.

Gerald wrapped a towel around her.

Then he and Otto rushed to the trunk to get Joanna.

Gerald squinted. Joanna was past the rigor mortis stage.

"She's fuckin' heavy," Otto said.

"Just get the bra on her. I'll pull her up so you can snap it."

Otto laughed. "I've perfected that move."

"Just do it."

As soon as Otto finished, Gerald released Joanna, and she flopped onto her back. He managed to get her feet through Kaylee's panties and pulled them up to Joanna's waist.

"There's a reverse move," Otto quipped.

Otto made Gerald's hands feel even dirtier.

Together they finished dressing Joanna in Kaylee's clothes.

Gerald slung Joanna over his shoulder. He glanced down the road in both directions. No sirens. No flashing lights.

He slid down the muddy bank and landed on his back. Joanna fell off his shoulder and rolled down the swampy, brush-covered hill.

"Shit!"

Joanna crashed onto the car's bumper, and the car lurched forward.

"Stop it," Gerald commanded the crashed vehicle.

As if the crunched car could comply.

But the vehicle seesawed to a halt.

Turned out Joanna did him a favor. The car's new position made it much easier to shove her in the back seat. Where the car ended up after that wasn't his concern. All the occupants were dead anyway. Nothing he could do about that.

Gerald slogged up the slippery bank.

Sirens got closer.

"Fuck! Get in the car," Otto yelled.

Otto started the car.

Muddied, Gerald jumped into the passenger seat.

Otto made a U-turn onto the road, away from the sirens.

Gerald looked back. The red strobes were getting clearer.

This had to work. Kaylee and Joanna looked pretty much alike. The Greek would never know the difference, Gerald convinced himself.

Then he leaned back in the seat.

"Over there!" An EMT pointed.

His colleague pulled to the roadside, directly above the crashed car.

"Shit! They hit the tree."

"By the looks of the skid marks and the mud tracks, the driver must have lost control of the vehicle. Not hard to do with these wet roads. Every rig's been busy today. Grab the bag and let's get down there."

The EMTs rushed out of the rig, leaving the red flashing lights engaged.

They sidestepped into the slippery bank, land-surfing down to the wreck.

"Hey! Rescue's here. Can you hear me?" the EMT called.

No response.

"Ambulance!" the EMT yelled louder. "Anyone hurt?"

No response.

One EMT looked in the vehicle.

"We've got three people down and unresponsive. Male driver. Female in the passenger seat and one in the back seat."

"Here comes another rig. We'll need the help."

"Sir? Sir? Are you hurt?" The EMT called louder.

"Nothing," he said to his partner.

"Miss? Ma'am?"

"Hey! Female in the back seat moved her leg."

The EMT leaned into the back seat to check it out.

"Miss! Miss!"

"She's moving her finger. Let's get her out. Any response from the victims in front?"

"No. They're gone. Neither has a pulse or respiratory effort. I'm ninety-nine percent sure neither is revivable, but the young female has a chance."

"Pull all of them out before the car goes under. I'll pull out the young female in the back while you get the two out of the front."

"I've got the male and female in the front."

Another responder slid towards them.

"We're the only other rig available."

"Assess the two victims in front. We'll work on the female from the back seat."

"Got her," the EMT said. "Oh my God. She's just a teenager."

Another EMT returned with a backboard and the EMT slid the girl onto the board.

"I feel a faint carotid pulse. Beginning CPR!" The one at the girl's head squeezed oxygen into her lungs with a bag valve mask.

One applied the pads from the AED, automated external defibrillator, to the girl's chest in between CPR attempts.

"Stand back. Analyzing rhythm," the AED computerized voice called. "Sinus bradycardia. Resume CPR."

The EMTs continued CPR and paused again for an AED assessment.

"Look! Spontaneous respirations!"

"Sinus rhythm. A beautiful thing! Let's get her transported."

The EMT looked at the ones tending to the front seat victims. They shook their heads.

"No rhythm. They're clinically dead," the EMT said. "We'll

transport them to the hospital where they can be officially pronounced dead. At least it looks like the girl is gonna make it."

5

Kaylee blinked rapidly and strained her eyelids half open. A stark white ceiling stared back at her. She gripped her head trying to counteract the relentless jackhammer pounding, which was when she saw a clear plastic tube stuck into her right hand that snacked up to a fluid-filled bag.

Where the hell was she? How did she get here?

Kaylee patted her chest and looked down to discover her clothes had been replaced with a hospital gown. She was at some hospital.

Kaylee bolted upright.

"Mom! Dad!"

They must have brought her parents here too. She had to find them.

She swung her legs over the side of the bed and saw they'd bandaged her left ankle.

The IV on her right hand tugged her backwards, tethering her to the bed.

She grabbed the IV bag, and eased down to stand on the cold tile floor.

Kaylee staggered in a haze to the closed door and blindly patted around for a doorknob. And when she finally found the knob and tried to open the door, it didn't budge. It was locked from the outside. *What the hell kind of hospital IS this?*

She swayed, but still managed to slam her fist against the door.

"Nurse! Nurse! I need help. Please."

Her breathing echoed in her ears. She waited, listening for voices or footsteps. But no one came.

The room swirled around her at weird, contorted angles. But her fight to steady herself failed, and Kaylee collapsed to the cold, hard floor.

The IV bag sloshed next to her.

Something in that IV had to be making her woozy.

Kaylee grabbed the tubing and yanked the IV out of her hand.

Warm blood dripped from the punctured site.

She instinctively put pressure on it with her other hand.

Blood oozed between her fingers. She pressed harder.

While Kaylee lay on her back maintaining pressure on the bleeding site, her vision slowly improved and room stopped spinning.

Yes, her suspicions were correct. They'd put something in her IV. But why? Maybe it was pain medicine for her ankle. But she didn't need it, and she'd tell that to a nurse or doctor, or whoever showed up.

She couldn't possibly be here alone. Maybe the nurses were just too busy right now, but someone had to get to her eventually. Of course they'd be pissed off about what she did to her IV, but she felt clearer already.

Kaylee stuck out her elbow and used it to prop herself upright.

This was a weird room. Aside from the locked door, her quarters consisted of a hospital bed and an open bathroom.

Kaylee hobbled to the bathroom. There was only a toilet and a sink. And a grimy shower. No mirror. A stack of brown paper towels was set on the side of the sink. No dispenser. A square of toilet paper hung from a skinny cardboard roll that wouldn't get her through the day. A black toilet seat sat on old porcelain. There was no toilet lid and no recognizable tank.

She glanced into the bowl. *Yuuuuk!*A fuzzy black ring surrounded the yellowed water.

The IV fluid must have filled her bladder, but she'd hold it as long she could until she could request another room. How old was this place?

Kaylee limped back into the bed.

Her IV site had stopped bleeding.

She lay back on the pillow. At least the sheets were clean.

Kaylee stared at the four stark walls surrounding her. No windows. She was boxed in. If she only had her cell phone. But it was at the bottom of the Everglades.

Plus now she had to pee—badly.

Kaylee sighed and tapped her foot against the sheets.

She had no choice. She had to use the toilet.

Back up again. At least she didn't have an IV to contend with this time.

She swung her legs over the bed and launched upright. The dizziness was gone.

She made her way to the bathroom while trying to put more weight on her injured ankle. The sooner she could get around, the sooner she could get out of this place. She'd search for Mom and Dad. They might be at another hospital. One better than this hellhole. Someone had to know something.

Kaylee positioned herself over the toilet without sitting on it and winced.

Here goes.

Her injured ankle gave way and Kaylee landed smack on that nasty seat.

She let her bladder loose and the stream of urine continued for a good thirty seconds.

She sighed with relief and then looked at the sparse toilet paper roll.

She'd use as little as possible. Who knew when housekeeping—or more likely the Hazmat team—would arrive? This bathroom was definitely a crime scene.

Kaylee neatly folded two squares of tissue and used both sides, then grabbed the sink to help her stand, and flushed.

Shit. No soap. Why wasn't she surprised?

Kaylee ran her hands under the water and rubbed them together.

She studied the stack of paper towels and decided against that venture, drying her hands on her hospital gown instead.

Then she hobbled back to the bed and collapsed onto it.

She wasn't ever going to get out of here without some assistance, and she had no idea who might be willing to help her.

The toilet flush and water running in the sink echoed into the kitchen.

Otto set his coffee cup on the table.

"Sounds like your patient is up."

"Sounds like it," Gerald answered.

He'd finished his coffee and his inane conversation with Otto.

Gerald pushed back his chair. "I'll go check on her and get her tucked in for the evening since I have office hours tomorrow and have to get back." He pointed at Otto. "You are not to disturb her."

Otto raised his right hand. "Scout's honor, Doctor," he mocked.

Gerald shook his head.

He was in charge of medically clearing the girls before they were ready for market. Joanna was a causality, and he'd make damn sure Kaylee was not.

As morbid as the thought was, Kaylee's parents were dead and she was alone, just like Joanna was. That was to his advantage, and ultimately to hers. A mega-millionaire Greek awaited her. Although thanks to Joanna's untimely demise, there was little time to spare in preparing his new candidate.

Gerald stopped in the hallway and peeked behind him to make sure Otto wasn't within ear's reach. Kaylee was an intelligent young woman and would quickly figure out that she was not in a bona fide hospital, and therefore she required sedation and its consequent amnesia. That's why he needed to enlist Margo. They were already behind schedule.

Gerald tapped Margo's contact number into his cell. She answered on the second ring.

"What's Otto done, now?" Margo asked.

"Besides killing Joanna, nothing yet, and that's how I want to keep it with this next one. Name's Kaylee. Found her at a roadside accident. She's the spitting image of Joanna. It's like looking at a ghost. But we have to work together now."

"Agreed. You want me to do the nurse thing again?"

"Yeah."

"All right. I must admit I'm getting good at this. When do you want me?"

"I'll tuck her in tonight, feed her, and keep her IV happy. You can come at 7 am for your *shift*, and I'll send you a hefty reward to your bank, plus given the late notice, I'll throw in a bonus."

"As long as I'm not cut out of the final payment upon goods delivered, okay. I don't advise for you or that asshole to fuck me over. I've been doing this longer and have connections—connections here and abroad."

"Have I ever crossed you?"

"No. But Otto's a bottom feeder."

"We need him for a while longer."

"He has a stamped expiration date."

"Yes, that's long been the agreement."

"I guarantee you'll thoroughly enjoy your practice in Greece. The final plans are in the works."

"Looking forward to the change."

"See you in the morning, Nurse Margo," Gerald chuckled.

"Seven am sharp, Doctor."

Gerald tucked his cell into his back pocket. He'd have to stop into the kitchen to get a dinner tray for Kaylee.

Shit! Otto wasn't in the kitchen. Where did that squat little fuck go?

The only other key to the room hung on the key rack.

Gerald sighed with relief. He took the key and pocketed it as his insurance policy.

Otto must be in the office, no doubt on the computer wrangling future promises. They were in a competitive field.

Gerald needed to restore Kaylee to top form, and fast.

Gerald reached into the freezer, pulled out a frozen meal, and tossed it into the microwave.

When the microwave beeped, he took the meal out and stuck in a potato.

Kaylee required calories to heal.

Next he prepared a chocolate protein shake and stirred in crushed Valium. She wouldn't detect it over the deep chocolate flavor, and it would put her out until Margo arrived in the morning.

He arranged the heated meal, the baked potato, and the chocolate shake on a tray and headed to the room.

Balancing the tray in one hand, he reached into his back pocket with the other hand for one of the keys.

Gerald stuck the key into the knob and unlocked the door.

He gasped when he entered the room.

He nearly stepped into a congealed pool of blood on the floor.

Kaylee sat on the bed, staring at Gerald.

"What happened here?" he asked, fighting to stay calm. The last thing he needed was an altercation with Kaylee. That served neither of their purposes.

She was angry…and frightened.

He didn't blame her.

"Oh, my. Your IV came out. No problem. We can fix that."

Without blinking, Kaylee retorted, "No."

Gerald calmly set the dinner tray on the nightstand.

Kaylee squinted and paused.

"Dr. Newell?"

"Yes, dear. You remember me."

"Where are my parents? Where did they take them?!"

Kaylee didn't remember when he returned to the car with the

unfortunate news.

"What hospital am I at?" she demanded.

Gerald sat at the end of the bed and placed his hand over Kaylee's.

"You and your parents were in a terrible car accident."

Gerald pressed one finger against Kaylee's bounding radial pulse. He patted her hand.

"You're at Miami General Hospital."

He'd used the fake name so many times that he sometimes forgot that it didn't exist.

"It doesn't seem like a hospital. Where are the nurses? Why hasn't anyone come? I called out. No one came. That's not right. And where are the other patients?" Kaylee flicked Gerald's hand away. "And you haven't answered me. Where are my parents? I'm here, so they have to be here somewhere too."

Confusion spun in her eyes. Memories must have gripped her.

Kaylee's lower lip fattened and trembled. Tears flooded from her eyes and streaked down her cheeks.

"I'm so sorry," Gerald said softly.

"I want to go home," Kaylee gulped.

"Soon," Gerald lied.

He guided Kaylee back up onto the bed.

"Let's fix you up."

6

Kaylee smacked her lips and winced.

She must have passed out after dinner, desperately needing the sleep.There was no window for the sun to rouse her, but her body clock was foolproof. Up at 6:30 am to shower, dress, and have breakfast before her best friend Shawna pulled in the driveway to drive them to school. They'd bob to the music all the way to what remained of their senior year.

Kaylee burrowed her face into the pillow, her shoulders shaking while she sobbed.

But crying only made her headache worse.

Kaylee turned her head and swiped the heel of her hand across her wet cheek and hugged her knees, trying to rock away her misery.

Everything changed in a split second.

Why did Dad have to do that?

Guilt intervened between her sobs.

Daddy didn't mean it. She loved him. He was tired and stressed, trying to meet her long list of college campus visits. It was all her fault. She wanted him and Mommy back so badly. But she was all alone now.

Kaylee pounded the pillow.

What was she going to do? Where was she going to go?

She'd be eighteen soon.

College was out.

She had to get better and get out of here, and then she'd find Aunt Lou Ann, who was the only family she had left.

The door clicked open. Someone was coming in! Finally.

Kaylee bolted upright in the bed.

A woman with a neat ponytail and wearing blue scrubs entered.

She smiled at Kaylee.

"Good morning. Kaylee. Aren't you up early? I'm Margo, your nurse today."

"Oh, my gosh. I'm so happy to see you. I called and called and nobody came last night. Except for Dr. Newell."

"He told me all about you and…the accident."

Kaylee sniffled.

"It's all right. It will take time to heal, and I don't mean just your ankle."

"Thank you."

"You're most welcome. Are you hungry?"

Kaylee shrugged.

"My head hurts, and I want to get clean. But the bathroom is just awful. Can I have another room?"

"Unfortunately, no, because we're full up."

"And why was the door locked?"

"We've a psychiatric patient that we can't move anywhere. He's been known to wander around, and Dr. Newell was afraid that he'd wander into your room."

"But why is the lock on the outside?"

"If the patient locks the door from the inside, we can't respond quickly enough if there's an emergency."

"But I needed help last night."

"We were short-staffed last night. I'm sorry it happened. Let me see what the problem is in the bathroom."

Margo peeked into the bathroom and fisted her hands on her hips.

"My word! What the heck has gone on here?! Completely unacceptable! We've had difficulty with housekeeping. I'll attend to this immediately! I'll be right back."

Margo left and locked the door behind her.

She returned with a cart loaded with cleaning supplies, rolls of toilet paper, paper towels, soap, and a stack of white towels."

Margo frowned. "This was the last room available."

"I don't know who stayed here last, but whoever it was, was really gross."

Margo nodded. "Yes."

Kaylee cocked her head, listening to the back-and-forth bristle strokes emanating from the bathroom.

Water sprayed in the shower, and she heard the sink water running.

Kaylee wrinkled her nose as the smell of chlorine drifted into the room.

She leaned forward and strained to see what was going on and then saw the Margo's bent-over back. Why would a nurse clean a dirty bathroom instead of a hospital housekeeper? But then Margo did admit to a slipshod housekeeping service. The state of the bathroom made that obvious.

Margo returned from the bathroom and dusted her hands.

"All clean," she announced.

"Wow," Kaylee said. "So not in your job description."

"You, however, *are* in my job description." Margo set a folded white towel at the bottom of the bed. "Why don't you get cleaned up while I prepare your breakfast?"

"Thank you," Kaylee said softly.

"You're welcome."

Kaylee pointed to her bandaged ankle. "What do I do about this?"

Margo unwrapped the bandage and arched her eyebrows.

Kaylee winced at her swollen, purple ankle.

"I'll help you to the shower and stay next to you."

"I'll feel safer that way."

Margo helped Kaylee get out of bed and shouldered her to the bathroom.

"Here. Hold onto the sink. I'll start the shower."

Kaylee wrapped her arms across her chest. Even though Margo was her nurse, she'd wait to undress until Margo left.

Margo stared at her.

"Well, let's go."

"Um...I can do it from here."

"Are you absolutely sure?"

"Yeah, I'll be fine. You'll be back with my breakfast anyway, in case something happens."

Margo studied Kaylee.

Perhaps she'd offended the nurse.

"Really. I'll be okay."

Margo shrugged. "All right. But I'll be back...with your breakfast."

With that, Margo wheeled the cart out of the room.

The door clicked.

Kaylee didn't mind being locked in this time. After all, she'd be naked and vulnerable to that wandering psycho guy. Who knows what he'd do to her?

Kaylee untied her patient gown, slipped it off, and draped it across the sink. Margo forgot to leave her a clean gown, but Kaylee was sure that all she had to do was ask the nurse for a clean one. She'd also ask for her clothes. Her mouth dried. She had no idea how she ended up in this room and in a patient gown. Her clothes must be in a bag somewhere.

Kaylee stared down at her bruised, ballooned ankle. Her heartbeat shot to her head, recalling how she managed to climb out of the swamp water and up the muddy bank to the roadside to flag the ambulance down. Sirens echoed in her head. Dr. Newell and that weirdo man were there.

There wasn't anything she could do about it now.

Kaylee stepped into the shower with her good foot and gingerly lifted her injured one in, too.

The lukewarm water was a welcome pleasure. It washed away the hot sweat and dirt. Particles of dried, gritty, sand swirled around the drain and disappeared.

Margo had blessedly left her a clean bar of soap and a small trial-sized shampoo, not to mention the clean towel and soap at the sink.

Margo was the best nurse.

Kaylee soaped every inch of her skin and lathered her hair with the shampoo. She topped her time in the shower with an invigorating rinse, relieved to be finally clean. It gave her the first glimmer of hope.

She shut the water off and toweled dry.

The locked door clicked.

Kaylee wrapped the towel tighter around her wet body.

Water dripped from the tips of her drenched hair onto her neck and dribbled into her cleavage.

"Who's there?" she called.

"It's me, silly," Margo replied.

Kaylee exhaled.

"I'll be right there," Kaylee called.

But Margo was already at the open doorway.

"Better?" she asked.

"Much."

Kaylee gripped her towel.

"May I have a clean gown?"

"I laid one on your bed."

"Thanks."

Kaylee started toward the bed with the towel.

"Please leave the towel in the bathroom."

Kaylee paused. "Umm."

Margo held out her hand.

"I wouldn't want you to slip with your injured ankle." Then she beckoned with her hand. "Come. C'mon."

Kaylee surrendered the towel and cringed at being naked in front of Margo.

"Good," Margo said. She moved away from the doorway. "Your gown and breakfast are there."

Kaylee limped to the bed and quickly tossed on the gown.

She even shied away from being naked in front of her mother.

Nurses saw naked patients all the time, but still, Kaylee sensed Margo's stare.

Kaylee pushed up onto the bed while holding her gown closed.

Margo pointed to the tray on the bedside stand. "There's breakfast."

Margo waited for Kaylee to sit up on the side of the bed.

Since she still didn't have underwear, Kaylee tucked the gown around her backside and slowly and carefully, made her way to the side of the bed.

Kaylee scooped her plastic fork into the chunky, pale, reconstituted scrambled eggs and brought it to her mouth. It wasn't her mom's cooking, but she was starved. The last time she ate was lunch in Tampa after the university tour. They'd planned on having dinner once they were home in Miami, but they never made it.

Her mind refused to go there.

Kaylee swallowed the tasteless eggs. She supposed all hospital food was this bland. But the soggy, unbuttered piece of toast was a definite no.

"Everything all right?" Margo asked.

"Uh, fine."

Kaylee sipped the orange juice. It was full of pulp, but it wasn't bad.

"Not going to eat your toast?"

"The eggs and the juice were plenty."

"Okay. Lie back, and I'll bandage your ankle."

Kaylee did as she was told. She didn't want to be labelled a difficult patient.

Margo struggled to wrap Kaylee's ankle with an elastic bandage, readjusting it several times. Margo's mummy job ended up cockeyed, with sections of Kaylee's bruised ankle peeking through the gaps.

"There," Margo pronounced.

"Thank you. Thank you, for everything."

"You're welcome."

"Um, Nurse Margo. Can I have my clothes back?"

"Unfortunately, they were torn to shreds during the accident."

Kaylee puffed out her bottom lip.

"No worries. We'll get you clothes, nice ones. Now rest."

Margo left the room and locked the door.

Kaylee unwound Margo's cockeyed work, and rewrapped her ankle. She'd once tended to Shawna's sprained knee during a soccer game, so she knew exactly how to use an elastic bandage.

Soccer.

Kaylee shut her eyes.

There she was, running, Shawna at her side, them passing the ball, moving it down the field. Score!

But Mom and Dad wouldn't be there to cheer her on. Now she was stranded at this strange hospital with a ballooned ankle and bruised heart, she'd never play soccer again, and playing on a college soccer team was only a dream now.

Kaylee gasped, unaware she'd been holding her breath.

She opened her eyes and stared at the tile ceiling.

She began counting the squares. What else was there to do? There wasn't a TV. She had no laptop. No cell.

One, two, three.

Fiftee-ee-eeen….

Huuu

Her lids grew heavy, like the rest of her body.

Margo sat at the kitchen table, locked her fingers together, and stretched her arms, then took her silver fork and dove it into the freshly scrambled eggs and crisp bacon. A piece of toast, perfectly browned from the toaster, shone with melted butter. She made a perfect breakfast for herself, excluding Otto.

He could fend for himself. There was no way in hell she'd sit at the kitchen table with him. She'd lose her appetite. What a fucking slob!

Margo bit into the toast just when Otto made his appearance.

Shit.

She stuffed the remainder of the toast in her mouth as an excuse so she wouldn't have to engage with him.

He hovered over her like a vulture anyway.

"So, how's our sleeping beauty?" he asked.

"Would I be sitting here if she wasn't?"

Otto shrugged.

"She drank every drop of the orange juice. Things should be quiet for the rest of morning."

Margo wished she could have as much peace and quiet as Kaylee.

Cleaning up the mess Otto and his filthy parade of scum left behind in that bathroom after raping Joanna to death had exhausted her.

Kaylee was as much her property, but it was imperative that the girl trust her. It otherwise would be a much harder fight.

"I'll check on her at noon," Otto said.

"That won't be necessary."

Otto waved his stubby finger at her, inches from her face.

She could easily twist his neck, but until all his computer files were in her hands, she held off killing him. She'd have to settle for imagining his ultimate demise.

Margo got up from the kitchen chair and took a step toward Otto to tower over him.

Otto slunk back and dropped his pointed finger.

"She's not my type, anyway," he said. "Perhaps the next one will be."

"Perhaps."

There wouldn't be a next for him, but let him dream.

Otto left the kitchen.

Margo picked up her breakfast plate and headed to the sink, and Otto passed her, puffing on his stogie.

"I'll be out back," he said.

"Okay."

Margo set her plate into the sink and peered out of the kitchen window at Otto.

He sat on a patio chair with knees wide and his cigar hanging from his crusty lips.

Margo shuddered in disgust.

Since Otto was out of the way, it was the perfect time to text Gerald.

"Available?" Margo texted.

They kept texts innocent, just in case they found their way to the FBI.

"Yes."

Margo's cell rang.

"Greetings," she answered.

"How's the morning been?"

"Fairly smooth."

"Fairly?"

"Seeing as how I had to clean the bathroom, that's how I'd rate it."

"Yeah, I forgot about that. But we had to leave in an unanticipated hurry."

"I recall."

"How's our guest?"

"Resting comfortably. I reiterated that she is not to be disturbed."

Margo glanced at the empty key ring.

"But I believe that won't be an issue."

Gerald chuckled. "I agree."

"When will you be *home*?"

"I'll work through lunch and because my day looks light, I should be there around 4 pm—Miami traffic and all. Is that a problem?"

"No."

"Good. See you then."

"Don't forget to bring supplies."

"I won't. See you then. You will hold dinner for me?"

"We'll all wait for you."

It was code for "don't feed Kaylee." The last thing she wanted to do was clean up vomit during the procedure. She'd learned from the past. Joanna yakked all over her shoes while she held the girl down. Disgusting. She'd tossed that pair in the garbage.

Margo and Gerald ended the call.

While Kaylee slept, Margo would get the procedure room ready.

7

Gerald glanced at the scheduled patient list on the computer in his office. He'd be out of here by early afternoon, no problem.

He frowned. All his patients today had commercial insurance. Gerald leaned in closer to his screen.

Yes!

The last patient just added to his schedule was a nineteen-year-old with no insurance. A little old, but some like them that way. She was a potential.

His nurse popped her head into his room.

"You've got three waiting," Cassidy announced. She winced. "And, uh, I booked a self-pay at the end of the day."

Gerald grinned. "No problem. I'll waive my fee, as always."

"Bless you, Dr. Newell. You're the best! She sounded desperate."

Gerald reclined in his chair. "Every woman deserves care."

Cassidy smiled wide, said, "That's why I love working here," and trotted away.

She wasn't the smartest, but she was a hard worker, and most important, she gushed over him.

Gerald stood and headed to the hallway of exam rooms.

He walked into an exam room without knocking.

A thirty-year-old woman wearing a patient gown and naked beneath it sat on the edge of the exam table.

She was a new patient to his practice, so he'd play nice and interested even though he was only going through the motions. He kept batting away thoughts of Kaylee and what was going on at the house. Good thing he pocketed Otto's key to the room. Margo would further keep him in check.

"I see you're here for your annual visit."

The woman fidgeted.

"Yes."

"Then, let's get to it. I'm sure you have better places to be," Gerald joked.

The woman laughed nervously.

Gerald slid the woman's gown off her shoulders, exposing her breasts.

The woman hunched her shoulders.

"It's necessary for me to do a complete breast exam," Gerald reassured her. "Move your arms up, then arms down at your hips."

She complied.

"Good. Now lie back, and put your feet in the stirrups."

Cassidy rounded the exam table and covered the woman's breasts with the patient gown.

Gerald walked to the other side of the table and snaked his hand under the patient's gown, rounded his hand over her breasts, and then gave each nipple a tweak.

The woman remained as silent as the exam room.

Gerald broke the tense quiet.

"Normal breast exam," he announced.

The woman dug her bare, sweaty heels into the metal stirrups and curled her toes.

"Speculum," he commanded Cassidy.

Cassidy squirted lubricant on the metal gynecologic instrument and handed him the cold instrument.

Gerald inserted it into the woman.

She flinched.

Gerald rubbed her thigh.

"Relax."

Gerald held out his hand and Cassidy placed a pap smear brush into his palm.

"Thank you, Cassidy."

He performed the pap test and handed the Cytobrush for the pap smear back to Cassidy, who swirled it into the fluid-filled jar.

The woman started to sit up.

"Not so fast my dear. I still need to do a pelvic exam.

Gerald shoved his gloved fingers deep into the woman.

She let out a muted gasp.

"Breathe," he told her.

The woman clenched around his probing fingers.

He was tired of telling her to relax. She was no virgin.

He swirled his fingers around her and pressed his other hand above her pubic bone, and he thrust his fingers deeper.

Cassidy moved to the woman's side and held her hand.

Such drama!

This exam was taking too long, putting him behind schedule.

Gerald removed his fingers from the woman.

"You may get dressed now."

He snapped off his gloves, tossed them into the exam room receptacle, and headed out of the exam room, his back to Cassidy and the woman.

"I'll meet you in the next room," he called to Cassidy.

Gerald sighed and moved to the next patient.

He stepped up his exams, minimizing chitchat.

He didn't have the time.

He had the add-on nineteen-year-old on his mind. He needed to spend extra time on her, convinced it would pay off. It always did. Bless Cassidy for booking the young girl last on his schedule. The uninterrupted time would be to his advantage, and he suspected to the poor girl's too.

Cassidy tiptoed past Dr. Newell's office, taking a quick glance inside.

Busy eating his noon sandwich while studying his computer screen, he didn't notice her.

Cassidy hurried to the staff break room and peeked in.

Janice, the head office nurse, looked up at her.

"Have a seat and take a well-deserved break. Dr. Newell had lunch delivered."

"Janice, may I talk to you in private?"

Janice patted her lips with a paper napkin.

"Sure. Let's go to my office."

Cassidy followed Janice to her boxy, windowless quarters.

Janice left the door ajar and then sat behind the computer on her desk.

Even though it was a tiny office, Janice had decorated the walls with serene prints of women.

Janice pointed to a chair.

Cassidy sat.

Her knee began to bounce.

Janice leaned forward and her forehead wrinkled with concern. "Heavens, Cassidy. What's the matter?"

Cassidy paused. Perhaps she could make some other excuse on the fly. No, she would not chicken out. She had to say something.

"Umm." Cassidy drew a breath. " I need to talk to you about this morning."

"Okay."

"The first patient of the day…the new patient."

"Yes," Janice prompted Cassidy to continue.

"Well, I could tell she was very uncomfortable with Dr. Newell. I was uncomfortable for her, too."

"How so?"

"Well, he…Dr. Newell…exposed her during a breast exam. And then he gave her a very long, inappropriate, and rather rough pelvic exam." Cassidy swiped a stray strand of hair off her forehead. "The woman was sweaty. Her feet, her hands. She was so mortified, she couldn't get out of the exam room fast enough."

There, she said it. Cassidy exhaled.

Janice studied her.

"Cassidy, this a gynecology office. It's not uncommon for women to be nervous. Some are more nervous, or show it more than others."

"Yeah, I get that. But this didn't seem like a normal gyn exam."

"The woman was a new patient. Dr. Newell always takes his time examining a new patient, as he should. He's a thorough doctor. Have you considered that the woman may have psychological issues? Maybe she was abused. I did her intake. God help me if I missed that."

"I don't believe you did."

"How about the rest of the morning?" Janice pressed her.

"He went very fast with all the other exams."

"Was Dr. Newell inappropriate during those exams?"

"No, but he rushed through them."

"This is a busy office. We would all like to spend more time with patients, including Dr. Newell. But that's the ugly part of the logistics in this era of medicine." Janice smiled. "The majority of patients like and trust Dr. Newell. We have many returning. Now, not all patients gel with him and so they leave our practice. And that's all right. It happens in every office. To every doctor. It's best for everyone that those patients seek care elsewhere."

Cassidy looked down.

"Go get some lunch," Janice said.

"Yeah, okay."

Cassidy met Janice's gaze.

"Is this conversation confidential... just between you and me?"

"Absolutely. Now let's go get lunch."

"Okay."

Gerald gritted his teeth and strode back into his office. And Cassidy thought she was safe. He'd seen her walk by, and then he saw her walk into Janice's office, disturbing her lunch...the lunch he'd been kind enough to order for the whole office, including that ingrate Cassidy.

She'd played him! Pretending to fawn all over him!

He'd naturally listened to the whole conversation.

Gerald tapped his desk.

He'd have to be proactive.

Gerald picked up his office phone and punched in John Fisher's office.

He'd known the family practitioner for decades.

John answered.

"Hi, John. It's Gerald. I'm lucky to have caught up with you."

"Hey, Gerald. What can I do for you?"

"I have a sticky situation."

"Patient?"

"No. No. It's about one of my office staff. My medical assistant. Sweet gal. But I'm afraid the office is too much for her. Don't get me wrong. She's very competent and great with the patients. Can you, by any chance, use a new medical assistant?"

"I can't believe this! I was about to place an ad for one. My MA just gave her notice because her husband's being transferred to South Carolina. I'd be happy to have your gal."

"Great. I'll let her know."

"So glad this works out for both of us," John said.

"Me too."

Gerald hung up and grinned.

This was shaping up to be a good day.

"Janice," he called after seeing her walk by his office.

Janice stuck her head into his office.

"Yes," she said.

Gerald beckoned for her to come inside.

"Do me a favor and shut the door."

"Sure."

Janice did as Gerald asked and then sat in a chair opposite him.

Gerald sighed. "I passed by your office while on my way to check if the lunch I ordered had arrived when I overheard Cassidy being… well…concerned about one of my new patients."

Janice shook her head. "I'm sorry you heard that."

Gerald massaged his chin. "I want you to know that I like Cassidy. She's a hard worker, but I've been observing her, and she's overwhelmed. I've spoken with John Fisher, and it turns out he's in need of a good medical assistant…and I think Cassidy will be happier there."

Janice shrugged.

"It's for the best," Gerald said. "I don't want to be the bad guy, so at the end of today, let her know. And even though I've found her one hell of a great job, tell her I'll pay her for not only this month, but the next one too. I wouldn't want her to be *discouraged.*"

"I understand. I'll let her know."

"You're the best."

Janice nodded.

"How was lunch?"

"It was very good, thank you. I've saved you a plate."

Gerald grinned. "Awesome."

Janice stood and exited his office.

Gerald turned his attention to his computer screen and stared at the last patient of his day, the one Cassidy added on. He had to give her credit for that. But he needed to ditch Cassidy before she became a threat. Besides it was also for her safety. It was the right thing to do.

He rubbed his fingers while he focused on nineteen-year-old Sophia Pavlis. Heavy menses was listed beneath her name regarding the nature of her visit. Gerald arched his brows. He knew exactly how to solve that.

Gerald studied the demographic data Cassidy had entered for Sophia. No insurance. Occupation- car wash attendant. Address- apartment in skeptical neighborhood. Hmmm. Very promising. Recently moved from Apopka, Florida.

He sent Sophia's information to his office printer, and the printer slid out the copy. Gerald folded the papers into perfect thirds, shoved them into an envelope, and tucked the envelope into his briefcase. He'd begun to keep his private files secure from Otto, and some even from Margo. He'd share info with her once she delivered on her promise to use her international connections. If that went bust, he'd move to plan B.

Cassidy assisted Gerald with the two patients before Sophia's appointment. He kept the interaction with Cassidy cordial and she likewise maintained decorum.

"Thank you for your help today," he said to her.

"There's one more patient," Cassidy said.

Gerald raised his hand. "It's fine. I've got it. You can go."

Gerald and Cassidy locked eyes.

"I do appreciate you," he softly said.

"Okay. Your last patient is in room two."

Cassidy turned and walked away.

Gerald looked both ways down the hallway.

He was alone.

Off to exam room two.

Gerald rapped on exam room door before opening it.

"It's Dr. Newell," he announced.

Sophia, wearing a patient gown, sat on the exam table.

Gerald glanced at the girl's bra and panties which had been tossed onto frayed denim shorts and a rumpled pink T-shirt. He always noticed his "special" patients' attire because it gave him invaluable insight to their backgrounds, and Sophia's smelled of desperation.

His eyes met her deep brown ones. Her brown hair cascaded down the front of the cornflower blue gown, and her high cheekbones, pouty bow lips, and long neck immediately hooked him. A diamond in the proverbial rough. She could definitely play younger.

Gerald approached her.

Sophia didn't flinch.

Gerald's pulse fluttered. God, she was perfect.

Gerald sat on the exam room stool and wheeled toward her, stopping within inches of her privates, his mind dizzy with where his hand would soon be. She oozed sexuality.

Gerald crossed his legs, holding back his hard-on. Last thing he wanted was to scare her off.

But Sophia didn't seem to notice.

"How may I help you today, Sophia?"

"My periods are so heavy that it's really causing me problems at work. I work at a busy car wash and I depend on tips. I can't keep ducking out to change tampons every hour. Well, maybe not every hour, but way too many times. And even my boss has noticed it, and he's threatened to fire me if I keep taking breaks like that. I need to get a handle on this, and fast. I can't lose this job. I've got rent to pay."

"I understand, perfectly."

Gerald tapped the stirrups.

"Put your heels right in here and let me take a look."

Sophia spread her legs in front of Gerald and scooted to the very edge of the exam table.

Oh, shit!

Just the sight of her shot straight to his cock.

He hadn't had this kind of incontrollable reaction to any of the others, not even with Joanna.

Gerald squeezed his thigh together—hard.

He donned gloves and parted her labia with his fingers.

She allowed him to probe further without a shred of resistance.

Maybe he'd keep this one for himself!

Gerald slid his lubricated fingers inside Sophia.

She tightened around them.

"Sorry about that," she said. "I'm little nervous."

"You're doing fine."

Gerald pressed his other hand down her flat lower belly and outlined Sophia's inner parts.

He withdrew his fingers.

"You're perfectly normal," he said.

What an understatement!

Sophia removed her heels from the stirrups and sat up. "So what about my problem?"

"I'm saying that your problem isn't anatomical. It's hormonal, and the good news is it's very treatable."

"Okay, then. What's next?"

"I believe an IUD, a hormone-delivering device placed inside your uterus, will solve your issue. Although not right away, of course."

"I've heard about those. But I can't afford it. I only have cash for today's visit. I guess I'll have to use extra-super-duper tampons."

"Not to worry. I'll insert an IUD at no charge."

"No charge?"

Gerald grinned. "Absolutely, no charge."

"Thanks! Sure, let's do it."

Gerald left Sophia in the exam room. He had to hurry before Janice discovered her there.

Luckily, Janice was ensconced in her office going over the routine patient billing for the day.

He opened the supply cabinet and found two neatly stacked rows of IUDs. Janice's recent order of the devices had come through.

Gerald took out two IUDs and rearranged the stacks to make it look like none were missing.

He then dodged into his office, stored one of the IUDs in his briefcase, and brought the other one into the exam room.

"Scoot into the stirrups, again."

Sophia shimmied into the position.

Gerald opened the package and set up the instruments required to insert the device.

He inserted a speculum into Sophia's vagina and cranked it open, noting how clean she was inside. No abnormal discharge. He'd forgone the routine tests he normally followed for his other patients prior to inserting an IUD. That wasn't the point for any of the other girls. He had to guarantee the clients that pregnancy and menstruation wouldn't be an issue. The girls had to be readily available without inconvenience...without the female mess of it all.

He slid in the IUD in seconds, trimmed the filament strings dangling from the cervix, and removed the speculum.

Gerald rolled back in his wheeled exam room chair.

"You're all set."

He tossed the IUD packaging and his gloves into the exam room trash, washed his hands, and covered his tracks with wads of paper towels.

Sophia sat up.

"That was quick. It didn't even hurt."

"You may have cramping and spotting today. Over-the-counter ibuprofen should take care of that."

"Trust me. Nothing like periods. Thank you, Dr. Newell."

"My pleasure."

"I'll figure out a way to pay you."

If she only knew how true that was.

Gerald shook his head. "It's not necessary. I know what it's like to be cash-strapped."

Sophia arched her brows. "You?"

"Yes."

"It took a lot of hard work to get where I am today."

"Wow."

"You can get dressed now."

Gerald waited outside the exam room for Sophia so he could escort her out the back office door and out of Janice's sight. Anyway, this patient didn't need to stop at the front of the office to pay.

Sophia exited the exam room in cutoff jeans shorts that teased her curvy derrière and a tight, hot pink T-shirt that spread across her perfectly round breasts.

Gerald took her hand.

"Come this way. It's shorter to the parking lot," he added quickly.

Gerald disarmed the back door alarm and walked Sophia out the door.

She reached into the back pocket of her Daisy Dukes and handed Gerald a rumpled business card for Squeaky Clean Car Wash.

"Here," she said. "Come down to the car wash and ask for me. It's a small favor, but I'll get your car washed and detailed for free."

"I'll take you up on that."

"Great! See you sometime, then."

"You can count on it."

Gerald reset the back door alarm and returned to his office. Sophia swirled in his head tempting him to break the cardinal rule of not getting personally involved with any of the girls—a rule that he used to chastise Otto—a rule he was within inches of breaking.

But if Sophia secretly stayed off market, then the rule didn't apply. Gerald tried hard to convince himself of that exemption, but it would be hard to defend and, worse, outright dangerous.

He stared at Sophia's name on his schedule.

He'd never hinted about his past to anyone before, except Sophia.

Her unabashed demeanor and her blatant sexuality intoxicated him enough for him to slip. He couldn't do that again. He couldn't throw away what he'd worked so hard to build up for the high of an animal attraction.

Gerald fidgeted in his chair.

Joanna's death niggled at him. He'd failed to watch over her, to protect her from Otto's dirty lust. And he knew all about dirty lust. He existed because of it.

He had no idea who his father was and neither did his mother, Stacey Newell, who spread her legs for any piece of shit who promised to pay the rent. But they'd all renege, giving one excuse after another. She was so stupid to believe them. Her teenage brain screwed her over and over again, and her lack of judgement got them evicted every time. He never managed to finish a school year.

"Big deal," she would say. "School never did me any good. You're not fit for it anyway, Gerald. Now run to the store a get me a pack of cigarettes."

Gerald's face burned, and he started to sweat.

One of these days he was going to shove Otto's cigar right up his ass. They were two of a kind.

Best thing Stacey Newell ever did was kick him to the curb.

It taught him how to be on his own.

He landed a job at a bookstore, and read every book on his breaks. Got fast at it, too, which helped him ace his high school equivalency exam, then college, and ultimately medical school. He did all right. Top quartile of his class.

He craved for women to need him, seek his expertise, and becoming an OB/GYN suited him perfectly. Babies weren't his thing, but women were. He'd solve their problems, and be a benefactor to the disenfranchised, the poor girls, who deserved a better life. Yes, that was his destiny. And he deserved to make millions doing it.

"Dr. Newell?"

Janice interrupted his journey into his past.

Gerald blinked to the present and turned his head toward her.

"Yes?"

"You're still here. Go on, enjoy the rest of the afternoon. I'll lock up."

Gerald looked at his watch.

Shit, he was late!

"I needed to catch up on a few things. But now that I've finished, I'll head on out."

Gerald signed off on his computer, pushed back in his chair, and picked up his briefcase.

"See you tomorrow, Janice."

He headed out the back door and clicked open his Benz's door, climbed in, and shut the car door.

Then he called Margo.

"I'm on my way."

8

"Who's next?" Dr. Gabe Walter, the medical examiner, asked his assistant.

"We've got the male and female victims, status post fatal car crash on the Collier side of the Tamiami Trail." Victor Flores announced. He paused and corrected himself. "Lyle Jasinski and Melinda Jasinski. Third passenger, located in the back seat, Kaylee Jasinski, daughter and sole survivor, is at Good Samaritan Hospital, same hospital that declared her parents dead."

"I'm glad to know we're not doing her autopsy today," Dr. Walter said.

Dr. Walter and Victor approached Lyle, whose body lay on the stainless steel table. Melinda lay next to her husband. Victor hosed him down while Gabe Walter engaged the scale.

"Seventy kilograms," the doctor announced.

Dr. Walter and Victor reviewed both Lyle and Melinda's postmortem CT scans.

"Looks like Lyle has a several rib fractures and both lung and spleen contusions and Melinda a skull fracture and displaced C5, with hemorrhage into the left ventricle of the brain, a double whammy. Her head must have hit the windshield and then a contrecoup seconds before the airbag deployment. I've seen that before," Dr. Walter mused.

"They hit that tree hard," Victor said. "It's fortunate that the father's back seat and the subsequent air bag deployment saved the daughter's life," Victor said.

The men sighed simultaneously.

"I can't imagine the heartache she's going to go through. My daughter's the same age," Dr. Walter said.

Victor shook his head. "My son's two years younger."

"Let's proceed." Dr. Walter said.

They examined Lyle and his organs in a standard and complete fashion.

"His ribs punctured his liver and lacerated the hepatic artery. He bled out internally in minutes. No one could have gotten to him fast enough despite his daughter's 911 call," the ME said.

Dr. Walter and Victor Flores finished Lyle Jasinski's autopsy and began Melinda's.

"Fifty-two kilograms. A petite woman," Victor said.

The electric saw's high-pitched grind echoed in the morgue while Dr Walter opened Melinda's cranium and removed her brain. He examined it and cut it into sections revealing dark maroon collections in the ventricles.

"At least she didn't suffer. She went out fast," Victor said.

They'd just finished Melinda's autopsy when Dr. Walter looked up to see Captain Brad Jarett enter the morgue.

"Good afternoon, Captain *Jarett*. What can I do you for?" Gabe Walter asked, with a smile.

He'd known the captain of the Collier County Sheriff's department for years.

Jarett nodded to the men. "Gabe...Victor."

Brad Jarett gazed at Lyle and then shifted his focus to Melinda without a grimace.

Gabe looked straight at Brad. "Both are consistent with accidental injuries from an automobile accident."

"Yep. After examining the skid marks, we came to the same conclusion." Brad pointed to Lyle's sutured body. "Doesn't look like anybody ran him off the road. However, based on the impact, he must have been cranking on a slick road, a deadly combination. Along with Lyle's and Melinda's driver licenses, we did discover a Miami High School ID for Kaylee Jasinski. Plus we found a recent receipt for lunch, by the time stamp, at a Tampa restaurant and a collage road trip itinerary in Melinda Jasinski's purse. So we know they left Tampa for their residence in Miami."

"I take it your next stop is Good Samaritan," Gabe said. "Yep. According to my sources, she's dazed but awake. So I get to change her life...forever."

Brad wrinkled his forehead. Gabe recognized the look. Brad wasn't finished.

"One more thing. I went to the academy with Lou Ann Jasinski. Jasinski is hardly a common name."

"No one's come forward to claim them so far. No relatives…yet."

"I think I have one."

Joanna flinched. Beeping monitors surrounded her. She gasped at the IV stuck into her elbow.

Otto!

She squeezed her thighs together.

That bastard Newell saved her! But he also betrayed her. No fucking way was she going to Greece!

She surveyed the strange surroundings and sniffed. It smelled different. In fact, it didn't smell at all. No urinary ammonia. No pungent sweat. No cheap men's cologne. No stale, mixed ejaculate.

They must have moved her to another room.

Joanna spied the open door and listened for the familiar thud of footsteps.

This was her chance to escape.

She grabbed the IV tubing and yanked the IV out.

Hot blood dribbled down her arm and dripped from her fingers. Her cheeks burned. Her fever hadn't broken, but, that wasn't going to stop her.

Joanna vaulted out of the bed and rushed to door, but her left arm clotheslined her. They'd attached some cord to her. It was coming from the clip at her index finger.

She ripped it off and an alarm sounded.

Shit!

Otto and Dr. Newell were on their way!

Go! Go! Go!

Joanna sprinted out the door and slammed into a woman in blue scrubs.

"Let me out, Margo!" Joanna screamed.

Another woman and a man approached.

Who the hell were they?

"Stop," Margo said to the other two.

They backed away.

"It's okay, Kaylee. My name is Lynn Davis. I'm your nurse," the woman said softly.

Why was she calling her Kaylee?

"You're at Good Samaritan Hospital in Naples in the intensive care unit.. An ambulance brought you here two days ago after a car accident. You hit your head pretty hard, and you've sustained a concussion."

Car accident?

Joanna breathed hot.

"You hit me!"

"Kaylee, you're safe here. No one hit you. You're safe here."

The nurse offered her hand to Joanna.

Joanna studied her. Her hands were small. Not like Margo's big paws. And there were no scars on either of her wrists. This wasn't Margo. Where did they move her to? No one was going to look for her but Otto and Dr. Newell.

"Who's the doctor here?"

"The doctor taking care of you is Dr. Zimmer."

"I want to see him right away!" Joanna demanded.

"Dr. Zimmer is a woman doctor. Dr. Stephanie Zimmer."

Joanna bit her bottom lip to stop it from trembling.

Was this a dream?

"Come, let me help you back to bed. I'm not going to force you, Kaylee."

Why does she keep calling me Kaylee?

Joanna backed away. She'd already lost her opportunity to run, anyway.

Lynn left the door open. The man and woman were gone.

Lynn pulled back the sheet and patted the bed.

"Rest."

Joanna slowly lowered onto the bed while keeping her eyes locked on the nurse.

"Are you hungry?" the nurse asked.

Joanna paused. The food could be spiked.

Joanna shook her head.

"All right. How about something to drink?"

Joanna shook her head harder.

"I'll be right back," Nurse Lynn said.

Joanna inspected the room. There weren't any windows, but the door stayed open.

Joanna snuck back out of bed and wandered around the room.

A clean tray table was parked on the other side of the bed, and the light oak bedside stand had no scratches. Whoever stayed here last was neat. And the walls were painted a tranquil apricot instead of stark white.

Why the upgrade?

Joanna pattered into the bathroom and closed the door. The room gleamed with a spic and span shine and the toilet seat even had some weird paper strip across the seat. And there was a full roll of toilet paper! A toothbrush sealed in plastic and toothpaste still in its carton lay on the stainless-steel shelf mounted above the sink, and a mirror hung above it.

Joanna gasped at the wan girl staring back at her. *Who is that?* She touched her cheek and the stranger in the mirror did the same. Tears streamed down Joanna's cheeks and the girl cried too.

She *was* the girl.

Joanna hadn't seen herself in months, or she thought it must have been months. But she lost track. She smeared her wet, ruddy cheeks with the heels of her hands and stared at her blond hair. They hadn't dyed it. But it didn't matter what color hair she had, because no one was looking for her. The Greek must have put in his order for a blonde.

She brought a strand of hair to her nose and sniffed the shampoo-fresh scent. Someone had taken the time to wash her hair, but she couldn't recall when and who. She must be living in a time warp. At least she was alive— and she was going to stay that way no matter what.

Joanna licked her cracked lips, but her throat was too dry to swallow.

She grabbed the toothbrush, ripped off the plastic seal, and then tore open the toothpaste carton and shook the tube out of it so hard it flew across the floor. She scooped it up before anyone could come. She squeezed the white paste onto the brush and scrubbed her teeth and tongue with forceful strokes, getting rid oft the accumulated crud on her teeth from men forcing their filthy dicks down her throat. She spat their remnants into the sink.

She'd just wiped her mouth when she stopped and listened. Two different footsteps approached, neither of which belonged to Otto or Dr. Newell. She'd memorized those two already.

"Kaylee?" Nurse Lynn, or whoever she really was, called. Nurse Lynn walked into the bathroom. "There you are. I brought you a can of ginger ale and a straw."

"Thank you."

Lynn backed out of the bathroom, and Joanna eased out, staying more than an arm's length away from the nurse.

The other set of footsteps belonged to the woman wearing the same color scrubs as Lynn, but she also wore one of those white coats she'd seen doctors wear on TV. Dr. Newell never wore a white coat.

"Hello," the woman greeted her. "I'm Dr. Stephanie Zimmer, your doctor."

The sides of Dr. Zimmer's short, shiny brown hair were neatly tucked behind her ears. Her light makeup accentuated her petite features, and when she smiled with her rose-tinted lips, Joanna's eyes went straight to the doctor's white teeth.

Joanna opened her mouth barely wide enough to utter, "Hi."

"I'm happy to see you up and about," Dr. Zimmer said. "Do you remember me?"

Joanna shook her head. She'd never seen Lynn or this doctor before today. What kind of game was this?

"That's all right. Memories can be a bit scrambled after a concussion. Please, have a seat on the bed. I need to examine you."

Joanna's heart hammered in her chest and she locked her knees, moving neither backward or forward.

"I'll be right here," Lynn said.

That was exactly what Margo said—before she held her down.

"I'm a neurologist, a special doctor who studies how the brain functions including all the messages it sends throughout the whole body."

Joanna stared at the doctor and then at Lynn. If they were lying, she'd kick both of them in their heads, and then she'd run.

Joanna started for the bed while keeping her eyes on Lynn and Dr. Zimmer. She sat on the edge of the bed with her feet planted firmly on the floor.

Dr. Zimmer approached her.

"I'm going to start by giving you a simple test. I want you to follow my finger without moving your head. You know, just with your eyes."

Joanna followed Dr. Zimmer's finger. Up. Down. Left Right.

"Good. Now I want you to do the same thing, but this time I want you to tell me how many fingers I'm holding up."

"Okay."

Dr. Zimmer wiggled her fingers to Joanna's right.

"Three."

"That's right."

"How about now?"

"One."

"Correct."

Dr. Zimmer wiggled her fingers to Joanna's left.

"Four. Now two."

"Bingo."

"That was easy."

The doctor took something resembling a flashlight out of her coat pocket.

"I'm going to shine this light into your eyes. I know it's hard but try not to blink."

The doctor moved closer and closer with her little black flashlight, shining it into both Joanna's eyes.

"Can you see my brain with that?" Joanna asked.

The doctor chuckled. "No, I'm not that good."

The doctor clicked off the flashlight.

"The blood vessels and nerves inside your eyes are normal., so now I'm going to feel your head."

Dr. Zimmer palpated Joanna's head in an organized fashion, stopping at the back of her head and applying firm pressure to the area.

Joanna flinched. "Ow!"

Dr. Zimmer probed the tender lump.

"Still sensitive, huh?" Dr. Zimmer asked.

"Yeah."

One of Otto's customers thrust her until he slammed the back of her head against the bed's headboard with his dick still inside her.

"You must have hit the car door hard."

"Car door? Car accident? I wasn't in a car wreck."

Concern furrowed across Dr. Zimmer's forehead. She drew a deep breath.

"You and your parents were in a car accident a day ago...Sunday afternoon. It had been raining hard and the roads of the Tamiami Trail were slick. Your father lost control of the car and it slammed into a tree. The medics responding to the accident pulled you out of the back seat." Dr. Zimmer paused. "Unfortunately, Kaylee, your mother and father did not survive."

Parents? She'd left those pieces of shit years ago.

Her father was no different from the other men, and her mother cared about her as much as Margo did. But she trusted Newell. He was kind and rather sweet...until he too sold her out.

Dr. Zimmer and Nurse Lynn stared at her as if they were waiting for her to melt down.

They'd mistaken her for a girl named Kaylee who was in a car wreck and whose parents did not survive. But how the hell did she end up in that car, and where the hell was Kaylee?

This wasn't Miami. She must have escaped. Otto and Newell would surely be looking for her. But as along as she pretended to be Kaylee, she was safe.

Joanna stuck out her bottom lip. "They're dead?"

Dr. Zimmer nodded. "Yes."

"Can I please be alone?"

"Sure," Dr. Zimmer said.

Joanna looked at Lynn.

"I'll leave you be," Lynn said. "The ginger ale is on your tray table. Here's the call light. Just push the nurse button if you need me or if you're hungry. I'll be right outside at the nurse's station."

"Okay."

Joanna waited until they left and then popped the ginger ale can open, stuck a straw in it, and drank the carbonated drink dry.

Then she lay back on the bed and crossed her ankles.

This could work.

9

Gerald pulled his Benz into the house's driveway and got out with his briefcase. He grinned and tapped the case, and with a spring in his step, he unlocked the door. Once inside he tripled-bolted the door and set the alarm. One couldn't be careful enough of who entered or left.

Strangely, Otto designed the program that ran the extra protection. The secured premises was a definite plus in his column, but the real Holy Grail existed in Otto's computer. It was hard to believe that little shit had a brain.

Otto spent hours in that room uploading the merchandise and sitting back to watch the bids come in.

The cut Gerald agreed to receive for providing clean girls paled in comparison to the millions Otto raked in. But agreements, like anything else, were subject to change.

With Margo's alliance and connections, it was now two to one.

Gerald turned around to find Otto splayed on the living room sofa.

Damn those cigarette and cigar burns.

He'd already decided to throw that disgusting sofa out the minute its occupant was no more. Maybe he'd bury Otto in it. How fitting.

Otto cracked his eyes open. "What the fuck did you do with my keys?"

Gerald clenched the briefcase handle.

"Given your issues with self-control placing us in financial jeopardy, ie. Joanna, I can't risk any damage to Kaylee. We're damn lucky we stumbled upon her. Actually, it was a miracle. And I don't want you and your shitbag entourage to fuck with that miracle."

Otto pushed up off of the sofa. "Shitbags, huh? Might I remind you that those shitbags keep you in more than just that Benz." Otto stuck out his stubby hand. "Give me the key."

Gerald shook his head. "No."

He came to the house in a good mood. Sophia put him there, and Otto wasn't going to spoil that for him.

Gerald took a deep breath. Challenging Otto wasn't the way to go.

"Look," Gerald said as calmly as he could. "We both need to deliver Kaylee in top condition to our Greek, don't you agree?"

"Okay…yes."

"Margo and I will be taking care of you. Your job is to keep the Greek happy. Anticipation is the best aphrodisiac."

Otto backed off. "I'll be in my room."

Gerald grinned. "How about I order Greek for dinner tonight?"

Otto smiled revealing that god-awful gap between his front, nicotine-yellow-stained teeth. "How fucking fitting! Knock on the door when it's here."

"Absolutely."

Gerald's mood bumped again.

Now to prepare Kaylee.

Gerald waited for Otto to seal himself in his room. That way he could be doing something—something that would benefit all of them.

Gerald went into the kitchen, where Margo sat sipping coffee. Gerald preferred tea. After drinking coffee to stay awake during those years in medical school, and then during the all-nighters as an OB/GYN resident, he couldn't stand the taste anymore. It was all bitter, no matter the roast. Now all he drank was herbal tea. It calmed him.

"Are we ready, *Nurse* Margo?"

Margo rolled her eyes over the brim of her mug and set it on the table.

"The procedure room is all set. All it needs is our little patient."

"Do you have the syringe filled?"

"Of course."

"I want this to go more smoothly than it did with Joanna."

"So do I. That bitch bit me. This time I increased the dosage. She'll be a little lamb for us," Margo said.

"Shall we?"

"I tee'd her up for you. Told her you were going to fix her ankle. I'll get the IV and syringe set up, and then I'll meet you in her room."

Gerald shot Margo a thumbs-up and headed to Kaylee's room.

Gerald unlocked the door and entered.

"How's my patient?"

"Okay. When can I leave?"

Gerald sat at the end of Kaylee's bed.

"Unfortunately, not yet. I reviewed your X-rays, and I'm afraid I missed a fracture."

"I don't recall having any X-rays, and my ankle is starting to feel better. The swelling's gone down, and I can actually move it more."

"Now, who's the doctor? First of all, you were really out of it when you got here, and that's why you don't remember the X-rays. Secondly, if I don't fix your ankle properly, you'll never walk the same. You'll limp forever. No sports. No high heels."

"Although I don't wear high heels, I do play soccer. There's no way I can live with a limp. Can you really fix it?"

"Absolutely."

"All right." Kaylee frowned. "Is it going to hurt?"

"No. I'll make sure you won't feel a thing. I'm going to start your IV before your surgery and for anesthesia, and because you also need an antibiotic."

Kaylee grimaced.

"I know how you don't like IVs, but it will only be for the surgery. I promise to take it out right afterward." Gerald shook his head. "You don't want to have an infection or feel any pain, do you?"

"No."

"Attagirl!"

Margo entered the room carrying the IV supplies. She winked at Gerald.

"Thank you, Nurse Margo." Gerald looked at Kaylee. "Hold out your arm."

Kaylee complied...not like Joanna who bucked them from the get-go.

Gerald tightened a rubber tourniquet above her elbow and slapped her forearm. A deep blue vein rewarded his effort.

"Perfect!"

Gerald easily threaded the IV into Kaylee's distended vein while Margo held a bag of fluid above Kaylee's head. He released the tourniquet and the IV fluid dripped steady into Kaylee's forearm.

He nodded at Margo. She reached into the front pocket of her scrubs and pulled out a syringe

Gerald poked the syringe's needle into a rubber port

"Okay, here we go," Gerald whispered to Kaylee.

Kaylee's eyelids fluttered more and more slowly until they completely collapsed.

Gerald scooped up Kaylee's limp body, carried her into his procedure room, and lay her on the exam table.

"Margo, help me put her heels in the stirrups."

Kaylee snored.

Margo grabbed one of Kaylee's legs and Gerald the other, and they pushed them into the metal stirrups.

Kaylee's knees wobbled inward.

"Shit, Margo!"

"Okay, so I upped the dose a bit."

"Yeah, quite a bit."

With Otto's black-market Fentanyl, he couldn't always gauge the dose. But after the Joanna incident, he couldn't blame Margo.

Margo helped him pull Kaylee's knees apart.

Good thing this didn't take more than a minute. She could sleep off the rest while Margo, Otto, and he enjoyed a Greek dinner.

Gerald inserted the speculum and pinched her cervix extra hard with the sharp steel-toothed instrument. His force startled him. Gerald paused. Kaylee didn't buck.

He poked his head above Kaylee's open legs. "Good job on the Fentanyl," he said to Margo.

She shrugged.

Gerald pushed the IUD into Kaylee's uterus and removed the sharp tenaculum from Kaylee's cervix. Blood pumped from the deep puncture, filling her open vagina and spilling out over the blades of the speculum. Kaylee's blood dripped onto the tops of his Italian leather shoes. He slapped Kaylee's knees.

"Damn you! Look what you've done to my shoes! You've ruined them!

Kaylee was so heavily sedated, she was oblivious to Gerald's rage.

"Margo! Hand me a bunch of those gauze squares! Now!" he demanded.

Gerald stuffed the gauze squares against Kaylee's hemorrhage.

"Shit! Shit! Shit!," he muttered.

It was his fault. Pressure. All she needed was pressure on her bleeding cervix, he reassured himself.

Gerald removed the blood-soaked gauze and pushed in fresh ones, and waited.

"Everything all right?" Margo asked.

"Yes," Gerald snapped.

Gerald glanced at his watch, positioned above the cuff of his rubber glove. He waited two full minutes, his annoyance causing the minutes to drag.

He removed the wad of gauze. The pressure had worked! He scooped the congealed blood clots out until he could finally see the long strings of the IUD and cut them with surgical scissors.

Kaylee continued to snore.

Gerald whipped the bloody speculum out of Kaylee and threw it into the exam room sink, the clatter echoing in the silent room. He tossed the remaining instruments into the sink and the IUD packaging into the garbage.

He frowned at Kaylee's bloodstained thighs. He needed to clean that up.

Gerald ran the dry extra gauze under the sink's faucet, while the water splashed on the bloody instruments, and Kaylee's blood swirled down the drain.

He sponged the deep maroon crusts off Kaylee's thighs, positive that she'd never know what happened. Next he positioned a sanitary napkin between her legs because he knew she was going to bleed. He'd just tell her it was her period.

Then he pulled the bottom of the exam table out.

"Let's get her legs down."

Margo and Gerald lifted Kaylee's heels out of the stirrups and laid them on the exam table, and Gerald tucked the stirrups back inside the table. Should Kaylee awake—which he doubted—the last thing he wanted her to see were the stirrups.

"Oh, shit. Her ankle," Gerald said.

He needed to maintain the ruse.

Gerald opened an exam room cabinet and pulled out a roll of Kerlix. He unwound the tan elastic bandage around Kaylee's ankle and replaced it with the long, white gauze. He had to make her think he'd fixed her ankle.

Gerald wound the gauze around her ankle several times making the dressing look extra-thick.

"There. How does it look?"

"Plausible," Margo said.

"Let's get her back into her room before she wakes up."

Otto popped his head into the procedure room.

He stuck out his tongue. "Ew! What happened here? Gross!"

"We're just leaving here," Gerald said.

"Is it done?"

"Yeah," *You fucking idiot.*

Gerald scooped Kaylee up off the exam room table.

"I'm not cleaning this shit up," Margo said. "I cleaned up Joanna's puke. Your turn."

"I'll take care of it."

Gerald carried Kaylee's limp body.

"Move," he commanded Otto.

"Not a problem," Otto replied, looking down. "Shit, man. What happened to your shoes?"

Gerald seethed hot.

"A minor complication."

"A little spritz of Windex should take care of that," Otto offered.

Double fucking idiot.

Gerald carried Kaylee past Otto, saying, "I'll settle her in. Meanwhile, call for Greek takeout. I'll have the moussaka and a Greek salad."

"I like those spinach pastries, myself," Otto said.

"Order anything you want."

Gerald laid Kaylee on the bed and covered her with a blanket. The sides of the IV antibiotic bag piggybacked into her IV was collapsed and dry, the dose completed. He removed the miniature bag but kept the mainline IV running. She might be out for a while and Gerald didn't want her to get dehydrated. He made that mistake with Joanna. He was in too much of a rush, and he'd forgone an antibiotic. Then Otto and his marauders pillaged her. But not this time. He wouldn't lose Kaylee. He had all night to watch over her.

Gerald stared at his stained loafers.

Windex, my ass!

Gerald returned to the procedure room's wreckage, donning rubber gloves on his way over to the sink. The running water had rinsed off the bloodstained instruments. Then he grabbed a red plastic biohazard bag and dumped the dirty instruments into it. He'd get to the office before Janice and sterilize them in the autoclave.

Gerald next wet a gauze under the tap and wiped his loafers. He got to them in time and cleaned the guilt off his designer shoes. He tossed the gauze from his shoes into the other red bag full of Kaylee's blood and knotted it. Since he couldn't pitch the bag into the general trash where it would be noticed and consequently lead straight to the house, he'd take no chances and get rid of Kaylee's soil at the office.

He frowned at the bloody mess on the tiled floor.

He went back to the sink and opened the door beneath, grabbed a bottle of disinfectant, and then poured it over the caked blood. Gerald grinned. Not only were his shoes clean, but the mess on the floor also began to dissolve.

Using his rubber gloves and paper towels, he wiped Kaylee's remnants off the floor.

Voilà! It was like nothing happened.

Gerald snapped off his gloves and threw them into the red bag with the rest of Kaylee's blood.

His stomach growled.

Damn he was hungry!

Greek. Just what he needed!

10

Joanna studied the hubbub of nurses outside the open door of her room. Neither Otto nor Dr. Newell had shown up. She was well hidden here, but she wouldn't risk them hunting her down. She'd have to get out of here soon. She'd hitch out of Florida, putting hundreds of miles between her and those assholes.

But first she had to get better, get stronger, and this was the place to do it.

Her stomach rumbled. The ginger ale had quenched Joanna's thirst, but it did little to satisfy her hunger.

Convinced the food was safe, Joanna pressed the nurse call light.

Nurse Lynn entered Joanna's room almost immediately.

"What can I do for you, Kaylee?"

Joanna responded to the name.

"I'm a bit hungry."

"I'm glad to hear that. How about a turkey and cheese sandwich? That's all we have right now, but I'll get you a patient menu for dinner."

"I'll take the sandwich, but do you have anything other than ginger ale, like cola?"

Lynn grinned. "One sandwich and a cola coming right up."

"Thanks."

"You're welcome."

Joanna licked her lips in anticipation of real food. Not the dog food crap Otto shoved into her prison cell. Newell had brought her sandwiches, and once even a burger, but then he'd visited her less and less, leaving her with Otto and Margo. And that bitch did nothing while Otto and smelly man after man raped her over and over again.

Joanna pressed her eyes shut and clenched her hands into trembling fists, exorcising the evil trio from her head.

"Kaylee! Kaylee!"

Joanna startled to find Nurse Lynn's hands over her horror-filled fists. She slowed her panicked breaths.

"Did you remember the accident?" Lynn asked.

Joanna shook her head. "No."

She wanted everyone to quit asking her questions about the car accident. She drove her brain crazy trying to answer her own questions about what the hell happened.

"That's all right. It will come."

"Maybe," Joanna lied.

Her head throbbed thinking about it.

"I brought you a sandwich and a cola, as you ordered."

Joanna looked at Lynn's relaxed face.

"You're really kind."

"Thank you. That means a lot to me." She patted Joanna's knee. "Eat."

Joanna bit into the soft bread. Her eyes teared up. She didn't remember turkey and cheese ever tasting this good!

She stuffed nearly half of the sandwich in her mouth and like a crazed addict, chewed the bites into doughy balls and swallowed them, washing down the pieces that stuck in the back of her throat with the cola.

Mmmm.

She belched and then giggled since she was alone.

Joanna ate the rest of her glorious sandwich more slowly because her empty stomach couldn't keep up with the frenzied pace. She couldn't remember the last time she ate.

Nurse Lynn returned.

"Wow! You really were hungry."

Nurse Lynn picked up the tray and replaced it with a hospital menu and a pencil.

"There's more to choose from."

"I liked the sandwich."

Lynn winked. "I'll save another one for you tomorrow."

"Cola too?"

"Yes, cola too."

Lynn just made it to the door when a man in a uniform appeared.

Shit! They've come for her. They must have discovered who she really was. No way was she going back to Otto and Newell. She'd go to jail first.

"I'm Captain Brad Jarett with the Collier County Sheriff's Department," Joanna heard him announce. "I'm here to speak with Kaylee Jasinski."

Nurse Lynn blocked the door.

"Just one minute. What is this about?" she asked.

Jasinski? No one had mentioned the last name before.

"Given that her parents are deceased, I believe I know her...uh... next of kin."

"Oh, Captain Jarett, can you please wait at the nurse's station. I'll have to clear your visit with her doctor and of course with Kaylee. She's suffered a concussion and has difficulty remembering the accident. You do understand?"

"Yes, ma'am. I'll wait for the doctor."

Joanna heard the overhead page for Dr. Zimmer.

She pulled the covers over her chin. As if that was going to provide an impenetrable shield.

She noticed Dr. Zimmer walking past her room and then talking with the sheriff, and she strained to listen to their conversation, but only made out something about an aunt.

Joanna lowered her shield. The sheriff clearly thought she was Kaylee Jasinski. But who was this mystery aunt?

Dr. Zimmer and the sheriff entered her room and stopped at the foot of her bed, neither crowding her.

"Hi, Kaylee," Dr. Zimmer said. "This is Captain Jarett with the Sheriff's department. He'd like to talk to you. Is that okay?"

Joanna shrugged. Maybe she'd learn more from the captain. After all, he wasn't here because she was a missing person. He was here to reunite her with someone. She'd hear him out.

"Okay," Joanna said.

"Hello, Kaylee," the sheriff greeted her.

Joanna clutched the blanket. "Hi."

"I'm sorry to hear about the car accident and your parents."

Joanna focused on the sheriff's relaxed blue eyes. Except for misjudging Newell's genuine concern, she was pretty much on the mark regarding people's intentions. Having survived on her own, she'd become adept at reading everyone she encountered. To the best of her spidey sense, the sheriff wasn't a foe.

"Thank you."

"I know things are very confusing for you right now, like where you're going to go once you recover."

"I'll probably go back to Miami," she lied.

She wasn't about to disclose her plan to hightail it out of Florida.

"That's understandable. I'm sure you'd like to go back to your home. I know I would. But you need a family or someone to look after you, at least for a year or two."

She didn't need anybody to babysit her. But then again she needed a place to stay and food to eat. That didn't come easy on the street, and shelters were unsafe, especially for girls pegged vulnerable, and she had a big "V" stamped on her forehead.

Besides, she had no idea where this Kaylee lived. And she could be hiding out at that house. Maybe she caused the accident and had disappeared. But that still didn't explain how Joanna ended up in that crashed car with people she didn't know.

"Well, I don't know anyone. It was just my mom, my dad, and me."

Joanna made that up on the sly, and she prided herself on how damn realistic that sounded. She was pretty good at making up tales. Con jobs were important skills for surviving on the road.

"Your last name is not common, but I went to the sheriff's academy with a wonderful woman with the same last name—Jasinski—Lou Ann Jasinski. Have you ever heard that name, or did your dad ever mention having a sister?"

Joanna shook her head.

"Kaylee has been struggling with her memory," Dr. Zimmer said.

"Okay. Well, it was nice meeting you, Kaylee," Captain Jarett said.

"Yeah, likewise."

Captain Jarett and Dr. Zimmer stood and left the room.

Joanna watched them converse at the nurse's station.

This "aunt" presented a whole new problem who might out her as a fake. And that could not happen.

11

Lou Ann's cell rang.

"Sorry about this," she said to Isabelle.

She lifted the dachshund off her lap so she could reach her cell.

Isabelle shot Lou Ann a doggy frown and lay down on her feet pinning, them against the cushion.

Lou Ann picked up her cell. It wasn't a number she recognized.

Who could it be, and, most important, who was invading her vacation?

She let it ring two more times. She'd set the cell to go to her voicemail after the fourth ring.

Hmmm? Should she screen the call?

But something made her answer the mysterious caller.

"Hello."

"Hello. Is there a Lou Jasinski at this number?" a male voice asked.

Why did he call her Lou instead of Lou Ann? Only her friends called her Lou.

"Who is this?" she shot back.

"It's Brad Jarett."

"Brad! Sorry. You surprised me. I didn't recognize the number. How the hell are you?"

"I'm good."

"Still in Naples?"

"Yep." Brad paused, and then continued. "I have some bad news, Lou."

She'd given unfortunate news to plenty of people. Her heartbeat took off. Now she knew how they felt.

"Hit me."

"Do have a brother named Lyle?"

Shit. What did he do now?

"Yeah. Hadn't seen him in years."

"How about Melinda or Kaylee?"

"Melinda's Lyle's wife and Kaylee is my niece. I haven't spoken to or seen any of them in years. In fact, the last time I saw my niece she was a toddler. Melinda did sneak me a Christmas card with Kaylee's second grade school photo. But Lyle must have found out about it, because nothing more ever came from Melinda. Kaylee must be in high school. I still have her photo. Unfortunately, the birthday cards and holiday cards were always returned to me unopened."

She hadn't spoken about her family in years, not even to Harry.

Brad remained silent.

Lou Anne winced. Shit. She shouldn't have babbled out her entire life history.

"Lou, I'm so sorry to tell you that your brother, your sister-in-law, and your niece, Kaylee, were involved in a car accident Sunday afternoon on the Collier side of the Tamiami Trail."

Lou Ann's ears began to buzz.

Brad continued, "Unfortunately, Lyle and Melinda were pronounced dead upon arrival at Good Samaritan Hospital in Naples. But Kaylee survived and is in the intensive care unit at Good Samaritan. I was at the ME's today for the autopsy, and I just finished visiting Kaylee. She's stable, but she's suffered a concussion and has some memory deficits. Lou?"

Lou Ann gasped, sucking air into her lungs. She'd just realized she was holding her breath.

"I'm here."

"Take as long as you need. I'll wait. I'm sorry I couldn't be there in person."

Lou Ann steadied her bouncing knee with her hand. Isabelle stood and circled reacting to Lou Ann's distress.

Why hadn't she made an honest effort to make amends with her big brother? Despite the acrimony, deep down she loved him. But now it was too late.

But Kaylee was alive.

"Okay. Go on," Lou Ann said.

"When I visited Kaylee, I asked if she knew you, or any family member. She said no, but I did tell you that she struggles with memory. Are you aware of any other family members?"

"No. Lyle and I were the only kids my parents had, and they had us late in life. They're both deceased, and they were both only children themselves. We never knew of any living relatives, and none visited us."

"Did Melinda and Lyle have any other children after Kaylee?"

"This is bizarre, but I don't know."

"We've contacted Miami-Dade police, and they're going over to their house right now, to the one listed on both Lyle and Melinda's driver's licenses, to check if there are any pets or children on premises or perhaps in the care of neighbors. It appears they'd left Tampa and were on their way home to Miami. We found a college itinerary in Melinda's purse so apparently they were on a college road trip.

Pain punched her in the chest.

They'd been only miles away and didn't even contact her—like she didn't even exist.

If she'd been in Miami, would she have done the same? God, she wanted to say no.

Worse, she could have gone to Miami and confronted Lyle. Things could have been different. Now she'd never know. But there was Kaylee. What had Lyle told Kaylee about her? Maybe Melinda told her the truth. Melinda was on her side, but she was meek and subject to Lyle's wishes. This all spiraled horribly out of control, and it was her fault as much as it was Lyle's, but they were both too stubborn—too prideful—to set aside the past.

"I'm going down to Naples tonight. Can I call you when I get there?"

"Absolutely. I'll text you my address. You'll stay with me. I have plenty room because it's just me."

"Okay. I just need to grab some stuff. Oh, I have a dog, Isabelle. She's a dachshund and really sweet. I can't leave her behind."

"No problem. Isabelle is welcome to stay."

"Thanks, Brad."

"No problem. I know you would do the same for me. See you tonight."

Lou Ann ended the call. Thoughts tangled in her head, but then Isabelle barked, grabbing her attention.

"We're going on a trip," Lou Ann explained to her canine sidekick.

Isabelle slowly swished her tail with understanding rather than the happy wag of excitement, and tagged along behind Lou Ann to the bedroom.

Lou Ann grabbed her carry-on suitcase from the top shelf of her closet and spread it open on the bed, and tossed in underclothes, PJs, jeans, and shirts. Shit! She couldn't wear any of those to a funeral.

Lou Ann returned to her closet and pushed aside hanger after hanger, until she finally halted at a pair of black pants she completely forgot about. There was also a white blouse somewhere in there that she used to wear with the pants.

She ran through a few more hangers before finding it, along with a black houndstooth jacket. It was her sole interview suit. She turned her attention to her shoe rack and pulled out a pair of black flats. She folded her funeral attire and packed it along with the shoes There, that would do.

Isabelle barked and trotted out of the bedroom.

Lou Ann closed her suitcase.

"I didn't forget to pack your stuff," she called to Isabelle.

She entered the kitchen to find Isabelle straddling her food bowl and her water bowl.

Lou Ann emptied both bowls and put them into a plastic bag.

"Don't worry, I'll bring your food and a bottle of water for the trip.

She'd bring a bottle of water for herself too.

Isabelle dragged up her blanket and then returned with her favorite toy and dumped both at Lou Ann's feet.

"Yeah, okay."

She could also use some comfort.

Lou Ann set her suitcase by the front door and looped Isabelle's harness around the doggy's belly.

She slung her purse over her shoulder and grabbed the handle of her suitcase, jangling the car keys.

"Be a good girl and wait here. I'm going to load the car and then I'll come back for you."

Isabelle sat.

Lou Ann opened the door to find Harry standing there with a box of pizza.

"Uh…I should've called. Looks like you're going somewhere."

She'd been so busy packing that she hadn't stopped to fully absorb Brad's news.

"My brother and his wife are dead, and my niece is in a hospital in Naples," she blurted, and then dropped the suitcase. Her eyes began to sting.

"Oh, hey. I'm so sorry," Harry said.

He set the box down and opened his arms.

Lou Ann pressed her face against his chest and sobbed.

Harry wrapped his arms around her and said nothing, letting her wail.

He stroked the back of her head.

She'd found her comfort.

Lou Ann sniffled and pulled away. Harry let her loose.

"Where are you off to?" Harry softly asked.

"Naples."

"I'll drive."

"Okay."

Harry grabbed Lou Ann's bag.

"Give me your keys. I'll transfer the load to my car."

Lou Ann handed Harry the keys.

Lou Ann dodged inside and grabbed Isabelle's belongs and Isabelle.

"We'll sit together," she told her dog. "Harry's driving."

Isabelle complied without so much of a whine.

Harry returned.

"Everything's ready," he said. He leaned over and petted Isabelle. "You and I are going to take care of her, aren't we?"

Isabelle wagged.

"We can eat the pizza on the way," he said.

Isabelle drooled.

"Yeah, you too."

Harry opened the car door for Lou Ann and Isabelle and then returned to the driver's seat.

"Cruiser locked?" he asked.

"Yes."

"Okay. Off to Naples."

While Harry drove toward the interstate, only the turn signals punctuated the silence.

Lou Ann heard her own sigh.

This was supposed to be a restful vacation. She'd planned to just to hang out with Isabelle, binge watch Netflix, and take sunset walks on the beach. But then her cell rang.

Harry accelerated up the ramp to 275 South and merged with oncoming traffic teeming with locals and Florida summer tourists trying to split their time between theme parks and top-rated white sandy beaches.

Lou Ann's heart twisted. Instead of her niece spending the summer at the beach, she'd be burying her parents. No child should have to do that.

She'd have to see Kaylee through the worst part of her life, a part that would never go away.

Lou Ann tried to imagine how Lyle and Melinda would look like after so many years. They wouldn't be able to see how she had aged. At least she could picture crow's feet and gray hair here and there. But she couldn't age Kaylee, not even from a second-grade photo. Who the hell looked like they did at age seven?

Computer graphics could age a person, but the human brain—no. Especially when it came to one's own family. Does one resemble Mom, or are they the spitting imagine of Dad? What about grandma or aunt? Oh, my God! She said aunt. Could Kaylee resemble her, even in the slightest? Would anyone be able to tell they were related?

Lou Ann jumped down the rabbit hole.

What kind of clothes are her style? What kind of music does she like? Does she have a boyfriend? Who's her best friend? Is she shy or outgoing? They were on a college tour, what are her top picks? They were in Tampa. Would she be happy at USF, or did she want to stick closer to Miami?

Lou Ann had all these questions to ask her, and more. She wanted, needed, to know all about Kaylee.

But first things first. She couldn't barrel in and fire these questions at her now. It wasn't right. There would be plenty of time for them to get to know each other. There was no need to force anything.

Lou Ann gasped.

Shit! Kaylee might not want to have anything to do with her.

Isabelle twirled around and Harry glanced at Lou Ann.

"Are you okay?" he asked.

"Yes."

But of course neither Harry nor Isabelle believed her.

Lou Ann curled up in her seat and stared out the window at the bright blue, cloudless sky that taunted her.

How would she explain to Kaylee why she hadn't been a part of her life and it took this tragedy to bring her to her? She wouldn't blame Kaylee if she was pissed off. Anger was part of the grieving process. She'd be kind and patient with her. Allow her to open up at her own pace.

Harry took an exit off the interstate.

"Where are we going?" she asked.

"A short stop. You'll see."

Harry pulled into a donut shop drive-thru and spoke into the microphone: two coffees with cream and sugar, two glazed donuts, and one chocolate cream-filled one.

He remembered!

Chocolate cream-filled donuts were her favorite.

Harry eased the car forward to the first window, and paid for the order, and then proceeded to the next window for pickup.

The server handed Harry the two coffees and the bag of donuts.

"Pizza, coffee, and donuts. I'm a bad influence," he joked.

Harry and Lou Ann locked gazes.

Harry was right. He was a bad influence, and she hated to admit it, but she badly needed him.

12

Kaylee clutched her belly. The cramping roused her. A warm wetness seeped deep between her thighs. She reached her hand down between her legs and then inspected her bloody fingers.

Shit! To top everything else that had happened to her, she started her period.

She wiggled in the bed. Why did her whole body feel bruised? That never happened when she got her period.

She frowned at the IV still in her arm.

Dr. Newell hadn't taken out her IV as he'd promised.

Then Kaylee stared at the fresh white bandage wrapped around her ankle.

That ankle didn't hurt, but the cramping was unbearable. She needed something for the cramping, plus a tampon.

"Hey, somebody!" she yelled.

Without a window in the room, Kaylee had no idea what time of day it was, or how long she was out.

A key scraped into the lock. Two clicks later, the door opened and Dr. Newell walked in, followed by Nurse Margo.

"What's all the fuss about?" Newell asked.

"I've got bad cramps, and I just got my period. I need a tampon and something for these cramps. Something that won't make me sleepy."

Newell looked at Margo. "Get our little patient some protection and a pill for those terrible cramps."

"Yes, doctor. Right away."

Margo left the room.

Kaylee lifted her arm with the IV attached.

"You promised to take this out."

Dr. Newell grinned.

Kaylee was starting to dislike him and his lies.

"So I did," he said with a chuckle.

Kaylee tapped her arm. "Take this out."

"Must be the anesthesia," Newell quipped. "All right. Stop your whining."

This man was truly Dr. Jekyll and Mr. Hyde. She was only asking him to keep his promise.

She was sick of this place, and even sicker of Dr. Newell and Margo. This was the worst hospital. She'd never seen or heard any patients. There was no psych patient. She was here all by herself.

Cold chills crept up her spine.

Newell removed her IV and put pressure on the puncture site.

Kaylee stared into his eyes.

"Don't I get a Band-Aid?"

Newell arched his brows as if she was bothering him and opened a nightstand drawer.

Kaylee craned her neck to see what was inside the drawer she hadn't explored.

Wrinkled and partly opened Band-Aids lay strewn about.

Kaylee widened her eyes in disbelief at the dried blood smears smudged against the sides of the drawer.

"That's all right." Kaylee pressed her thumb against the IV site. "I don't need a Band-aid."

Newel slammed the bedside drawer shut.

"You could've told me that earlier!" he snapped.

Kaylee reared away from him.

Newell exhaled.

"I'm sorry, Kaylee. I didn't mean to snap at you. It was absolutely my fault. I had a long day at the office, and your surgery took extra time. But now you're on the road to recovery, and we'll get you all the supplies you need for your unanticipated circumstance."

Margo returned with a handful of tampons and a pill bottle.

Kaylee zeroed in on the ibuprofen label.

"This should tide you over. Let me know if you need more," Margo said.

"Thank you," Kaylee said.

"Hold out your hand."

Kaylee stuck out her palm and Margo deposited two white pills into it.

"That should take care of the cramps." Margo picked up a tampon. "Let me help you into the bathroom."

"I can do it," Kaylee said.

"I'll have no such thing. You just had surgery and anesthesia. It's not safe. You could fall and hurt yourself. Then we'd have to fix you again. You wouldn't want that, would you?"

Kaylee shook her head in response to Margo's threat. "No."

There was no way out of it with this vulture hanging over her. That woman planned to watch her.

Kaylee scooted to the edge of the bed and pushed to a stand, but then swayed.

She held out her hands to block Margo from touching her.

"I just need a minute," Kaylee said.

Margo didn't budge.

"I'm fine now," Kaylee insisted.

Her dizziness receded. With an alternating step and limp, Kaylee made it into the bathroom without Margo laying a hand on her.

Margo and Newell's sweetness had turned sour.

Kaylee unwrapped the tampon while Margo stood guard at the open bathroom door.

There was nowhere to hide.

"I'm a little uncomfortable. Umm…can you please turn around a second?"

Margo rolled her eyes "It's just us girls, but okay."

Just us girls? What a farce!

Margo turned her back to Kaylee while Kaylee inserted the tampon.

"Done," Kaylee said.

"Fine. Wash your hands and back to bed with you."

Kaylee did as she was told while Margo spied on her every move.

Kaylee walked back to the bed unassisted.

She halted and stared at the bloodstained sheet.

"I'll need clean sheets."

"Tomorrow. There's no point tonight because you'll just stain it more."

"Then can I have underwear?"

Margo sighed.

"Tomorrow. That tampon should hold you for the night."

"What time is it?" Kaylee asked.

"It's 6 pm. Rest. That cramping should go away."

"I'm hungry. I haven't had anything to eat for hours."

"I'll bring you dinner."

"Thanks."

Kaylee waited for Margo to leave.

As soon as the door lock clicked, Kaylee stuck her finger in her mouth, scooped the two pills from her cheek, and tucked them under the mattress.

Ibuprofen my ass!

"Have you settled her for the night?" Newell asked Margo the minute she walked into the kitchen.

"Taken care of. Let's eat," Margo replied.

Newell laughed. "Damn. She thinks she got her period. If she ever knew."

"There was a lot. More than the usual."

"Hey. I'm eating here," Otto complained.

"While you were tapping on the computer, Gerald and I were doing the dirty work."

"We all have our strengths and weaknesses," Otto said.

Keep inputting the data, asshole. And when you're done, I'm gonna chop off more than your fingers.

Gerald smiled and raised his glass of wine toward Otto. "Absolutely."

"Salut," Margo added.

Otto raised his can of beer. "Yeah, whatever."

Otto popped the top of the can and guzzled it, belching when he came up for air.

Margo winced. "That was truly disgusting."

"What? It's the beer."

"Let's just eat," Gerald said.

Margo scraped what was left of her moussaka onto a plate.

"Come on, Gerald. Our girl is hungry. We'll have to keep her strength up. Our Greek ordered curvy, not emaciated. And besides, I promised her dinner."

"Those sleepers have knocked her out by now. She won't miss dinner," Gerald said. "She's taken up enough of my time tonight."

Margo stared at Gerald.

"All right. You can leave it on her tray table. But it won't be edible by morning."

Gerald shoved some of his food onto Kaylee's plate.

"Ahem," Margo tossed it to Otto. "Give her one of your

spanakopita."

"Fuck, no. She'll have to work for it."

Gerald gritted. "Give her one."

He towered over Otto, and he had twice the muscles. And he wouldn't even try to compare their mental acuity.

Otto flipped one of the Greek spinach pastries onto the plate.

"See? Doesn't it feel good to give?" Gerald mocked.

"Yep. And those who give shall also receive," Otto shot back.

Gerald raised his fist.

"You'll receive this if you as much as touch a hair on her."

"What kind of hair are you talking about?" Otto joked.

Gerald pushed back his chair and stood. He'd had enough of this little fuck!

He lunged at Otto—only to have Margo step between them to referee.

"Stop it! Both of you. We can't fuck this up again!"

Gerald backed away. Margo was right. All their reputations were at stake. But all bets were off once the Greek deal was done.

Kaylee's stomach growled. The cramps had subsided on their own.

Was Margo lying to her about dinner? Probably.

Margo must've counted on her being asleep by now.

But then the door clicked open, and there stood Margo, holding a dinner plate that actually smelled heavenly.

"Looks like you're still up."

Margo set the plate on tray table.

"I hope you like Greek food. The cafeteria does a pretty good job."

Who cares where she got the food?

Kaylee let out a long, fake yawn.

Margo studied her.

"Enjoy," she said with obvious disbelief.

Kaylee drooped her eyelids.

"Oooooooh-kay," she sleepily answered.

Satisfied that dinner was at least offered, Margo left.

Kaylee grinned.

Fooled you, bitch.

13

Lou Ann's mind bobbed and weaved during the drive, and the schizophrenic pace quickened when they arrived in Naples.

Shit! She'd forgotten to text Brad earlier to let him know that it wasn't only her and Isabelle, but now Harry.

Lou Ann took out her cell and texted Brad.

Hey, it's Lou.

Glad you made it. House 2238 Sweetgum Lane.

Change of plans. Harry's with me.

K. No problem. Plenty room.

Hotel K?

No. Come.

K.

Lou Ann put the house address into her map app. ETA 20 minutes.

See you 20 min

K. Be waiting.

"I can stay at a hotel and then pick you up in the morning to go to the hospital."

"No, Harry. Brad wants you to stay at his house…with me."

Harry widened his eyes.

Everything that happened between her and Harry had melted away after Brad's call…temporarily. Harry was like a comfortable pair of shoes worn to holes in the sole—shoes she'd dug out of a discard box.

"I didn't mean stay together," Lou Ann blurted.

Harry stared at the road ahead.

"I knew that," he said. "We're almost there. I'll drop you off. I need to go to the store to get clothes and toiletries, given that we left rather abruptly."

"I'm so sorry."

"Don't be. I need new underwear anyway," he joked.

It took for Lou Ann to laugh. "Yeah, it's that time of year again."

She had to admit, being with Harry was cathartic.

Harry pulled into Brad"s driveway.

Brad came out to meet them, and as he approached the car, Lou Ann rolled down the window.

"Hey, Lou, Harry. Happy to see you both."

Harry leaned toward Lou Ann and craned his neck to greet Brad.

"Good seeing you too, Brad," Harry called.

Isabelle barked.

"Happy to have you as my guest," Brad said to Isabelle.

Isabelle tilted her head up and sniffed.

"I have your rooms ready, and a soft blanket for Isabelle."

Isabelle let out a soft growl.

"She brought her own blanket, and I brought the rest of her doggie accoutrements," Lou Ann explained.

"We all need those things that comfort us," Brad said.

Silence vibrated between Lou Ann and Harry.

Lou Ann rolled up the window and Harry cut the idling engine.

She exited the car, opened the backdoor, and reached inside to grab Isabelle.

"You go on. I'll bring your suitcase and Isabelle's belongings."

"Thank you, Harry."

Lou Ann cradled Isabelle...her only "child"—up until now....while she and Brad waited at the front door for Harry.

Lou Ann surveyed Brad's spacious yet homey house. The last time she saw him he lived in a one-bedroom apartment in Clearwater.

"Here it is, home," Brad said.

"Nice," Lou Ann nodded.

"After I married Melissa, as you know, we moved to Naples."

She never warmed up to Melissa, but remained cordial to her for Brad's sake. Melissa was all about Melissa, and insisted on a lifestyle beyond what my salary could provide—way beyond.

"Ironically, the house Melissa chose is now mine and the kids'. Melissa moved on to marry an attorney whose face is plastered all over billboards and buses, not to mention the TV and radio ads. She'd outgrown me and the house. We share custody of our two daughters, and they're with their mother this week, so I have the place to myself."

"I'm so sorry we lost touch. I didn't know you had children."

"Life's like that. It sort of sneaks up on you," Brad said.

"It sure does," Lou Ann said quietly.

Brad broke the awkward silence.

"I'll show you to your rooms, and I'll apologize ahead of time for the girly decor."

"It's fine. I'm just so grateful for your hospitality," Lou Ann said.

"I second that," Harry added.

Brad led Lou Ann and Harry down the hallway.

"First stop is you," he said to Lou Ann. "This is my Emily's room, my five-year-old."

Lou Ann entered "Hello Kitty" land, complete with pink walls.

Isabelle scowled at the multitude of cats staring back at her.

"I forgot to mention in the heat of our conservation that we have a real cat. Mr. Whiskers."

Isabelle growled. Of course "cat" was in her vocabulary.

"No worries. Mr. Whiskers will stay safely hidden in my bedroom."

Harry put down Lou Ann's and Isabelle's belongings in their kitty room.

"On to your place, Harry."

"I have to see this," Lou Ann said.

She followed Harry and Brad into the next bedroom.

"This is my eight-year-old Macy's room. As you can tell, she loves daisies."

"I like daisies," Harry said.

Brad grinned. "Perfect."

"I don't mean to rush out, but I need to buy some clothes and other stuff."

"Yeah. I get it. Everything just tumbled," Brad said. "There's a Target down the road. Go to the end of this street and make a right onto the main drag. It'll be a mile away, on your right."

"Thanks."

"I'll see you in a bit," Harry told Lou Ann.

"We can all sit down to dinner when you get back," Brad said. "I've got pot roast with potatoes, and carrots in the pressure cooker."

"Wow. Since when do you cook?" Lou Ann asked.

"Since I've become a single dad. It's amazing what you can do when you have to."

Lou Ann pressed her lips tight. She was anything but amazing, and tomorrow frightened the hell out of her.

Brad gave her hand a gentle squeeze.

"You and Isabelle get settled. Meet me in the kitchen whenever you're ready."

"Okay."

"I'm off," Harry said. "I won't be long."

"Take whatever time you need," Lou Ann said.

Harry leaned over and kissed her on the cheek.

"You too."

Harry backed out of Brad's driveway and followed his directions to the main drag, leaving Lou Ann behind.

He stopped at a red light and looked at his reflection in the rearview mirror.

"You stupid shit!"

He would not use Lou Ann's trauma to his advantage.

He was already responsible for inflicting enough drama in her life.

He'd broken her trust in him.

They'd argued. He'd gone to a bar to get drunk. That's when he'd spilled his soul to Lindsey, the woman sitting next to him. He should have let the bartender call for an UBER but instead he left with a woman he'd known less than an hour. A woman deep in her own problems.

When he woke up naked in her bed, he was positive nothing happened because his dick had been as drunk as he was. He was sure she'd undressed him and then claimed they were now a thing.

Then came the text messages he hid from Lou Ann. But then the crazy woman showed up at the house, followed by Lou Ann's notice of eviction. He pleaded his case to Lou Ann, but she slammed the door on him. Fuck Lindsey and fuck that night. If only he hadn't gone to that bar.

Harry scouted for a parking spot. And when all the spots closest to the entrance were filled, he decided to park at a distance. The walk to the store would do him good—a brief respite from the sudden life-changing turn of events. It was supposed to be a simple pizza dinner, and if she rejected him, he'd still have the pizza. They did have the pizza. But it was anything but simple.

He entered the store, picked up a shopping cart, and headed to the men's department.

Other than groceries, he was not a shopper, so he'd make this a quick trip. He didn't want to hold up dinner.

Although his FBI attire hung in his closet at home, he could always use a spare pair of pants and a dress shirt.

He chose standard navy trousers and a white button-down shirt. He wasn't sure what to wear at a hospital, so he tossed in a light blue casual shirt and a tie, just in case, and added a black belt.

He ended with a package of underwear, navy dress socks, and a couple of pairs of sport socks.

Damn. At least he wouldn't have to do laundry for a while.

Then he looked down at his running shoes.

Shit.

He mowed back down the aisles until he saw the shoe department. Harry glanced at his watch and hurried toward it.

What are the chances he'd find a pair of size eleven shoes?

He scanned the racks and—bingo—a pair of size eleven black shoes!

This was a good omen, so maybe everything would shake out all right.

Harry transferred his items onto the cashier's belt while she scanned each item, folded it neatly, and placed it in a large bag with the rest. Then she set the shoe box in a separate bag.

He paid her and grabbed the bags.

"Thank you," he said.

"You're welcome. Have a great night."

He hauled his brand-new belongings to his car, pulled away with the stash, and headed to Brad's house and back to Lou Ann.

He parked the car and bags in hand, he approached the front door and knocked. He was after all a guest. It didn't seem right to just barge in.

Brad opened the door.

"You don't need to knock. Just come right in. I'm used to the kids coming in and going during the summer months."

"It must be hard for you to trade your kids for Lou Ann and me."

Brad chuckled. "At least I don't have to cut your meat."

"Speaking of dinner, it smells great."

"Another ten minutes. Go ahead and put your bags away."

Harry walked down the hallway and halted in front of Lou Ann's open door.

She was sitting on the kitty bedspread with her back to him, just staring out the window.

"Ahem," he announced, not wanting to startle her.

Lou Ann spun around.

"Oh. You're back. That was quick."

"I just grabbed a few things I needed."

"That's good," she said in a monotone.

Harry set his bags down and entered the room to sit down next to her, but he remained silent..

Minutes later he gently laid his hand on her knee.

"Dinner's ready," he said.

"Okay."

Harry pecked a kiss on Lou Ann's head.

He expected her to reflexively pull away, but she didn't.

"I'll be in the kitchen in a bit," Lou Ann said.

"See you there."

Harry stood and walked to the doorway where he'd deposited his bags, picked them up, and proceeded to the daisy room.

He set his bags on the bed and removed the items, laying them on the bed. He'd put them away later. It would give him a purpose, albeit brief, in the silence of the night.

He returned to Lou Ann and held out his hand.

"Come on. You need to eat something nutritious besides pizza and donuts."

Lou Ann took his hand.

"Just so you know, I am partial to pizza and chocolate cream-filled donuts."

Harry winked. "I'll keep that in mind."

14

Kaylee shoved plastic forkfuls of the mishmash of Greek food peppering her paper plate, and the afterthought meal settled warm in her stomach.

She shoved the empty plate away and risked drinking the room temperature water in a paper cup.

She waited, but the drowsiness didn't come.

Kaylee stared at the locked door. She had no idea what lay outside of it. She'd been too sedated to be familiar with anything other than this room. She couldn't even remember being in that operating room.

Nothing made sense, but she vowed not to languish here.

Then it hit her like a kick in the gut.

Newell was a liar. Her parents weren't dead! They were in a real hospital.

Her knees began to tremble.

They probably told her parents were dead.

She was going to get out of here, but she needed to have a plan.

Kaylee wiggled her toes.

Hmmm.

She could already predict the comings and goings of the people here. So while she was locked away, she'd initiate her escape plan.

Step one: She'd do her own physical therapy. She needed the strength to run.

Step two: She'd eat every crappy meal they gave her.

Step three: She'd appoint the day.

Step four: She'd fashion a weapon.

Step five: She'd hurt anyone who got in her way.

The door clicked open and Margo entered.

Margo stared at the empty plate. "Looks like someone was hungry." She collected the plate and the plastic fork. "Now get some rest," she said.

"I will. See you in the morning," Kaylee replied.

Margo nodded. "Yes, until then."

Margo left and locked the door.

Kaylee grinned.

"Yes, until then."

Joanna stared at the clock on the wall. When she was in that dim, windowless prison cell, she had no idea what time of day it was, or even what week or month. Time was some hidden continuum.

But no more.

It was six pm.

Sated after the grilled chicken, roasted baby red potatoes, and green beans she ordered from the menu Lynn left her, she had no place to go…for now.

Joanna lay back in the bed with her hands behind her head and her ankles crossed.

Tomorrow she would meet this so-called aunt, Kaylee's aunt.

What would an aunt be like? Like maybe a second mother? Joanna barely knew her mother, and she had no aunts, uncles, or any assortment of relatives as far she knew. Perhaps there was someone out there, but they would be as useless as her mother, and worse than her unknown father. Her eyes burned, and she gritted her teeth. No, she would not cry for any of them. No one cared that she was gone. No one even missed her. Newell and Otto had capitalized on that.

But soon she'd be free of them, one way or another.

Lou Ann entered the kitchen to find Harry and Brad at the table, their plates heaped with roast beef, potatoes, and carrots. Another full plate lay next to Harry.

Harry patted the empty chair next to him.

"Have a seat," he said. "I hope you don't mind…," he continued.

She interrupted him. "No, I don't. And thank you."

Lou Ann sat and scooted closer to the table. "Looks and smells delicious."

Brad smiled and nodded. "It took me a couple of tries, but I finally got it right. Even Emily and Macy eat it."

"Surely a sign of an accomplished cook and dad," Lou Ann said.

Could she learn to do the same? Be a single parent, a single mother?

"I could make something else if you like," Brad said.

"Umm, no. Absolutely not."

Lou Ann picked up her fork and knife and dug into her meal.

Tines poked and knives scraped during the silent dinner.

Until Harry leaned back in his chair and patted his belly. "I'm stuffed."

Lou Ann chewed her last forkful, and Brad had cleaned his plate, too.

Cops and agents learned to eat fast, a hard habit hard to break.

Brad picked up the plates.

"Let me help," Lou Ann said.

"I won't hear of it. You're my guests. There's a patio outside the living room glass doors. Why don't you guys relax there, and I'll bring us some after-dinner wine."

Brad read her thoughts.

Lou Ann and Harry settled around the glass patio table.

She met Harry's gaze.

"How are you doing?" he asked.

"All right."

It was best to maintain an even keel, not dip too low, nor ignite any excitement. There was no way to predict how tomorrow would go. Either way, Kaylee's well-being and future were paramount. Lou Ann couldn't expect to waltz into her shattered life. She had no idea how she was going to react, and she was positive Kaylee wouldn't either.

Brad returned with two glasses of white wine, and then fetched his own glass before joining them.

Lou Ann sipped her wine, letting its fruity warmth percolate through her veins.

"I'll have breakfast ready around seven-thirty. I told Dr. Zimmer, Kaylee's doctor, that we'll meet in a hospital conference room to confer before you meet Kaylee tomorrow morning."

"I'll stay here," Harry said.

The last thing Lou wanted was to inundate Kaylee with strangers. And technically, Harry was not back in her life. It would be unfair for Kaylee to meet someone who wouldn't be a stable presence in her life. The girl had been through enough trauma. Everything would be baby steps from here on out, and Harry was only accustomed to running.

"I think that would be best," she said to Harry.

Harry's cheeks drooped and his eyes turned murky

It used to give her pleasure to wound him, but not this time. He'd dropped everything to be with her. Drove her here. Stood by her. Offered himself to her. And this is how she repaid him?

Harry gulped his wine and stood.

"I'm going to turn in. I'll see you guys in the morning."

With that, Harry left.

"I didn't mean to do that," she said to Brad.

"I know. Families are sticky."

Despite everything that had happened between them, Harry was her family.

15

"Meow-meow! Meow-meow!"

What the hell is that?

Lou Ann rolled off the single bed and fell onto the pink carpet while wrapped in a Hello Kitty comforter.

"Meow-meow! Meow-meow!"

Shit! It's a kitty alarm clock.

"Meow-meow! Meow-meow!"

"Shut up!"

Lou Ann untangled herself from the comforter, picked up the annoying kitty alarm, and turned it around.

How the hell do you shut this thing off?

Nothing in the back.

Lou Ann poked Hello Kitty's nose.

The mewing alarm stopped.

She flopped back onto five-year-old Emily's bed and glared at the kitty clock. According to Kitty, it was 7 o'clock. Lou Ann was so buzzed and exhausted that she forgot to set her cell alarm. Thank God this thing was programed for seven. Kindergarten must start early, and if she didn't get going, she'd be late.

Lou Ann grabbed her travel-size toiletry bag, eased out of Emily's bedroom, looked both ways, but saw neither Harry nor Brad.

She pattered into the bathroom, closed the door, and locked it. She'd take a quick shower and then free it up for Harry. She assumed Brad had his own attached bathroom.

It must have been hard for Brad to get used to sleeping alone in a big bed. It was hard enough for her, even after she switched from a king to a queen-sized bed. But she'd become used to her own space.

Besides, Harry was a snorer and a blanket hog.

Lou Ann set the shower temperature to a pleasant warmth and tested it before ducking behind the tropical fish-patterned shower curtain. At least it wasn't stamped with Hello Kitty faces.

She stood under the waterfall, allowing it to massage her shoulders and back into submission. Lou Ann rolled her head around her neck. She'd love to stay here for a good ten minutes, but she couldn't. She had an appointment to keep. Plus she wanted to be fair to Harry and not use up all the hot water.

She needed him know she'd changed her mind. She did need him there, at least in the conference room. Then he could wait in the lobby for her. It was the best compromise. She hoped Harry would see it that way.

Lou Ann shampooed her hair and chuckled about giving Harry back his coconut shampoo with just enough left to cover the bottom of the bottle.

She tilted her head back. The rich lather oozed down her shoulders and then trailed in between her shoulder blades. She did a quick conditioning and lathered up the rest of her body, rinsing yesterday away.

She stepped out of the shower and grabbed a towel. She didn't use one at home, and before the split with Harry, she dried off in the buff.

But this was Brad's house, and she certainly didn't want to give Harry the wrong idea. Besides, she would have to get used to towel coverage if Kaylee came to live with her. However, that was still an if. Both she and Kaylee would have to take it one day at a time.

Lou Ann opened the bathroom door to find Harry standing in his underwear while holding a brand-new bottle of coconut shampoo in one hand and a Target bag in the other.

His gazed down at her damp cleavage.

Harry grinned. "Done?"

She tightened her towel.

"Yes, you could say that."

Harry's smile faded.

"Okay. I'll see you at breakfast," he said over his shoulder just before he shut the bathroom door.

Shit. Why was she so snarky to him? After yesterday he deserved better.

He could've given her his condolences and walked away. He certainly didn't owe her anything. But he didn't run away. He actually ran toward her.

Lou Ann returned to her Hello Kitty temporary habitat and removed a blow dryer from her suitcase. She wasn't sure if Brad owned one. Harry let his hair air dry 99% of the time so she'd assumed it was a guy thing. She didn't dare look in the bathroom for one because it would probably be a Hello Kitty hair dryer with pint-sized strength.

She set out her dress slacks, white button-down blouse with pearl buttons, and her jacket. Lou Ann shook her head. The jacket was too businesslike to wear for the first meeting with her niece. She hung the jacket back up.

Hmmm.

Lou Ann took the jacket back out. She'd wear it during the conference with Kaylee's doctor, and then she could hand it to Harry before going to meet Kaylee. First impressions counted.

She dressed, put on her makeup, and checked herself in the dresser mirror before heading out of Hello Kitty Land.

She passed the open bathroom door. Harry was gone, but his coconut scent lingered.

Lou Ann inhaled Harry's trail.

No! Stop it!

That coconut smell used to annoy her. Truth was, she actually missed it now. The snoring? That was a totally separate issue.

Lou Ann had worked so hard to learn to be alone, and now it could all change.

Harry sat on Macy's double-sized bed. Although he had a wider berth than Lou Ann's single bed assignment, his feet hung off the end of the bed. He missed that king-sized bed he and Lou Ann used to share.

They bought that bed together, and when he and Lou Ann were over, no one got custody of the bed. She did ask him about selling the bed after he declined to take it with him. It was too big for his one-bedroom apartment, and even if it did fit, he couldn't lie in it...alone. But that was on him.

He put on his trousers and the basic long-sleeved shirt, then donned his new socks and shoes and fastened his belt. And at last, he wrapped the tie around the shirt's collar and knotted it.

He studied himself in the mirror.

Not bad.

He could still knot a tie that rivaled how Lou Ann used to fasten them. He'd almost learned to survive without her, but there was that part of him that refused to move on—the stronger part.

But he'd have to push forward...or rather away...after Lou Ann brought Kaylee into her life. They would need space to start a new relationship. Lou Ann and he were the old relationship. Perhaps in time they, too, could start anew, but that was subject to her approval or thumbs-down.

But their relationship wasn't a priority. Lou Ann and Kaylee's was.

He refused to stay behind today. He would go with Lou Ann and Brad and then take up residence in the hospital's lobby. Whether her meeting with Kaylee went well or not, he would be there for her. He'd see her through this, and then retreat the minute he was no longer needed in her life. But until then, he was all in.

Lou Ann froze and Harry halted too. They faced each other after walking out of their respective quarters.

What were the odds of this happening?

She'd forgotten how fine he looked, whether he wore slacks and a tie or jeans and a T-shirt.

How long was she going to keep him begging?

She didn't hate Harry. She only thought she did.

"Hey."

"Hey."

They had to do better than this.

"You look nice," she said.

"So do you."

"Harry..."

"I'm coming with you and Brad." Harry shook his head. "I'm not going to get in your way. Today is so important for you...for Kaylee. And I don't want to interrupt that. I'll wait for you and Brad in the hospital lobby, or wherever."

There he goes again. Reading my thoughts.

Lou Ann took Harry's hand. "I was about to tell you I decided the same."

She'd left out the part about how much she needed him with her.

Lou Ann let go of Harry's hand.

"Let's go get breakfast," she said.

Harry nodded. "Sure." He gave her a small bow and gestured toward Brad's kitchen. "After you."

Damn! Could he pull my heart strings any tighter?

* * *

On their way to breakfast Lou Ann took the lead along the corridor with Harry's footsteps shadowing hers, keeping the same beat.

Sizzling bacon beckoned.

"Smells like Brad went all-out for breakfast," Lou Ann said without turning around.

They walked into the kitchen to find that Brad had set two plates side by side and one plate across the kitchen table, and Lou Ann knew that solitary plate wasn't meant for her.

Brad deliberately sat them next to each other.

She couldn't remember the last time she and Harry sat together to eat breakfast for more than ten minutes. As busy law enforcement agents, they were accustomed to wolfing down bagels, buttered toast, or anything else that was quick and easy to consume so they could move on with their day. And then there was the obligatory to-go coffee sipped in separate cars. They should've gotten up at least fifteen minutes earlier, but they didn't.

Lou Ann and Harry took their places.

"Breakfast is served," Brad announced.

Lou Ann stared at her plate full of scrambled eggs, two slices of bacon, and hash browns. Plus a slice of toast topped off her plate.

"Butter and jam are on the table, and so are salt and pepper. Help yourselves."

Harry looked down at his plate. "Wow!"

"Beats a bagel and toast," Lou Ann said.

"I figure we need a hearty breakfast before a long day," Brad said.

"Yeah, who knows? The conference could take a while and uh...I don't want to just walk in and then walk back out of Kaylee's room."

Her stomach growling during the conference could give the impression of distraction.

"I know today will be unpredictable, but I also know you, and you'll power through it," Harry said. "And Brad and I will be your backup."

"That's right, Lou," Brad nodded.

Lou Ann chuckled.

"What are you laughing at?"

She looked at Harry.

"All you planned on was a simple pizza dinner, and yet here we are."

"Our dinner plans were always subject to change."

"They were, weren't they?"

Harry patted Lou Ann's hand. "A lot of things are subject to change."

A vacation had been the only change she had planned.

16

The door unlocked and Margo brought in Kaylee's breakfast.

Margo shoved the tray with the standard breakfast of curdy scrambled egg substitute, toast with a pat of un-melted butter, and a glass of pulpy orange juice so thick that her plastic fork could stand upright in the middle of it.

"Eat up. I'll be back in half an hour to pick it up whether you're finished with it or not."

"Thank you," Kaylee said, making it a point to sound genuinely thankful.

She'd be polite and compliant with Margo and Newell, but fuck Otto. She couldn't stomach being anywhere near him, and based on the dynamics she heard behind her secured door, Margo and Newell couldn't either.

Kaylee would capitalize on that.

Margo grinned.

"I just want you to heal," she said.

"So do I."

"I'm happy to hear that." Margo glanced at her watch. "Tick-tock. Thirty minutes, my dear."

"I'll start on it right away."

The minute Margo left, Kaylee grimaced and forced down two forkfuls of the fake scrambled eggs and washed them down with gulps of the thick pulp.

Kaylee stuck out her tongue.

Yuck!

She picked up the paper plate and paper cup and limped to the bathroom where she slid the rest of the disgusting breakfast into the toilet and poured what remained of the orange-flecked juice over it.

Then she flushed.

Kaylee smiled.

Done!

She brought the empty plate and cup back and deposited both on the tray.

Since she didn't have pencil or paper, Kaylee started a mental list, and put "breakfast around 7 am" at the top.

Then she lay back on the bed and began to count the ceiling tiles, row after row, pausing at each for a second. She'd counted thirty tiles, estimating thirty seconds. She repeated the count again, equaling a minute. If she scanned the tiles up and back that would be a minute. She would practice that until she could use the ceiling tiles as sort of a clock. Minutes for her would make the difference between freedom or confinement, or—she swallowed hard—punishment.

The door unlocked and Margo sauntered in, inspected the empty plate and cup, and applauded.

"Good girl!"

Margo picked up the tray.

"I'll be right back," she said.

What the hell was next?

Kaylee tapped her finger against the mattress.

Margo returned carrying a mysterious black box by its handle and carried a small black case in her other hand.

Kaylee scooted to the top of the bed as her heartbeat took flight.

She stared at Margo.

"What are those things?"

"This is definitely before your time, but it's called a CD player."

"CD?"

"Compact disc player."

Margo set the strange device on the bedside stand.

"Here, let me show you."

She opened the small black case.

Kaylee looked at the small shiny discs neatly lined up in parallel slots.

"These are CDs. These are musical CDs. Watch."

Margo took out a disc and pushed it into a slot.

"You press this button to play."

A saxophone medley came out of the device.

Margo grinned.

"I was into jazz."

"These are your CDs?"

"Yes. You deserve a reward."

Margo pressed a stop button and an eject button, The shiny disc slid out of the machine.

"Cool!"

"Just don't break or scratch any of my CDs."

"I'll be careful."

"All right. Just don't play it too loud. By the way, you could use a shower. And there's a fresh tampon in the bathroom if you need one."

"Thank you."

"You earned it. And just leave the wet towels in a corner. I'll pick them up later."

Margo left.

Kaylee inspected the discs.

Along with jazz and dated pop, she discovered a row full of classical music, perfect for her to practice her ballet so she could not only strengthen every muscle, but also to keep her sanity.

But first a shower to celebrate starting fresh and anew.

Kaylee walked to the bathroom with barely a limp. She already could tolerate weight on her left ankle longer and with less pain than yesterday, so Dr. Newell's surgery was a success. Strange that neither Margo or Newell unwrapped her ankle to inspect it. Wasn't that what a doctor or so-called nurse would do? And why would Margo tell her to take a shower without removing the dressing?

Kaylee shrugged. So she'd do it herself.

Kaylee set her foot on the toilet seat, leaned over, and unwound the bulky white bandage. She peeled roll after roll until the loosened bandage slid off her ankle.

She inspected it from all sides but couldn't find any incision. Why was she out for so long, then? What went on in that "operating room"?

Her shoulders tensed and thoughts tangled in her head. He didn't do a damn thing to her ankle! He only changed the dressing. Her ankle was healing on its own.

It was all just a ruse—to convince her she was in an antiquated yet bona fide hospital, because they probably suspected she had questions. They were right. But she had more than questions, she had intuition—increasingly icy-spine intuition.

She'd start her own physical therapy today.

Kaylee untied the gown's strings and let it drop to the tiled bathroom floor, and then kicked it with her bruised foot to the corner for Margo to pick up.

Next she turned on the shower faucets. The hot was cold and the cold was colder, but it didn't matter because she'd get clean either way.

She removed the tampon to find it lightly stained. It was the shortest period she'd ever had, but she'd been under a lot of stress so it made sense. Better for her in this ratty place, too. But not for much longer.

Shivering yet invigorated from the cold shower, Kaylee grabbed what used to be a white bath towel, now thinned and with bald patches, and half-dried off. She tossed it into the corner, too, where it landed on top of the soiled gown.

She grinned. She was just following Margo's instructions. She'd delight in watching the woman stoop over to pick them up.

Having no other attire, Kaylee donned a stained, stale, haphazardly laundered gown. They told her that her clothes were tattered from the accident. Probably true, but it could be another lie.

She'd request clothes.

The door unlocked.

Kaylee hurried out of the bathroom.

Margo entered with a plastic bag.

Two surprises and it was still morning.

Margo shook her head. "That gown is pitiful. They should've chucked that long ago."

Kaylee shrugged. *No shit.*

"I brought you clothes as we promised you."

What a scary coincidence.

Margo took out a package of panties and a bra.

"I had to guess the sizes, but I think they'll fit."

"Thank you."

Margo emptied the contents of the plastic bag.

"These shorts and T-shirts are from our lost and found bin. They're clean."

Kaylee scanned Margo's "gifts." Whoever lost them, they were hers now. At least she'd be rid of the recycled patient gowns.

"Thank you for these."

"You're welcome."

Margo stared at Kaylee's bare ankle.

"I see you removed the dressing."

"Yes. I didn't want to get it wet in the shower." Kaylee cocked her head. "I hope that's okay. Dr. Newell fixed it well."

Might as well play the game.

"Yes, he did. I assisted."

"I don't see any stitches that need to be removed," Kaylee said, phrasing her inquiry to sound authentic.

"There are no stitches. Dr. Newell rotated your ankle into place. It would've been too painful to perform this without anesthesia. He's an excellent surgeon and doctor. You are a lucky girl."

"I am."

May lightning strike me.

"You can get dressed now. I'll remove the dirty items from the bathroom." Margo pointed at Kaylee. "And I'll take that gown too."

Kaylee waited for Margo to leave, but she didn't. Instead she stood in front of Kaylee while tapping her foot.

"Come on. Give me that gown."

"I'll leave it on the end of the bed and you can get it later., since you already have your hands full."

"I don't have time for this, Kaylee. I've others to attend to."

Kaylee removed the gown and stood naked in front of Margo.

Margo eyed her, focusing on her breasts and then roving her study downward.

Any other decent nurse would have turned away and given Kaylee appropriate privacy.

"Put on the bra and panties. I want to see how you look in them."

Kaylee hurried into the panties and bra. At least now she was covered up.

"Turn around. I need to see if they fit."

Kaylee's stomach churned. She did as Margo instructed. The sooner she complied, the sooner Margo would leave her alone.

"Those will do. You can finish dressing."

While Margo collected the pile in the bathroom, Kaylee slipped on the shorts, buttoned and zipped them, and ducked into the T-shirt.

"There. Isn't that much better?" Margo asked.

"Yes."

"I'll see you at lunch."

"Yes, ma'am."

"Oh. I'll bring a razor." Margo waved her hand. "We'll have to fix all that down there."

Before she could protest, Margo left.

There were boundaries no one should cross, and Margo just crossed one of them.

* * *

Joanna shoved her breakfast tray away. She'd only managed to eat half the breakfast she ordered because her nervous stomach couldn't take anymore. She was going to meet this aunt today, and she'd have to play the part of Kaylee well enough to pass for a girl she knew nothing about.

What if this aunt asked personal questions she wouldn't be able to answer and revealed she was nothing but a fake?

Oh, that's right. She has amnesia. Perfect.

Nurse Lynn entered.

"Not very hungry?"

Joanna rubbed her belly.

"Nervous."

"I can imagine."

Lynn sat on the end of Joanna's bed.

"I bet your aunt is nervous too. This is life-changing for both of you. But I'll be at the conference this morning with Dr. Zimmer and your aunt, and I'll be your advocate. I'll be going there to make sure everything will go right for you. Lord only knows you deserve it. Can I get you anything else before I leave for the conference?"

"Courage."

Lynn tapped Joanna's knee.

"You're a survivor. You already have that."

Lynn was the kindest woman she'd ever met.

How truly lucky was she?

17

Lou Ann, along with Harry and Brad, entered the hospital's conference room to find two women seated at the conference room table. They both rose, one dressed in a tan skirt and a cream blouse beneath an open white lab coat, and the other wearing maroon scrubs.

She eagle-eyed their hospital IDs.

Stephanie Zimmer MD. Lynn Davis RN.

Trained to commit head-to-toe features to memory, Lou Ann covertly studied the women.

The doctor's light brown hair neatly rested on the shoulders of her white lab coat, and the nurse sported a sleek blonde ponytail and a genuine, relaxed smile.

"Good morning. I'm Stephanie Zimmer, Kaylee's doctor, and this is Nurse Lynn Davis, who's been taking care of Kaylee."

"It's nice to meet you. I'm Lou Ann Jasinski, Kaylee's father's sister...Kaylee's aunt."

She left out that she was a sergeant, because, unlike Brad, her law enforcement status was unimportant today. She was here as Kaylee's guardian.

Dr. Zimmer extended her hand and Lou Ann shook it.

The petite doctor's grip was firm, but kind.

Lynn's hand settled warm in Lou Ann's palm. They gave each other a light squeeze.

"This is my...good friend, Harry Boxer, and Captain Brad Jarett, who I believe both of you and Kaylee have met," Lou Ann said, compelled to announce them.

"Absolutely. It's nice to see you again, Captain Jarett," Dr. Zimmer said.

Both women briefly gripped the men's hands.

"Please, let's all sit," Dr. Zimmer said.

Lou Ann, Harry, and Brad sat together opposite Dr. Zimmer and Lynn.

"Today's conference is not only to discuss Kaylee's medical issues, but also how we can all work together to help Kaylee progress."

She already liked Dr. Zimmer and Nurse Lynn, and trusted them to properly care for Kaylee. Soon it would be her turn. Would they trust her, and most important, would Kaylee?

Dr. Zimmer leaned across the table toward Lou Ann, her empathy clear.

"Lou Ann, I'm so sorry about your brother and sister-in-law. Your world upended in twenty-four hours, and yet here you are with more to come. I can only imagine the turmoil you've been tossed into. Although I and Nurse Lynn are responsible for Kaylee's care, we are also here to help you. This will be a huge change for you and Kaylee, and we want you both of to succeed."

She didn't doubt Dr. Zimmer's and Nurse Lynn's sincerity, but doubts about her ability to parent Kaylee lingered. She was single, and the only being she was responsible for was Isabelle.

After she miscarried her and Harry's child, she distanced herself from him, and he sought solace elsewhere. That part was on her. It wasn't all Harry's fault, but it falsely healed her heart to blame him exclusively and to call herself the victim.

It was time to stop making him the villain. The true, innocent victim was Kaylee.

Her brother's and Melinda's deaths left behind a frightened child and granted Lou Ann a second chance to right horrible wrongs.

Lou Ann looked at Dr. Zimmer and Nurse Lynn.

"Thank you. Kaylee and I will be starting a long and challenging road." Lou Ann then glanced at Brad and shifted her gaze to Harry.

Harry rested his hand on Lou Ann's shoulder. The gesture was an outwardly safe PDA, but inwardly it was a risky move. But he came back harder every time she rebuffed him.

She and Harry had an undeniable history. But history was about the past, and the past was set in stone. Present and future were malleable.

The question was, how much would she bend for Harry?

Harry removed his hand, leaving her shoulder cold and lonely. She hated that he still left her feeling that way, and that she couldn't completely respond in kind…yet. There was a lot left of their mess that needed untangling.

But her top priorities needed to be Kaylee, and providing her with stability.

Dr. Zimmer began the conference. "The paramedics who responded to the scene of the car accident involving your brother's family found their efforts to resuscitate your brother and sister-in-law futile, and they also deemed Kaylee—who they found unresponsive in the back seat— the same. But surprisingly, they were able to revive her and transported her to Good Samaritan, the closest hospital."

Lou Ann's breaths strained against her ribs, and every beat of her heart echoed in her chest while she played in her head every second of the accident and the terror that must have filled the vehicle while it careened to Lyle and Melinda's deaths and left Kaylee clinging to the life.

Lou couldn't contain her stuttered breathing.

With everything tumbling so fast, and given the lateness of her arrival, she hadn't been to the medical examiner's office yet. As a sheriff, she'd attended many autopsies with professional detachment, but this time it would be gut-wrenchingly personal. While she was sitting in a chair, Lyle and Melinda were lying on cold steel autopsy tables.

She shuddered.

"Are you all right? Dr. Zimmer asked.

Lou Ann licked the inside of her dry mouth. She opened her suddenly-parched mouth.

"Yes," she lied. "I just need a glass of water."

Lou Ann picked up her water glass and drank half of it in silence while everyone watched and waited.

She set the water glass down.

"Please continue, Dr. Zimmer."

"Kaylee's admission assessment included CT scans of her brain, chest, and abdomen and pelvis. Given the logistics of what appeared to have been a high-speed collision with a tree, it was truly a miracle that Kaylee survived. Her face and chest were bruised, which may partially be from the air bag deployment that ultimately saved her life."

The doctor continued, "Her head trauma included a concussion and although she is physically stable now, she continues to suffer from memory loss, which maybe be acute or chronic. Only time and therapy will tell. Her neurological exam is normal, and her memory issues to some extent may stem from psychological trauma. She suffered no fractures, however her white blood cell count, one index of infection, was high, and that along with her fever, we decided to start her on antibiotics, which she has responded to well. She remains without a fever."

"Why would she have an infection and fever?" Lou Ann probed. "A concussion usually doesn't cause that, does it?"

They were holding something back.

Lynn cocked her head.

Dr. Zimmer pursed her lips and nodded. She glanced at Harry and Brad, and then returned her focus on Lou Ann. "There's a matter that I need to discuss in private with you after the conference," she said.

"All right," Lou Ann answered.

"A final issue I must address is that Kaylee is significantly underweight. It's not unusual to see eating disorders in teenage girls, but this didn't happen overnight."

"I noticed that Kaylee didn't want to eat or drink anything at first. I also was suspicious that she didn't trust the food or drink, but ultimately she did eat a sandwich and drink that I brought her," Lynn said. "I then gave her a hospital menu and she's been filling that out. "I haven't observed her inducing vomiting, but, as Dr. Zimmer mentioned, her weight will be an ongoing problem and will need to be addressed."

"I agree that Kaylee will need psychological care on many fronts, and I'll make sure it happens," Lou Ann said.

"We can help with that," Dr. Zimmer said. "Do any of you have any questions?"

"I don't have any questions. You've covered the issues that Lou Ann and Kaylee will have to conquer, but I'm here at Lou Ann's request as a good friend. I'd be more than happy to set up any of consults or therapies allowing Lou Ann and Kaylee the time they require." Harry looked at Lou Ann. "Of course only if I'm asked."

Lou Ann set her hand on Harry's. "I'm asking."

"You got it."

"Ditto for me," Brad said.

Dr. Zimmer grinned. "It's good to have reinforcements."

Harry and Brad stood.

"We'll be waiting in the hospital lobby. Take your time," Harry said.

"No worries. We'll keep busy."

"Text us me when you're ready," Harry said.

"I will."

"See you later," Harry said. He took Lou Ann's hand and squeezed it. "You'll do fine."

Harry had stepped up to the plate the way she'd longed for him to do so many times before.

He leaned as if to kiss her cheek, but stopped short. They weren't a couple, and he must have realized it would be unfair for him to claim that in front of the doctor, especially since she introduced Harry as her friend, just the same as Brad. But there was a difference. It just couldn't be right now.

The door closed behind Harry and Brad.

Lou Ann studied Dr. Zimmer and Lynn, waiting for their explanation of the private matter.

The doctor tapped her fingers on the table.

"I take patient information very seriously, but given that Kaylee is underage, and because you will be responsible for her care, I feel it is important that I discuss with you a difficult and serious matter."

Lou Ann shifted her chair closer to the table to signal she wasn't going to back away from what appeared to be grave news. She wanted the doctor to know she had her full attention.

"I'd mentioned that Kaylee had a CT of her pelvis while we were looking for hidden injuries and, of course, the source of her infection, we noted an IUD inside her uterus."

The last time Lou Ann saw Kaylee she was a toddler. That she was sexually active was wildly surprising.

"Was the IUD the problem?"

"Yes. Her tests also returned positive for gonorrhea and chlamydia. I consulted a gynecologist, who examined Kaylee and concurred that Kaylee had a pelvic infection and recommended removal of the IUD and appropriate antibiotic therapy, which she received. The gynecologist and I talked to Kaylee about the IUD. She said it was inserted in a clinic a few months ago and that she'd had sex with two men."

"Men?"

"She called them men."

"Was she raped?"

"She denied that. And she was happy to have the IUD removed and added that she was done with men."

There was that term again, "men".

Dr. Zimmer cleared her voice. "When the gynecologist examined Kaylee, she noted that Kaylee was very detached. Although it hasn't been confirmed, we sometimes see this with sexual abuse victims."

No wonder they wanted to say all this in private.

"Just say what you're going to say. Full disclosure, I'm a deputy sheriff with a Clearwater sheriff's department and I also have seen a lot of grisly things, but if you're trying to imply that my brother abused her, the answer is a big, fat no!. He would never have done that. We weren't raised that way. There wasn't any abuse in our home, and Melinda also would never have allowed that to happen, because it didn't."

Her volume escalated to loud and angry.

"Lou Ann, you know I had to ask."

Lou Ann cradled her forehead in her palm.

"I understand. You're just doing your job and looking out for Kaylee. I'll discuss sexuality with her once she trusts me, and I'll see to it that she has follow-ups with a gynecologist and a psychiatrist."

"I trust you will."

"Are you ready to meet Kaylee, or do you need more time?" Dr. Zimmer asked.

"I'm ready."

"Good. Nurse Lynn and I will take you to her."

Joanna drummed her fingers on the mattress. This lie was taking up a lot of oxygen. And what if she really couldn't stand this woman—this so-called aunt? Maybe her initial plans to hitch out of Florida were better after all. But everything had been set in motion, and it was too late now. Then again, if this this aunt was a real jerk she could still take off. She'd become a wizard at contingency plans. This was no different.

Joanna ran her fingers through her hair.

She could at least present herself well.

She vaulted out of bed and hurried into the bathroom. The conference should be ending soon. How much more was there to discuss about her?

She looked into the mirror and frowned.

Hmmm. Bad bed hair.

Joanna grabbed a comb, pulled it through the tangled mess, and nodded to her reflection.

Then she splashed cold water on her face and slapped her cheeks for color.

Margo used to plaster her face with makeup and gobs of mascara, and outline her cheeks with disgusting pink blush. Candy apple lipstick topped off the "come fuck me" look.

Joanna's slapped cheeks at least looked more natural.

Joanna rushed back to the bed, jumped in, pulled the sheet to her waist, and squirmed into a faux relaxed pose. The back of her neck got sweaty and her heartbeat thumped against her ribs while she stared at the door and waited for the potential key out of this place before Newell, Otto, and Margo found her.

Footsteps coming down the hallway further heightened her pulse rate. Joanna held her breath.The sounds of approach echoed in her ears remembering how her stomached soured when she heard the footsteps of the multiple men who lined the hallways outside her "cell" waiting for their turn.

Dr. Zimmer peeked her head around the corner and smiled.

Joanna sucked air back into her lungs.

"Are you ready?" she asked.

"Yes," she said, fighting a breathlessness.

What if the next few minutes would end up an epic fail?

But her overthinking the situation expired the minute Dr. Zimmer and Nurse Lynn ushered the woman into her room, her temporary safe abode.

Joanna widened her eyes to have a better look at the aunt.

The woman returned a strained a smile.

Joanna assessed the strange relative.

She wasn't as sterile-looking as Joanna expected, or as scary.

She never had an aunt, and somehow she'd expected a matronly crone to come claim her. But that clearly wasn't the case.

Her aunt's hair was a smooth chocolate brown that rested on her shoulders. She was slim, yet muscular as well as womanly.

She must work out.

She was classy. Not like Margo or her mother—the two women in her life who failed her. *May this woman not be the third*. But her eyes had a genuine glow.

"Kaylee, this your Aunt Lou Ann," Dr. Zimmer announced.

Aunt Lou Ann flashed a wider grin and gave a slight nod.

Joanna nodded back.

"Hi," Joanna said while meeting Lou Ann's direct gaze. Coyness wasn't in her repertoire. She'd be long dead if she was.

"Hi, Kaylee," she said.

The woman covered her guilt well. That she hadn't laid eyes on her real niece in ages was to Joanna's advantage. Whatever happened in this family was as messed up as what happened in hers, although without the violence.

"I'll let you two get acquainted," Dr. Zimmer said.

Dr. Zimmer and Nurse Lynn left and slid the ICU glass door shut.

At least Joanna could see through it. Not like the bolted door of her prison cell. She'd caught on quickly that her "room" wasn't a hospital. That really pissed them off. She could've just pretended. It would have saved her until that opening—that split second—where she could've escaped instead of lying there hot and fighting for that last breath while Newell fought to resurrect her until she decided death was her best option.

Her pulse jackhammered in her head.

Joanna jerked, shoving what was way too scary out of her mind. After all, she hadn't died.

"Are you all right?" her aunt asked. "Do you need me to call Dr. Zimmer?"

"No. I'm okay. I just had a chill. It happens sometimes," Joanna lied.

The excuse rolled right off her tongue.

"I better call Dr. Zimmer," Aunt Lou Ann insisted.

Joanna grasped Lou Ann's hand and then jerked it away.

"I'm sorry. I didn't mean to grab your hand."

"It's all right," Lou Ann reassured her and rested her hand, bird-like, on top of Joanna's.

Lou Ann's tentative touch only emphasized that they knew nothing about each other.

And at that moment, Joanna made up her mind. She'd go with Aunt Lou Ann.

Why did she stay away? She and Lyle could've made amends. Lou Ann could've made the first move, extended a family olive branch, but instead they left a dying tree between them. And as a bitter reminder, Kaylee didn't recognize her, and sadly she wouldn't have recognized Kaylee if she had walked right past her.

Her heart soured and her hand flittered away from Kaylee's.

Kaylee flinched as if she'd done something wrong.

"I'm sorry!" they blurted at the same time.

Then they stared at each other, waiting for whoever moved first.

Lou Ann had to fix this.

She rested her hand again on top of Kaylee's, but now with emphasis, and then she waited for Kaylee's move—a precarious game of chess between them.

Checkmate.

Kaylee let Lou Ann's hand stay.

They breathed in rhythm.

It was an emotional standoff.

What kind of mother was she going to be to Kaylee? She'd thought hard about the past twenty-four hours. She swore she wasn't going to be the distant aunt. Kaylee would be eighteen years old on October tenth.

Warmth shot to her fingertips.

She was there with Melinda that day, holding her hand during each contraction and wiping Melinda's sweaty forehead with a damp washcloth while pale Lyle paced.

But when Kaylee's wet head emerged, Lyle was all in, and they both yelled, "Push!" while Melinda squeezed Kaylee out into the doctor's waiting arms.

It was the best day ever!

But at eighteen Kaylee would be free to leave and never return—or perhaps only returning for college breaks. She imagined that happened to the best of parents—college calling their child away to shaky independence.

But Lou Ann wasn't ready for that.

Damn! They just now met again, fourteen years later.

But they were both starting at zero as if the past between them never existed, and it took Lyle and Melinda's deaths to bring them to this point.

None of this should've happened. But they both were left to cobble together a relationship, and Lou Ann would see to it that they weaved a family together. There would be splinters, but Lou Ann had decided during the drive to Naples to provide her niece with stability. They both could use that. And maybe that family tree hadn't completely died. She and Kaylee could become the first leaves to sprout from its naked branches.

"Hey! You're smiling," Kaylee said.

Heat seeped into Lou Ann's face.

Just how long had she been smiling? Long enough to get caught.

"I'm just happy to see you again."

That was true, but maybe it was too much for Kaylee at the moment.

Kaylee tapped Lou Ann's hand.

"I am too."

So, it wasn't too much.
For the moment, it was just right.

This woman was genuine. She was safe. She had no inkling that the hand she held belonged to a true stranger.

Joanna would carefully probe what really happened between Lou Ann and this Kaylee. And more importantly, what happened to the real Kaylee.

Joanna was becoming more and more comfortable being called Kaylee. It was second nature to respond to the new name, her new identity.

She couldn't go back. She could only go forward.

And if the real Kaylee showed up, she'd be out of here as fast as she had entered.

She and Lou Ann retreated to their comfort zones with their hands poised at their sides.

This relationship was going to take a while.

She might as well be Kaylee.

Joanna stiffened between the sheets, and her head buzzed.

The recollection strobed in her head like a bad movie clip.

Her mouth went dry and her lips numbed.

Shit! That's what really happened. She woke up in this hospital in strange clothes, and she could only presume they were Kaylee's.

Newell and that creep Otto had dumped her at that car wreck they were all talking about.

Damn! They thought she was dead, but she had one hell of a resurrection.

That Kaylee chick had switched clothes with a dead girl and then run off. But why? There she was—a privileged girl—on her way to college. Well, she didn't deserve to return. That she hadn't surfaced told Joanna she stood a chance at a new life—the life Kaylee ditched. Kaylee had no clue how good she had it.

Now it was Joanna's turn to have a real family.

And she more than deserved it.

18

"Hey! There are three cars backed up!" yelled Freddie, Sophia's boss.

Sophia stood up straight with the vacuum hose in her hand. She gripped the black snake in her hand and waved it at Freddie. She knew exactly where she wanted to shove it.

Bend over, asshole. I'll make your day—and mine!

She'd just finished vacuuming the never-used back seat floor after waxing the attorney's silver Jaguar and massaging the leather upholstery.

J. B. Princer, the third, or, as she called him, "the Prickster," was a repeat customer, and this was his usual Saturday monthly demand. And he'd always asked for Sophia to detail his luxury ride. He just wanted to gawk at her ass while she bent over to clean up after his indiscretions. Thank God she would never be one of them.

He just wanted to massage his dick while she worked. Maybe there was something erotic about slumming. She was sure only platinum blondes with boob jobs and cutsie giggles sat in the front passenger seat, no doubt primed to lean over and suck him off.

J. B. sidled over to Sophia.

"Nice job, as always," he said.

"Thank you, Mr. Princer."

He grinned with a cock of his eyebrow.

"You know you can call me Jason."

He said that every time, and every time she referred to him as Mr. Princer.

"Here you go."

He jutted out a fifty-dollar bill and waited for her to take it, and when she went for it, he held back a second before releasing it to her, emphasizing his "superiority."

Sophia eased it away.

J. B. smiled wider, while the corners of his eyes crinkled in symmetrical trifolds that recessed deep into that fake tan of his, and then he twirled the fat gold pinky ring on his right hand. It was thicker than the plain wedding band on his left ring finger. Sophia felt sorry for his wife. But then maybe she had someone else in her back pocket. Who knew about the rich? They had their own rules. Their own games.

The Prickster winked.

"See you next month," he slid out.

Sophia waved.

"Next month," she called back.

Sophia quickly stuffed the fifty into the back pocket of her Daisy Dukes before Freddie could eye the huge tip and abscond with all but ten bucks of what she'd worked damn hard for, and predictably threatening to fire her if she didn't pony it up.

But she'd managed to hide every one of Prickster's fifties without Freddie so much as getting a glimpse.

The more often J. B. showed and requested her, the more likely that Freddie would inevitably catch on.

He'd accuse her of fucking J. B. What a joke! She'd never touch him, even if the tips dwindled to nearly nothing, or nothing at all.

She hated this job, but it paid the rent on that apartment on the outskirts of Little Havana.

Sophia found the place advertised in the *Pennysaver*.

Even though the thunder of jets scurrying and out of Miami International shook her walls and rattled her windows, she was lucky to find an affordable place to live without having to resort to dreaded roommates. She could come and go as she pleased, and the tiny bathroom was all hers, all the time. No one to complicate her life. No one to steal her food or freeload off her. It was perfect.

Sophia peered through her sunglasses at the Porsche waiting next in line for her services, but the black Mercedes behind it grabbed her attention.

Shit! It couldn't be!

Sophia lowered her shades, balancing the frames on the tip of her nose.

It was him!

Looked like the doctor decided to take her up on her offer to detail his car.

Sophia looked past the Mercedes's windshield and met Gerald Newell's smiling gaze.

She shot him a wider grin.

The hot doc shot her a thumbs-up.

Her stomach flipped and her heart beat cheerfully in her ears.

She did come on to him, and she regretted it, a bit. But using her sexuality got her things. Take the landlord. He initially wanted more, but she'd worn her peek-a-boo low cut bra like armor, and bang, he cut $300 off the rent. But what happened on that appointment day with Gerald Newell, an appointment that she actually was able to pay up front...well, that just happened. She could tell he was turned on too. And damn! Here he was!

She returned a quick wave.

The driver of the Porsche rolled down his window.

"Hey! It's my lunch hour. Snap to it! I don't have all fucking day!" he yelled.

She didn't have all fucking day either.

Freddie approached with fists jammed on his hips.

"Is there a problem?" he demanded.

"Nope. I'm taking care of the next customer," Sophia responded.

"Yeah, finally!" the man groused with his head propped out his open car window.

Freddie gestured to the cantankerous man. "I'll take care of you right here."

Freddie shot Sophia a narrowed *"I deal with you later,"* glance.

She blinked back a *"Just try me. I'll fuck with you later."*

She put in more hours than anyone else, and she was good at her job. And Freddie knew that.

The driver of the Porsche shot her a satisfied smirk while he pulled his vehicle towards Freddie.

Those two deserved each other.

Plus they just freed her up to give the good doctor her undivided attention.

Sophia beckoned him on.

Gerald inched his Mercedes towards her.

She mouthed, *Closer*, and she winked when he stopped his car.

He rolled down his window.

"I'm so glad you came," she said.

"So am I."

* * *

Gerald swung open his car door, got out, and leaned over the hood to get Sophia's attention, which took all of five seconds before his gaze met hers. He raised his brows.

"Looks like you're suddenly free," he said.

She winked at him. "Absolutely."

"That guy in the Porsche is an asshole," Gerald said. "Would you like me to meet him out back?" he teased.

He wouldn't do it, but it made him feel taller to offer to defend her from that slime.

Sophia giggled. "That won't be necessary."

He shifted his weight.

"The offer still stands."

"Duly noted."

They stared at each other.

"If you just drive through the wash, I'll meet you on the other side to hand wax and detail the inside. I'll give you the works, as promised."

Shit! Would he ever like a hand job and a thorough detailing!

Gerald fought the stiffy coming on. Sophia had him by the balls and he was loving it.

She was his little nymph.

He hadn't felt this way since Jenna. Beautifully polished Jenna from medical school. Jenna had matched at a top surgical residency program and he at a prestigious obstetrics and gynecology residency. They tried to maintain a long-distance relationship that was doomed to fail, not only because of the 3,000-mile distance, but also from the heavy and demanding hours of residency. They'd finally drifted apart.

Gerald had seen other women on and off, but nothing lasted for more than six months. He'd become bored with them. Sex was perfunctory, probably for them too.

Then he met Otto. He was at the top of his career, but insurance companies gouged him, and his income soon stagnated. So he toyed with Otto's plan instead of burning out. It seemed reasonable at the time. After all, he offered his services for free to women who had no clear, bright future, and who would be taken care of financially. They were sexually active anyway, and most he deemed promiscuous, so it was a win-win, he assured himself.

As Otto had promised, it would be done discreetly. No one would be the wiser. Gerald would be safe and well off. And his practice could flourish. But it was all a lie, and now he was too deep in. The only way out was to close the practice and take off for Greece.

He gazed at Sophia. What did she really have here? He'd sweep her off to Greece, or who knows where in Europe. Perhaps France.

Finger snaps crackled in his ear.

"Hey! Earth to Dr. Gerald!"

Sophia's voice popped him back to reality.

Sophia chuckled. "You were smiling."

"And why wouldn't I? It's a gorgeous day."

That was an understatement.

"It sure is. Well, let's get you going."

The double entendre was killing him.

Is she doing this on purpose? God, I hope so.

"Umm. Just drive through the automated wash."

Gerald cocked his head.

"Why don't you hop inside? I'll give you a ride. No point in you walking around to the rear."

He grinned. Rear. He wanted her rear in his car. Better yet, his hand under her rear. Cupping and squeezing her firm, plump cheeks.

Sophia shrugged.

"Okay."

She hopped into his car, swung her legs inside, and shut the passenger side door.

Gerald climbed in and grasped the wheel.

Sophia wrapped the seat belt across her. The belt wedged in her ample cleavage.

She winked at him.

"Uh-hmm. Safety first."

"Absolutely."

Gerald snapped on his seat belt.

"Ready?" he asked.

Sophia tossed a forward gesture.

"Onward."

Which was exactly what he had in mind.

Gerald pulled his car up the car wash ramp and put it into neutral, and then he leaned back.

"Did I pull in right?" he asked with a flirty grin.

"Couldn't have done better."

Was his aim that perfect for everything?

Sophia wiggled on the butter-soft leather seat at the naughty fantasy.

Sudsy tentacles flapped the car, leaving Sophia and Gerald ensconced in their white-foamed private cave.

Her heart pulsed while she waited for his next move. But Gerald kept his hands to himself. She'd been sure he'd crawl toward her, even for the five minutes where no one could see them.

Sophia grinned. Freddie would shit his pants if he knew she was inside a client's car. She'd never done this before, but Gerald was different. He was her ticket out of this shitty job. And above all, he was sexy, and she wanted what she wanted, and she knew he wanted it too.

And then it happened.

Gerald's hand landed smack on her naked thigh. He gave her a gentle squeeze, and of course she didn't stop him. Not one peep of protest.

He slid his hand slowly up her thigh and then slid it under the high hem of her Daisy Dukes.

She grew moist and eyed his hardness.

Damn! She'd caught a doctor. Better yet a gynecologist, inside and now out of the office, out of his turf and into hers.

The foam faded and so necessarily did their foreplay.

Their steamy cave was rinsed clean and the car was dragged back into the sunlight.

Shit! There was Freddie. Luckily his back was towards them while the Porsche driver dictated his demands, using gestures to drive home his points, which apparently were many. Freddie shrank with every gesture.

Sophia chuckled.

Gerald caught on and laughed.

"Entertaining, isn't it?"

"Yes, but I gotta get out of your car before he catches me."

"Would that be so bad?"

Sophia sighed. "Yes and no. It pays the bills."

She tested his response.

He simply nodded.

Not the response she expected. Perhaps all that was between them was animal instinct, which wasn't that bad. But she was hoping for more.

Sophia crawled out of Gerald's Mercedes as if Freddie could hear the whoosh of her exit, and then grimaced while easing the door closed until it softly clicked shut.

Gerald sprang out of the driver's side and swung the car door shut.

Freddie turned at the sound.

Gerald waved to him. Freddie didn't even notice Sophia. She had no idea what to think of that.

Sophia pointed to the car wash lobby.

"Why don't you go in there and relax while I get to work on your car? There are vending machines inside."

Here she was telling a wealthy doctor to slum among vending machines.

"Great. It's sweltering out here."

Fuck you, Gerald.

Sweat snaked along her neck and pooled in the small of her back leaving a telltale wet spot on the back of her cotton shirt.

She pressed her hand against the back of her neck and the sunbaked skin burned her palm. Smack in the middle of summer high noon in Miami could easily be confused with hell. But she owed Gerald a spit shine and she was going to deliver just that. He could show her some extra appreciation.

The Mercedes's hood sizzled clear through the polish rag and nearly blistered her palm.

Sophia waxed Gerald's luxury vehicle in concentric circles. The sun's rays brightened her work to blinding perfection.

She straightened to relieve the strain in her spine, and a drop of sweat fell off the tip of her nose and landed in her cleavage. Her bra broke its descent.

Sophia sighed. Gerald was sitting in air conditioned comfort while she slaved in the heat.

But she's the one who told him to go.

Muted footsteps sinking into the broiling asphalt thudded behind her.

Oh, Freddie, will you please fuck off?

It was too hot to argue with him.

Breath poked at her neck.

Before she could spin around and torpedo a roundhouse punch to his measly, fucking face, someone grabbed the back of her shirt and pressed a shot of cold against her hot skin. The pop of a soda can followed. Cold carbonated bubbles fizzed across her back, lowering her skin temperature a blessed ten degrees.

"How's that feel?' Gerald whispered in her ear.

Sophia smiled wide.

"Like heaven," she cooed.

She'd been sprung from hell.

She didn't move. She could really give a fuck if Freddie saw them. In fact, she wished he would.

"Thank you."

"Don't mention it," Gerald said, while he kept the cold soda can to her back.

"My car looks blindly awesome."

"It's my job. I'm glad you approve," she said, not turning around, not wanting to give up the cold, bubbly gift.

Gerald slid the can out from under her shirt, placed his muscular hand on her shoulder, and spun her towards him.

He held out the can of Coke.

"Here, you deserve this."

"Thanks."

At least he was considerate.

Sophia grabbed the Coke and gulped it until the can crunched empty.

"Ahhh! That hit the spot. Oh! I drank your soda."

"It was meant for you."

"That's so sweet."

Gerald chuckled. "Don't give me too much credit, because I drank mine in air-conditioned comfort."

Sophia grinned. "You brought the air conditioning with you."

They locked gazes.

"How about I take you out for an air-conditioned dinner tonight?"

Apparently the Coke was foreplay.

"Umm. Sure. I get off at five."

"What a coincidence. So do I."

Gerald reached into his back pocket and pulled out a fat, black leather wallet. He opened it and handed Sophia a crisp stack of twenties. She opened her mouth but before she could utter a word, Gerald interrupted her.

"Give that asshole boss his minimal due and keep the rest." He winked. "It'll be our secret."

Sophia grinned. "For sure. Thanks."

"See you tonight. Where shall I pick you up?"

Her head buzzed. He surely lived in a mansion while she had a tiny apartment within earshot of jets. But she desperately desired a relationship with him, and he was bound to find out about her living situation eventually, and she didn't want to lie. She was who she was.

Excuses were not her thing.

Sophia straightened.

"Let me see your palm," she said.

Gerald arched his brows in an intrigued way.

Sophia took out a pen from the back pocket of her shorty shorts and wrote her address on his palm.

"There you go," she chirped. "See you at six."

Gerald chuckled. "Now I know where to find you."

"I'll be waiting."

Gerald hopped into his shiny Mercedes keeping his eyes trained on Sophia.

She gave him a queen's wave, and he returned with a roguish salute.

Then he drove away.

Sophia followed the car's bumper, and she knew he was watching her through his rearview mirror.

"Hey! When you're through going gaga over that rich prick, get to work on the next in line. Don't make me rescue you again," Freddie called from across the lot.

She tossed the real prick a queen's wave with her middle finger extended.

"Got it!" she yelled back.

19

Lou Ann and Kaylee had said their temporary goodbyes. Yes, temporary. It was an odd—and at first—awkward, initial meeting for them both, but it was to be expected. She couldn't just waltz into her traumatized niece's life, especially since she'd been excommunicated from Lyle's life and consequently severed from Kaylee's.

And still Lou Ann's heart squeezed guilt through every vessel in her body. But she couldn't change the past. Only atone for it and move forward.

Harry stood the minute Lou Ann entered the hospital lobby with eyes that asked, *How did it go it go?*

She moved closer until the toes of their shoes met halfway.

Harry held out his arms, arms she once sank into so happily .

She stepped into his embrace and waited, and he gave her a cautious hug.

Her shoulder blades stiffened, but then relaxed, her body memory of the way Harry and she used to be surfaced, and she rested her head on his shoulder—her heartbeat hankering for the comfort Harry so willingly provided at this vulnerable moment.

He patted her back, carefully staying away from her lower back. Plus, they were in a hospital—not that sorrowful or jubilant embraces weren't a normal part of hospital life-and-death matters.

Lou Ann leaned away, and Harry lowered his arms.

"How are you?' he asked.

"Okay."

That was mostly true. But Kaylee and she made a connection—a start.

"All right. Now what?" Harry asked.

Lou Ann looked at her cell phone. Her chest sagged during an extra-long exhale.

"I have to go to the medical examiner's office and make funeral arrangements for my brother, Lyle, and my sister-in-law, Melinda. I'm the only surviving family—besides Kaylee—so I have to see to the burial."

Everything crashed down on her so fast! Things that, unbelievably, she hadn't thought about like the responsibility for the burial and its expenses. Money she didn't have. She'd have to figure it out. She'd have to get a loan. She couldn't leave them to a Potter's field destination. She wouldn't.

Harry extended his hand. "Let's go."

Lou Ann gazed out the passenger window while Harry drove. The hospital shrank in the distance, but her thoughts of Kaylee grew larger.

Harry remained silent while making the turns dictated by a woman's voice on his maps app.

"In 700 feet, make a right at the traffic light and then stay left."

Harry followed her commands all the way until the voice reported, "Your destination is 300 feet on your right."

He pulled into the Medical Examiner's office parking lot.

The automated woman's voice announced that they'd arrived at their destination.

He parked and cut the engine.

They sat in silence for a few seconds that seemed more like minutes.

"Do you want me to go in with you or wait out here?"

Lou Ann turned to him.

It was considerate of him to ask. The Harry she knew never died. It was she who'd tried so hard to extinguish him.

"I want you to come with me."

Lou Ann and Harry unbuckled their seat belts and exited the car.

Harry clicked his remote, and with a toot he secured the doors.

He walked next to her but didn't offer his hand.

He could still read her like a good FBI Special Agent and a better ex. He recognized that she needed space, and even more so control.

He did, however, reach for the polished brass door handle and open the door, allowing her to enter first.

His size eleven shoes shadowed her determined stride.

Lou Ann halted in front of the reception desk.

A woman gazed up at Lou Ann and Harry past the spectacles

teetering on the tip of her nose.

"May I help you?" she asked politely.

"I'm Lou Ann Jasinski and this is my friend, Harry Boxer."

She'd just whittled Harry down to "friend." It was the quickest and dirtiest way to identify their complicated relationship.

Harry gave the receptionist an appropriate, yet solemn half-smile.

The receptionist arched her filled-in eyebrows and examined her computer screen.

"Oh, sorry," Lou Ann said.

She took out her wallet and extracted her driver's license for identification.

Harry did the same.

They produced their IDs.

The receptionist accepted them, gave each another cursory glance, and then returned the driver's licenses.

The receptionist tapped some more on her keyboard and looked up at them. She pointed to a waiting area with a deep green and white-striped high-backed sofa flanked by two matching wingback chairs and a magazines-strewn mahogany coffee table breaking up the set.

"Dr. Adamson will be out shortly."

Lou Ann nodded. "Thank you."

She and Harry avoided the intimacy of the sofa and instead claimed the wingback chairs, sitting at an angle to each other.

Lou Ann pressed her hands down on her thighs to thwart the rapid-fire tics threatening to expose her frayed nerves.

Harry's eyes went straight to her defensive body language.

This horrible quaking was foreign to her. Not even one twitch distracted her when she was on the job.

But she couldn't do that now. She was forced into yet another catastrophic pain, a pain she'd shelved in the back of her mind for close to two decades. Her breathing hitched and her heart raced. The last time she'd been in a lobby like this was when she and Lyle sat opposite each other in a Miami funeral home.

"Lou Ann," Harry called.

His voice registered in her brain, but her body remained trapped.

"Lou Ann?" Harry said again, this time louder.

Lou Ann blinked.

She watched Harry stand and walk towards her in slow motion.

His warm breath on her forehead pulled her out of her panic. He was squatting in front of her, his concerned blue eyes scanning her face. He picked her hands up off her thighs and squeezed them gently.

"It's okay," he said softly.

Harry helped Lou Ann to her feet, and when they turned, the receptionist was staring at them. The woman quickly ducked her head and resumed typing.

The far lobby door opened and a slim man in surgical greens and a graying hairline approached them.

He extended his hand to Lou Ann.

"Hello, Ms. Jasinski. I'm Dr. Adamson, the pathologist on duty." He shook her hand and continued, "I'm sorry for your tragic loss. I was the pathologist who received both your brother and sister-in-law."

His sympathetic expression deepened. At least he used the word "tragic."

Dr. Adamson then introduced himself to Harry.

"Good to meet you, Dr. Adamson. I'm Harry Boxer, a good friend of Ms. Jasinski."

"I'm glad you're here with her," Dr. Adamson said.

Harry nodded. He gave Lou Ann's arm a gentle squeeze. "I'll be right here waiting for you."

Lou Ann reached for Harry's hand and their fingertips touched for an instant.

"Would it be all right if Harry accompanies me?" Lou Ann asked.

"Sure."

Lou Ann, with Harry by her side, followed Dr. Adamson down a long, empty and echoing hallway.

Lou Ann studied every room they passed, wondering if Lyle and Melinda were lying there and whether she would be able to see them.

Dr. Adamson escorted Lou Ann and Harry into his office and gestured to two brown leather chairs facing his desk.

The doctor closed the door and then took his place behind his desk and reverently folded his hands.

A closed folder lay to his left.

Were the contents about Lyle and Melinda, or something unrelated? She couldn't get past the distraction. She had to ask.

Lou Ann pointed to the mysterious folder with her eyes.

"Is that about my brother and sister-in-law?"

"Yes."

He picked up the folder and handed it to Lou Ann.

"It contains your official copies of Lyle and Melinda's autopsy reports."

Lou Ann set the folder on her lap and clutched both sealed ends lest any information sneak out and grab her.

"I want to let you know that they both died as a result of internal bleeding. Melinda additionally sustained head trauma. Their deaths have been ruled accidental with injuries sustained from a motor vehicle accident. Based on the extent of their injuries, they would've rapidly been rendered unconscious, and I believe they didn't suffer long. I won't go into further details unless you want me to."

Lou Ann shook her head. What good would it do? This day was hard enough. She knew the outcome of the autopsies, but having the report on the results in her possession solidified the whole grisly scene.

The doctor nodded and continued, "The details are all there when you're ready to read them, or you can file them away. I find most families decide that on their own. Also know that if you have any concerns or questions, you can contact me, and I'll return your call the minute I'm available."

"Thank you," Lou Ann said.

She inhaled, filling her lungs with air until it hurt, and then relieved the hot pressure through her nose.

"May I see them?" Lou Ann asked.

"Yes," the doctor said.

He pointed to small flat-screen TV screen mounted on the wall, and then he picked up the phone and pressed the second extension. "Joanie, this is Dr. Adamson. Can you please bring 7784A and 7786B?"

Dr. Adamson set down the receiver.

"I'm so sorry. I didn't intend any disrespect. Unfortunately, I need to refer to your brother and sister-in-law as case numbers so the assistant can locate the proper bodies. I, however, think of them as Lyle and Melinda Jasinski."

"I understand," Lou Ann said.

As a sergeant, she followed the same protocol. Her reports included case number this and case number that. Subject this…insert name. Subject that…insert name. All so sterile. How she detested reports.

Guilt tapped her on the shoulder. How many times had she been wanting to just get the damn thing done so she could end her shift and go home? It was more than a few times, for sure.

The TV hummed and a snowy pattern akin to bad reception filled the screen.

And then it cleared, showing Lyle and Melinda, lying side by side on steel gurneys, each covered from chin to feet with a white sheet.

Lou Ann whisper-gasped and gripped the chair's arms.

She laser-focused on Lyle's pale, waxy face while taking intermittent deep breaths. His blue lips stood in contrast to the death pallor, as if someone had drawn them on. And threads of silver woven through his hair revealed how he'd aged since she and he severed ties. He was seven years older, but now he'd age no more.

Her stare softened and her tension eased. Despite the jarring sight of Lyle, the slim nose, which he always hated, and the high-set cheekbones were those of her big brother.

The same brother who pulled her in her wagon at demon speeds while she clung to the sides and belly laughed during the rocket journey and laughed even harder when she and the wagon tipped over.

She smiled, remembering how he would run to her and help her up, skinned knees and all. Then Momma would spring out of her kitchen and wag her finger at him while examining Lou Ann's minor kid wounds. But she was tough and Momma knew it.

Lyle was Momma's firstborn and her favorite, although she wouldn't admit to that. Lou Ann, however, was Daddy's girl. She was tough like him and she dreamed of being just like him, a Florida State trooper. Instead she went the sheriff route. And before her dad committed suicide, he told her how proud he was of her, always and often. Ironically, Lyle was the spitting image of him, and she was Momma's look-alike.

"He looks the same," Lou Ann murmured.

Her gaze strayed to sweet Melinda. Her blonde hair lay flattened behind her still head and accentuated her pallor, and her lips were as blue as Lyle's.

Lou Ann recalled how she and Melinda became such fast friends, each standing by the other when family criticized one or the other of them, which happened more than anyone wanted.

Melinda tried so hard to heal what soured between Lou Ann and Lyle. She adored them. But after what happened to Momma and then Daddy, Lou Ann and Lyle blamed each other. Melinda couldn't resolve the rift, and Lyle pulled her closer to him. But Lou Ann understood Melinda's ultimate, but heartbreaking, loyalty to her husband and forgave her.

Lou Ann's heart beat for Melinda's silenced one.

The doctor's assistant, Joanie, who stood in between Lyle and Melinda, looked at the screen as if she was watching Lou Ann and waiting for instructions.

Dr. Adamson gazed at Lou Ann.

"It's fine. Thank you," she said.

Adamson once again picked up the receiver.

"Thank you, Joanie. That'll be all."

Joanie nodded and the screen returned to snow.

"I'm sorry for your loss," Dr. Adamson repeated.

Lou Ann nodded in response.

"About…."

She anticipated the beginning and the end of the conversation.

"I…uh…would like both of them to be transported to Marshall Funeral Home in Miami."

It was the same funeral home that took care of Margaret and John Jasinski. Now they would receive Lyle and Melinda." Lou Ann let out a painful sigh. "Do you need the address?" She reached for her cell.

Dr. Adamson shook his head. "Not necessary. We'll handle everything and get it all done today. The funeral home will then contact you."

"Who should I pay?"

"No one. The city covers the autopsies because of the mandated accidental death inquiry and the disposition to the funeral home."

"Okay."

Kaylee! She'd just met her and started a tenuous relationship with her. Now she'd have to take her to her parents' funeral. She hadn't found a chance to discuss that yet, but she'd have to approach the subject carefully, to tiptoe, especially about the estrangement. They would both need to say goodbye—a forever goodbye.

Lou Ann and Harry stood.

She clutched Lyle and Melinda's finality to her chest.

"I'll walk you out," Dr. Adamson said.

Lou Ann and Harry followed the doctor in a solemn parade to the exit.

The hot sun blasted her face and assaulted her eyes. Lou Ann squinted in defense until her body adjusted to the Florida heat.

Harry and she walked in silence to the car.

He unlocked and opened the passenger door. It was like opening an oven door.

Lou Ann hesitated.

"Wait here. I'll get in and start the air full blast."

Harry shut the door and rounded to the driver's side.

"Don't burn yourself," Lou Ann called.

Harry chuckled. "It wouldn't be the first time."

She caught on to the double entendre.

Harry opened his door, removed the towel he'd placed across the steering wheel, and then started the engine. She watched him press the AC button.

He beckoned to her that it was safe to enter.

Lou Ann opened the door to a refreshing blast of cold and scooted inside.

"Good thing I got this baby serviced," he said.

He left the car idling, and they sat silent.

"I know how hard this is for you," Harry said softly.

"I couldn't have done it without you."

"Whatever you need. No strings attached," he added.

"I know, and thank you."

"You're welcome. Are you ready?"

"Yes."

While Harry drove out of the Medical Examiner's parking lot, Lou Ann turned and looked back at the place where she left Lyle and Melinda. The next time she'd see them was with Kaylee, at the funeral home.

20

Kaylee shuffled through the CDs Margo brought her.

Jazz. Jazz. Jazz.

She tossed the genre CDs aside until pausing at an album of Chopin's classical music.

This will do!

Kaylee shoved a CD into the slim slot of the black player.

The player ate the CD so fast that Kaylee yanked her fingers away in case the player gobbled them up, too.

Damn these ancient things. No wonder they'd become obsolete.

The "Nocturne in B-flat minor, Opus 9, Number 1" began to play.

She danced to the same classical piece during a recital years ago. Kaylee closed her eyes and inhaled deeply. The tranquil fragrance of petal-soft roses surrounded her. Mom and Dad had stood, applauding her pointe performance, and then rushed backstage to present her with a dozen pink roses.

Kaylee touched her cheeks where her parents had flooded her with sweet kisses.

She popped her eyes open to her stark reality. She was going to get out of here no matter what and the first thing she was going to buy was a dozen pink roses. Tears dripped down her cheeks and plopped down on her chest. She'd find where they buried her parents, and she would lay her roses on their graves.

But crying was useless.

She dried her cheeks with her palms, stood, and walked over to the bedside stand, where she gently rested her hand on top of it, using it as a makeshift ballet barre.

Kaylee began her warm-up barre routine. Her muscle memory

roused, and she proceeded without wobble through plié in all five ballet positions, first halfway or *demi,* and then deep, *grande,* and then followed by relevé, or rising to the balls of her feet. Her left ankle complained, but cooperated once she stretched it carefully.

Every note, so familiar, circled in her brain.

Kaylee hummed while gracefully sweeping her arms and tilting her head. She was back in ballet class where nothing bad had ever happened.

The music stopped abruptly, startling her.

She whipped her head around to look at the black box.

And her heart paused when she saw Margo.

She never heard the door unlock.

How long had Margo been standing there?

Margo grinned with narrowed eyes.

A creepy chill skittered up Kaylee's spine at Margo's changed demeanor.

"I like the way you move," Margo said, her tone rippling like a snake.

Kaylee shrank back, hunching her shoulders.

Margo held up a clearly used off-white plastic caddy containing a shaving cream can and a washcloth.

Nausea shot up to the back of Kaylee's throat, leaving an acidic burn in its wake.

"Time for grooming," Margo chirped.

Kaylee didn't reply. There was nothing she could say or do to stop what was about to happen.

Margo strode to the bedside stand, the same bedside stand Kaylee used minutes ago as a ballet barre, and set the caddy on top of it.

Every wonderful moment Kaylee just enjoyed was now ruined.

"Hop up on that bed and take off your shorts and panties."

Kaylee stared at the caddy.

"I can do that myself."

"Oh, don't be silly. It's easy to miss certain parts that way. I'll make sure everything is done right." Margo beckoned with her open palm. "Come on. Come on. Let's go."

Kaylee sidestepped to the bed while watching Margo's prying eyes.

She wasn't going to get out of this.

Kaylee sat on the edge of the bed, and then with her knees pressed together, she swung her legs up on the bed.

"I can't do this through your shorts."

Kaylee eased her shorts and panties to her ankles.

"Oh, for God's sake!"

Margo snatched the shorts and panties off Kaylee's ankles and tossed them on the floor before she reached into the caddy.

Kaylee gritted her teeth.

"Shit! I forgot the razor." Margo wagged her finger at Kaylee. "Don't go way," she said in a sing-song voice.

Margo walked out of the room and engaged the lock.

Kaylee sat up and riffled through the caddy, her eyes widening at the razor stuck inside the washcloth. She eyed the door, and with her heart thumping in her ears, grabbed the razor, dumped it into the bedside drawer, and shoved the drawer shut. She repositioned herself on the bed just before the lock disengaged *Whew!*

Margo walked in carrying a basin and proceeded to the bathroom. The water faucet hissed open and the sound of water pounding against the metal basin echoed into the room. Then the faucet squeaked shut and Margo walked in balancing the full basin, and with a threadbare towel draped across her shoulder, she placed the basin next to the caddy.

"Hips up," Margo commanded.

She shoved the towel under Kaylee.

"Open."

Kaylee had no choice but to comply. She had no idea how long she'd been in this fake room, leaving her privates wild.

Kaylee's chest heaved and her belly quivered while Margo squirted out enough shaving cream to completely cover her genitals.

She watched Margo dunk the razor into the water and with a swish of broad strokes she cut away the overgrowth. Mercifully, the whole encounter took what Kaylee estimated to be a minute. The woman had done this a lot.

Then Margo dunked the washcloth in the same shaving water, and wiped away the mess she left behind.

"There! That wasn't so bad," Margo practically cheered.

Kaylee clamped her legs together and didn't reply.

Margo retrieved the shorts and panties from the floor and tossed them on the bed.

"You can get dressed now."

Margo went over to the boom box and turned it back on. She waved her hands in maestro fashion and grinned. "Go on, my ballerina. Dance!"

She picked up the basin and caddy and left the room.

But Kaylee didn't dance. Instead she opened the drawer and removed the razor.

Now you dance, you bitch!

Otto lay sprawled on the green couch with a cigarette in his hand.

Damn, she hated that couch. It would be the first thing she threw out.

"So is she bald as a baby?" he asked Margo.

"None of your business. And don't set that couch on fire again."

"Yeah, yeah, yeah."

He sat up and stubbed out his cigarette in the ashtray on the floor, where the squashed cigarette joined a mountain of other wrinkled butts in piles of ash.

Margo grimaced.

"Put that piled-up, disgusting shit in the garbage."

She couldn't wait for Otto's demise.

But it was too early.

Otto was still useful, although his expiration date approached.

Otto shuffled behind Margo into the kitchen.

She just wanted to turn around and slap him hard—real hard.

Instead she curled her fingers suppressing the urge to pulverize him.

That lucky bastard!

"Say, when do I get a peek at your handiwork?"

Margo reached into her pants pocket and fingered the key to Kaylee's room.

She turned around and narrowed her gaze at Otto.

"Not gonna happen."

Otto chuckled. "Says you."

Margo marched to within inches of Otto and looked down at his slobbish, little face.

"Says me."

"Who appointed you queen?"

Margo reared back from his fetid breath. It was the last stinking breath Joanna inhaled before she died, and Margo couldn't afford to have Kaylee succumb to the same fate. The girl was precious cargo, her and Gerald's ticket to a hefty, lucrative independence.

"Gerald and I did after what happened to Joanna. We can't ever have a repeat of that situation. You're just lucky to have your scalp intact, and that Kaylee jumped into our lives and rescued all of us. We can't fuck with the Greek and his money and connections. He could off us with a snap of his fingers." Margo flicked her fingers at Otto's nose. "Get it?"

Otto grumbled and retreated.

"Lesson learned," Margo snarled.

Margo reached into a kitchen cupboard, took out a mug, and poured a cup of coffee. She drank it black, needing the jolt.

She perked her ears when she heard shuffling behind Kaylee's door. She listened harder. Muted classical music seeped from under the door.

Hmmm. She grinned. *The Greek is going to love watching her dance.*

21

Joanna stared into her blue eyes in the bathroom mirror.

"I don't owe you an explanation, so stop staring at me!" she warned her reflection.

She knew only little about the aunt who this afternoon would become her sole caretaker.

Nothing wrong with that. She still hadn't figured out the details of assuming Kaylee's identity, but she would in time. After all, the real Kaylee was gone, and Joanna was actually stepping in to give everyone a new future, most of all herself. It was a fair trade.

She slipped off the cornflower print hospital gown and put on bra, panties, jeans and the peach cap-sleeved cotton shirt "Aunt Lou Ann" brought for the D-day, discharge day.

Joanna posed in front of the mirror.

Hmmm, not bad. Auntie had a good eye. The clothes were a perfect fit.

Then she stepped into the strappy bronze sandals and buckled them into place.

Perfect, too.

And she also needed to be perfect too and not slip up. Her life depended on it.

She brushed her hair, putting on the final touches before Aunt Lou Ann showed up.

The hospital room door slid open.

Joanna sucked in a deep breath.

You can do this!

She stepped out of the bathroom.

"You look great!" Nurse Lynn cheered with happy arms.

"Thanks." Joanna's eyes misted. "I'm going to miss you."

Nurse Lynn hugged her. "Me too." She wagged her finger at Joanna and smiled. "Now you be good."

Joanna grinned wide. "I will."

Nurse Lynn was the first person she'd trusted.

Dr. Zimmer joined them.

"Wow! What a change," Dr. Zimmer said. "Are you ready?" she asked.

"I think so."

"Good. It's going to be challenging for you and your aunt so take it slow. She's a kind and patient woman, so I'm sure you'll both find your way."

Joanna nodded. There wasn't anything more to say. She wasn't about to risk leaving before they came for her.

"When can I leave?" Joanna asked, trying not to sound inpatient.

"As soon as your aunt arrives." Dr. Zimmer turned toward the open door. "And here she is!"

Lou Ann eyed Kaylee, from her shiny blonde hair to her strappy sandals.

"Everything okay? she asked Kaylee. "I picked everything out," she looked at Nurse Lynn, "with your nurse's help. Although I did guess the shoe size. Ummm. I won't be offended if it's not your thing. We'll get the rest of your clothes from the house."

The color in Kaylee's cheeks vanished.

Shit! Lou Ann hadn't intended to mention the house, and most pressing, she hadn't broached the subject of the impending funeral. She'd only made preliminary arrangements for Lyle and Melinda's transfer to the Miami funeral home this morning. Those arrangements were a conversation she planned to have later, and not during Kaylee's discharge from the hospital.

"We don't have to do it today," Lou Ann added quickly.

Dr. Zimmer blessedly intervened. "I've sent the antibiotic prescription for Kaylee to our outpatient pharmacy. You can pick it up on the way out." She looked at Kaylee. "It's important for you to finish the full course."

"I will," Kaylee said.

Dr. Zimmer looked back and forth between Lou Ann and Kaylee. "Once you've settled, I recommend that Kaylee see a psychiatrist, and a gynecologist, and have neurology follow-up,. Just let me know, and after you've consented to have Kaylee's medical records released, I'll forward them to your chosen providers."

"I'll...we'll...take care of that," Lou Ann replied.

She emphasized the term "we" because she and Kaylee were a team —a family now.

That apparently worked. Kaylee's face relaxed and the pale pink blush returned to her cheeks.

It was all about striking the correct balance. Naturally it would be like walking on eggshells for a while.

Lou Ann scanned Kaylee's room for her possessions only to find nothing.

Her heart ached for her newly discovered niece, a young girl left with nothing,

Lou Ann smiled.

"Shall we?" she asked.

"Yeah," Kaylee replied.

"Good luck, Kaylee," Dr. Zimmer said.

The doctor hugged Kaylee and then Lou Ann.

"Good luck to you both. I sincerely want you to stay in touch. Actually I expect it."

"Thank you for everything," Lou Ann said.

Kaylee chimed in, "Ditto."

Nurse Lynn and Dr. Zimmer escorted Lou Ann and Kaylee out of the unit.

All the nurses waved.

"We'll miss you, Kaylee," they called after her.

Kaylee waved.

"Miss you, too," Kaylee called back.

The elevator doors parted, and Lou Ann and Kaylee stepped inside.

The bittersweet yet jubilant waves continued until the elevator doors closed, leaving Lou Ann and Kaylee truly alone for the very first time.

"Are you hungry?" Lou Ann asked.

"Starved."

"How about that? Me too!"

Joanna followed her new family out of Samaritan Hospital where she'd awakened frightened and confused not so long ago. The pieces of how she landed there and why, not to mention why they all thought she was someone else bewildered her. The frame of the puzzle was easy.

The rest of the scattered, jagged pieces were the problem.

But so far so good.

However, it would get harder from here on.

And where exactly was here? She was about to find out.

Lou Ann slowed.

"Just one second, Kaylee. I need to text my friend that we're ready."

Joanna halted while Lou Ann thumbed a text message.

Who was this friend?

What's more, she had no clue where they were going—where she would be staying before moving to Clearwater. Joanna just wanted to stay far away from Miami. Newell, Otto, and Margo assumed she was dead, and she wanted to keep it that way. If they found out she had survived—and their tentacles were long—they'd make sure she was dead for real. Miami was going to be all sunshine…until she met Newell, that charismatic SOB!

Plus, who in Miami knew Kaylee? They'd recognize right away that she was not Kaylee. Her ploy would be revealed. Maybe she'd go to jail!

Joanna's heart raced, and she shifted from side to side while Lou Ann waited for a response.

"He's just around the corner," Lou Ann said.

He?

"Okay."

She and Lou Ann walked side by side through the hospital lobby and out the door when a silver sedan pulled up to the hospital entrance.

Lou Ann smiled and waved at the man who then got out of the vehicle and smiled and waved back.

"Hey, there," the very attractive man called.

He opened the back seat door while leaving the car idling and looked at Joanna.

"Welcome, Kaylee. I'm glad to meet you. I'm Harry Boxer, Lou Ann's friend."

This was the friend? But the way they glommed onto each other, Joanna knew right away that they were way more than just good friends.

Joanna slid into the back seat while Lou Ann sat in the passenger seat up front.

This guy seemed on the up-and-up.

Joanna looked at Lou Ann and then Harry.

Man, did she ever trade up!

Joanna buckled her seat belt.

What would Kaylee do or say, just in case anyone asked how Kaylee was doing, including neighbors and friends—neighbors and friends she was going to avoid? After all, Kaylee had experienced the trauma of the car accident and the death of her parents. That would give Joanna a workable excuse to remain a recluse.

Lou Ann turned to look at Joanna.

"What kind of food do you like? What could you go for? Are you a pizza or burger kind of girl? Maybe pasta or a sub?" Lou Ann prattled on.

"Any of those are fine."

It was the absolute truth.

She'd known real hunger, and had scoured more than one trash can.

"Hey, look," Harry said. "That diner on the right looks interesting. It says all-American food, something for everyone."

"Sounds okay to me," Joanna said.

"Diner it is!" Lou Ann chirped.

Harry pulled the car into the last vacant spot.

"Must be a popular place," Harry said.

Harry got out of the car and opened Joanna's door.

She unbuckled her seat belt.

He was a nice man and funny, too.

Lou Ann needed to relax. But then, again, so should she. After all, they were going to live together. And maybe Harry, too. Joanna hoped so.

Lou Ann climbed out of the car, and Harry locked the doors with the remote.

As soon as the three entered the crowded diner, a host approached them.

"Booth for three," Harry said.

"Come with me. You're in luck. I have a great booth for you and the young ladies."

Lou Ann and Joanna snickered at the same time.

The host gestured to a clean, empty booth.

They paused.

"Is this booth all right?" the host asked.

"It's great," Harry said.

They glanced at each other. Then Lou Ann slid into the booth, leaving Joanna the option of which side to take.

She slid on Lou Ann's side while keeping toward the end of the bench seat.

Harry took his place opposite them.

The host brought them three menus.

Harry flopped his up like it was an interesting book.

"Hmmm. Let me see." He set the menu down. "I'm in the mood for a juicy burger and mondo fries."

Joanna giggled, which set off wide smile from Lou Ann and Harry.

"Me too," Joanna announced. "Mondo fries?"

"What? You've never had mondo fries before?" Harry teased her.

"You made that up!" Joanna chuckled. "That's not on my menu."

"Maybe you didn't look hard enough?" He grinned. "It was on my menu."

Joanna stuck out her hand. "Let me see."

A waitress approached.

"Do you folks need more time?" she asked.

Harry looked at Lou Ann.

"No. We know what we're having," Lou Ann said.

The waitress looked at Joanna.

"I'll have the All-American burger and mondo fries."

The waitress cocked her eyebrows.

"Make it three," Harry said. "Burger and fries."

He winked at Joanna.

"How would you folks like your burgers?"

Joanna hesitated. She'd never eaten in a restaurant. Joanna had no idea what that meant.

Lou Ann piped up. "Medium well for me."

She looked at Joanna.

"Same," Joanna parroted.

"Medium well for me too," Harry said.

"You guys are easy," the waitress said.

"How about drinks?"

Harry shrugged.

"Cokes?"

Joanna nodded.

She recalled how Nurse Lynn had brought her a Coke. It was the best one she ever had.

"A round of Cokes," Lou Ann said.

The waitress collected their menus.

"I'll be right back with your sodas."

Joanna tapped her fingers on the table, but then reined in her nervous energy.

She needed to watch every move.

But neither Lou Ann nor Harry commented on her tic.

Thankfully the waitress brought their drinks right away, so Joanna could keep her hands busy.

She wrapped her fingers around the glass and sucked up such a long sip of the cola through the straw that the carbonated bubbles shot up her nose. Joanna released the straw and sniffed, sucking the fizz back down her throat to avoid one hell of an embarrassing situation.

"Sorry. I was thirsty," Joanna explained.

"Don't apologize," Lou Ann said. "My throat's parched too."

Lou Ann and Harry deliberately tackled their drinks in "Three Musketeers" fashion, which was a pretty cool move.

Joanna slowed her pace, taking intermittent sips.

The waitress brought their food and placed the steamy burgers and fries in front of them.

"Ketchup and mustard are right there. Can I get you folks anything else?"

"We're good," Harry said.

The waitress nodded and sped off to her next station.

Joanna chuckled.

"What's so funny?" Lou Ann asked.

"I've never been called 'folks'."

Lou Ann and Harry laughed.

"Well, *folks*. Let's dig in!" Harry mocked with a wink.

Joanna grabbed the fat burger and took a hefty bite. The beefy juice dribbled down her chin.

Oh, no! Please don't ruin this new peach shirt!

Joanna snatched a napkin and dabbed her chin, barely avoiding damage to the brand-new shirt Lou Ann bought for her.

"The sign of a good burger," Harry reassured her.

Joanna grinned over her paper napkin.

She leaned farther over her plate for the remaining bites.

The cheese and the blending condiment concoction surrounding the thick patty, all stacked between a doughy fresh bun, were nirvana in her mouth, cleansing the hellish gruel Margo pushed onto her plate.

At first the food where Margo and the rest kept her wasn't bad. They brought her the standard yet bland meat and potatoes, pretending it was hospital fare.

But then Otto began sneaking into her room at night and pushing himself into her so hard that the food regurgitated to the back of her throat. And when she fought, kicking him as hard as she could, and even biting his stinky, bumpy tongue, that only made him go at her harder. He even stuffed a washcloth in her mouth to muffle her screams. But it didn't matter if she did scream, because no one ever came to her rescue. Newell and Margo had to know, but they did nothing. And worse, Newell took a turn, too.

A hand perched on her shoulder.

"Hey, are you okay?"

Lou Ann's voice buzzed in her ear.

Joanna shook to the present, her burger poised in her grip.

"Yeah."

She took a bite to pretend she *was* okay.

She needed to bury her captors, like they buried her, or thought they did. But as long as they circled in her head, they'd still control her.

Get out! Get out! Get out!

The next bite was big and vengeful. And the next and the next, until her burger was all gone.

Joanna picked at her fries as an afterthought.

Harry examined her empty plate.

"I'm glad you enjoyed your meal, and that we stopped at this diner," Harry said.

Lou Ann tossed her napkin on her plate.

"Excellent choice," she said.

"I agree," Joanna added.

It was one hell of a cathartic meal, and just what she needed.

And then she saw him! That straight cut hair skimming the back of his collar!

He'd found her!

Her meal bubbled in her stomach.

Joanna flung her fork off the table and dove deep under the booth.

She cowered there, hiding. Trembling.

Lou Ann rested her hand on Joanna's back.

She batted it away.

Lou Ann was going to give her away!

The waitress' shoes appeared.

"Is everything all right?" Joanna heard her ask. "I'll get another fork."

"Thank you," Lou Ann said.

"Kaylee?" She called her quietly.

Joanna lurched from her hiding place and squeezed against Lou Ann, burying her face against Lou Ann's chest.

Lou Ann hugged her tight.

"It's okay. It's okay," she murmured.

But Harry didn't make a sound.

A fork tapped on the table.

"Is she okay?" the waitress asked.

"She's fine. We'll have the check, please," Lou Ann said.

"Uh…no problem. I'll get that right away."

Lou Ann stroked the back of Joanna's head.

"We'll leave in just a minute."

How was she going to get out of here?

She'd run!

No, that would only get his attention.

She had to camouflage herself between Lou Ann and Harry. There was no other way.

Joanna opened one eye to assess Newell's location.

He turned around.

Her heart exploded in her chest.

It wasn't him.

22

Kaylee lay in bed listening to the music. No clock or calendar marked the time of her captivity in this so-called sham hospital. But she estimated by her body hair growth that it had probably been a week, give or take a few days. The solitude tricked her into feeling it was longer.

She opened the bedside drawer and removed the razor she'd stashed there. Stupid Margo had unknowingly given her a true gift.

She worked away the plastic casing surrounding the double blade, careful not to crack the handle. She'd need that to get a good grip on her makeshift weapon.

The casing abruptly splintered and the exposed blade sliced her finger.

Shit! Ouch!

Kaylee sucked the blood off her finger and then put pressure on the wound with her other hand.

She grinned, imagining Margo's and Otto's faces gashed. Better yet, she'd aim for their eyes, blinding them. What a beautiful, bloody sight that would be.

She slipped out of bed and turned up the music loud enough to cover her plan, but not loud enough to cause Margo to barge in complaining about the noise.

She needed time to practice her moves—how to wield her weapon for maximum damage—enough damage for her to make a run for freedom.

Kaylee's mouth went dry.

The odds were overwhelmingly against her.

But even the smallest sliver of hope for freedom was worth anything they would do to punish her.

They'd worked overtime to break her down. To lie to her. Especially Newell. What kind of doctor would do this? Take part in this horrific charade? They clearly had some reason to keep her here.

The only thing she'd come to believe was that her parents didn't survive the car accident. But she did. And she had every intention of living.

Kaylee grabbed her weapon and leaped to the floor with feet wide and knees bent, and eyes wide and wild, ready to pounce, her teeth clenched, and hands in fists, her right hand choking the handle of the bare double blades. She shifted quickly, side to side, while alternating her shoulders, like a boxer evading punches until he knew when to strike for the knockout.

"Yah! Yah!"

This was no ballet, and she was no longer a ballerina, but a warrior, and she was at war with her captors.

"Bring it!" she hissed.

Gerald Newell grinned while he tapped his pen rhythmically on his desk. He had only three more patients to see before he could spruce up for his date with Sophia. He tapped his toe along with the rhythm of his pen. He was hooked, and he liked it. He hadn't felt this way in years.

He'd been working too hard in both businesses. Time for him to have fun. To have a release. He'd been a bit mean with Joanna, and now with Kaylee.

But he'd need to keep both his worlds humming.

Gerald pumped his fist. Without his hunt, Otto would still be in the dirt.

A cultural moron!

Gerald relaxed his hand. Otto wasn't going to bust into his steamy fantasies of naked Sofia curled up in his arms.

His dreamy smile returned to his lips, lips that would soon trail all over Sophia's delectable body.

He stiffened at the thought.

He exhaled and took control of his response before it was too late.

It was best to take his time with her. He knew she wanted it too, but he'd drive the narrative. Sofia's rawness made him shiver in his pants. He ached to touch her in every place, in every possible way. But the last thing he wanted was for him or her to sexually burn out. He genuinely wanted to know more about her. To control her as much as she controlled him.

Gerald tossed his rhythmical pen on the desk, pushed back in his office chair, and folded his hands behind his head.

Life was picking up. He had Sophia, and he had that mega deal with the Greek, who he'd provide with a nubile blonde, but in exchange the billionaire agreed to front him a gynecology practice in Greece. Fucking beautiful Greece.

He'd lounge on the sand with Sofia while gazing at the bright blue sea. They'd go for a swim. He'd touch her playfully under the water. They'd towel off together and lie in sun until they were toasty dry. He'd give her money to shop while he finished seeing women and cultivating just the right ones.

There was an abundance of brothels that would take these women. Plus, before Otto was "phased out", Gerald would set up a US connection, a profitable one, before pulling the rip cord.

Poor, poor Otto. He had no idea. It was better, and yes, more humane, to surprise him.

"You look relaxed!" Janice called from his open office door. "Good for you! You know what they say, all work and no play..."

If only Janice knew the truth.

But his longtime office nurse was more of a—"mother"—than his own blood. Janice looked after him. Fed him. Brought him coffee. Made sure he was happy, and always complimented him. He'd sorely miss her. Too bad he couldn't ever explain what he did. He could never break her heart. Disappoint her. Janice didn't even believe Cassidy. He could do no wrong in her eyes.

"You only have three more patients to see, and off with you for the weekend, and by that smile on your face, I bet you have awesome plans."

Gerald nodded. "I do."

"Hmmm," she said, sheepishly.

Gerald shot her his best smile, stood, and slid playfully past her.

"Are you coming, slowpoke?" he teased.

"I'll give you slowpoke!"

They giggled while they raced to exam room 1, pausing short of the exam door to collect themselves, and walked inside.

The middle-aged woman was there for her annual GYN exam, and so were the next two.

Janice kept a decent pace, and luckily engaged each patient in chitchat, since his mind was busy with Sophia.

He remained pleasant enough to satisfy the women in order to expedite their checkout and subsequently his, too.

"Well, that's it," Janice cheered. "You're free. I'll clean things up and lock up. Now, you skedaddle!"

He loved this woman! He'd eventually have to break his departure to her, but he'd ease the pain by giving her one hell of a reference.

No one would ever take care of him the way Janice did.

But time to shelve his melancholia.

Gerald vaulted out of his office chair and rushed to the adjoining bathroom.

He gave his reflection in the mirror a thumbs-up and then winked.

Hot damn! Lucky dog!

He ran his hands over his rough cheeks.

That would never do.

He didn't want to scratch her thighs…just in case, of course.

Gerald removed an electric razor he kept in the vanity drawer and buzzed the stubble away. Then he stroked his smooth cheeks and nodded his approval.

He straightened his tie and smoothed his slacks. Then he combed his hair and slapped cologne on his clean-shaven cheeks.

He was ready!

Gerald gave himself a once-over, and satisfied, he strode out of the bathroom and picked up his black briefcase with a hidden compartment containing the contractual agreement between him and the Greek.

He walked out the office door, nearly smacking into Janice.

She whistled.

"Woo-hoo! Hot date, huh?"

"A date."

He gave her that much information.

"Lucky woman!"

Gerald shrugged.

Sophia was lucky, but he was luckier.

"I have to go or I'll be late."

"We wouldn't want that."

"No, we wouldn't. Good night, Janice. You have a fun weekend too."

"I wouldn't consider laundry and cleaning to be fun, but it needs to get done."

Gerald reached into his back pocket and pulled out his wallet. He opened it and took out two tickets. He had season Miami Broadway tickets, so he felt no sorrow in parting with them. Besides, Janice deserved them.

"Here. Take your daughter to the opera. Enjoy yourselves."

"Oh, I can't. Take your date."

"My date isn't exactly a fan of the opera. Take them, please."

Janice accepted the tickets. She hugged Gerald.

"Thank you."

"You're most welcome. How is Natasha?"

"She's good. I'm proud to say she's finishing her degree in biochemical engineering next semester."

"That's awesome. She takes after you."

"Oh, stop."

After Janice's husband died from a heart attack, Gerald began hosting Janice and her daughter for Thanksgiving. He'd taught himself how to cook since his addicted mother couldn't boil water. It was just the three of them, but it was more than enough. They were his family.

But there would be no Thanksgiving dinner this year. Instead he'd send them a turkey meal with all the trimmings with an invitation to join him in Greece, once he got things settled.

Gerald squeezed Janice's hand.

"You and Natasha have a great night, and that's an order."

"We will. I promise. But you also have to promise to get out more."

Gerald grinned and crossed his fingers.

"You can count on it."

Kaylee turned down the music. She wanted it to play softly while she killed. None of them should live to do this to any girl…ever.

Kaylee breathed deeply. She'd never killed anything other than insects. But these horrific malcontents were lower than any insect.

She squeezed the razor's handle. She had to do it. It was not only self-defense, but self-preservation too. She'd do it for the girls, past and future. She'd end it tonight. She'd end them. Then she'd expose all their horrific deeds.

Kaylee stepped out of bed and waited, poised by the door, ready for Margo to walk right through—and the best part—unaware of what was going to happen to her, just like what happened to Kaylee.

Karma was a bitch.

* * *

Gerald cranked up the music and bobbed his head while on his way to pick up Sophia. He'd requested the restaurant's host to seat them at a quiet, privately tucked away table.

He'd order the best vintage and cajole Sophia into more than one glass. He wanted her relaxed.

While they waited for their five-star meals, he'd discreetly slip his hand under the table and run it up her golden, suntanned thigh.

No hot sun to labor under. Only the raw heat between them.

Despite the Mercedes's AC blowing full blast, sweat collected on his forehead.

Shit! What was she doing to him?And the evening hadn't even started.

Gerald swiped the sweat off his forehead. Good thing he put on an extra layer of deodorant.

The heat of his fantasies activated the cologne. Perhaps he went a bit heavy on it. But Janice would have told him.

And even if he slapped on too much, the excess should evaporate, leaving him with just the right touch before he reached Sophia's cramped apartment in a shitty neighborhood. He'd take care of that for her.

His Map App should steer him clear of even more undesirable areas.

He stopped at a red light.

He was safe in his vehicle. The door locks were secure, plus he had a panic mode that called the nearest cops to his rescue.

Gerald idled at the red light that was taking forever to turn green.

He glanced sideways at the Ford Fusion that pulled up next to him.

No gangbanger would ever be caught in that.

Gerald slowly turned his head toward the driver.

The buxom twenty-something-year-old woman with deep, exposed cleavage and her equally hot passenger waved to him.

Hmmm.

Gerald returned a wink and a wave.

They giggled behind the glass.

The passenger hottie rolled down her window and yelled, "Hey! Tight car!"

Gerald took his hands off the steering wheel, and while his foot was on the brake, he leaned back against the buttery upholstery and gestured with open, show-off arms. He nodded to the girl, responding to her compliment.

The light turned green and the Fusion shot forward. If he had the time, he'd follow them. His Mercedes could easily outpace them.

But he let them go.

Sophia was waiting for him.

He wouldn't disappoint her.

Sophia stared at the black cocktail dress Gerald had delivered to her earlier. What jaw-dropping surprise that was, especially since she'd just gotten home from her hours at the car wash, her Daisy Dukes soaked with car wash and sweat.

She'd need a shower before Gerald showed up.

She picked the dress up off her bed by the spaghetti straps and held it up to her while looking in the mirror. It was absolutely gorgeous. She'd never owned anything like this, not on what Freddie paid her.

Sophia carefully replaced the dress on the bed as if it was so fragile that it might break.

Then she walked over to the dresser and picked up the stack of bills Gerald left her as a tip. And she'd planned to do him for free.

She twirled around the bedroom.

This was really going somewhere!

Before she could remove her soaked shorts and gritty T-shirt—an occupational hazard—there was a knock on the door.

Shit! He was early. He'd just have to wait.

Sophia stashed the bills under the mattress. It was the first place anyone would look, but this was an emergency. She'd find a more creative hiding spot later.

Sophia hurried to the front door and peeked through the little hole stamped into the cracked layers of the overly painted gray door.

She sighed with relief. It wasn't him.

Her next-door neighbor and friend, Maria, stood on the other side of the door holding up a brown bag.

Sophia grinned.

Maria worked as a waitress at a Cuban restaurant down the road, and always brought her some goody from there. She wondered what was in the bag tonight.

Sophia opened the three door locks.

The place came with one measly lock, which she tightened herself and then installed two more. One couldn't be safer in this neighborhood. But the price was right.

She opened the door wide, letting Maria pass inside.

"Ah, chica, my dear, pray tell, what do you have for me tonight?

Sophia shut the door.

"The best flan, baby. The very best. I brought two for us."

"Put them on the table. We'll sit and devour them after my shower."

"Hard day, huh? At least I work part of the time in the AC inside. But more and more people want to eat outside." Maria shrugged. "Why? I don't know."

"It was a typical sweltering day. Plus, I had to deal with Freddie."

"Yes, your boss is slimy."

"But," Sophia waggled her eyebrows, "I took care of my own VIP, my doctor, who showed up in his kick-ass Mercedes at lunchtime. I left him my card after my appointment with him, and he took me up on it."

"Doctor? What kind of doctor?"

"Gynecologist."

Maria bugged out her eyes.

"Oh, come on now. I was the flirty one. I couldn't help myself. He turned me on the second I saw him. And he was into me." Sophia laughed. "No pun intended."

Maria shot her hands to her ears.

Sophia grabbed Maria's hands and pulled them away so she could hear Sophia's great news.

"I'm not ashamed. He really helped me with my bleeding problem. Things just sort of took off between us. He's actually taking me on a date tonight."

Maria shook her head. "You're bad. This is too pervy."

"What? No. We're both into each other. He's sexy…for an older guy. I mean, look at my other bad choices. All they ever did was stink up my sheets before hitting the door. I'm done with that crap. I have a chance with a doctor…a rich one."

Sophia grabbed Maria's hand and yanked her to the bedroom.

"Wait until you see the dress he had delivered to me."

Maria's eyes went big, really big.

"Dios mio!"

"Sweet, huh?"

"He bought this for you?"

"It arrived from him."

Maria inspected the dress.

"Oh, shit! The price tag is still on it," Maria squealed.

"I didn't even notice. The package was left on my doorstep, and I went into shock when I opened it."

Now Sophia widened her eyes.

"Holy shit! This dress cost $500 dollars!"

The bedroom began to spin.

Sophia plopped onto a chair and held out her hand.

"Take my pulse."

Sexy fun and all, she was in over her head.

She thought they were on the same playing field, the sexually charged kind, the kind where she yielded control. The tip, she earned, but the dress put him at an advantage.

Sophia stood and huffed, "I'll send the dress back! He can eat at my kind of place!"

"Wait…wait. Not so fast," Maria warned. "Accept the dress as a gift. But make him know that you owe him nothing in return. Show him you're not a pushover. Let him take you out to a nice place. But never leave the table if there is water or any drink on the table, not even to the bathroom. Be careful. I don't trust this guy, even if he's a doctor. And he can have all sorts of drugs."

Sophia shook her head. "No, he's not that kind of man. And I can take care of myself."

Maria sighed and shrugged. "You always do what you want anyway."

"And that's bad?"

"It can be."

"I'm going to take a shower, and as soon as I'm done, we'll sit down and eat flan together."

"Okay. It's better to get something in your stomach before you go out."

Maria always had her back. She was Sophia's one true friend.

After Maria left for the kitchen, Sophia stared at the black dress on her bed. She walked over to it and tucked the price tag out of sight. Maybe she'd wear it and return it for money after tonight…or not. She let her decision simmer and hurried into the shower. She wanted to be ready way ahead of time.

Sophia took a quick shower and shaved every excess hair off her body.

She got out of the shower, toweled off, and rubbed a thick layer of deodorant into her armpits, and then applied the floral scent body lotion that Maria gave to her this past Christmas. She could finally use it. There was no point in applying it before her car wash duties. That would be a waste of time, and she wouldn't squander any of it on

Freddie.

Sophia applied her makeup in the nude, not wanting to get any stray smudges on her best lacy black bra and panties, and, even more important, that black dress...especially if she decided to return it.

With her makeup artfully in place, Sophia donned her lingerie and slipped into the dress, its silkiness gliding onto her fresh skin and falling perfectly into every curve of her body. It was if the dress was tailor-made for her.

She gazed into her dresser mirror and took a few steps back to get a fuller view.

Damn! She looked fine! She'd keep the dress. No amount of money was worth it.

Sophia waltzed into the kitchen and spun around in front of Maria.

"Ta-daa!"

"You look stunning!"

Sophia turned her back to Maria.

"Finishing zipping me, will ya?"

Maria pulled up the last bit of the zipper.

"Thank you, my friend."

Sophia sat opposite Maria at the tiny, scratched kitchen table that barely fit two people. Maria's apartment was as small, so they'd both learned to eat cram-styled without as much as batting an eye.

Sophia protected her dress by tucking a clean dish cloth into her cleavage.

They dove their spoons into the flan.

"Mmmm. So good!"

Although her car wash job was messy, she had some level of independence, unlike Maria, who had too many bosses and too many cranky customers. Sophia could never be a waitress. Plus, she liked wearing shorts and a comfortable tee. It sure beat uniforms and dirty plates.

The caramel custard melted in her mouth.

Maria smacked her lips. "It's good, huh?"

"Oh, yeah."

"Not as good as what my mother used to make."

She and Maria shared the lack of a mother, but at least Maria had the kind of mother Sophia had always dreamed of, the kind who pecked a kiss on your forehead and made sure you were fed, clean, and safe. Maria's mother died in Cuba, of who knows what, and since her father had mysteriously disappeared, Maria received a cable from a distant cousin about her mother's death.

Sophia recalled how she sat on Sophia's bed, hugging her tightly while Maria wailed against her shoulder. Such pain. But she hadn't shed a tear after her own mother's demise. In fact, she rejoiced. But she never told Maria, or anyone else. They wouldn't understand, and they'd blame her for her "inappropriate" stoic response. But if only they knew a sliver about her mother, they'd understand why she had no remorse.

Sophia looked down at her bare feet. She was so jazzed about the dress and seeing Gerald that she completely forgot about shoes. The dress didn't come with shoes, and the only shoes she owned were sneakers and flip-flops, neither of which were appropriate to wear with a five-hundred-dollar dress.

"Shit! I don't have the right shoes. It's too late to get any, and besides, I don't have the money. I just paid rent."

"Don't cry and ruin your makeup," Maria said, calmly. "Let me see your feet."

"What?"

"Just do it."

Sophia stuck out a naked foot.

Maria viewed it from different angles.

"Looks like you and I have the same size feet. I have dressy black sandals that I wore for my friend's niece's quinceañera tucked in my closet. I'll go get them."

Maria got up from the table, sidestepped away, and hurried out of Sophia's apartment.

Sophia rested her head on her hand and bobbed her knee.

What if the sandals don't fit? She'd come up with some excuse and cancel the whole night until she could maybe score some shoes at a thrift store.

Minutes later Maria returned with a jubilant smile while dangling a pair of black patent leather sandals.

"Here! Try these on."

Sophia slowly slid her foot into one of the sandals. Hope flickered to life. She wiggled her toes. The sandal fit perfectly. It was a true Cinderella moment, and Maria was her Fairy Godmother.

She put the other sandal on and buckled the straps.

Bingo!

Sophia stood and teetered like a toddler taking her first steps. Maria wrapped her arms around her.

"Mi amiga!"

Sophia backpedaled and swayed, but regained her balance. Funny that she'd never in her whole life even tried on a pair of heels.

"Easy, now. You can do it. Just look up and walk normally. Maybe swing your hips a bit. Like this."

Maria strode around the room with a slight hip toss.

Sophia chuckled. "Looks like I have to practice."

"You'll get it."

Maria wagged her finger at Sophia. "Now remember what you promised, chica. Don't leave the table under any circumstances. And text me when you get home. I'll be up waiting."

"I promise, Mommy," Sophia teased.

Maria kissed Sophia on the cheek.

"You look absolutely stunning," Maria said.

"Thank you—for everything."

"Eh. I'll see what I can bring us tomorrow night. Good night."

Sophia walked Maria to the door and then engaged the triple locks.

She strode to a threadbare living room chair without as much jerking or wobbling, sat, crossed her legs, and stared at the clock on the wall.

Gerald was due any minute now.

23

Kaylee stood guard at the door feeling her heart pound clear to her feet. Her stance was wide and ready. Her eyes trained on the doorknob. Her ears alert to footsteps.

She licked her lips. It was her or them.

Newell hadn't arrived until after supper for days, at least that's when she heard his voice. He hadn't visited her since that fake operation. Kaylee wasn't clear if that was good news or maybe bad news.

It didn't matter. She knew she had to contend with Margo and that Otto dude, who she hadn't seen since that drive away from the car accident. At least that's what she remembered.

But she recognized his throaty voice, so he was definitely on the other side of that door…somewhere.

He hadn't breached the door, though. They'd purposely kept him away from her. Her captors had a pecking order. She assumed Newell was at the helm, Margo was in the middle, and that creep, Otto, was dead last.

She had to take Margo and Otto out before Newell arrived.

Newell would be harder to take down.

God help her, she might never know.

With Newell away, she'd at least have a head start.

He'd be really pissed off to find her gone and his little gang disabled…permanently.

Footsteps tapped closer to the door above the soft, classical music playing in the background.

It was Margo and she'd be carrying a food tray so her hands would be busy, perfect for a surprise attack.

The door locks clicked.

Kaylee slid to the side of the door.

It was go time.

The door opened.

"Suppertime," Margo announced.

Kaylee stuck out her foot as Margo predictably entered with dinner tray in hand.

The woman tripped and lost her balance.

The food tray toppled to the floor, spilling mashed potatoes and chunks of meatloaf all over the floor.

Kaylee shoved surprised Margo to the floor and punched the back of the woman's head with her fist.

Margo was stunned, but not for long.

Kaylee rushed over to the dinner tray, picked it up, and raced back to Margo who was slowing righting herself while snorting like a mad bull.

Kaylee raised the tray high overhead and slammed it against Margo's head.

Margo slumped to the floor, knocked out.

She was about to butcher the women's face when Otto rushed inside.

"What the fuck?!" he yelled. "You little bitch!"

With her teeth clenched, she rushed Otto.

She slammed into him. The power of her anger mowed him back until he toppled to the floor.

Kaylee straddled him and slammed her fists into his face.

Otto moaned.

Kaylee kicked him in the balls.

Otto crunched into a pathetic ball

"Ahhhhh!" he wailed.

Kaylee grabbed a plastic fork from the floor and stabbed Otto in the eye.

She then reached for her razor weapon and slashed Otto's cheek down to his lips.

"You pathetic bastard!" she yelled.

While Otto was incapacitated and Margo unconscious, Kaylee reached into Margo's pants pocket and removed a key. It was the key to the room! She raced out of her prison cell, slammed the door, and locked Margo and Otto inside. How wonderfully ironic.

But she had very little time left before Newell arrived.

She had to get out of here, now!

She ran into what appeared to be a living room.

What is this?

She looked wildly about. There had to be a way out.

Then she saw a door and rushed to it. She twisted the knob. It rotated in her hand.

"Oh, please, Jesus, let me out!"

The door didn't budge.

She looked up to find a stack of locks that all appeared to require keys.

"Shit!"

The whole door was sealed.

She ran past the living room and found the kitchen. There was a door there, but it also required a key.

They'd sealed her and anybody else but them inside.

She scanned the kitchen.

Kaylee ran her hands over the counter.

Then something went "ting."

She'd knocked a key to the ground.

Kaylee snatched it up, her hands shaking.

Stop it! Stop it! Pull yourself together!

While steadying her hands, Kaylee jabbed the key into the lock on the kitchen door. It fit! She twisted it and the door unlocked.

Sweet, Jesus. She was almost free. Just a little bit more to go.

Kaylee ripped open the door and ran outside.

"Help!" she screamed. "Someone help me!"

She glanced around.

There were no houses. Nothing but woods surrounded her. *Shit, where am I?* She looked back to find that she'd been stashed in a house with windows set high and papered over. No one would ever find her here. She was positive there'd been girls before her. They had a routine. They must have been out trolling for girls and happened upon her! She had no choice but to run barefoot in any direction. Anywhere far from here.

Kaylee ran around the back of the house, hidden from where Newell parked in case he showed up. She'd been held captive in a house that looked like any other house except it sat spookily isolated, perfect to keep her and God knows how many more girls held captive before her.

Shit! There was a car parked behind the house. She tried the doors and they opened. But there was no key, and she couldn't risk going back inside to find one. Precious little time was on her side.

She'd have to run for it.

Kaylee shook every pine needle that pricked her feet until she reached an asphalt drive where another car sat empty. Her heart raced double-time. It was the same vehicle Newell and Otto used to bring her here under the pretense of taking her to a hospital—a hospital that didn't make sense—one she now realized didn't exist.

But with Margo and Otto trapped in that room, this was her chance to maybe commandeer this car.

She pulled the car door's handle and it opened. Shit! They'd left this one unlocked too.

Kaylee shoved into the driver's seat and found the ignition. Empty again! No key!

She smacked the steering wheel.

"Damn you! Damn you!"

She shot out of the vehicle

She'd have to run for her freedom.

Kaylee bolted down the drive to its end, and paused. Which way to go? She decided to go right, and took off into the woods where she could hide from Newell.

Pine needles punctured her feet, causing her to stop and pick them out when it got too painful to continue. But whenever she stopped to pick them out, she lost precious time. She'd have to endure the pain and keep going. It was either pain or death, and death wasn't an option.

Kaylee zigzagged past tree after tree, caught in an endless maze of trees that began to look alike. Had she passed this one or that one before? Was she running in circles? Or making progress? She stopped and bent over, panting, and listened for cars, but heard none. Maybe she should've turned left, but it was too late now. She'd gone down the wrong path.

She headed straight. There had to be a road. They brought her here from the Tamiami Trail. She just needed to get back there.

But they'd drugged her, so she had no idea how long it took to bring her to that remote house of horrors. She woke up in a hospital bed with an IV. Ugh! The lengths they went to to disguise the truth.

Her eyes burned, and the angry heat propelled her faster.

Kaylee pumped her arms with every stride.

She was going to make it.

A cabin appeared in the distance. It wasn't the Tamiami Trail, but it was a place where she could get help. She'd call the police from there.

Her lungs hurt and her left ankle throbbed, but all she had to do was reach that cabin.

Kaylee's run turned into a quick limp that soon sagged into a hobble.

It didn't matter. The end was in sight.

She was within striking distance of the cabin when a searing pain shot up her left leg. Kaylee fell to the ground and clutched her leg, rocking back and forth to ease the pain.

A twig stuck out from the sole of her left foot. She grabbed it and tried to pull it out, but gasped at the pain. It was impaled deep. This was so bad.

She tried again but couldn't wedge it out.

"Shit! Shit! Shit! Shit! Shit!"

Now what?

It had to come out.

She braced herself, grabbed the twig, and yanked it hard.

The twig snapped, leaving its jagged stump in her already injured foot.

"No!" she screamed.

Kaylee sat among the pine needles with her knees to her chest and rocked some more.

"Help me, please!" she shouted.

No one came out of the cabin.

She swiped the tears off her cheeks with her dirt-caked hands.

Blood oozed around the twig stump.

Kaylee took off her shirt and tied it around the bottom of her foot. The snapped-off twig had retracted into her sole.

It was only a matter of time before it got infected.

She needed help.

She crawled on her hands and knees and reached the steps of the cabin.

Kaylee hoisted herself up the three steps. She raised her hand, curled her fingers into a fist, and managed a knock on the wood-splintered door.

"Help!"

She threw another knock.

"Please! Someone! I'm hurt. I need help! Puleese!"

Her calls had weakened.

Kaylee fell on her back. Her head began to spin, and the tree branches blurred into monster arms.

Blood seeped through her shirt. She lay in her bra, defeated.

There was nowhere for her to go.

Margo rubbed her head and winced when she grazed the lump on her head.

"Fuck!"

Otto lay in a fetal position, whimpering, his face covered with blood.

The bitch had attacked them and escaped, locking them in here.

Margo searched her pockets. One key was gone, but not the other. She always carried Otto's key along with hers. That bitch had no idea.

Margo stood, stepped over Otto, and opened the door.

"I'm coming for you, bitch."

She couldn't have gone far with that ankle.

Margo cackled.

The Tamiami Trail was the only road out of here and it was ten miles away.

Margo went over to the living room credenza. Her cell was still on top of it.

Stupid girl didn't see it.

She picked it up and scrolled through recent calls, just in case the bitch had fooled her.

Nope. The only calls were ones she made. No 911 either.

Then she called Gerald.

He answered on the second ring.

"Get here now! We have a problem. She's escaped!"

Gerald pulled over to the side of the road and slammed on his brakes. The Mercedes squealed to a halt.

"What the fuck are you talking about?" he yelled into his cell.

"She surprised me, and apparently Otto as well, at dinner. She knocked me out, and she did a number on Otto. He looks real bad."

"Fuck, Otto. I'm coming now. Search every room. Make sure she's not hiding. How the fuck did this happen?"

He mashed "end call" before Margo could answer.

All he wanted was a night out without all sorts of shit on his mind. And now this.

He made a sharp U-turn and just missed colliding with another car. The driver of the car rolled down his window and waved his middle finger at Gerald.

"You asshole!" he yelled.

Any other time Gerald would tail the jerk and accost him, but he couldn't waste any time. He gritted his teeth. Kaylee had to be found. He didn't go through all those maneuvers to secure her just to let her escape.

The pulse in his neck throbbed. The Greek was going to kill him. Delay was one thing, but failure to produce was an entirely different offense, guaranteed to end painfully.

Gerald rammed his foot down on the accelerator and blew past two red lights. Kaylee wasn't going to be the instigator of his demise, physically or financially.

He glanced in his rearview mirror for red and blue strobes tailing him, but none appeared.

The last thing he needed was to be stopped by the police. He had no criminal record, but the whole encounter would unnerve him. Perhaps draw suspicion about where he was headed.

A medical emergency, he mused. That would do it.

Gerald sped up faster and faster.

All he had to do was to reach that dirt road, then he'd be free to stomp on the gas like the devil without any consequences.

He scanned each side of the road for Kaylee.

She was here somewhere. She couldn't have gotten far with that bum ankle.

Dirt spewed from beneath the tires when he vaulted onto the asphalt drive.

He squealed the Mercedes to a halt and jumped out before the engine shut down.

Otto's car stood with the driver's side door open.

He checked the ignition. No key.

Even if she found the key, the car was useless since the gas tank was bone dry.

Fucking Otto never filled it up.

He had to rescue the idiot more than once for stranding himself with an empty gas tank.

But this time he'd thank Otto.

Margo ran out the front door with her hand pressed against her head.

"I don't want to know," Gerald hissed.

His whole fucking night was ruined.

"How could you have let this happen? I left you in charge! I've always trusted you. Where the hell is Otto?"

His mind was racing, but he needed answers, now!

"Otto's inside. He's in the room, and he's hurt bad."

Gerald pounded through the house, searching for her. The back of his neck burned hotter with every angry stride.

He didn't care whether Margo followed him or not.

He ripped into the room to find Otto curled up on the floor with his head in a pool of blood.

Shit! Was that a fork in his eye?

He rolled over Otto with his foot.

Otto let out a muted groan.

Oh, man! She'd sliced him from his cheek to his mouth.

Gerald didn't have time to suture him, and there was no way he could salvage Otto's right eye.

Margo stood waiting next to Gerald.

He looked at her ready to explode.

"How did she do this? And don't tell me it was with her nails."

"She had a razor."

"Where the hell did she get a razor?" he yelled in Margo's face.

"I don't know," Margo pleaded. "I shaved her today, but I took the razor back. I swear!"

"I don't have time to figure this out. Wait here."

Gerald stormed off to the procedure room. He went straight to the anesthetic cart and yanked out the top drawer. He took out a syringe and a vial of Ketamine and drew enough of the drug up into the syringe to take out a wrestler.

He'd underestimated Kaylee. She was shrewd and strong—characteristics he normally admired in others. And when he caught up with her, he'd have to break her.

Gerald bolted out of the procedure room with syringe in hand.

"What about Otto?" Margo asked.

"What about him?"

He pointed to the door.

"Get in the car. We have to catch her."

Kaylee woke on the porch in front of the cabin door.

How long had she been out?

No one had come out the cabin. No one had discovered her…yet.

She tried one more desperate thump on the door.

Nothing.

The sun would be setting soon, and she could travel no farther.

She needed to hide and rest.

Kaylee stood on her hands and knees and slowly righted, using the door to help brace herself, and winced.

Her shirt bandage had dried blood on it. At least her foot had stopped bleeding. But it was only a matter of time before it got infected from the dirty, impaled twig.

Kaylee tried the front cabin door, but it was locked.

"Hey!" she yelled again, and then waited.

Whoever owned the cabin or maybe rented it was gone.

She needed a way inside where she'd at least be safe for the night.

Kaylee's knee gave out, and she tumbled down the three cabin steps and landed on her side.

Get up. Get up. You can do it.

She rolled to her hands and knees again and walked her hands back until she could manage a bent-over stance.

She wheezed. Just standing winded her.

How was she ever going to get out of here?

She needed to get to the main road before sunrise so she could signal for help and be taken to a real hospital.

Kaylee gritted her teeth and hobbled around the deserted cabin.

The windows weren't set as high as the prison one, which no doubt had been built specifically to further their diabolical plans.

She shivered.

Was the infection setting in, or was it the realization that she might not make it to a main road, or, worse, not make it through the night? Or all of the above?

Kaylee shoved her morose thoughts away. They couldn't help her survive.

She reached a side window and shoved it up.

The wood frame cracked and then loosened.

She opened it as far as it could go and then stood back assessing if she could fit through it.

It would be tight, but she could—had to—squeeze through.

Kaylee pressed her hands against the windowsill and drew a deep breath.

One…two…three.

She hoisted herself up and shoved her head and shoulders through the opening.

Push! Push!

She wiggled in up to her waist and hung there, half in and half out.

She kicked her legs and bent farther until she plopped completely inside, falling to the musty floor.

Her lungs tightened.

She'd made it in.

Thank you, sweet Jesus.

She lay on her side with her head resting on the planks, taking the time to catch her breath.

Kaylee fought the urge to just lie there like a wounded animal.

Perhaps there were supplies she could use: food, water, soap or maybe even a first aid kit. A flashlight would be a Holy Grail.

Kaylee stood and scanned the abandoned surroundings. Layers of dust confirmed that no one had been here for a long time.

She was alone.

First, she'd secure her refuge.

She limped to the front door and tested the doorknob. It was locked. However, there was no dead bolt, and only a metal hook for extra security.

Kaylee pushed down on the metal hook further until it was firmly sealed—not that anyone was coming. The place was hers…for a couple of hours.

She then went to each of the two windows and twisted shut the rusty window locks, testing them afterwards.

Check.

Kaylee inspected the room.

From the looks of a tattered brown and tan plaid couch with rips deep enough to expose yellowed foam, and the chair with matching worn upholstery and a missing arm, Kaylee assumed this used to be a living room.

She limped past the sad furniture to a closed door.

Kaylee gave the door a hearty push, and it groaned open.

She ventured inside the closed-off room to discover a double bed with a bare mattress except for old puddles of brown and irregular stains.

Kaylee grimaced.

Is that blood?

She retreated the two steps she had taken into the closed-off room and slammed the door.

Her heart pounded in her ears.

Shit!

She limped away and paused at a kitchen. Should she wander inside? It couldn't be worse than that bedroom. Perhaps there were provisions in there that she could use.

Kaylee shuffled over the bubbled linoleum toward the cupboards, but when she opened one after another, she found nothing but dust lining the shelves.

She inhaled three quick breaths and sneezed.

She ambled to the sink while holding onto the kitchen counter to steady herself, hoping to rinse her festering wound.

She cranked the faucet handles. They vibrated and spit out brown water and air. Once the spigot pushed what must have remained in the pipes, no water came behind it.

Kaylee pounded the cracked porcelain sink.

Of course!

Then she looked down. She hadn't explored the kitchen drawers.

She had nothing to lose at this point.

The first drawer she pulled squeaked open, contained cutlery—mostly spoons and forks.

Kaylee laughed recalling how she'd stabbed a plastic fork in Otto's eye. Too bad it wasn't a metal one. She poked her fingers on the tines and picked it up. It would be useful. Then she saw a more perfect weapon, a serrated knife.

Bingo!

She grabbed it with renewed energy.

In the next drawer, Kaylee discovered a flashlight. And batteries, too!

This was too good to be true.

Kaylee ripped open the pack of batteries, unscrewed the bottom of the flashlight, and tossed the batteries inside.

She mashed the power button but no light came on. She mashed the flashlight button over and over again, pressing harder and harder, but still no light. She picked up the package containing the batteries. They'd expired five years ago.

Kaylee frowned and sniffled.

It really *was* too good to be true.

She tossed the useless flashlight, and the opened package of batteries into the drawer and slammed it shut.

She snorted. At least she had the fork, and most important, the knife.

She limped out of the kitchen with the knife and fork in her hands, and into a bathroom. After her kitchen finds, it was worth a look for any further hidden treasures.

She already knew the water was shut off, so she didn't even try the bathroom sink. Instead she opened the toilet lid. A thin layer of rusted water covered the bottom. She shut the lid. She was dehydrated and luckily or not, she had no urge to urinate.

Kaylee glanced at the strange reflection in the mirror. Sweat tracked across her sallow forehead and her bones jutted out from her sunken cheeks. Dull strands of what used to be sunny blonde hair lay limply behind her ears. No one would recognize her. She didn't even recognize herself.

Kaylee looked away and ran her parched tongue across her thin, cracked lips.

She was never going to be the same.

Her chest squeezed, but her tears had likewise dried up.

She touched her skin. She was burning up. With nothing to drink and fever from her infected foot, every last speck of hope just died.

She shouldn't have looked in the mirror.

Kaylee flicked the mirror out of the way and forced herself to look into the medicine cabinet.

She found an old bottle of acetaminophen. So what if it too was expired? She opened the bottle. The pills were still white. She tossed two pills far in the back of her throat and swallowed. The bitter, jagged pills stuck in the back of her throat. Kaylee stuck her finger in her mouth and pushed the pills further back. She gagged.

Swallow!

With what spittle she had left, the pills wedged down her throat, but managed to burn her upper chest.

Kaylee stuffed the pill bottle in her shorts pocket and then stared at the medicine cabinet. A quarter-filled bottle of alcohol sat lonely on one shelf, but down below it was an elastic bandage.

Oh, my God!

And she'd been about to give up.

Kaylee set the fork and knife on the toilet seat and grabbed the alcohol bottle and bandage. The broken-off twig was deeply impaled in her foot and unreachable, but now she could doctor it up herself until she could get medical help. She prayed that the expired acetaminophen and the alcohol and bandage would hold her until then.

She hobbled back to the living room and plopped down on the

disaster of a sofa, winded.

She shoved down the mountains of yellowed foam that bulged up from the grave of the split couch, but the pieces of foam sprang back out and attacked her.

Damn you!

Kaylee slid to the end of the sofa and away from the rising foam.

She tipped the bottle of alcohol and doused her wound.

Ow! Ow! Ow!

But it needed to be done. She wrapped the elastic bandage around her injured foot and wiggled her toes.

After her wound was cleansed and secured, Kaylee sat back on the sofa. Miraculously, the tattered and battered sofa held up, but her foot still throbbed.

Kaylee closed her eyes and listened to her steady breathing.

She was neither hungry nor thirsty. She recognized it was a bad sign, but she just needed to rest before moving on.

Her head lolled to one side, waking her. The pain had lessened. It was still there, but tolerable. Kaylee touched her forehead and her hand encountered sweat. She shifted on the sofa. The back of her shirt was soaked. Her fever must have broken. But she was too weak to get up.

Maybe she should die here…alone. At least she'd be with her mom and dad.

"Kaylee, get up and run," her mom whispered in her ear.

Kaylee startled awake.

"Mom!"

No one was there.

She'd begun to hallucinate.

"Kayleeeeee."

Kaylee grabbed the side of the sofa and pushed herself up.

"Mommy, help me!"

"Run."

"I'm going, Mommy. I'm going."

Kaylee stumbled into the bathroom, grabbed the knife, hobbled to the front door, released the locks, and ran back into the woods.

24

Gerald gritted his teeth, alternatively lurching the car forward, and then jamming on the brakes while searching for Kaylee. "You look on the right, and I'll take the left," Gerald said. "Can you do that?" he added with heavy sarcasm.

"I want her as badly as you do," Margo hissed back.

Gerald knew every tree and bush in these woods since he'd grown up here. He studied the branches and watched out for any telltale split in the bushes for signs that Kaylee ran through them, but nothing stood out.

"Damn it!"

Margo pointed to a drooping tree branch with missing leaves.

"There! How about that?"

Gerald grunted, pulled the car to the side of the dirt road, and got out.

"I'll come with you," Margo called.

Gerald plodded on, leaving Margo to catch up. He had no time for her. No time for that little bitch, either. Sophia was waiting for him.

Heat spread from his neck to his face, and his fingernails dug into his palms while he stomped through the woods with everything he had focused on any breadcrumbs Kaylee might have left behind.

And then he saw it!

Gerald squatted and touched the fresh drops of blood. He was now on her trail.

He followed the blood like a hound, smashing through leaves and kicking fallen branches. His heart rate pulsed faster and faster. He was closing in on her.

Shit!

Mother's cabin came into view.

Rage gripped him.

Kaylee had found it.

How dare she invade it!

Gerald raced to the cabin he'd escaped.

Kaylee forced him to go back inside—to relive every shitty nightmare that took place in there.

He stomped up the three steps.

The rotted wood groaned beneath his feet, and his foot busted through the third step, scraping his ankle and tearing the hem of his pants. Off-kilter, he grabbed the cabin's door handle to steady himself.

"Fuck! I'm going to kill that fucking bitch!"

He hoisted his leg out of the jagged hole and shoved his hand into the back pocket of his torn pants. Whipping out a key ring thick with assorted keys, he fumbled for the cabin key. As hideous as his childhood had been, he'd never removed the key to hell on earth. Tonight he was glad he hadn't ditched it. He still owned the cabin—and all its nightmares, too.

His mind raced, thinking about how the hell Kaylee got inside. That blood couldn't have been from anyone else.

Margo's hot breath pricked at the back of his neck. It was a good thing the woman kept her mouth shut, because it was all that stopped him from turning around and slapping the shit out of her.

But that's exactly what Kaylee wanted to happen…to have them turn on each other, playing to her advantage. This was not a stupid girl, and that worried him. If she got away, she'd bring them all down.

He'd tackle her inside and drag her to the punishment she deserved.

Gerald unlocked the door and bolted inside.

"I'm coming for you!" he yelled.

He scanned the living room. It was as decrepit as the day he left. Mother's broken chair stared right at him. Her heartless weight had broken it and dusty time had finally finished it off. He kicked it over. It was missing one leg

Gerald ran his tongue over his front teeth while mulling over the missing piece of wood.

Was she hiding around some corner waiting to bludgeon him? He wouldn't put it past her. She'd already set one trap. Well, he could play that game too.

Gerald ripped off the chair's leg, toppling it over. He despised that chair and reveled in its death.

Armed with the chair leg, he ventured around the cabin, slowing at each corner. But Kaylee hadn't popped out…yet.

"I'll check the hallway." Margo whispered.

"No. You stay here. She's already bested you. I don't need you to interfere."

Margo complied and stood with her back against the door.

At least she was thinking straight and blocking Kaylee's exit.

He had the uppity bitch trapped.

Gerald stepped into the kitchen, his attention going straight to the loosely-shut top kitchen drawer. He ripped it open. It was where mother kept her cutlery, among other monstrous devices.

He stared into the drawer, but mother had craftily gotten rid of her "disciplinary" devices, leaving only everyday cutlery behind. Gerald focused on the knives, and then he gazed at the forks and remembered Otto with that plastic fork in his eye. He shuddered, imagining what damage Kaylee could do with a metal fork. He wasn't about to find out.

"Kaylee," he called, taunting her to come out. "I'm not angry with you," he lied, hoping to tempt her out.

But Kaylee didn't surrender.

"There's no use hiding. I know you're hurt. Let me help you."

Still no Kaylee.

That girl has balls.

Gerald tiptoed down the hallway, chair-leg raised.

Kaylee hadn't attacked.

He swung into the bathroom, leaving the door open.

The medicine cabinet was open, and a capped bottle of alcohol sat on the toilet seat cover along with a thinned and yellowed cardboard bandage box. He opened the box, but it fell apart, empty.

He recalled the Band-Aid brand and rubbed his forearm where mother used to scratch him every time she dug her fingernails into his boyhood skin.

"You're such a sissy!" she would chant while she taunted him with his Band-Aids.

Gerald picked up the ancient box and threw it on the floor. Then he stomped on it.

He grunted and with gorilla strength and smashed the alcohol bottle in the sink. It bounced out of the sink and ricocheted off the bathroom wall and skidded to a stop.

Gerald stomped out of the bathroom while clutching his chair leg harder and harder.

He'd hit her hard for the mess she created. It didn't matter that she was apparently more injured than he'd thought. She was going to get a lesson she'd never forget.

Gerald proceeded to the bedroom. He was mouth went dry and the pulses in his neck hammered in in his ears. He'd sworn he'd never go back into that bedroom.

He had no choice. Kaylee was certainly in there.

Gerald jerked his hand off the doorknob as if it singed him, sucked in a deep breath, and grabbed the doorknob again and twisted it. Then he slammed the door open, ready to confront Kaylee.

"Got you!" he roared into the empty room.

The closet. She must be in the closet.

He swung the door open only to find Mother's kaftans hanging on wire hangars. He parted the saggy, flower-printed kaftans, expecting to find Kaylee huddled into a ball.

"Shit!" he hissed.

She'd fooled him again!

He whipped around, only to face the bloodstained mattress. His blood. He rubbed his hands where mother had secured clamps with its big teeth on his fingers when she caught him masturbating. Then she tied him to the bed and locked the bedroom door until she returned with branches full of leaves.

He could still hear the sound of her hurried footsteps and click of the bedroom door unlocking. He winced and then hollered with every lash of that branch to his scrotum. And then came the worst part. She'd leave him naked, and then, hours later, return to untie him and kiss his wounds. She'd make him sleep with her instead of his normal place on the sofa.

Gerald bolted out of the foul bedroom and slammed the door to his former prison cell.

He stormed out the front door.

"She's not here!"

Kaylee grabbed tree branch after tree branch to help propel her forward through the woods. Between the swinging from branch to branch, the elastic bandage began to pool down at her ankle.

No! No!

She stopped, bent over, and tightened the bandage, tucking the end inside the mummy-wrap.

Then she looked up and spotted a thick, bare branch.

It would do as a makeshift crutch. That way she could avoid putting so much weight on her foot.

Kaylee stood and reached for the branch, but it was too high.

She jumped and swatted at it.

Her fingers brushed against it, and on the third try she grabbed enough purchase to yank until the branch cracked away from the tree, the force toppling her to her back with the branch clutched in her hand.

Kaylee rolled to her side and dug the splintered end into the dirt, bracing it to help her stand up.

It worked. She was up and ready for another go at freedom.

She repeatedly stabbed the end into the ground, providing her with newfound balance and traction.

Her coordination improved with every limped stride, and she moved through the woods at an even pace.

She decided to stay deep in the woods. Newell's car wouldn't fit through the maze of trees, shrubs and rocks, and that played to her advantage, not to mention the knife she'd holstered in her shorts' pocket. It was amazing she didn't stab herself when she fell. That was a good omen. Right?

Her branch crutch splintered the dry pine needles.

Shhhh!

Kaylee scanned her surroundings. Neither a creature nor a monster made their presence known.

The sun would begin to set soon, and she had little time left to find help. The last thing she wanted was to be forced to camp out in the dark. That exponentially increased her chances of being cornered and caught like a wild animal. If only that flashlight had worked. That only pushed her harder to keep moving forward.

With her eyes focused forward, she maneuvered farther through the woods.

She paused and listened hard at the distant humming.

Cars! Are those cars?

Hallelujah! She was closing in on freedom!

Kaylee picked up her pace, limping faster and faster.

Her heart raced pumping life-saving adrenaline through her.

Even her ankle had stopped hurting.

A white truck rumbled by.

"Hey!" Kaylee yelled.

But the truck disappeared.

She pouted with a fat lower lip.

Keep moving.

There had to eventually be more traffic on the that road. She just needed to get closer. Someone was bound to see her.

Salvation pushed her to move at even a faster clip.

She panted. *Almost there.*

Another vehicle hummed closer.

Kaylee waved her hand while leaning on her natural crutch.

"Over here! Help!"

Her crutch slipped under her, and she hit the ground on her belly.

Someone grabbed her legs.

"Gotcha!" Newell growled.

Kaylee swung her hand to her back pocket, reached for the knife, and yanked it out.

She refused to go back to that prison.

Kaylee kicked away Newell's hands and rolled to her side with the knife drawn.

Pain seared through her hand and she dropped the knife.

Margo stood on Kaylee's hand crushing the bones.

"That's for hitting me on the head!"

Margo forced Kaylee to her belly and held her hands while Newell sat on her.

Dirt filled her nostrils.

"Nighty-night," he hissed.

The needle jabbed her clear through her shorts.

The woods went blurry.

A car zoomed past in the distance.

Then everything went black.

25

Gerald dragged unconscious Kaylee by her feet. Her head bobbled on her neck and smacked rocks and tree roots. He couldn't care less. Gerald grinned and yanked her limp body harder, all the way to his car parked on the side of the road.

Margo walked next to him.

"The little bitch got far," Margo said.

Gerald grunted.

Yes, she did, and she almost succeeded in bringing him down. And now she was going to pay for it.

He'd gotten to her just in time.

He and Margo had methodically combed the woods every few yards, returning to the car and then moving forward again.

But Kaylee's calls for help roused him right away.

It was a close call, but it was over now.

Gerald popped the trunk with his remote.

Kaylee couldn't be trusted anywhere else.

She deserved a trunk ride.

He folded Kaylee in half, tossed her into the trunk like a rag doll, and slammed the trunk lid shut.

Gerald and Margo got in the car.

He tossed the knife in the glove box and locked it.

Margo remained silent and all was quiet in the trunk.

He'd rush back to the house. The last thing he wanted was another Joanna situation.

Kaylee deserved maximum punishment, but he needed to keep her alive.

The bruises should heal before they left for Greece. Thereafter, he'd only use humiliation to break her. She'd learn her place.

He'd underestimated her this time, but never again.

Joanna certainly was easier. Too bad she died.

Gerald pulled into the drive and parked.

He hadn't heard any noise from the trunk, but that meant nothing. He gave her a hefty dose of Ketamine, but it might not stop her for long. Her strength and determination could be genetic. But if there were any relatives left, they'd acknowledge that Kaylee died in that car wreck. Actually, it was Joanna who died, but no one would know the difference.

Gerald chuckled. They were probably having her funeral right now.

Meanwhile, he had to secure Kaylee inside, and then he needed to call Sophia.

Gerald and Margo rounded the car to the trunk and both stared at it.

"Ready?" he asked Margo.

"Ready."

He knew they were both waiting for Kaylee to leap out of that trunk like a zombie.

Gerald hit the remote to unlock it.

The trunk hood slowly rose.

Gerald winced, and Margo took a step back.

But Kaylee lay in the trunk in the same position he'd left her.

He poked her, but she didn't move.

Then he leaned closer to make sure she was still breathing.

Indeed, Kaylee was alive.

Gerald lifted Kaylee out of the trunk.

"Go open the door," he commanded Margo.

He carried the collapsed girl into the house.

Kaylee lay sprawled in his arms with her head lolling on her neck, to and fro with every step.

Thankfully she was out, and he didn't have to fight her.

Gerald brought her into her cell.

Otto lay on the floor in a fetal position and at this point barely moaning.

Dried blood caked his face, but on closer inspection, Gerald winced.

"Shit."

While they were out searching for Kaylee, Otto had pulled the fork out of his eye, and along with it, half his eyeball.

Gerald couldn't fix that, and taking Otto to a hospital was out of the question.

He stepped around Otto, tossed Kaylee on the bed, and stripped her.

"Get the ties," he ordered Margo.

"Right."

Margo returned with some thick rope.

"You tie her hands to the headboard while I get her feet," Gerald said.

Margo did as instructed, while Gerald tied Kaylee's legs wide apart.

He inspected the impaled twig in the bottom of Kaylee's left foot.

Gerald widened his eyes.

Guts and grit.

He took a step back.

"There. Leave her like that. I want her to feel every second of pain once she comes to. And don't feed her or give her any water. I'll deal with her when I get back."

Gerald tossed a glance at Otto.

He grabbed Otto's arms and hauled him out of Kaylee's room, depositing him on the living room floor.

"I'll deal with him too when I return."

He'd made Sophia wait long enough. He'd make it up to her.

Gerald plucked his cell out of his back pocket and texted Sophia.

Sorry I'm late. Had a medical emergency I needed to take care of. Be there in about 30 minutes.

Sophia texted back.

K.

Gerald looked down at his torn pants and dirty shirt.

Fuck! Kaylee ruined his evening.

Good thing he kept spare clothes at the house. It weren't his best, but they'd suffice. It would take him too long to go to his condo in Miami Beach, change clothes, and then be on his way to Sophia's place. She lived closer to the house anyway.

Gerald went to the bathroom and spritzed his face with water. He returned to the spare bedroom he kept at the house and opened the locked bedroom. He kept it locked to keep Otto out of it, but that wouldn't be a problem anymore.

He flung his dirty clothes and torn pants on the floor and hurried dressing. All that was left to do was clean his shoes. It would be hard to explain why they were sprinkled with dirt since he already told her he was delayed because of a medical emergency. Although it was a medical emergency—of sorts.

Gerald stopped in the kitchen and wiped his shoes with a damp paper towel.

Margo sat at the kitchen table.

"Remember, no food or drink. Don't even bother going in there, even when she starts hollering."

"I got it," Margo replied.

"I'll be back around nine or nine-thirty."

"Okay."

He knew Margo wanted to leave for her own place, but this was her fault. She'd been coddling Kaylee. She was getting too soft. He'd have to monitor her. No way would he get rid of her. Her US and global connections were too valuable. Otto? Well…he was dispensable. He'd served his purpose.

Sophia tapped the toe of her loaned, strappy black sandals on the cracked linoleum kitchen floor. Maria left over an hour ago and the flan they shared had also left her stomach an hour ago. She was hungry again.

She got up, went to the cabinet, and pulled out an outdated box of crackers.

She popped one in her mouth and frowned. The cracker had lost its crunch.

Sophia sighed. At least it was something to chew on until Gerald arrived and treated her to something much better to eat.

Her stomach grumbled, displeased with the stale crackers.

Maybe he made up that medical emergency excuse to test her.

She'd never really been stood up before. Sex was sex. She got what she wanted. They got what they wanted. That was fair. Then they'd go their separate ways. Sometimes they returned, and more often not.

But Gerald was different. She just wanted him again and again and again.

Oh shit! Maybe he's married and that's the delay.

She'd been through that once before, and said never again. It wasn't worth it, and besides, it made her all skeevy inside.

Sophia picked up her cell and was about to send a text canceling the night when a knock came at her door.

She clopped to door in the spiked-heeled sandals and squinted through the door's peep hole.

Gerald stood on the other side.

Sophia deleted the text and smiled.

It took him less than the thirty minutes he promised.

Sophia unbolted the triple locks and opened the door.

"Hi," she chirped, forgetting her second thoughts.

Gerald grinned wide.

"I'm so sorry I'm late."

Sophia shrugged.

"Let's go," she said.

She sashayed through the door without letting Gerald get past her doorstep.

He wasn't the kind of man she'd entertained in the past.

Gerald didn't fit in her tiny apartment.

Sophia locked her door and turned to face him.

Her stomach forgot its demands and fluttered.

Gerald held out his hand to her.

"You look lovely tonight."

Sophia smoothed her dress.

"Thanks to you."

Sophia accepted his hand, and he squeezed it gently.

His fingers were warm and masculine.

"I'm so glad it suits you. I described you to the saleswoman. She did the rest."

Sophia gave him a playful nudge with her shoulder.

He actually described her perfectly.

"Ready?" he asked.

"Absolutely."

Gerald followed Sophia's delicious curves. But it was her short shorts and the tantalizing view of her firm, half-moon cheeks that got him. No matter what she wore, Sophia made every one of his nerves stand on end.

"Where to?" Sophia asked.

"I'll surprise you."

"Ooh! I like surprises."

Gerald grinned. "I was counting on that."

He led Sophia to where his Mercedes was parked on the side of the road. At least his car still had all four hubcaps.

"Wow. What happened to your car? It's all dusty."

"I was trying to get to you as fast as I could, so I took a shortcut along a dirt road," he lied.

Shit! He'd forgotten all about having to use his car to track down Kaylee in the woods.

"I could fix that for you tomorrow…or when it's convenient for you."

"I'm sorry I destroyed all your hard work."

Sophia shook her head. "Nah. You're my best customer."

"How about the day after tomorrow? That gives you a day to relax after I get you home late tonight."

He also needed to recoup after chasing Kaylee.

"That'll be fine. It'll give me something to look forward to 'cause as you already know that Freddie is such a prick."

He'd remedy that. But he decided to wait to tell her he'd be leaving for Greece and taking her with him…a lot sooner than he planned. He couldn't risk Kaylee escaping, and the Greek's invitation was gold, and he didn't want to keep the Greek waiting.

Things changed rapidly in this business and there were many competitors. But he had an edge. He could get women. Nice women—when they were cleaned up—not dirty, ragged, whores. Men could get dirty and ragged anywhere. No, his girls were special. Plus, he was a great schmoozer. Being a doctor not only offered instant social status, but also the gift of gab. Potential clients would be tripping over themselves just to speak with him. And as a gynecologist, he was able to screen and treat his girls for sexually transmitted infections, and with a steady supply of IUDs, his girls would also be guaranteed pregnancy-free. And of course he could handle any stray pregnancy that happened.

"Well, that's a big smile," Sophia said.

"Just dreaming."

Sophia smiled and nodded.

Gerald opened the passenger car door open and escorted Sophia inside. Then he gently shut the door and rounded the Mercedes and scooched into the driver's seat.

He looked at Sophia and how the setting sun dallied in her hair, highlighting the glistening brown strands surrounding her smiling face.

His day plummeted to shit hours earlier, but now everything was looking up.

26

Joanna placed herself between Lou Ann and Harry as they left the diner. Even though it wasn't Newell in the that diner, the thought of him made her knees weak. She needed to get to the car before they buckled.

When they'd finally made it to the car, Joanna stood at the back passenger door bouncing her knee.

"Uh…do you need to use the uh…the facilities?" Harry asked.

Joanna shook her head. "Nope."

"Uh…okay. The ride to where we're staying is short," Harry said.

Harry unlocked the back door, and Joanna bolted inside and buckled her seat belt.

Lou Ann and Harry climbed into the car and looked back at Joanna at the same time.

Joanna sat quietly. She was safe inside.

Harry returned his attention to the steering wheel and started the engine.

Lou Ann faced the front slowly.

An awkward silence filled the car.

Joanna took a deep breath and patted her buckle.

She looked out the window at the trees and cars passing by. She'd missed life on the outside while she spent weeks or maybe even months locked away, or so she guessed because without windows or even a clock or calendar she'd lost track of time, and that's what Newell wanted. It was all about control. But she was free now.

Harry slowed the car and turned right into the driveway of the most beautiful house she'd ever seen.

Neatly trimmed dark green shrubbery with thick, waxy leaves

surrounded the sparkling, white, concrete block house. The one-story house, with its matching dark green shutters sprawled forever before making sharp turns on each end. A palm tree with a nest of brown coconuts way at the top stood to her left, and a smaller trio of palms took residence at the other end. It was truly magnificent. Someday she wanted to live in a house just like this.

Was this where she was going to stay, at least temporarily?!

This was a dream she never wanted to wake from.

She wondered what Lou Ann's house looked like. If it was half as beautiful as this house, then she'd be perfectly satisfied.

She purged Newell, Otto, and Margo from her brain.

She really was going to be okay.

Harry cut the engine.

Joanna unbuckled her seat belt and flung open her door before either Lou Ann or Harry could help her out.

"This is our friend's house where we've been staying."

The front door opened and a smiling man with a sharp crew cut that worked for him came out to greet them.

Unbelievable!

It was the captain who visited her while she was in the hospital. Joanna didn't initially recognize him without his uniform.

"Welcome back" he said to Lou Ann and Harry, and then he shot an attentive gaze toward Joanna. "Kaylee, it's so nice to see you again. He beckoned to her. "Come on in."

Lou Ann walked next to Joanna, and Harry caught up with them.

Once they were inside, Brad locked the door and armed an alarm.

The sound of the locks clicked loud in her ears.

Joanna whipped around and stared at the locks on the door. There were only two, and not the four clicks that perked her ears while bracing for whoever was next to invade her.

Joanna's breath hitched in a preamble to a full-scale panic attack.

Someone rested their arm on her shoulder.

"Kaylee. It's all right," Lou Ann said, her voice as soft as her reassuring touch.

Joanna turned around.

"I'm sorry" she gushed.

"No need to apologize. Life has been asking a lot of you."

Joanna nodded.

If they only knew.

But whatever it took, she'd keep her past a secret.

"Let me show you to the bedroom where you'll be staying," Lou Ann said.

"I think that will be a good idea," Brad agreed.

"I second that," Harry said.

Joanna followed Lou Ann down a hallway.

She stared at the pictures of two smiling girls mounted on the wall.

"Those are Brad's daughters. But they're not here right now. They're with their mother."

"So he's divorced?" Joanna asked.

"Yes. You'll be staying in one of his daughters' rooms."

Joanna hesitated.

"It's all right," Lou Ann said.

"Harry has been staying in there, but now it's yours for tonight."

"For tonight?"

"Yes."

Lou Ann opened the door to a little girl's dream world full of Barbie Dolls and all their accessories.

Joanna had only seen the dolls on TV, having only ever dreamed about having just one.

"Well, get settled."

Lou Ann eased the door shut.

Joanna waited to make sure she was alone and then picked up a Barbie doll. She stroked the doll's long blonde hair and hugged Barbie to her chest.

A knock came at the bedroom door.

"Kaylee, it's Lou Ann."

Joanna tossed the Barbie doll under the pillow.

"Come in," Joanna called.

Lou Ann entered the bedroom with a plastic bag in her hand.

"I forgot to give you this."

Lou Ann handed Joanna the bag.

"I bought you a nightie and some underclothes. I hope that's okay since I didn't know your preferences."

"I'm sure they're fine. Thank you."

"Kaylee, can we sit down?"

"Um...sure."

Joanna sat next to the pillow hiding the Barbie doll.

Lou Ann sat on the bed next to Joanna and took a deep breath.

"In the morning...after breakfast...we're leaving for Miami. We'll gather your belongings at the house before the funeral."

"Funeral?"

Shit! She hadn't thought about that.

Lou Ann touched Joanna's leg lightly.

"I know this is so hard for you, but it's important for you to be there for your parents. And it's important for me too. I'll be with you the whole time. I think you'd regret not going. I went to my mom's funeral and then within a month, my dad's, so I can understand the pain you feel."

The funeral was unavoidable. She couldn't say no. If she didn't go, they'd question why. She'd go with Lou Ann and Harry, and then she could get the hell out of Miami for good. She just needed to jump through this one hoop.

Lou Ann waited for her reply.

"I'll go."

"That's a good decision."

"I'm going to get some rest now."

"Okay. I'm available to talk, any time. Just knock on my door, the bedroom across from this one."

"Thanks. I'm going to turn in now."

Lou Ann stood, leaned over, and kissed Joanna on the head.

"Good night, Kaylee."

"Good night, Aunt Lou Ann."

Lou Ann grinned and left the room, closing the bedroom door behind her.

Aunt Lou Ann. What a nice touch.

Joanna lay back on the bed, took the Barbie doll from under the pillow, and hugged it close.

She left the bag with the nightie unopened.

She slipped off the jeans and bra Lou Ann bought her and ducked under the pink covers in her underwear and T- shirt and closed her eyes.

One more day in Miami wouldn't kill her.

Lou Ann entered the bedroom where Harry had been staying. She wanted to give Kaylee privacy, and she was close by if Kaylee should need her.

She found Harry spreading a purple blanket on the floor.

"You can have the bed," he said.

"I hate to put you out."

Being in bed with Harry wasn't going to happen tonight or any other night. He'd been nothing but caring and surprisingly wonderful to her though all this upheaval, exactly the way he used to be. But it didn't mean a whole new beginning for them, and based on the blanket on the floor, she knew he accepted that too. The bad history between them overshadowed the once-vivid relationship they enjoyed for years.

Harry stretched out on the girly blanket with his arms behind his head.

"Don't mention it."

Lou Ann chuckled. "I won't."

"So how is she doing?" Harry asked. "That was weird how she rushed out of the dinner, and then that thing she did at the door was even weirder."

Lou Ann sat on the bed.

"Yeah. But we have to remember that she's been through even what most people three times her age experience, if ever—the traumatic car wreck, being the only survivor. And man, she must feel real guilty for having lived, and not her parents. Then the whole head trauma, and uh, you know, memory loss—physical and psychological."

"Yeah, I get it," Harry agreed. "Poor kid. I think we were making good progress in the diner."

Lou Ann laughed. "Apparently she likes your jokes. And I think she really likes you."

"Funny. That's what you used to like about me."

"I still do, Harry."

A knock came at the door.

Was that Kaylee?

"Hey, are you guys decent?" Brad called.

"Just a minute," Harry called.

Then he jokingly called, "Hurry up, Lou Ann. Get your clothes on!"

Lou Ann rolled her eyes and shook her head.

"Come on in," Lou Ann said.

Brad opened the door.

Harry lay with the purple blanket up to his chin.

"She a fast dresser. Always was."

"You're such a card, Harry. I just want to make sure you guys are okay."

"Thanks, Brad. We're fine. We're both tired, and we need to get up early tomorrow to hit the road to Miami," Lou Ann said.

"Okay. I'm an early riser."

"Since when?" Harry asked.

"Since my divorce."

"Ouch. Sorry," Harry said.

"No problem. I'll get you started with a good breakfast before you leave."

"We can get something on the road."

"What? You don't like my cooking? Gee, I'm offended."

"You've done so much for us already, and on such short notice."

"Again. Not a problem. Actually, with the kids gone, I've enjoyed the company, even though it wasn't under the best circumstances. How's Kaylee doing?"

"Harry and I were just talking about that. She's gonna need a lot of help for a long time."

"We've all seen gruesome stuff, and I hate to say this, but it is completely different when it's personal," Brad said.

Brad's words sank deep in her chest. She couldn't break out of that cycle of "personal."

"But I don't want to end the night on a bad note, so I'll just say, 'See you in the morning.'"

"Good night, Brad," Lou Ann said.

Harry shot a thumbs-up. "In the morning."

27

The pain searing up the back of her leg woke Kaylee with a start. When she went to rub the pain away, the headboard jerked, and her feet were split way apart and tied so tight to the end of the bed that when she tried to get comfortable, the ropes around her ankles tightened like thorns.

She winced. How did she end up this way? Then it came to her. Running and running. Cars in the background. And then they tackled her. The needle punctured her.

Those bastards had to knock her out so they could to tie her like this.

She almost made it out.

Tears spread across her cheeks and trailed behind her neck, but she wasn't able to wipe them away.

They'd won.

How long would they keep her like this—a slow torture—before they returned?

Her heart pounded.

What were they going to do to her?

Whatever it was, it was going to be painful.

Torture would be her punishment.

There was no way out now.

This was it.

Kaylee stared at the same white ceiling tiles.

There wasn't any point counting them anymore.

She watched her naked stomach rise and fall.

Maybe if she begged for them not to do what they were planning.

She'd promise to be good.

She'd do whatever they wanted.

She'd comply.

What choice did she have?

None.

Kaylee lay in her bonds, waiting for Newell or Margo, or both to bust through the door to direct their rage at her.

She'd put them through their paces, now it was their turn to put her through hers.

Newell even left in the impaled twig in her foot.

It was just like him to make her suffer—to teach her a lesson.

But no one came.

Maybe they'd left, leaving her to languish alone with no one knowing she was here.

That would be the ultimate revenge.

Margo drummed her fingers on the kitchen table. Newell was out having fun while she was stuck with whimpering Otto and a locked-up Kaylee. She'd had enough of both of them.

Margo stood and walked past the living room where Otto lay on the very couch he'd ruined with cigarette holes.

"Help me. Please help me," Otto repeatedly mumbled.

Margo shook her head.

She had to give Kaylee credit for disabling Otto.

Margo tiptoed to Kaylee's door and put her ear against it.

Not a sound came from the other side.

Even though she and Newell had tied Kaylee naked to the bed, she still didn't trust her.

But Newell ordered her to leave Kaylee alone until he got home from his date with that slut of his.

It was best to have both of them in the room with Kaylee.

Margo returned to Otto and stuck her hand in his pants pocket.

His bedroom key had to be in there.

Otto grabbed her arm.

"Help me," he cried out.

Margo winced at the sight of Otto's hanging eyeball.

She tossed off his hand and pulled a keyring out of his pocket and then left him.

She couldn't do a damn thing to help him, even if she chose to.

Margo walked down the hall to Otto's locked bedroom door.

The keys jangled.

How many did he have?

Margo recognized the car key, but not the other three.

One had to be to the front door, and one to the kitchen door. That left one key, and when she stuck it into the keyhole, it fit perfectly, and the lock clicked.

Margo opened the door.

She sniffed and winced at the rotten stink.

A half-eaten lump of what once was a hamburger and shriveled, brown French fries lay strewn on a paper plate in the middle of crumpled sheets.

Shit.

But she wasn't here to clean up his mess. She was there for his laptop including every connection that was on it, no doubt, the ones she had stupidly given him. She was here to reclaim it all. It wasn't useful to him now.

Margo scanned the tornado of a room and spotted Otto's laptop perched on scratched desktop with no chair.

He did everything in that nasty bed.

Margo snatched up the laptop.

She then went through the desk drawers, and found a small notebook in the second one, which she opened to find a treasure trove of not only passwords, but phone numbers and contact information.

Thank you, Otto.

She grabbed the notebook, shut the rickety drawers, and left Otto's pathetic bedroom.

Hmmm. She decided not to tell Newell about the notebook and laptop, and hang onto them as her insurance policy.

Gerald pulled into the restaurant's parking lot and parked among the other luxury vehicles.

"Here we are," he announced.

He was sure Sophia had never been to a place like this before.

He got out of the car, rounded to the passenger side, and opened Sophia's door.

Gerald held out his hand, and she answered his polite invitation with hers.

Ordinarily he would snap her up because of her background, or lack thereof. She'd be well worth the investment and the ultimate payoff, but he couldn't do that to her, not even after tonight.

Sophia had broken all his rules, but he couldn't keep his eyes off her.

She was all his, and he'd worked himself to the top of the business, so he could make these kinds of calls without suffering any consequences.

Sophia's eyes went wide.

"Wow!"

"I take it you'd like to go inside?"

"Would I!"

Gerald closed the car door and clicked his remote to lock up.

He linked arms with Sophia while they approached the restaurant's entrance.

Gerald opened the restaurant door and escorted Sophia inside.

A statuesque blonde with her hair upswept and her snug red dress's neckline plunging deep enough to highlight her well-rounded breasts smiled directly at Gerald.

"Dr. Newell, how nice to see you this evening!"

She attempted a glance at Sophia.

"It's great to see you too, Melissa. I called earlier to move my reservation for two to 7:30."

"Yes, I have that right here. No problem. I have your regular, private table ready. Follow me."

Melissa had tits and ass that begged to be touched.

But he'd restrained himself because Melissa was an untouchable, sharp as she was sexy. Melissa was the kind of woman who would make the evening news the minute she went missing. Plus, she wasn't malleable. Kaylee invaded Gerald's mind for the first time since he'd picked up Sophia.

Damn Kaylee!

She was an untouchable who accidentally became his property. No one would miss her since she was said to have died in an auto wreck with her parents. But she was a handful. He'd enjoy dinner with Sophia and deal with Kaylee later.

Melissa showed Gerald to his favorite table and nodded to Sophia.

"Enjoy your evening."

"We will," Gerald replied.

He pulled out Sophia's chair and once she was settled, he sat.

Her eyes roamed the restaurant, her expression thoroughly awestruck.

Gerald grinned, enjoying Sophia's childlike delight.

She really was going to love Greece.

When she blinked at the myriad of cutlery on the table and looked up at him with a small frown, he said, "Just go from the outside in."

Sophia shot him one of her brightest, beaming smiles.

"Thanks."

"Don't mention it. I used to get confused too."

Sophia widened those innocent brown eyes.

"Really?"

"Yep."

Gerald lowered Sophia's menu.

"I'll order for you. You trust me, don't you?"

Sophia nodded.

Good girl.

They dined on duck confit and between them they polished off a bottle of red.

Gerald leaned back in his chair, doubly satisfied.

Sophia had followed all his suggestions.

It was a good night.

Too bad he'd have to take Sophia home and then leave.

His night was far from over.

28

Gerald parked in the same place as when he picked up Sophia.

Sophia reached over and rested her hand on Gerald's thigh.

"I had an awesome time," Sophia grinned. "Want to come inside so I can thank you even more?"

Gerald placed his hand over Sophia's.

"I really want to come inside with you, but I can't tonight."

Sophia's lower lip swelled and quivered.

"No. No. It's not you. I promise. Trust me, I'll make it up to you. We got a late start, and I really wanted to take you out somewhere special. But I have to get up early because I have a full day in the office tomorrow."

It was lie. He needed get back to Kaylee and that might take hours.

"You're married, aren't you?" Sophia blurted out. "That's why you were late, and that's why you're not staying!"

Gerald chuckled.

Sophia flung open the car door and slammed it shut. Then she rushed to her apartment.

"Sophia! Wait!"

But Sophia didn't look back.

Women!

He rushed to Sophia and grabbed her arm.

"I'm not married!"

Sophia whipped around.

"Then it's me."

"No." Gerald sighed. "But I haven't been completely honest with you."

Sophia wrinkled her forehead.

"I need to get to the office early to start seeing more patients because I'm planning to take some time off."

"Okay."

"I'm planning to take you on a vacation with me."

Sophia jumped up and down.

"Oh, my gosh!"

"How would you like to go to Greece?"

"Would I?!"

Sophia gave Gerald a big, smacking kiss.

"I'll start packing!"

"I can't wait to show you around Greece."

"I'll let Freddy know I'm not ever coming back because you know he's never going to give me the time off. I've been fantasizing about quitting anyway. I'll let him know first thing in the morning. Oh, Gerald, you're the best at surprises."

"And there are a lot more to come."

Gerald pulled his Mercedes into the driveway.

Not only did Kaylee ruin his clothes, and make him late for his date with Sophia, but worse, he had to ditch a night of hot sex because he had to come back here and deal once again with that little bitch. If he hadn't already sold her, he would have strangled her in the woods.

He got out of his car and slammed the door. It was Kaylee who forced him to spend the night here.

Gerald reached into his back pocket and removed his crowded keyring.

"Shit! Shit! Shit!" he muttered while unlocking the front door and the four deadbolts. Once inside, he secured the door.

Margo came out of the kitchen. "Short night," she said.

Gerald sighed with his eyes.

Otto lay limp on his favorite ratty couch, his moans reduced to more of a whisper.

"I'm here for the night. You can leave now."

"I thought we'd both go in and tackle her."

"Go home, Margo." Gerald growled.

He was in no mood to deal with women…other than Sophia. But that wasn't going to happen tonight.

Gerald stomped around the sofa and dug his heels into the carpeted hallway leading to the bedroom he kept at the house.

"I'll fix both of them."

* * *

Margo backtracked into the kitchen. Luckily, Gerald went straight to his bedroom and didn't stop in the kitchen where Margo had left Otto's laptop and password booklet on the table. She'd counted on Gerald texting her before heading to the house, which would've given her time to stash both in her car. She'd do that right now before Gerald returned from his bedroom.

Margo grabbed her booty and eased out of the kitchen door, careful not to close it loudly enough to stir Gerald's attention.

She hurried to her car at the back of the house. She'd always parked out of sight just in case Otto, but also potentially Gerald, fingered her as complicit in the business. That way she had a chance to escape before all the shit went down.

She opened the unlocked car, another ready escape, and slid the laptop and booklet beneath the driver's seat. She clicked the car door shut and rushed back into the kitchen, where she scooted into a kitchen chair just in time before Gerald ambled into the room.

He'd changed into a pair of jeans, a navy T-shirt, and sport shoes.

Gerald set a gun on the table.

Oh, God! Did he know she absconded with the laptop?

Margo swallowed her spit to moisten her dry mouth.

"Get going," Gerald said. "I'll see you in the morning."

"Okay."

Margo grabbed her purse and headed out the kitchen door. She locked it, walked to her car without looking back, and got in.

She dug her keys out of her purse.

Shit! She had Otto's bedroom key!

Nothing she could do about it now.

Gerald probably wouldn't notice.

Besides, Otto wasn't going to be able to get to his bedroom anyway.

Margo started the car and drove around to the front of house and onto the driveway.

The gunshot exploded in her ears.

Margo slumped over her steering wheel.

Kaylee yanked at her bonds when she heard the gunshot.

The series of locks on her room's door tumbled.

He's going to kill me next!

Gerald entered the room.

"Good evening, Kaylee."

Gerald's sinister chuckle made the bottoms of her feet sweat.

"Please, don't get up."

Gerald set the gun on the bedside stand where she could clearly see it. Kaylee turned her head away from it and held her breath.

But Newell walked away.

He went into the bathroom, and Kaylee heard the water running.

What was he doing in there?

Newell returned with a basin and tossed water at her.

Her breath hitched and then Kaylee sputtered. She arched her back as the frigid water cascaded off her body to the sheet beneath her. Her teeth chattered.

Newell left the room laughing, leaving the door open to taunt her.

He returned holding what looked like miniature tongs.

Kaylee stared at his gray eyes, preparing herself for him to torture her.

He clacked the metal tongs together while he approached.

"Let's get on with it, shall we?"

He jammed the tongs into the bottom of her left foot.

Kaylee screamed from the pain.

Newell held up the broken twig that he just crudely extracted and wagged it in Kaylee's face.

"This is what you get!"

29

Lou Ann mumbled, "No!"

She held out her arms to try not to fall off the cliff, but her arms gave way and she rolled off it weightless with her arms flailing and her back arched until she hit the rocks below.

"Whoa! Hey, Lou Ann! Get off me!"

Lou Ann jerked awake to find herself smack on top of Harry.

She rolled off him.

"I'm so sorry. I had a nightmare."

Harry rolled closer and hugged her. He stroked her hair. "It's okay. It's okay. Man, your heart is really racing."

"I dreamed I was falling off a cliff."

Harry chuckled softly. "I'm glad I broke your fall."

It was a recurring dream she had whenever her life went through an abrupt change. It happened when Dad committed suicide after her mom died, and the last time when she and Harry split. Now it was her unresolved relationship with her own brother, leaving her with a niece she didn't know.

She lay in his reassuring arms until her pounding heartbeat returned to normal.

"Thank you."

"Don't mention it. For a minute there, I thought you missed me."

"Hmmm." Lou Ann began to pull free of Harry's arms until the scream rattled them both.

"Shit! That wasn't you!"

Harry and Lou Ann bolted upright. Harry rushed to the door and flung it open. Lou Ann ran past him and straight to Kaylee's bedroom door. She didn't bother knocking, just burst into the room.

Kaylee was lying on the bed, rocking herself back and forth, with her hands clutching the headboard and her legs splayed open.

What the…?

"Kaylee! Kaylee! Wake up!"

Lou Ann sat on the edge of the bed and gently patted Kaylee's thigh.

Harry and Brad stood next to each other in the doorway, wide-eyed —Harry in shorts and a T, and Brad in boxers and an undershirt.

"I've got her. It's all right," Lou Ann said.

Harry and Brad backed away.

Kaylee stopped screaming, sat up, and threw herself into Lou Ann's waiting arms.

"It was a just a dream," Lou Ann whispered into Kaylee's ear.

She eased Kaylee back onto the bed and lay down next to her.

"Close your eyes and go back to sleep. I'm right here."

Kaylee sighed and shut her eyes.

It didn't take long for Kaylee to start snoring.

Lou Ann watched Kaylee's chest rise and fall.

She quietly rolled over and looked at the unopened bag of nightclothes she'd bought for Kaylee, right next to the Barbie doll.

Then Lou Ann sighed. While everyone had warned her that Kaylee would probably have deep psychological issues, she was still so ill-prepared to care for her.

At least they had nightmares in common. They'd both need therapy.

Lou Ann tiptoed out of Kaylee's room, leaving the door open, and returned to the room she shared with Harry.

Harry sat cross-legged on the floor on top of his blanket.

"Is she okay?"

"Yeah, for now. She passed right out. I'm sure the nightmare exhausted her. I don't think she was even awake."

"Deja vu." Harry patted the bed. "Come. Sit."

But instead of climbing back into the bed, Lou Ann sat cross-legged across from Harry.

"I'm in deep shit," she said.

Harry shrugged. "Wouldn't be the first time, and it won't be the last." He gazed at her with those deep brown eyes. "You can do it. I'll help…that is if you let me. No strings attached."

"Okay."

"All right, then."

Lou Ann stood and went back to bed.

"Do you need me to lie down with you?"

"Appreciate it, but no thanks for tonight."

"Ooh. Do you mean there's a chance for later?"

Lou Ann grinned. "No strings attached. Remember?"

Harry stretched out on his blanket and linked his hands behind his head.

"Yeah. I remember."

30

Soaking wet, Kaylee shivered so hard in her bonds that she no longer felt the pain in the sole of her left foot. It hurt like hell when Newell ripped that twig out. He totally enjoyed that. But it was out now.

She traced her tongue across her lips, hoping for a sliver of moisture, but her tacky tongue only stuck to the top of her lip.

Kaylee winced and dislodged her tongue. She had no spit left to swallow. Ironically, she was grateful she was too dehydrated to pee so she wouldn't have to lie in her urine, or worse.

How pitiful that she'd been reduced to worrying about normal body functions.

Her muscles were tired of shivering, and her spirits were buried in the dirt.

There was nothing left but to wait to die.

Her head buzzed and she struggled to keep her eyes open should Newell come through that door.

She wanted to look straight in his cold, dark eyes when he seized her again. She wouldn't give him the satisfaction of controlling her.

But her eyes grew heavier and her blinks slowed…

Stay awake!

Her head lolled to the side.

"Kaylee!" her mom called. "Come on, let's get going. We're going to miss our flight."

"I'll be right there."

Kaylee squinted in the bathroom mirror while she put on the last coat of mascara.

Perfect!

"Kaylee!"

The car horn beeped.

Kaylee tossed her makeup bag into her suitcase and snatched it up. Tonight she'd sleep in a cushy hotel bed in Paris!

The car horn tooted again.

Kaylee ran out the front door, past her mom, who set the alarm and locked the front door.

Kaylee shoved her suitcase into the trunk in between her parents' and closed the trunk. She then leaped into the back seat and buckled her seat belt.

"What are you waiting for, Dad?" she teased.

"You!," he teased back.

Mom took her place in the front passenger seat.

"Next stop, Miami International Airport!" Dad announced.

"Paris, here we come!" Kaylee cheered.

Kaylee struggled in her bonds and woke up.

It was the best dream.

But she was never going to Europe, or anywhere else but here.

Joanna blinked her eyes open to the sun streaming in between the blinds' slats. She'd been in that dark cell for so long, and then in the hospital, that she had forgotten how glorious it was to wake to the sunrise. The bogeymen of the night were gone, taking her nightmares with them. True daylight had given her enough hope that she could actually imagine having a decent future.

She stretched in the bed, untethered.

Joanna looked down at the bag of items Lou Ann bought for her.

Yeah, that was pretty shitty of her. She wanted to do better—to be more grateful. The last thing she wanted was to piss off Lou Ann and ruin her chances to live safely and with someone who might actually care about her, neither of which she ever had before.

Joanna got out of bed, walked over to the bag, and opened it. Along with the nightie she didn't use last night, was a brand-new pack of cotton underwear, and thankfully not the kind Margo made her wear, plus, bras that looked like they'd fit, two pairs of shorts that would cover her butt completely, and two matching bright shirts.

She looped the plastic bag over her arm and then replaced the Barbie doll where she had found her. It was embarrassing, but she really liked that doll. Maybe someday she'd buy one of her own and hide it, only taking her out in absolute privacy.

Joanna tiptoed to the open bedroom door and peeked past it both ways. No one. She was the first one up. She walked past Lou Ann's and Harry's room. They so obviously belonged together, even if neither of them would admit it.

But then again, if Lou Ann didn't want Harry, Joanna might give him a go. Harry made her laugh. No man had ever done that before. There was nothing funny about a man pumping on top of her. She would count the yellowed, nicotine-stained ceiling tiles while man after man got off. It was kind of funny that she never made it past five tiles, sometimes just two. She preferred the quick ones because sometimes she got a break in between.

She made it to the bathroom without being noticed, and once inside she locked the door. Imagine that! She was the one in control of the locked door!

Joanna dropped the bag. And she thought the hospital bathroom was the nicest bathroom she'd ever been inside…until now! Not that the hospital wasn't clean and cozy, but she could live in this bathroom.

She traced her fingers along the cool, beige and gold-speckled granite bathroom vanity. The bronze faucet handles dove over the porcelain sink that matched the countertop. Not a stray hair or a hint of soap scum invaded the sink.

Brad must have a maid to keep this bathroom beyond clean. Maybe there was another bathroom he and his kids used, leaving this one for guests. How many guest rooms did this guy have?

Joanna skipped to the oval bathtub.

Three people could fit in there!

Pity she had no time to dally in a luxurious bath, but the glass doors to the shower stall invited her right in.

Wow!

She grabbed a perfectly folded, thick fluffy white towel set on the end of the vanity and within reach.

She parted the two glass shower doors as if they were the gates to heaven, cranked the water to a shade beyond warm, and jumped in. The water rained on her shoulders and down her back. She moved closer and tipped her head back to wet her hair. The shower even had shampoo, conditioner, and body wash. Joanna lathered her hair and body and twirled under the water. She rinsed off, cut off the water, and opened the doors. After wrapping the towel around her, she brought the hem to her nose and sniffed the laundry freshness of it.

Joanna purred a sigh. People actually lived like this!

The knock on the bathroom door made her jump.

"I'll be right out," she called.

"Sorry," Lou Ann said from the other side of the door. "I didn't know it was occupied."

Occupied? She talks funny. What doesn't she just say she didn't know anyone was in here? Is she always that formal? Probably not. She's probably as freaked out as I am. I'll cut her some slack. After all, Lou Ann did rescue me from that nightmare. She's a good person. I'll thank her for the clothes and everything else so far.

"I need to get some clothes on. Then it's all yours."

"No hurry. Take your time."

Joanna grinned at her reflection in the vanity mirror. May she never wake up from this kind of dream.

Lou Ann didn't want to loiter in front of the bathroom and risk making Kaylee uncomfortable. She recalled how timid she was as a teen about being seen naked.

She backed away from the bathroom door and retreated to the bedroom, where Harry lay on his back on his blanket bed, his mouth open and snoring.

She used to bounce on the mattress, and if that didn't quell his snoring, she'd nudge him. He'd sputter and quit snoring for five minutes tops, then he'd start up again.

How odd to realize she actually missed that.

Harry shifted, as if he knew she was standing over him.

Then her cell alarm chirped a loud tune.

Harry let out one final snore and jerked awake.

"Whaaat?" he slurred, his voice throaty.

Lou Ann silenced the alarm.

"Morning," Lou Ann sang.

Harry groaned. He was never a morning person.

He sat up and widened his sleepy eyes.

"Morning. You're up early, considering last night."

"I couldn't sleep anymore so I got up before the alarm. But Kaylee beat me to the bathroom."

"I guess she didn't sleep well, either."

The difficult day was just beginning. She had to take Kaylee to the house in Miami—the house where Kaylee grew up, now stripped of her parents—her family. She was Kaylee's guardian now. Then there was the funeral tomorrow. She had no idea how Kaylee would react, but she'd stand beside her to get her through the next-to-worst day in her niece's life.

Harry tightened the muscles of his face and his eyes deepened with concern.

"Are you okay?" he asked Lou Ann.

"Yeah. It's just that it's going to be a busy day. And probably a tough one."

More like busy with pain.

Kaylee arched her back, and then wiggled her fingers and toes—the only exercise she could manage while tied to the bed.

She escaped to Paris in her dreams. But today she returned to the stark reality of her pitiful existence.

She listened, but no noises snuck underneath the locked door.

They'd abandoned her like this. On the positive, if there was one, if she could bite through these ropes or manage to slide out of them, she'd be truly free.

Kaylee rubbed her wrists against the ropes.

Damn, they were tight. There was no leeway.

She'd work to stretch them. That could take hours—if not day—and without food or water, her strength would fade over time. But she had to try.

This time she squeezed her fingers and thumb into an arrow-head shape and tried to pull her hands out through the loop of the rope, gritting her teeth to get past the burn. But the friction intensified, and her skin got sticky and moist. She'd rubbed her wrists raw.

Defeated, she halted her attempts and sank her spine into the mattress. The burst of activity had roused what remained in her bladder, and urine tricked to the small of her back and then seeped into the mattress, leaving her wet and humiliated…and still tied to the bed.

She'd wait until the burn faded before she tried again. She couldn't do anything about lying in her urine. She mentally shrugged, knowing it would eventually dry and smell of ammonia.

Kaylee wiggled in her ankle restraints while letting her wrists cool. The sole of her left foot no longer ached. That could be either good or bad. Newell might have cruelly eliminated the source of her pain, but even if he'd extracted the broken-off twig, the infection might have worsened to the point of gangrene. Kaylee shuddered. She could lose her ankle. Her foot might have to be amputated. She jumped right down into the rabbit hole of terror.

Kaylee pulled herself out of her morose musings, letting her left foot rest while she worked with her right foot.

She bent her right knee and—hallelujah—her right ankle slid out of the rope.

She did it!

Victory!

Pain never felt so good!

She swung her free right foot to help extricate her left one, and worked her toes feverishly under the rope.

Her big toe got stuck a few times, but she backed it out and then went back at it again. On the twenty-first try, her left foot was liberated.

Double hallelujah!

Now for her wrists.

But no matter how hard she tried, she couldn't manage to free her arms from the headboard.

Then it came to her.

Kaylee swung her legs to a pike position just over her head, her years of ballet combined with gymnastics allowing her the tight position. Then she released her legs with maximum momentum, flinging them up and over, and the force ripped the ropes off her wrists, causing the headboard to fly back and smash against the wall.

The bang was firecrackers to her ears, because today was her Independence Day!

Gerald bolted upright in his bed.

What the fuck was that?

He rushed out of bed and hopped with one leg and then the other into the shorts he kept at the bottom of his bed, covering up his underwear.

Otto was dead, Kaylee was tied up securely, Margo wasn't here yet.

He rushed down the hallway and into the living room where he'd left Otto to rot overnight. He'd take care of that today.

There went another bang.

Gerald peeked past a slit in the living room window's drapes in case the police or FBI were making their approach.

But it was only Margo slamming her car door. She always parked her car in the back of the house, but because of last night's events, they were all out of step…except for Otto.

Gerald retreated from the window and went to the front door, where he unbolted the series of deadbolts, and opened the it.

Margo had her keys in her hand ready to open the front door.

Gerald stood barefoot at the door. "You scared the shit out of me."

"Sorry."

Margo entered and Gerald secured the locks.

"So how was she?" Margo asked.

Gerald shrugged.

"I taught her a good lesson, which exhausted the hell out of me, and then I collapsed in the bed." He massaged his chin. "What time is it?"

"Seven."

"Shit."

Margo pointed to Otto. "What are we going to do about him?"

"I'll take care of him tonight. I can't risk anyone catching me."

"He's starting to stink."

"So turn up the AC and spray deodorizer around the room. I have my hands full, Margo."

"Oh, and I don't?"

"You don't have patients to get rid of."

"No, I just have a dead body to contend with and a smart-ass Houdini."

"Come with me, I'll show you that you have nothing but breakfast to worry about."

Gerald slid a carpet next to the sofa where Otto lay. Then he grabbed Otto by one arm and one leg, pulled him onto the carpet, and rolled him up in it.

Gerald dusted off his hands. "Now let's visit your Houdini, who's now also an assassin."

Kaylee squatted naked next to the door. Shit! They hadn't abandoned her. Newell and Margo were on the other side of the door.

Now what? Perhaps their plan really is to never enter this room—to starve me.

But she couldn't count on it.

Kaylee hurried over to the smashed headboard and picked up a splintered piece.

After breaking out of her bonds, she'd be damned if she'd go ever go back in them.

She returned to the door and waited, listening to her panicked breathing.

Steady. Steady.

But no footsteps approached.

Kaylee's breaths floated up from the door's slim bottom edge. No way would Gerald hear her from the bed, so she must be close…real close. Gerald had to hand it to her, she was better than Houdini.

He brought his finger to his lips to hush Margo.

Kaylee was all about surprises. But he was on to her now. Hmm. They'd roped her securely, so she must have worked at those bonds all night while he slept. Crafty girl!

Gerald motioned for Margo to remain while he went to the garage. He'd completely forgotten that he used zip ties on Joanna.

He slid a box off a shelf, grabbed a handful of zip ties, and returned to Kaylee's door, handing Margo a few.

"We're going extra tight," he whispered in Margo's ear.

She nodded.

Gerald whipped his keys in each lock with the click of a high-noon duel. It was him against Kaylee, and he was a sore loser.

Gerald and Margo burst through the door.

The force knocked Kaylee to her back, and the splintered headboard piece—her weapon—flew from her grip. Newell, with rage-reddened eyes, leapt in the air like Satan sent from hell and crushed her to the floor with such malice that her spine cracked. Kaylee struggled to take a breath, but even the reserved air in her lungs was trapped deep in her rib cage.

He flipped her stunned body to her belly and wrenched her hands behind her back. The ratcheting of a new bond cut into her wrists.

Kaylee kicked her legs.

"No you don't!" Margo yelled.

The bones in Kaylee's ankles collided. Another slicing ratchet. She was done for.

"Leave her here," Gerald said, his breath heaving between each word.

He drew a deep breath while Kaylee gasped and coughed to restore the rhythm of her own breathing.

"And leave the door open so you can guard her. I'm already late for the office."

Gerald stomped away.

Chair legs scraped across the floor and a cushion crinkled.

Margo was now her warden.

31

Joanna, with her skin dewy-fresh and her hair nearly dry, sauntered into the kitchen to find Lou Ann and Harry sitting at the kitchen table while Brad stood over the stove alternating between flipping pancakes and turning over sausage links in another pan.

Joanna sniffed the strange but enticing, crisp aroma.

She was used to pale, runny scrambled whatever eggs and soured juice of the week for sometimes breakfast. This was a feast!

"Sorry, I'm late."

"That's all right," Brad said. "My daughters are infamously tardier than you are. And you're just in time. Breakfast is almost done."

Lou Ann patted an empty chair next to hers. "Have a seat."

Joanna took her assigned seat, while Isabelle chomped the last of her breakfast kibble and lapped at the water bowl.

Joanna grinned. "Looks like Isabelle enjoyed her breakfast."

She'd made fast friends with Isabelle, who wagged her tail every time Joanna petted her. She never had a pet until now…sort of.

Brad served up plates of fluffy pancakes with sizzling sausage links on the side. He placed the breakfast bonanza in front of Joanna first. She giggled at the smiley face with blueberries and whipped cream topping her short stack. Lou Ann and Harry's were fluffy, but plain.

Harry leaned over and examined Joanna's specialized pancakes.

"Hey, Brad. Where's mine?"

Brad returned with a can of whip cream and a bowl of blueberries. He sprayed a lopsided smiley face on Harry's pancake and scattered blueberries on top of it.

"Thanks, man."

Brad sat at the table with his plate. "Don't mention it."

"And if you're really good, I'll make you one with Mickey Mouse ears next time," Lou Ann teased Harry.

Harry's eyebrows shot up. "Ooh, next time!"

Lou Ann shook her head while stifling a smile.

Joanna chuckled. After giving everyone a quick glance, she dove into her pancakes.

The whipped cream and blueberries danced on her tongue. She swallowed the luscious bite and let it settle happily in her stomach.

Is this what love really feels like?

Margo sniffed.

"You stink almost as bad as Otto," she announced.

She stood and walked carefully around Kaylee, who still lay prone on the floor.

Seriously. What was she going to do? Jump at her? Ridiculous.

"Shit. You soiled the bed."

Kaylee remained silent.

"You know you asked for this."

Kaylee didn't respond.

Margo exited the room and turned to look at Kaylee.

Between Otto's stench, which she couldn't do anything about at the moment, and Kaylee's odor, she couldn't take it anymore.

She left the door open, hurried to a linen closet, and returned with sheets in hand, relieved to see that Kaylee hadn't somehow escaped her bonds. But the girl lay in the same position.

Margo stripped the bed and tossed the soiled sheets in the corner of the room, replacing them with yellowed, but clean sheets.

Kaylee hadn't moved.

Was she plotting?

Margo approached her.

Dried blood surrounded Kaylee's wrists and ankles.

Newell reveled in his torturous handiwork, but Margo began to regret what he made her do. She pushed those feelings aside. After all, her softness toward Kaylee was partially responsible for the havoc the girl created, not to mention the lump on her head. Otto's causality was the only upside.

Margo rolled Kaylee over and pushed her to a sitting position, but when she let go, Kaylee slumped back to the floor.

"Sit up!" Margo commanded.

She pushed Kaylee up again, however this time she braced the girl up with her shoulder, and then moved her hands to Kaylee's back, and shoved her to her feet.

Kaylee wobbled.

"No, you don't. You're going in the shower, like it or not. Now, hop."

Kaylee swayed.

"I said hop!"

Kaylee attempted a small hop in her bonds.

Margo gave Kaylee a push.

"Faster."

Kaylee drooped her head and paused.

"I'm not going to carry you."

Kaylee raised her head and began to make short hops.

"Keep going."

Kaylee managed to reach the bathroom.

"Finally."

Margo prompted Kaylee to the toilet.

"Sit here and do your business while I get the water running."

Kaylee slouched on the toilet.

Margo cranked on the cold water. It was cruel, yet necessary.

"Stand up."

Kaylee see-sawed to a stance, nearly falling over.

Margo caught her.

She couldn't risk Kaylee knocking out her teeth, not this close to Greece.

"In you go."

She prodded Kaylee into the shower.

The weakened girl made one final hop.

Kaylee remained perfectly still, not even a grimace, under the frigid spray.

Margo squirted Kaylee with dish detergent while Kaylee stood silent with her eyes closed.

The foamy soap swirled around the drain before disappearing.

Margo cut the cold water, stepped into the shower stall, and toweled Kaylee off. She'd never hear the end of that.

Margo sighed. Kaylee was too exhausted to hop anymore, and she couldn't carry her. Plus, she didn't trust her. Kaylee could bite her.

"We're going to do this differently. Hop just a few more times to get out of the bathroom, and then you're gonna log roll back to your place…on the floor."

Kaylee's hops faltered, but she made it out of the bathroom and then squatted and collapsed to the floor. She rolled as Margo commanded.

Was all this silent compliance a ploy?

Margo stared at the wan girl.

She doubted it.

With a slow thump, thump thump, Kaylee rolled to her prescribed destination.

Margo laid a threadbare blanket on the floor. Gerald would be pissed, but he wasn't here. Besides, he left her in charge.

"Lie on this."

Naked and compliant, Kaylee did as Margo ordered.

Margo returned to her chair and sat.

Kaylee stared up at her with soulless eyes.

She wasn't going to survive the trip to Greece. Not like this. She wasn't going to look anything like her...well, Joanna's...photo. The Greek was a top client who'd paid for a blue-eyed, blonde, preferably virgin girl, and the girl on the floor wasn't it. Damn Newell! She'd have to fix Kaylee, and quick.

Kaylee hadn't moved, so Margo decided it was safe to go to the kitchen. Kaylee needed food and water, despite Gerald's directives.

Margo rummaged through the sparse supplies and scrounged up a packet of instant oatmeal and a one-day old carton of orange juice. It would do. She microwaved the oatmeal with water in a paper bowl and poured the orange juice into a paper cup. She grabbed a plastic spoon and chuckled to herself. No more plastic forks for this girl. The thought was morbid, yet at the same time humorous.

Margo returned to the room with the plain breakfast and sat on the floor next to Kaylee.

"You have to eat."

Kaylee turned her face away.

Margo sighed.

"Look, this situation isn't what you ever imagined for yourself, but hear me out. You have no one left but yourself. There is a way forward, but it's up to you. Besides, if you don't eat, Dr. Newell is going to stick a feeding tube down your throat. You don't want that to happen, do you?"

Kaylee turned to look at Margo and opened her mouth.

"Good girl."

Margo spoon-fed Kaylee the oatmeal.

Kaylee sputtered. Lumps of oatmeal dribbled from her mouth and plopped onto her bare chest.

"Let's take it slower."

Margo filled the spoon halfway and waited longer between bites.

Kaylee chewed, stoic, but at least she ate.

Margo brought the cup of juice to Kaylee's lips. Kaylee gulped the whole juice.

"Thirsty, huh?"

Kaylee nodded.

"Go rest. And I won't tell Dr. Newell about the oatmeal and juice."

Kaylee lay like a dying animal on the blanket.

Margo flicked the sheet off the bed and covered Kaylee's naked body.

"That'll be our secret too. Listen to me, and you'll survive."

Kaylee curled up under the sheet and shut her eyes.

Joanna returned to her too-soon-temporary bedroom and began to stuff her new belongings in a plastic bag.

Brad knocked on the doorway.

"Can I come in?"

Joanna laughed. "Of course you can. It's your house."

"You're my guest, but you deserve privacy."

Joanna shrugged. The door was open, yet he still asked.

Brad entered with a pink suitcase decorated with unicorns and stars.

"This was my older daughter's suitcase, and she doesn't use it anymore. I know it's childish, but you can have it to put your belongings in until you get one more your style."

It was perfect. Her life had become as much of a fantasy as unicorns.

Joanna accepted the suitcase.

"Thank you…and thank you for everything else."

"You're welcome."

Giddy inside, she plopped the suitcase on the bed, opened it, and sniffed. The only travel bags she'd ever used consisted of a moldy duffel bag she found lying next to someone's trash can and black garbage bags. Now she owned a real suitcase!

Joanna dumped the clothes out of the plastic bag and folded them neatly inside the unicorn suitcase, then stood back and smiled at her efforts. Being always on the run, she simply stuffed whatever she could in her bags. But no more flinging bags in the back of trucks or hugging them in shelters, protecting everything she owned.

She zipped the bag shut and lowered it to the floor.

Joanna yanked the black handle and it popped up, sending her rearing backward. What the—!

She'd never seen anything like that! Joanna examined her new suitcase. *Wow! It has wheels.* She grabbed the extended handle and gave it a shove. The unicorn suitcase moved. She tilted it, and the wheels magically whirred.

Awesome!

Lou Ann knocked on the doorway.

Why does everyone keep doing that?

"Are you ready to go?" Lou Ann asked, sounding hesitant.

"Yeah."

"Cool suitcase!"

"I know! Brad gave it to me."

"He's a nice guy, isn't he?"

"Yeah. Maybe we can visit him some time. Maybe even his kids will be here next time."

Lou Ann grinned. "Yes, and maybe."

"Great. But I'm sure I'll like it better in Clearwater."

Lou Ann nodded. "I hope you will. We'll work together to get you settled, but we have to go to Miami first."

"I know."

Joanna tapped her fantastical suitcase, right over the unicorn, so it would protect her from evil.

32

Harry sat comfortably in the car with the windows rolled down, since the Florida morning heat hadn't revved up yet. Plus, he didn't want to start the engine and maybe pressure Lou Ann and Kaylee before they were both ready to move on to Miami.

Brad came out of the house, walked over to Harry, and leaned over the window frame.

"How are you doing?" Brad asked.

Funny that no one had asked him that. But Lou Ann and Kaylee were everyone's priority.

"I'm all right."

Which wasn't completely true. He was as confused as everyone else by the seismic change that was happening.

"You're a good guy."

"Thanks, but I'm not looking for any awards."

"You know that's not what I meant."

"Yep."

"Lou Ann and Kaylee are going to need you. That's a lot to handle."

"I never abandoned Lou Ann."

It still stung, what happened between them, but now wasn't the time to dredge all that up. Both he and Lou Ann had put their war on hold, and it more than suited him. He even had a feeling Lou Ann felt the same way. Perhaps they could patch something together, especially now.

"I know you didn't. Trust me, I know relationships gone sour can eat you up."

"Any chance of you and Liz giving it a go?"

Brad shook his head. "No. She's perfectly happy with the asshole, but the jury isn't back yet for me and the kids."

"Sorry."

"Yeah, well, what are ya gonna do?"

Lou Ann and Kaylee came out of the house with suitcases in tow and with Isabelle on a leash.

"Hello, ladies," Brad said with a small bow. He looked at Isabelle. "And you too, little lady."

Isabelle wagged her tail.

Harry got out of the car and took Lou Ann and Kaylee's suitcases. He opened the trunk, pushed back Isabelle's bag of kibble, and set their suitcases next to the black leather duffle where he kept his tactical gear. He shut the trunk and returned to the driver's side.

He nudged Brad. "Thanks, man."

"No problem. You'd do the same for me."

Lou Ann hugged Brad.

"Stay strong," he whispered in her ear.

Lou Ann nodded.

The minute Lou Ann broke away from Brad, Kaylee jumped into his arms.

He hugged her and patted her on the head.

"You have a long journey ahead of you, but you can make it."

"Aunt Lou Ann said we can come back to visit with uh...." Kaylee grinned, "with Uncle Harry."

Harry felt warm, and it wasn't from the rising temperature. He'd never been an uncle to anyone, and although not technically related to Kaylee, he couldn't think of a role he'd rather play.

Even Lou Ann beamed at that. Maybe things *could* change.

"Uncle Harry says everybody in the car, and that goes for you too, Isabelle."

Isabelle growled. The dog still held a grudge.

Kaylee sat in the back seat. "Come on, Isabelle. You can ride next to me."

Isabelle leaped into the back seat.

Kaylee buckled her seat belt.

"Don't worry, Isabelle. I'll keep you safe."

Isabelle let out a happy bark.

"She used to do that for me too," Harry said. "But then it's a long road to forgiveness."

"Yes it is. But some roads are worth taking," Lou Ann replied.

"I've always preferred the scenic route."

"Speaking of routes, I think we need to take the one to Miami."

Harry nodded and started the engine.

Brad waved while Harry pulled out of the driveway.

Harry glanced in the rearview mirror.

Kaylee had sunk into her seat and was petting Isabelle, who'd curled up next to her.

Suddenly it was okay that Isabelle never warmed up to him.

The dog knew who needed her most.

They made it to Alligator Alley, which connected Naples to Miami, an endless and boring stretch of toll road.

Lou Ann turned and peeked into the back seat.

Kaylee and Isabelle snored in tandem.

Lou Ann yawned. Nightmares were exhausting—hers and Kaylee's. Who knew what dogs dreamed?

Normally, Isabelle pawed at the window, taking in exciting sights and smells. But she stayed with Kaylee.

Lou Ann shut her eyes and her head bobbed. She jerked awake at a bump in the road.

"Rest," Harry said. "We have another hour and a half before reaching Miami."

Lou Ann checked the back seat.

Kaylee and Isabelle were still out. She might as well rest, because today would require all her and Kaylee's attention.

Her sleep fitful and frustrating, Lou Ann finally wiggled upright in her seat.

"That was a short nap. We've just passed into Miami-Dade county, and we still have to head to West Kendall."

"Mom, Dad, Lyle and I used to pick strawberries in fields filled with rows and rows of them."

The mouthwatering, sweet scent was tattooed on her brain.

When her mom started to get lost in the fields she knew by heart, they all suspected something was happening to her, but they didn't want to confront the reality of her dwindling memory. Dad, Lyle, and she continued to go to the fields, leaving Mom at home, and then would bring back strawberries, blueberries, tomatoes, and assorted vegetables, whatever was in season. Then they'd sit on the porch with Mom, where they all devoured the ripe treasures.

Lou Ann gazed out her window at the leggy egrets beyond the chain-link fence appearing and disappearing out of the tall blades of grass. The fencing kept animals—especially Florida panthers—safely out of the highly-traveled, multi-lane toll road. Mom and Dad used to remind her and Lyle that it once was a two-lane stretch where cars played chicken, passing the car ahead of them with barely enough time to jump back to their lane milliseconds before a collision.

Lou Ann shuddered, thinking about Lyle skidding off the road on the still mostly two-lane Tamiami trail that ran parallel to Alligator Alley, mostly used by folks who wanted to avoid a toll and truckers.

Lou Ann again looked back at Kaylee in the back seat. Was her nightmare about those final minutes of her mother and father's lives? It was beyond comprehension—and outright fortuitous—that Kaylee survived the ill-fated wreck.

Lyle was a hotshot driver as a teen, and admittedly so was she. But she was sure Lyle drove responsibly as an adult, especially with a family in tow. She drove responsibly as a civilian, but she could give chase with the best of them while on duty.

Harry took the exit to Miami and by the time he reached Chrome Avenue, the pathway to West Kendall suburbs, Lou Ann barely recognized the busy road.

"Oh, my."

She hadn't been back home in more than a decade. She frowned at how few strawberries there were, and the fruit stand had only a handful cars parked in front of it.

"Everything's changed," Lou Ann said.

She wondered whether she'd even recognize her old house, down the street from Lyle, Melinda's, and Kaylee's house.

"You can't expect it to look the same as the day you moved out."

"I didn't move out. I chose to relocate to Clearwater after Mom, and then Dad died. Lyle didn't want to sell the house, but I did. It was for the best. Lyle had his own house."

"Okay."

Perhaps she was being rather snarky, but it was still a touchy subject.

Theirs was a house truly divided, and it only further divided her and Lyle.

She moved to Clearwater, and Lyle stayed behind and had to drive by their old house every day, a constant reminder that it was now owned by someone else.

She was a shit about the whole thing, but Lyle refused her apology. Then came the standoff, and she never saw Kaylee again… until now.

* * *

Harry slowed at the street corner.

He tapped the steering wheel. "I can turn around and go another block to come another way," he said.

"No," Lou Ann blurted.

Kaylee stirred in the back seat. "Where are we?"

"We're houses away from your home, and my former one."

Kaylee responded with panicked silence.

This wasn't going to go well for either one of them.

Harry drove down the street of angst.

Their old family house was on her right, in full view.

Her heart hammered faster and faster.

It was her decision.

A chill skittered up her spine.

"Take a good look at what you forced me into," Lyle's cold voice echoed in her ear.

A woman came out the front door.

"Michael J! You get back in here and clean your room!"

The boy skidded his bicycle to a stop.

"Aw, Mom! The guys are waiting for me at the park."

"Let them wait."

The boy swung his arm with an "aw shucks" gesture, turned his bike around, and pedaled back to the house.

The deja vu couldn't have been more blatant. The woman was Mom, and the boy, Lyle.

Lou Ann pressed her fingers to her mouth.

Harry accelerated and then slowed again ten houses later.

The maps app woman's digital voice announced, "You have reached your final destination."

33

Harry pulled up to the white double-door garage. It was the only thing white in the sprawling pink concrete house, which was even bigger than Brad's.

But Joanna was a guest in this house.

This one supposedly belonged to her…or rather Kaylee.

How was she ever going to pull this off?

She couldn't stay behind in the car. That would only spawn other questions she didn't want to answer because she couldn't.

She'd just tail Lou Ann. She'd been in there before.

Harry and Lou Ann exited the car.

Lou Ann poked her head into the back seat.

"Kaylee? Come on, it's all right. We'll do this together."

Damn straight we're going to do this together.

A woman much older than Lou Ann or Harry approached from next door carrying a chihuahua.

Isabelle leaped to the front seat and dashed out, barking at the chihuahua, or she could've been barking at the nosy neighbor too.

Lou Ann scooped Isabelle up.

"I'm sorry. She's friendly with other dogs. She's just excited," Lou Ann said.

The woman petted her miniature dog. "I'm Peggy Foster, and this is Peppi."

"Isabelle," Lou Ann announced

Traitor!

Isabelle and Peppi traded nose bumps.

"I'm Lou Ann Jasinski, and this is my friend, Harry Boxer."

"Nice to meet you, ma'am," Harry said.

"Jasinski?!"

"Yes, I'm Lyle's sister."

"Oh, my gosh. I'm so sorry for your loss. The whole neighborhood was shocked when they heard about Lyle and Melinda. Such good people."

The woman approached the car closer and peered in the back seat.

"Kaylee?" she whispered.

Joanna bowed her head. She hadn't even thought of running into any neighbors who knew the actual Kaylee.

This was quickly getting out of hand. Now this woman threatened to expose her as an imposter. Then everything was going to topple to shit. Joanna didn't want to hurt Lou Ann or Harry. This all started as a ploy for her own safety. Genuinely liking Lou Ann and Harry hadn't been in the plan—it just happened.

Lou Ann tapped the woman on the shoulder.

"Kaylee's been through a lot."

The woman backed away.

"Of course. We all heard she was in the hospital. I didn't mean to pry. I'm just so happy she survived."

"We are too."

"I'll let you and Kaylee be. But if you need anything, I'm just next door. I'll see you at the funeral tomorrow."

When the woman and her dog retreated to their house, Joanna slid out of the car.

"I'm sorry about that. But it's going to keep happening while we're here," Lou Ann said.

"Okay," Joanna responded, and then hurried to the front door before anyone else saw her, including evil lurkers.

Joanna pressed her back to the wall next to the front door and waited for Lou Ann and Harry to catch up.

Lou Ann stopped in front of the door but made no comment about Joanna's actions. She reached onto her purse and took out a single key with a white tag hanging from it with "Jasinski house" written on it. She unlocked the front door and hesitated in front of it. Then she opened it and walked inside.

Joanna hurried in behind her, nearly stepping on Lou Ann's heels.

Harry rested his hand on Joanna's shoulder while the three of them ventured into the strange pink house.

Stale, cool air greeted them.

"Looks like they left the AC on," Harry said.

"They were planning to come back."

Joanna stayed close to Lou Ann while they made their way through the living room, their shoes click-clacking across the ceramic tile floor, the sounds amplified in the deserted house.

An L-shaped beige leather sofa surrounded a glass top coffee table with a half-empty glass of water perched on a seashell-printed coaster. A flat screen TV took up practically the entire wall across from the sofa.

Wow! That TV is the size of a drive-in movie screen!

Ironically, her mother once took her to see the Disney movie, *Lady and the Tramp,* at a drive-in so that her mother and her cadre of drug addicts could shoot up in the car while Joanna watched the movie. When the management discovered the drug orgy, they were kicked out and banned from ever returning. To this day, Joanna had never seen the rest of the movie.

Lou Ann picked up the glass of water and headed to the kitchen.

The kitchen was completely white, and the countertop wasn't even stained!

Joanna pressed her hands to her hips so she wouldn't leave a fingerprint or God-forbid a smudge on the pristine countertop.

Lou Ann dumped the stale water into the sink and opened the dishwasher to load the glass inside, but the dishwasher was full of clean dishes.

"Your mom must have run the dishwasher before you guys left. Let's put all this clean stuff back, and I'll hand wash the glass. I don't want to leave anything behind."

Lou Ann grabbed a clean plate from the dishwasher and handed it to Joanna.

Joanna clutched the plate and scanned the cupboards.

Please pick the right one!

Joanna opened the closest cupboard while Lou Ann busied with the next plate.

It contained glasses.

Shit!

She quickly opened the cupboard next to it.

Bingo!

Joanna stacked the clean plate inside.

At least she already knew where the glasses belonged.

Lou Ann emptied the plates and glasses faster and faster. Then came the silverware.

Oh, no!

Joanna opened a random drawer. Baking utensils stared back at her.

"Oops. Mom must have just changed drawers."

It was the best excuse could come up with on the spot. She'd lied so much that her lies were starting to ring true.

Joanna opened the drawer beside the incorrect one.

"Here, put these back," Lou Ann said.

Joanna sorted the silverware and tucked them away.

Whew! That was close.

Lou Ann glanced sideways at her, or maybe that was just her imagination.

Harry came into the kitchen, unknowingly rescuing Joanna.

"I came to help, but I see you've got everything under control."

Hardly.

Lou Ann put her arm around Joanna.

"Let's go to your bedroom next."

Joanna nodded. What else could she do? She had no idea where this girl's bedroom was. She prayed the bedroom door would be open so she could peek inside and chose the correct one. How many bedrooms could there be, anyway? Two? So she had a 50-50 chance of getting it right.

"I'll park myself on the couch," Harry said. "Call me when you have everything packed away, and I'll load the car."

Joanna wished she could stay with Harry and let Lou Ann sort things out, but the whole purpose of this visit was for her to sift through a strange girl's belongings.

She'd blindly managed in the kitchen so the closet and bedroom should be cake. Maybe she'd find some stuff she wanted. "Kaylee" wasn't going to be using any of it, seeing that she was permanently AWOL.

Joanna followed Lou Ann along the hallway to the bedrooms.

Framed photos lined the walls.

Joanna winced.

Lou Ann stopped at a wedding photo and wiped the corner of her eye.

Was that how the parents looked, although much younger?

Joanna stared at the photo.

"Is that you?" she blurted out.

Lou Ann turned to face Joanna.

Joanna's heartbeat bumped.

She'd screwed up.

"Yes, that's me as maid of honor," she said.

Kaylee would have known that.

"Are you okay?" Lou Ann asked.

"Yeah."

"Must be really hard coming back to your house."

Joanna let out a fake sniffle.

"Yes, it is."

She and Lou Ann continued along the hallway.

Joanna gritted her teeth, anticipating the next photo.

Thank God it was one of a baby girl dressed in a puffy pink dress and with a matching pink bow in a tuft of fine, blonde baby hair.

These people surely like pink!

A perfectly posed family photo at sunset on a beach was thankfully the last in the hallway gallery. It wasn't a cell phone or random camera pic. This had to be professionally done and must have cost a lot. It was the kind of photo you'd find in a wallet, like the one she'd stole one time. She'd sifted through a bunch of wallets before she settled on one that fit in her bag. Then she walked right out of the discount store with it. No security. No questions asked. Once outside, she skipped away.

Joanna hoped they'd walk past it. Nope.

Joanna stared at the photo.

Shit! The blonde teen with a perfect smile and perfect makeup could have been her twin, less the makeup and cheesy grin.

Lou Ann took the photo off the wall and handed it to Joanna.

"We'll pack this one first," Lou Ann said.

Joanna followed Lou Ann farther along while clutching the family she'd been incorporated into. She'd signed onto a permanent gig.

"I'm going to my brother and sister-in-law's bedroom. Meanwhile, you can start in your room, and I'll meet you there. All right? You can put the photo on the bed."

"Okay."

Lou Ann clearly needed a moment alone. It must be tough to lose a brother. Joanna had no true siblings...that she knew of...but she couldn't attest to how many half-ones were left hanging around after she ran away. Too bad for them, if they existed. Maybe they smartened up and left too.

Joanna watched Lou Ann disappear into a bedroom, which only left Kaylee's room.

What treasures awaited her there?

Joanna confidently opened a closed door only to discover a

bathroom.

She quickly closed the door and ventured to another closed door.

Wrong one, again.

It was some kind of an office.

Behind the next door was a bedroom, but it didn't look like it belonged to Kaylee. A colorful quilt with blocks of triangles lay tight across a big bed, not a wrinkle on it. An oak nightstand with a bronze-base lamp stood next to the bed. Pictures of a seashore, lighthouse, and sailboats hung on the pale yellow-painted walls. A definite change from pink. She had no idea whose bedroom this was. Perhaps no one's. It just was there for whoever came along. Someone like her.

Joanna exited the bedroom and moved onto the next closed door.

With the photo tucked under her arm, Joanna opened the door and gasped.

Wow! This was definitely Kaylee's room.

Joanna carefully set the framed photo on the fluffy coral comforter with mini-white polka dots. A white teddy bear sat smack in the middle of stacked pillows, waiting for his owner to return. But Joanna would take care of him in the meantime.

Joanna spun around in the dream bedroom. The light cream-painted walls tied the whole room together.

She bounced over to the pale oak dresser, catching her reflection in the matching oak-framed cheval mirror.

Three framed photos lay on top of the dresser: a smaller version of the photo on the bed, one of a tanned, hunky guy with his arm around Kaylee, and one with two smiling girlfriends flanking one hell of a happy girl with the Disney Castle in the background. Disney World! How she'd dreamed of going there! But for now, the picture would have to do.

Joanna spied a double-door, off-white, accordion closet on the left, next to the dresser. Oh, the clothes in there!

She pushed open the closet doors and gasped at the assorted booty.

Joanna rifled through skirts, dresses, blouses and jeans. She tossed them with their hangers onto the bed.

"Fit! Fit! Fit!" she sang.

She'd emptied the entire closet to discover a shoe rack with every conceivable type of shoe stacked on it. Joanna spilled them onto the laminate floor.

She giggled and grabbed shoe after mismatched shoe and crammed her feet into them. She tossed the too-tight-for comfort ones over her head and threw the ones that fit into a burgeoning heap.

Joanna grinned at the bigger stack of haves than have-nots.

She swam out of the mountain of shoes and next flung open every dresser drawer.

No to the panties and bras. That was just too weird. But she grabbed a handful of socks and pajamas and nighties. She could definitely use those.

Joanna assessed the hurricane she'd created and sighed.

No way was this going to fit in her unicorn suitcase.

Harry popped his head into the room.

"Wow!"

Lou Ann appeared from behind him.

"Hmmm. I have a few items, too," she admitted.

"I'll go get a U-Haul and boxes," Harry said.

"Good idea," Lou Ann responded.

Joanna stood in the middle of the stacked clothes on the bed and the pile of shoes.

"I couldn't part with it all," she confessed.

"I understand," Lou Ann said. "That's why we came." She glanced around the room. "I'll help you straighten all this up, so when Harry returns with the boxes, packing up will go faster."

"Thanks. It's so overwhelming."

Lou Ann sat on the only clear spot on the bed.

"Do you want to stay in this house?"

"No!"

The only thing Joanna understood was that she didn't belong in this strange, pink house.

"Okay. Okay."

Lou Ann stood and, together with Joanna, they arranged the clothes and shoes in neat piles.

"Is this everything?"

Joanna hugged the white Teddy bear and patted the polka dot quilt.

"These two."

"All right."

It was the ultimate invasion, but Joanna wanted both, the bear most of all.

If she was going to live with a lie, then she was going to go all the way.

Lou Ann clapped at her and Kaylee's combined successful efforts to tidy up the hodgepodge of Kaylee's bedroom.

"We did it!" Kaylee cheered.

All Lou Ann had to do was to prod teenage Kaylee. The rest happened spontaneously.

She *was* going to be a capable guardian.

"Wait here," Lou Ann said.

Kaylee scrunched her face.

"I'll be right back," she reassured her.

For someone who initially insisted on maintaining physical and psychological distance, Kaylee had switched over to craving comfort. Her shrinking away first started when they met in the hospital and extended to her discharge. Then she rushed out of the diner in a panic. But now Kaylee followed Lou Ann so closely, she almost bumped into her.

The doctors warned about Kaylee's unpredictable behavior, but it was exactly that unpredictability that Lou Ann had learned to embrace instead of expecting any other behavior, and made it easy to allow Kaylee enough time and space to heal without pressuring her to move on.

Lou Ann had purposely gone into Lyle and Melinda's bedroom alone, shutting the door to spare Kaylee the agony of remembering that her parents were never returning—their tragic deaths only days old. In time the pain would lessen, but wouldn't go away, just like it never went away for her after Mom died, and, worse, when Dad committed suicide. Now Lyle was gone, leaving her and Kaylee the last of the Jasinski line.

Lou Ann scooted into Lyle and Melinda's bedroom and grabbed the photo album off the dresser top. She'd found it set deep on the top shelf of the closet. She'd share it with Kaylee.

She returned to Kaylee's bedroom and sat on the bed with the album on her lap and patted the bed for Kaylee to sit next to her.

Kaylee plopped onto the bed. "What's up?"

Lou Ann tapped the top of the album's cover.

"That's a big book!"

Lou Ann patted Kaylee's leg "It contains photos from when you were just a toddler."

"Oh."

She'd hoped for a more excited response from Kaylee, but she pressed on.

Lou Ann peeled back the front cover.

"Look! That's your mom holding you when you came home from the hospital, and your dad looking over both of you. He was a wreck, and loading you in and out of the car seat took the longest time."

Lou Ann gulped at the memory. He was so overprotective. The car wreck didn't make sense. Kaylee was their only child—their baby girl. Surely Lyle made a Herculean effort to save her and Melinda. But the car spun out of his control.

Lou Ann dragged her attention back to the photo album.

"Wow. She was so tiny. Uh…I mean I was so tiny."

Lou Ann glanced sideways at Kaylee's odd response—perhaps a manifestation of fresh, deep emotional scars separating herself from the terror of losing her parents.

Kaylee reached over and turned over a wad of pages, landing on one of Kaylee and Lou Ann sitting at a white, toy table with two little matching chairs. Lou Ann stared at the photo of her squeezed into a miniature chair while Kaylee fit into hers with wiggle room.

Lou Ann grinned, remembering how they used to dress up for their teatimes, and use tiny white porcelain cups with a ring of roses painted on in matching plates. Lou Ann had ordered the tea set specifically for Kaylee, after seeing them online. She couldn't resist buying it, and the gift was a hit!

Before every visit, she'd stop at the bakery and buy vanilla creme-filled cookies because her niece deserved the best. Kaylee would jump up and down, squealing for the special cookies that only she and Kaylee shared.

Kaylee was only three years old when the rift between her and Lyle happened—too innocent to fathom why her Aunt Lou Ann went away—the aunt who had played hide and go seek in the house, giggling loud enough for Kaylee to find her. Then they'd hug and belly laugh together.

Lou Ann's heart lurched. Would Kaylee remember how they shared their favorite cookies? Probably not. She'd been way too young. So much had happened since those precious teatimes. Perhaps after she was gone, they weren't Kaylee's favorite anymore.

Kaylee inched closer to Lou Ann.

"Mmmm! Look at those fat cookies!"

Lou Ann hugged Kaylee. "You remembered!"

Joanna merely commented on the cookies. She had no idea it would catapult Aunt Lou Ann into a gaga frenzy.

Lou Ann continued to turn page after page, and Joanna continued to periodically smile and let out fake "Ohs" and "Ahs".

Anything to finish going through these strange, cheesy photos.

Thank God Aunt Lou Ann finally reached the last page, and just in time for Harry to walk in with an empty cardboard box in each hand.

"I'm back," he announced. "Ready to start packing?"

Joanna vaulted off the bed.

"Yes!"

Lou Ann and Harry left Joanna to load her new, personal items into one box. She quickly filled one to over the brim. Clearly, she'd need at least two more extra-large boxes.

"Harry!" she called.

Harry entered the room and assessed her situation.

"More boxes, huh?"

"Yes, please."

"Good thing I rented the deluxe package."

He returned with two huge boxes and dropped then on the floor.

"Will these do?"

"Absolutely! You're the best!"

"Thank you, and I appreciate your enthusiasm. Carry on."

Joanna tossed dozens of pairs of shoes in one of the boxes.

The top of the bed was completely bare now.

Joanna stroked the coral and white polka dotted comforter and gazed at the remaining empty box.

She gently plucked off the white Teddy bear and picked up the real Kaylee's framed photo that she'd inherited, and set them both on the dresser top. Then she returned to the bed and stripped off the comforter, folding it up and packing it in the box. She set the framed photo on top of the comforter and covered it with the two soft pillows with matching shams. But Kaylee left the sheets. Aunt Lou Ann would surely get her new ones.

Joanna stared at the stuffed bear. She picked it up and gingerly packed it alongside the pillows.

"I'll see you soon," she cooed to the bear, and then closed the box.

34

Gerald parked his Mercedes back behind his office and entered through the back door.

While the office staff buzzed to life, Gerald proceeded to his office and closed the door.

It was 3 pm Athens time, and a good time to call the Greek.

The Greek answered on the third ring.

"Good afternoon, Demetrios! It's Gerald Newell."

"Ah, Doctor, how are you?"

"I'm great. And I have wonderful news for you. We're right on schedule to meet with you and bring you our lovely girl."

"That is wonderful news. I already have everything prepared for you and my lovely girl."

"We'll be ready to depart tomorrow evening so Joanna can rest up during the trip and be fresh and ready."

"Good. And I have your new office almost all set and ready, minus some renovations, and, most important, I found a beautiful home for you, with plenty of private space for you and your "team."

"That will be just three of us, Margo and I and my lady friend, Sophia Pavlis. Unfortunately, our third partner will not be able to make the trip."

"I will have top-of-the-line living arrangements for the three of you. I can't wait to meet everyone in person. I will arrange for my private jet to arrive at Miami-Opa Locka Executive Airport tomorrow evening.

"All right, then. I'll add Sophia to the passenger manifest."

"We'll meet in about two days, yes?" Gerald asked.

"Sounds fine. We'll connect once you've arrived to establish a meeting place. A driver will pick you up at the airport and take you to your accommodations, and Joanna will come with me after we meet, as agreed upon."

"Until then," Gerald said.

"Absolutely, until then."

Demetrios ended the call first.

Gerald hated when anyone did that to him.

A knock came on his office door.

"Your first two patients are ready," Janice called.

"I'll be right there."

Damn women! He had a lot to do today. Gerald looked up the day's schedule. He shrugged. Actually, it didn't look that bad.

He quickly saw the two patients and rushed back into his office and shut the door.

He'd alert Margo to the plans and to tell her it was time to ready Kaylee.

Margo's cell rang.

Oh, shit. It's him, checking up on me.

She glanced at Kaylee who stared up at her.

She let it ring four times before she answered.

"Yes, Gerald."

"Get her and you ready. We're all leaving tonight. There's a trousseau for her in my bedroom closet, and my room's unlocked. I'm going to cut out early and dispose of Otto. I already have Joanna's passport, and I'm sure Kaylee will pass. So get going."

"I'm packed, and I have everything under control. She's more than compliant. I'll take care of her, and you deal with Otto."

Margo hung up and grinned, satisfied that she managed to piss him off.

Fucking narcissist.

"It's showtime. We're going to Greece."

Kaylee continued to stare at her, blank-faced.

"Oh, why so glum? Greece is beautiful. And you'll be living with Demetrios, a multibillionaire who has a mansion by a sea bluer than blue, you lucky girl. We leave tonight, so I have a lot of work to do on you."

Kaylee bowed her head.

"I'm going to trust you and cut those bonds. Then you can have a nice shower."

Margo removed a pocket knife from her jeans and approached

Kaylee with the blade engaged.

"I'm not going to hurt you unless I have to. Is that understood?"

Kaylee didn't respond.

She was about to free the same girl who bashed her over the head with a tray and severely messed up Otto.

But Gerald's tough stance worked.

Her eyes had lost that spark of defiance. She was surely resigned to the fact that there were no escape options left. How oddly sad.

Margo snapped free Kaylee's bonds and waited to be tricked. But nothing happened. Kaylee let her arms flop to her sides and then stood motionless in front of Margo.

She shuffled her feet to the bathroom.

"Wait, Kaylee. Let's take you to the nicer shower."

Gerald would shit if he knew Kaylee took a shower in his personal one. But he wasn't here, and she was in charge. Besides, the water would dry before he showed up.

Margo led Kaylee to Gerald's room. She gestured for Kaylee to halt and cranked the hot and cold shower stall faucets and tested the water until it was a warm blend. Then she prodded Kaylee in under the spray.

"Snap out of it and quit pitying yourself! Use the shampoo and soap in there. I'm not going to do that for you."

Kaylee picked up a shampoo bottle and squirted it on her hair.

Margo sat on the commode and kept her eyes focused on Kaylee.

She has a sweet body. The Greek's going to be real happy.

When Kaylee finished, she turned off the water and stood in the stall with water beads running down her and plopping on the shower tiles.

Margo tossed her a towel.

"Here you go."

Kaylee winced while she haphazardly dried her hair and body.

The shower accentuated the raw bands of skin surrounding her wrists and ankles.

She couldn't be presented to the Greek in this condition.

Margo searched in the medicine cabinet and discovered a tube of antibiotic ointment, a bottle of antiseptic alcohol, a roll of gauze, and ibuprofen. Gerald kept everything else locked up in his procedure room and only he had the key to that.

"This may sting," she warned Kaylee.

Margo dumped alcohol on Kaylee's wrists and ankles.

Damn! She didn't even flinch. This is one tough girl.

After the alcohol dried, Margo squirted the antibiotic ointment over Kaylee's wounds and wrapped them with gauze.

"There. We'll need to do this at least twice a day."

Margo filled a bathroom cup with water and handed it to Kaylee along with two ibuprofen tablets.

"Take these."

Kaylee did as she was told.

"Open your mouth," Margo ordered.

She inspected Kaylee's mouth for any hidden pills. It would be like her to think these pills were something else or refuse to swallow them as an act of defiance.

Margo inspected the insides of Kaylee's cheeks and under her tongue, but there were no pills stuffed anywhere.

"Close."

Kaylee snapped her teeth shut like a wolf trap.

There was the Kaylee she knew.

She next grabbed Gerald's fine-tooth comb and chuckled. It would've been more amusing if he didn't have a bunch of combs stashed all over the place. He could say goodbye to this one.

Margo raked the comb through Kaylee's wet, tangled hair, pulling hard enough to yank Kaylee's head back.

Her mother used to do the same to her.

Margo's hand cramped after struggling through the bird's nest hair.

She tossed the broken-tooth comb into the garbage.

Hmmm. Maybe he'd discover it there.

"Come on. You can't stand there naked."

Margo went to the closet, and as Gerald had described, she discovered the cedar chest on the floor of the closet and opened it. Her eyes went straight to the worn superheroes, cartoon characters, and GI Joe decals randomly covering the inside of the lid.

Shit! This was no ordinary chest. It was his boyhood chest. How fucked up was that? But in a twisted way it made sense. Gerald had dropped snippets of his messed-up relationship with his mother, but he never mentioned anything about his father.

Margo ignored the bizarre decals and looked inside the chest, lifting sheets of white tissue paper to find neatly folded and separate piles of lingerie, blouses, skirts, pants including jeans, and shirts, and a stack of shoeboxes—a testament to his obsessive/compulsive disorder. All this was meant for Joanna—stupid girl. Spooky how the attire looked like it would also fit Kaylee.

Margo sifted through the blouses and pants and picked out a long-sleeved bell-shaped blouse and long, wide-hemmed pants to camouflage Kaylee's wrist and ankle wounds. They'd have to get her past border agents without questions for the flight to Greece.

Margo set the outfit and underclothes on Gerald's bed.

Now it was time to get Kaylee ready, and that would take time. They'd have to leave at least three hours earlier this afternoon in order to board the Greek's private jet this evening. Margo beamed inside. No commercial flying!

First she'd have to style Kaylee's hair and apply makeup before dressing her up, so they wouldn't stain the clothes.

She blow-dried Kaylee's hair.

Her hair was wonderfully thick and compliant, just as Joanna's had been.

Margo then applied concealer and a slightly darker version of pale foundation. Her skin was fair, but her yellowed bruises were not.

Margo touched up the base until the bruises were no longer obvious...unless one looked real close.

She polished off the foundation with a layer of pressed powder.

"Good," she said, satisfied with her work thus far.

She'd go for a more natural look with only a swipe of beige eyeshadow and a coat of mascara. The last thing she wanted was for Kaylee to attract more attention. A brush of peach blush completed the look.

"Well look at you," Margo said, pleased with her own artistic coup.

Kaylee stared into the mirror at the stranger looking back at her. She blinked and so did the stranger. She nodded to her reflection, accepting her altered self. The last time she'd seen herself in a mirror was in that cabin bathroom. Her features were angular then, when she was filled with a mix of rage and hope. All she saw now was despair.

Gone was her bouncy summer ponytail and her dewy bronzer. Her lips were thin, not the full ones that her boyfriend, Jimmy, loved to kiss.

Jimmy. Was he mourning her? He had no idea how she mourned him. But she was dead to him. He'd move on, and she would too, in ways unimaginable.

"What do you think?" Margo asked.

Kaylee shrugged.

"You ungrateful girl!"

What did Margo think she was going to do? Jump into her arms and hug her?

Never.

She didn't know what to think of Margo anyway. The woman had two settings—warm and ice cold. But that's not how she suspected Margo saw herself.

"Let's get you dressed. I'm tired of seeing you naked."

Tired? Really? She wasn't too tired when she helped Newell tie her up. How ironic that she was now tending the wounds she helped create.

Margo led her to Gerald's soft, clean bed—the one he slept in so cozily in while she lay naked, bound, and spread-eagled. He had no soul, and his heart pumped rancid blood.

"Put those on."

Margo was obviously going to watch. She swirled her hand in a "come on and hurry up" gesture.

Kaylee put on the bra and panties. At least they weren't used. She then slipped on the white pants and floral-printed, bell-shaped blouse. She wouldn't be caught dead in this kind of outfit. And still that might actually happen.

"Spin around."

She was nothing more than a toy.

Kaylee did as commanded. It was the only way she'd survive now.

"Perfect!" Margo cried out, congratulating herself, not Kaylee.

Yeah, just perfect.

She was about to be forever stranded in a foreign country where no one would hear her cries for help.

Gerald pounded through the morning's patients. He already instructed Janice to have the rest of the day's appointments cancelled. And when she asked whether he meant for them to be rescheduled, he emphasized that she heard him correctly.

Janice's confusion would now spread like an infection. And, like the doctor he was, he'd have to cure it before the gossip reached the pandemic crisis stage.

He knew what he had to do.

Gerald walked into the front office just before the lunch break.

"Hi, everyone. As you know I've cancelled the appointments for the rest of the day. Unfortunately, I have bad news.

Janice's and the remaining staff's faces sank.

"I have an emergency out of town"—he failed to add out of the country— "a family crisis that I must attend to immediately. And I'll be gone indefinitely. Please let the patients know, and I'll keep you informed as to when I'll possibly return. Meanwhile, all of you will continue to be paid in full during my absence. That's all. Have a nice lunch. I'll be leaving shortly."

The staff's chatter followed him down the hall to his office.

Janice knocked on the open doorway while Gerald gathered his belongings.

"I'm so sorry. The office will be so lonely," Janice said, practically whining.

Gerald hugged her. "Buck up. We've known each other for years. I have to leave."

"I understand. You can't plan emergencies."

"No, you can't."

She believed the ruse. Everyone did. He was free to leave forever. He'd let them know later, when he was all set up in Greece. Perhaps he'd find someone like Janice to spoil him and help keep his new practice organized.

35

Lou Ann followed Harry out to the U-Haul trailer, both their arms piled high with sealed cardboard boxes.

They set the boxes down while Harry opened the trailer's door.

"Harry."

"Yeah."

"I'm concerned about Kaylee."

"That's a given."

"In another way."

"And what way is that?"

Harry loaded the boxes into the trailer.

"It's something she said."

"Lou Ann, I don't want to guess. Just tell me."

"I showed her a photo album I found in Lyle's room from when she was a baby and a toddler. I was in a few of the pictures. I realized she wouldn't remember me, but when I told her that one was of her coming home from the hospital, she referred to the baby as if it wasn't her. It was odd."

"You know she's probably got this dissociative stuff going on."

"That's what I thought initially, but it still bugs me."

"Lou Ann, stuff always bugs you."

"That's what makes me a good sheriff."

Harry leaned on the trailer. "I can't argue with that. Let's just get the rest of the boxes."

Lou Ann shot him a quick grin.

"All right. I'll pay more attention."

Lou Ann and Harry returned for the next load and stopped in Kaylee's room.

Harry tossed Kaylee a permanent marker.

"Heads-up," he called.

Kaylee caught the marker.

"Thanks."

Lou Ann and Harry retreated to Lou Ann's boxes.

Harry gave Lou Ann a marker, too.

Lou Ann labeled boxes of photo albums and framed photos. She couldn't take all of Lyle and Melinda's belongings. Her house didn't have enough storage space. Plus, she'd wait for Kaylee to eventually sift through her parents' items when she was ready. Right now it was more important to secure Kaylee's belongings. Besides, being surrounded with her own things would ease her transition to a new life.

Lou Ann and Harry shoved the heavy boxes into the hallway.

Kaylee greeted them, standing next to her boxes with her hands on her hips .

"Beat you!"

"Yes, you did," Lou Ann said.

"I'll go get the dolly because I'm not going to carry any more girl stuff."

"Girl stuff!" Lou Ann and Kaylee chimed in at the same time.

"I should keep my mouth shut before I get booted to the car tonight."

Lou Ann and Kaylee grinned at each other and at him.

"Good idea," Lou Ann said.

Harry returned with the dolly and hoisted the last of Kaylee's boxes onto it.

He tilted the trolley onto its wheels.

"Please tell me this is it?"

"Yep," Kaylee said.

"Hallelujah."

Harry wheeled the stacked boxes away, and Lou Ann and Kaylee followed him to the trailer.

"I've got it from here," Harry said.

"I know you do, dear."

"Dear" slipped off Lou Ann's tongue when she wasn't paying attention.

Harry arched his brows and grinned. "So I'm 'dear' now?"

Kaylee's eyes ping-ponged between Lou Ann and Harry.

"I'm just saying that you've worked really hard today, and I—we—

appreciate it," Lou Ann quickly offered with a nod to Kaylee.

"So I don't have to sleep in the car tonight?"

"Of course not. You can sleep in the recliner while Kaylee and I call the sofa."

"Fair enough, since it's only for one more night."

Harry grabbed the trailer door handle and yanked it.

The moving truck's door slid along the metal tracks and the door clicked shut with a crisp snap, and Harry secured their belongings.

An awkward silence floated around them.

Lou Ann slipped her arm around Kaylee's shoulders.

"Ready?" she asked.

Kaylee nodded.

"Let's all go back into the house," Lou Ann said. "How about we order pizza for dinner?"

"Sounds good," Harry said.

Kaylee voted affirmative.

The three shuffled to the pink house.

Lou Ann glanced back at the trailer.

After the funeral tomorrow, they'd unload it in her Clearwater driveway before nightfall.

Gerald pulled into the driveway next to Otto's empty-tank sedan. Just like Otto, the car had served its purpose. It had more than enough trunk space to easily dump Joanna into, and a roomy back seat to lay Kaylee. But there'd be no need for it now, and it was only a liability should anyone come snooping around. He'd get rid of the vehicle with Otto trapped inside it.

Gerald grinned. Accidents happened. After all, it's what brought Kaylee to him.

He popped the trunk, got out of his Mercedes, and lifted the full gas can out of the trunk. It didn't take him long to fill it at the gas station after he topped off the Mercedes.

Demetrios had arranged for the luxury sedan to be picked up from airport parking and shipped to Greece.

He'd soon have at least half of what the Greek had, and if all went according to plan, between his US and European connections, he'd eventually become a multimillionaire too.

He emptied the gas can into Otto's car. It would be enough to drive it into the woods.

Gerald quick-stepped to the house.

Yeah, it would all work out.

Gerald unlocked the multiple front door deadbolts and entered the house. Otto lay rolled in the carpet next to the green couch. Gerald cupped his hand over his mouth and nose.

Damn! He stank like week-old meat left out of the fridge.

He peeked into Kaylee's room and saw nothing but sheets.

I told Margo! he growled to himself.

"Margo!" he yelled.

Margo came out of the kitchen.

"No need to yell. We're in the kitchen trying to avoid the stink."

"I have a solution for that."

"I hope you do, and fast. We need to leave for the airport in four hours, and you know Miami traffic. I've got everything packed, and I've gotten Kaylee ready."

"Hmmm," Gerald grumbled.

He walked into the kitchen to see Kaylee sitting at the table with a half-eaten sandwich on her plate.

Gerald reared back. Shit! He barely recognized her.

"Took some effort," Margo said.

"Kudos to you."

He pointed to Kaylee. "Behave. We have a long trip ahead. Don't give me any shit."

"She hasn't and she won't. We've come to an agreement."

"Lock her in the room. You're going to help me take care of Otto."

"I thought you were going to deal with Otto."

"I am. But I need you to drive him to a spot in the woods with a steep incline. I'll follow you. You get out. I put Otto behind the wheel with my gun planted on the seat and push the car. Instant suicide. The gun's registered to him, and it has his blood on it. Bullet to the head with his eye popped out. Perfect suicide scenario. By the time anyone finds him…if they find him…he'd be half eaten by animals and vultures. Too late now, but Joanna's going to get her justice from beyond."

Margo led Kaylee into her old room.

"Sit here. We'll be back. Then I'll let you out."

Kaylee sat on the clean sheets, and Margo bolted her inside.

"Let's go and get this over with, but you know I'm not going to touch him. It's bad enough that I have to be in the same car with him."

"Go start the car. I put gas in it, so it should turn over."

Margo went out the door while Gerald approached Otto.

"Come on you motherfucker. You're gonna make us all late."

He'd have to shower afterward and then swing by and pick up Sophia.

Gerald yanked the carpet containing Otto's rotting corpse and wedged him with all his might, squeezing Otto out the front door and then log-rolling him to the car, huffing and puffing the whole way.

Margo sat behind the wheel with the engine idling.

Gerald took a deep breath, nearly choking, but managed to hoist Otto in his carpet burrito onto the back seat and then slammed the door.

Margo rolled down her window and hung her head out, coughing and taking deep breaths.

"It won't take long. Follow me."

Gerald jumped into his Mercedes and headed to the same woods where he hunted down Kaylee. He then halted at a steep incline.

Margo skidded to a stop and burst out of the driver's seat holding her nose and gagging.

"You owe me!" she hissed at Gerald.

"You'll get a good cut."

Margo retreated to his Mercedes.

Gerald dragged Otto out of the back seat, unrolled him from the carpet, and dragged him to the driver's side.

"Up you go."

He stuffed Otto in headfirst, turned him on his side, worked his legs till they were under the wheel, and sat him up. Otto's body began to sag out of the open door.

"Oh, no you don't."

Gerald shoved him back in, flopped his head over the steering wheel, and slammed the door. There!

He went in through the passenger door, put the car in neutral, and hopped out.

Then he gave the car a shove, and the hill did the rest.

The car gained enough momentum to crash into a tree.

That was that...until he looked at the rug. How could he have forgotten about that? Shit!

He had a layer of gas left in the can and a lighter in his glove box. He could burn it. No. The smoke would attract attention—far-reaching attention. He had to think fast. Plus, he still needed to get ready, pick up Sophia, and make it to the airport.

Gerald's mind spun around and around.

Then it stopped.

He'd rush to the cabin and dump it there. Other than Kaylee, no one had bothered the cabin in years.

Gerald threw the carpet into the trunk of his Mercedes and then slid behind the wheel.

"We have to make one more stop."

"Shit, Gerald."

"Don't worry. We'll make the flight and be in Greece tomorrow."

Sophia heard the knock on her apartment door and squinted into the peep hole.

Maria stood on the other side, carrying the suitcase she'd come up with at a moment's notice.

She was the best friend Sophia ever had.

Sophia opened the door, and beckoned Maria inside.

"You're a lifesaver!"

Sophia's suitcase had split zipper, and the last thing she wanted was to show up on a private jet with rope wrapped around her pitiful suitcase.

"It's hardly fancy," Maria said

"At least it zips up."

"How long are you going to be gone?" Maria asked.

Sophia shrugged. "I don't know."

Maria's eyes went wide. "You don't know?"

"No. It's a spur-of-the-moment vacation. Gerald only let me know two days ago."

Maria shook her head. "Honey, this isn't a good idea. A date—a single date—is one thing. A trip out of the country is completely different. Aren't you suspicious about this spontaneous vacation? I am."

Sophia held Maria's hands. "This my only chance to visit another country with someone who cares for me. My passport is completely empty. I got it because I wished that someday I could use it. My wish came true!"

"It's not safe. My time off is coming up next month. We'll go together."

"Absolutely! I can't wait. But I'm still going to Greece with Gerald."

"I'm worried about you. What if this guy, Gerald, this supposed doctor, dumps you while you're in Greece?"

"No, he wouldn't do that."

Maria took out her cell. "I'm going to look up something up for you."

She handed her cell to Sophia.

"There. I did a search for the US Embassy in Greece. Here's the one in Athens. Because your cell may not work there, write this address down and put that in your wallet. Please, at least for me?"

"Okay. If it will make you feel better."

"It will."

Sophia copied the US Embassy Athens address and the weird-looking phone number on a piece of paper, then folded the paper and tucked in her wallet.

Maria hugged her.

"Safe trip, my friend."

Sophia walked Maria to the door.

"I'll see you soon," Sophia said.

"Promise?"

"Cross my heart."

After waving to Maria, Sophia took the suitcase to her bedroom. She'd already laid out the sparse clothes she had on the bed. Five minutes later her packing was complete. There was a lot to be said for traveling light. At least she'd have plenty of room for souvenirs and new outfits Gerald would buy her.

Sophia spun around the room.

"Greece! Here I come!"

Kaylee sat on the edge of the bed behind the same locked doors she'd been stuck behind since she'd arrived in this hellhole. But she wouldn't sleep here tonight, or ever again.

Greece would be her new prison.

She knew nothing about this Greek tycoon, and that's exactly what they wanted. Although Margo hinted more about her life thereafter. But how long was thereafter? How long before this multimillionaire tired of her? Then what? Where the hell would she land next?

But there was no point in worrying about the unknown, especially since right now she had no control over her circumstances. She'd take one day at a time. The Greek, as they called him, must have a clock and a calendar.

Kaylee's heavy heartbeat slammed against her chest.

What if the Greek had a cell like this, ready and waiting for her?

Maybe there was nothing better in her future.

Kaylee sucked in several slow, deep breaths to squelch her rising panic.

She needed to train herself to stay calm. Or at least appear calm.

Otherwise they'd all win, and she'd be the only loser, and she wasn't ready to resign herself to that.

They could have her body, but she was the owner of her soul.

Kaylee cocked her head, listening.

One click, followed by three more deadbolts.

Newell and Margo had returned.

Kaylee pushed to the edge of the bed and strained to hear her captors' voices.. Her wounds fresh, she knew better than to crouch right by the door. She'd stay put.

"I'm going to go take a shower," Newell called.

"Humph." Kaylee giggled.

She'd used his shampoo and soap. Margo made her do it.

Kaylee secretly hoped he'd notice.

"Keep her locked up until we're ready to leave."

Margo shot her middle finger behind Gerald's back.

Although Otto was a sleazebag, at least he hadn't let Gerald lead him by the nose.

Kaylee had demonstrated that she could behave.

He couldn't keep her captive forever.

She'd soon belong to Demetrios, and Margo was certain that irked Gerald. Gerald was all about solitary control. Soon he'd find out that wasn't the case.

He was getting in over his head, especially with Sophia. Margo couldn't believe he was bringing her along. That was sure to go sideways, and Margo wasn't about to pick up after him.

Margo waited until she heard the whoosh of the shower and then unlocked Kaylee's door.

She nodded when she saw Kaylee sitting where she'd left her.

"He said I have to stay in here."

"I say you can come out."

"Okay."

"You're to sit in the kitchen with your back to the wall. I will block your exit. I'm warning you. Don't do anything stupid."

"I won't."

Margo led Kaylee into the kitchen. She was a smart girl. She'd be a thousand times better off with the Greek than with Gerald. Margo, on the other hand, was stuck with Gerald.

Gerald returned to the kitchen with his wet hair slicked back.

His eyes went straight to Kaylee and then bounced to Margo.

"You do know she's going on the plane with us," Margo said sarcastically.

Gerald narrowed his eyes at Margo.

"Really?"

Gerald abandoned glaring at them and poured himself a cup of coffee, drinking it black.

What was he trying to prove? He always added creamer and sugar. Bitter bastard.

36

Lou Ann stretched and yawned. Between the packing, loading the trailer, and the pizza, daylight had disappeared.

"I don't know about you two, but I'm exhausted beyond exhaustion," she said to Harry and Kaylee.

"I second that," Harry replied.

"I third that," Kaylee called.

Harry and Kaylee stared at Lou Ann. She suspected they had questions regarding the sleeping arrangements.

"That L-shaped sofa is more than big enough for me and Kaylee. Harry, you can have the recliner." Lou Ann paused. "Is that all right with everyone?"

Harry shrugged.

"It's okay by me."

"Kaylee?" Lou Ann asked.

"That'll be fine," Kaylee answered.

"All right then. Let's get settled."

Pillows. They would need pillows.

Kaylee could use her own pillow while Harry and she—Lou Ann winced—could use Lyle and Melinda's. They had no need for them anyway, she convinced herself. Still, she'd put on different pillow cases.

"I'm going to the hallway closet to look for fresh pillowcases and some light blankets," Lou Ann said.

Harry set his hand on Lou Ann's shoulder. "I'll go with you."

Lou Ann glanced at Kaylee.

"Why don't you get one of your pillows while Harry and I get ours?"

"Okay."

Kaylee walked away toward her bedroom.

Kaylee could use the comfort of her own pillow. But it would be a long night for Lou Ann to be able to sleep on her brother's and sister-in-law's pillows. They'd be the same pillows despite a different cases.

Lou Ann circled Lyle and Melinda's bed, conflicted about which side was Melinda's and which side was Lyle's?

What did it matter? They were just pillows.

Lou Ann grabbed a pillow and brought it to her nose. A clean soap scent was imprinted on it. Hmm. Typical Lyle. The other pillow smelled of lavender. Definitely Melinda's.

She was sure Harry wouldn't want to smell lavender all night so she handed him Lyle's pillow.

Sleeping on Lyle's pillow wouldn't absolve her of the past acrimony between them. It would take more than that.

"Let's take off these pillowcases and get fresh ones," Lou Ann said.

She and Harry stripped off the pillowcases.

"Leave them on the bed. I'll...uh...return another time to clear out the rest of the house."

"Okay," Harry softly answered.

Lou Ann and Harry walked out of the bedroom and to the hallway linen closet.

She handed Melinda's pillow to Harry who stood there silent while holding Lyle's former pillow.

Lou Ann opened the closet door

Luckily, Melinda kept fresh linens in there.

Lou Ann piled two pillowcases and three light weight blankets on top of Harry's stack, who didn't complain.

She closed the linen closet door.

"Shall we?" she asked.

"Lead the way," Harry answered.

When Lou Ann and Harry returned with the pillows and blankets, Kaylee was already stretched out on the sofa and lightly snoring.

"Well, she's out," Lou Ann said. "I don't blame her," she added.

Lou Ann covered Kaylee with the blanket.

After a long, hot day of travel and packing, Lou Ann had kicked up the AC.

Lou Ann and Harry slipped on the fresh pillowcases.

Even with Kaylee stretched out, there was ample space on the huge sofa for Lou Ann.

Harry set the pillow on the sofa for Lou Ann.

"Lay down."

Lou Ann relaxed back and Harry covered her with a blanket.

"I know this may not even be possible, but close your eyes and try to get some rest. Tomorrow's gonna be a hard day."

Lou Ann held out her hand and Harry took it.

"I'm a wreck, and I can only imagine the depth of pain Kaylee will endure tomorrow, and for a long time to come. I'm frightened that I won't be able to bring her through this, especially with everything that's happened." Lou Ann looked up at him. "Harry, I don't even know her. She's not three anymore."

"It will be a challenge. A lot of things don't make sense right now. You…we…will get through this."

And then her leaned over and kissed her on the cheek.

She hated to admit it, but she needed Harry's comfort.

"Goodnight, Lou Ann."

"Goodnight Harry."

Harry went over the the recliner with his pillow and blanket and huddled in for the night.

Lou Ann fluffed her pillow and shifted on the sofa.

With the funeral ahead, she doubted she'd need Harry to shake her awake.

Harry was already snoring.

But it wasn't his snoring that kept her awake.

Lyle and Melinda's funeral rightfully circled in her head. She'd witnessed the finality of death many times, but never in her wildest dreams did she think death would grab her brother and sister-in-law, and that Kaylee's world would crumble. Lou Ann's world was in tatters, too, for the *fourth time*. The Jasinskis were cursed.

Lou Ann sat up and watched Kaylee sleep.

She had no idea about Kaylee's sleeping and waking habits. She assumed they were like any teenager, sleep till noon and stay up past midnight.

And then her thoughts spun to Melinda. Sweet Melinda, who tried to nudge her and Lyle back together but failed. Neither Lyle or her couldn't shake their polar differences over what was best for Mom, only to watch her decline to the point that she couldn't recognize her own children, and sometimes not even Dad. Blame. Blame. Blame. The final rift came when Dad couldn't exist without Mom. A love like that was rare. Shame on herself! She moved on and ditched Lyle for selfish reasons, leaving him to grapple with the house and the memories of happier times there.

"I'm so sorry, Lyle" she murmured.

She should've stayed.

37

Gerald arranged the suitcases in the Mercedes' trunk and shut the trunk lid. When he returned to the car, he made sure Kaylee and Margo were in the back seat with their seat belts fastened. The passenger seat was reserved for Sophia.

He got behind the wheel, engaged the door locks and started the engine. No one was getting out of this car without his permission. While he pulled away, he looked at Kaylee in his rearview mirror. She didn't look back at the house. Ungrateful girl. After all, he'd saved her life that day on the side of the road.

He'd be at Sophia's apartment in half an hour, and the airport was fifteen minutes tops from there. He patted the passenger seat, reserved for Sophia.

Sophia was actually coming with him.

And why not? He'd offered her the world—his world—and that was not a bad place to be.

He grew warm below the belt. He couldn't wait to see her juicy smile.

Gerald maneuvered through the height of Miami traffic, weaving in and out lanes and honking the horn.

"Damn idiots on the road!"

He pounded his fist on the steering wheel.

Getting rid of Otto took longer than he expected.

He swerved off the exit to Sophia's neighborhood, zipped along three blocks, and hit the brakes hard enough to squeal when he parked next to her apartment. He cut the engine.

"I'll be right back," he called to Margo and Kaylee.

Gerald leaped out of the car, and with Kaylee and Margo safely locked in the back, he trotted up the stairs to Sophia's door and knocked.

Sophia opened the door with a huge smile, suitcase at her heels.

He glanced down at the secondhand bag. He'd buy her a brand-new, acceptable suitcase—no, a whole set.

Gerald grabbed her cheap suitcase.

"Ready?" he asked.

"I think so!"

Sophia locked the door and walked with a lilt next to him. She playfully bumped his hip with hers, and he responded in kind.

This was going to be one hell of a flight!

He patted her behind, snugly wrapped in her tight jeans.

Gerald opened the trunk and slid Sophia's suitcase inside next to his and gave her a quick peck on those luscious lips.

"You ride up front with me."

Gerald opened the passenger door, escorted her inside, and then closed her door. He returned to driver's side and tapped the wheel.

Sophia settled into her VIP seat and turned to glance into the back seat and wave to Margo and Kaylee.

"Hi! I'm Sophia! Isn't this exciting?!"

"Absolutely," Margo said. "I'm Margo, and this is Joanna, Gerald's niece."

Sophia tapped Gerald's shoulder. "I didn't know you had a niece!"

He had to applaud Margo. She had a knack for coming up with the most imaginative excuses.

"We'll all have such a good time," Sophia squealed. "Maybe just us girls can go shopping together!"

"Mmmm. Maybe," Margo said.

Kaylee offered no comment.

Sophia grinned. "She's so quiet. But I'll warm her up."

"Well, Joanna will be busy with her uncle," Margo said.

Two kudos to you, Margo.

Gerald started the car.

"Next stop, the airport," he announced.

Gerald pulled into the Miami-Opa Locka Executive Airport with forty-five minutes to spare.

He had everyone's passports in his briefcase, including Sophia's, and he grinned when he noticed its blank pages. Now she'd have a stamp for Greece.

This was the beginning of her journey. Unbeknownst to her, Greece was about to become her new homeland. He'd divulge that minor detail in time. He planned to wait until Sophia fell in love with Greece too, since she'd already taken the leap with him.

Gerald checked them in, confirming the private jet's tail number, and was cleared to drive to where Demetrios's jet pilot and copilot waited for them. Customs and Border agents had already inspected the foreign jet and the Greek's pilots.

Miami's fading sun spotlighted Demetrios's white luxury jet, highlighted with a running bright blue stripe, parked and patiently waiting for them to board. The Greek's initials, DS, along with the Greek flag, were boldly stamped in bright blue on the tail wing, just below the jet's tail number.

"What a beautiful sight!" Gerald said with a grin.

One day he'd have a private jet, a bigger one, with his monogramed initials.

Sophia widened her eyes. "Wow! I've never been on an airplane before!"

"Jet," Gerald corrected her.

"It's marvelous!" Margo cooed from the back seat.

Gerald inspected Kaylee's sour demeanor.

She wouldn't dare ruin this trip.

"Margo, you and Sophia go forward. Kaylee and I will meet you before we all board."

Margo shot him a cautionary glance.

"Go. Go. We'll catch up."

Three men belonging to one of private companies operating out of the executive airport approached Gerald and Kaylee.

"May we take your luggage aboard?"

"Sure."

"And when you're ready, we'll take your keys and park your car."

"Yes. One moment please."

Gerald handed a manilla envelope to one of the men.

"Inside are the documents identifying a gentleman who is to pick up my car, along with my signature approval."

"Very good, sir. We'll take care of that for you."

Gerald surrendered the keys to his Mercedes. He'd next see it in Greece when it arrived on shipboard.

"Let's go," he ordered Kaylee.

Kaylee raised her hand to the men.

"Yes?" one of the men asked.

Gerald lowered Kaylee's hand and clutched it.

"My niece is concerned about her luggage. You know teenagers."

"No worries, young lady. We always take the utmost care of our passengers' luggage." He looked at Gerald. "I have a teenage daughter at home."

Gerald grinned politely and then extracted Kaylee from the car while squeezing her hand.

"See, dear? There's nothing to worry about."

Gerald whispered in Kaylee's ear. "Open your mouth, and I'm going to break your wrist. And I'll do it so cleanly, no one's going to notice. And remember, according to your passport your name is Joanna Stemple, which is who Demetrios expects. You will no longer answer to Kaylee. Let's get on this jet, *Joanna.* And for God's sake, smile."

Gerald prodded Margo and Sophia up the jet's blue-carpeted stairway, his hand gripping the back of Kaylee's neck as he pushed her up the stairs.

Sophia turned and glanced at Gerald.

"Go, Sophia…sweetheart…and get settled."

Sophia trotted up the steps in her high heels, bypassing Margo.

She was as easy as a kid to please, and the luxury jet should keep her giddy and—most important—turned on.

Let the fun begin, he mused while he dug his fingers harder into Kaylee's neck.

"Come on, Joanna," he teased.

Gerald released his grip on Kaylee once they entered the jet.

"Welcome aboard, Dr. Newell," the pilot said. "I'm Michael Katsopolus, Demetrios's pilot." He pointed to a blue-capped young man standing next to him and wearing the same official, blue uniform. "This is Adam Sakalis, my copilot and Demetrios's nephew."

"You don't say," Gerald replied.

"My uncle sends his regards." Adam eyed Kaylee. "I'm sure he'll be happy to see *all* of you."

Kaylee turned her head away from Adam.

"I'm sorry. She's shy," Gerald offered.

"That's all right." Adam winked. "He likes the quiet ones."

"Customs has cleared us, and I've provided them the passenger manifest. If you please, now I'll need to collect all your passports," Michael said.

"Absolutely."

Gerald pushed Kaylee forward before he opened his briefcase and gave the passports to Michael.

"You'll find everything's in order."

Michael fanned the passports without peeking inside any of them.

"Yes, they're all here," he said.

Michael gave the passports back to Gerald.

"You'll have to show them to Customs when we arrive in Athens," Michael cautioned.

"Thank you. I'll have them ready when we arrive."

"Please, make yourselves comfortable. We'll be taking off in about thirty minutes for the twelve-hour trip. The weather is cooperating, so we should have a smooth flight."

Gerald narrowed his eyes at Kaylee.

"I'm sure everything will go smoothly."

Kaylee widened her eyes to take in the jet's massive, ornate interior. She'd flown first class internationally with her family, but that couldn't begin to compare to this. She'd stepped into a mobile palace.

She inched forward, almost afraid to touch the oversized white leather seats along the way.

Gerald shoved her forward until they reached another section.

The buxom girl who introduced herself as Sophia lay on a plush white sofa with her feet crossed and her hands behind her head.

"Isn't this the bomb!" she squealed.

She sat up in her tight jeans and equally too-tight top and patted the sofa.

"Come sit!" she beckoned Kaylee.

"Not right now." Gerald interrupted. "I need to get Joanna settled since she has horrible air sickness."

Every time this man opened his mouth, a vomit of lies spewed out.

"Let's go, Joanna, and buckle you in."

Even on a luxury jet, she was still a prisoner. But in some messed up sense, a man who owned a luxury jet might perhaps be willing to handle her with a modicum of kindness. Anyone would be a step up from this monster. Clearly Sophia had no clue about the darkness she'd wandered into, and where she was now trapped. The giddy girl was obviously Newell's property, and so far she was perfectly happy with that. And even if Kaylee told her about her controlling paramour, Sophia was so far gone that she wouldn't accept the truth. But Kaylee promised herself she'd warn Sophia about Newell's sex enterprise at the right moment.

Newell led Kaylee to a seat across the wide aisle from Margo, who was strapped into a puffy seat that could easily fit three people.

He shoved Kaylee into the seat and walked away.

The buttery seat swallowed her.

"That's what happens when you're too small," Margo joked.

Kaylee grabbed the seat belt and snapped the gold buckles together.

Damn! People live like this?

"It's overwhelming, isn't it?" Margo commented.

Although Margo was a key part of the ring, Kaylee hadn't decided what to say about her should she ever get the chance.

The same woman she'd smashed over the head, see-sawed her feelings toward her in a twisted way—a nurturer with a witch's brain. A groomer.

What made this woman become what she was? It couldn't be as fucked-up as what made Newell an evil masquerader. People trusted doctors, especially women who trusted their gynecologists, sharing their most intimate details with them. But neither gender or profession mattered in this horrid secret world, because they shared equally in forced captivity and then selling their property to the highest bidder, who was just as culpable.

Until now Kaylee had no idea this world even existed.

Newell and Sophia walked hand in hand to their deluxe seats at the front of the cabin and strapped themselves in for takeoff.

"We've been cleared for takeoff," the pilot announced.

Nothing happened.

Was there a problem? Did they realize she was being whisked away against her will?

Her heart pumped hard in her chest while she waited for Customs or the police or whoever to storm the plane and to rescue her and arrest Newell and Margo.

But no white knights burst onto the jet.

Kaylee looked at Margo.

"How long will it be before we takeoff?" Kaylee asked with disguised hope.

Margo laughed. "We're already up in the air."

"We couldn't be."

"Look," Margo said.

She pressed a button on the seat's console and the window covering rose.

Blue sky filled the oval window.

Unbelievable. The slide to the air happened without the usual roar and the pull of gravity as they soared aloft.

"You won't feel a thing with this jet," Margo said. "Push that button on your console and look out the window at those glorious clouds floating in blue."

Kaylee pressed the magic button and her shade lifted silently.

When she looked out the jet's window, all she saw was the home she once knew vanishing.

Kaylee pressed the button again, lowering the shade, and huddled in her seat.

There was no way back home, and to think otherwise, was a foolish fantasy and a waste of time.

"We're up," Michael announced. "You're now free to explore every aspect of this marvelous jet. Enjoy!"

Gerald unbuckled his seat belt and reached over to unbuckle Sophia's.

"Thank you, Gerald. I'm still in awe of this plane…jet. It's like a hotel in the air." Sophia grinned widely. "I can't believe I'm here. Pinch me."

Gerald goosed her bottom.

Sophia giggled. "You bad boy!"

He winked. "And I'm going to get a lot badder."

"Oooh!"

"Dinner is being served in the dining cabin," Michael announced over the loudspeaker.

Gerald grabbed Sophia's hand and winked.

"We'll need all the energy we can get."

Sophia squeezed his hand.

"I promise to eat everything on my plate!"

"You bad girl!" he parodied her, which made her giggle harder.

This was going to be the best twelve hours.

Gerald and Sophia arrived in the dining cabin to find four white china settings with DS monogrammed on every piece, including the silverware placed equidistantly on a crisp, blue tablecloth. Kaylee and Margo were already seated next to each other.

Gerald stared at Kaylee's stone face.

He'd offered her a taste of luxury, but no, that wasn't enough! He'd be rid of her face soon enough. Gerald focused his attention on Sophia. Now there was a face he could get lost in.

He pulled out Sophia's chair which was next to him, and then sat and inched to the table.

A gentleman with his black hair slicked back and outfitted in a starched white shirt, black pants, black vest, and a black bowtie, rolled a silver cart into the cabin. A silver-dome covered platter completely covered the top.

The immaculate waiter halted his cart next to the table.

"Dinner is served," he announced.

He lifted the cover to reveal a pile of thick filet mignons, assorted greens topped with baby carrots, and cut potatoes sprinkled with parsley and cut at perfectly matched angles.

He filled Kaylee's, Margo's, and Sophia's plates first, and then Gerald's, as it should be. Gerald wouldn't have it any other way. Well, perhaps not Kaylee, but what the hell.

Sophia threw her up her hands. "Oh, my gawd!"

Gerald lowered them and caught Kaylee's smirk. Even Margo stifled a smile.

What Sophia lacked in refinement, she made up for with a smokin' body. Kaylee had a firm, youthful figure, but oddly, he was never attracted to her. Yeah, Margo was also a never. But Margo's high cheekbones and smooth complexion served to accentuate the strands of gold highlights woven into her brown bob cut. She had it professionally styled every six weeks like clockwork. He admired that type of dedication in women. He'd have to instill it in Sophia.

While they ate, their personal waiter filled their water and wine glasses the moment either fell to half full.

Gerald examined Sophia's nearly empty plate. She wasn't kidding. She only had a few bites remaining. He then assessed Margo's and Kaylee's plates. Kaylee hadn't touched a bite.

Damn it! Everything was a contest with her!

Margo was half done.

He and Sophia would soon excuse themselves, leaving Kaylee and Margo to dine as they pleased. He couldn't care less.

He'd get to spend the rest of the night wrestling with Sophia in their private bedroom suite.

Kaylee and Margo would sleep in the next double occupancy accommodation, where he trusted Margo to keep an eye on Kaylee. Gerald chuckled to himself. Although where was Kaylee going to go?

Jump out of the jet?!

Gerald got up from the table and offered Sophia his hand.

"You'll have to excuse us," Gerald said with a lilt in his voice. "Sophia and I will be retiring for the evening."

Sophia rose, and with her free hand, she waved to Kaylee and Margo.

"Good night," she cooed. "You get some rest, too."

Gerald whisked Sophia away before Margo or Kaylee noticed and commented on his hard-on.

Kaylee wiggled her fingers in the air. "Good night and get some rest, too!" she parroted Sophia with a squeaky high voice.

Margo nudged her. "Stop it." But then she chuckled. "Eat your dinner. It would be criminal to waste this food."

With Gerald gone, Kaylee's standoff with him ended. Now she could eat.

Kaylee cut a piece of the filet mignon and put the forkful in her mouth. Tepid, but still tasty—a testament to the make-believe crap tossed her way while in her make-believe hospital room by her make-believe nurse, Margo.

Kaylee stared into Margo's eyes while chewing extra-slowly.

"I get it," Margo said. "But I had no control over your menu then."

Kaylee continued to eat the rest of her dinner without acknowledging Margo, who likewise ate in silence.

She gulped her wine, praying for a buzz so she could forget why she was on this multibillionaire's jet.

When the waiter returned to refill her glass, Margo blocked the brim of Kaylee's glass.

"She's had enough, thank you," Margo told the waiter, who retreated silently.

"You did that on purpose!"

"I sure did," Margo replied.

"You're not my mother! Don't you dare insult her memory!" Kaylee growled at Margo through her bared teeth.

She flung the napkin on the table, shoved back her chair, and stomped out of the dining cabin.

Kaylee made a sharp left and ended up in a different section..

She twirled around, confused.

How did she end up here, and which way was out?

Damn this jet!

Kaylee flopped onto a white and beige checked sofa. It wasn't the one she noticed when she boarded, where Sophia lounged in delight.

Just how many cabins were there?

She sighed and got to her feet, deciding to backtrack.

Adam came out of the pilot's cabin.

"Hey, Joanna," he called.

Kaylee ignored him. That wasn't her name, but she wouldn't tell him that, because she had no idea what Gerald would do to her. He threatened to break her wrist, but it wouldn't be in his best interests at this point. Although he could send her back to that hellhole and sell her at a bargain price to someone like Otto, and then replace her with another girl for Demetrios. At this point, all she knew about the Greek, other than his mega-money, was his icky nephew.

"Are you lost?" Adam asked.

If he only knew.

Kaylee lied and adamantly shook her head.

Adam pointed straight.

"Go through the next two sections, turn right and then left. That will get you to your sleep accommodations."

"Thanks," Kaylee said.

"You're welcome," he said in warm voice.

Kaylee followed Adam's directions and found the door.

She yawned. But that wouldn't guarantee she'd fall asleep.

She could just lie on bed. Besides, she didn't trust anyone, including Margo.

Kaylee opened the door and gasped at Newell's naked ass pumping up and down, and Sophia moaning with every thrust.

Gerald vaulted off Sophia and glared at Kaylee.

"Get the fuck out of here!"

Kaylee bolted away.

Her heart slammed in her chest and her shoulders hunched, waiting for Gerald's fingers to dig into her neck.

His footsteps approached closer and closer.

Kaylee glanced back to gauge how close Gerald was behind her.

She slammed into someone who grabbed her.

Margo?

Kaylee reared back to find that it was Adam who'd stopped her.

"You!" she yelled. "You did that on purpose!"

She slapped him across the face.

"Have you gone insane?!" Gerald yelled while fumbling with his robe.

He clutched Kaylee's hand.

"Ow!"

Michael rushed out of the pilot's cabin.

"What the hell is going in here?"

Gerald's chest heaved.

"I thought Joanna was staying in the main bedroom. Demetrios ordered that every comfort be offered to her. It's my fault," Adam explained.

"Dr. Newell, let go of her!" Michael ordered.

Sophia rushed to Gerald's side while wearing the same dark blue silk robe. "Please Gerald, stop this."

Newell released his death grip on Kaylee's wrist.

Kaylee rotated it. He didn't fracture her wrist as he promised earlier, but he'd left his fingerprints embedded in her skin—his tattoo.

Margo rushed onto the scene. "What's going on?"

"You were supposed to be watching her," Gerald hissed.

"I was!" she snapped.

"That's enough!" Michael yelled. "I'm going back to the controls."

Gerald backed up and then he and Sophia walked away with their arms around each other.

Maybe Adam would tattle on them to his uncle, or maybe she would, since Demetrios seemed to have been rather generous with her so far. Or maybe he was trying to gain her trust so he could eventually control her. That's the way it always worked.

Adam escorted Kaylee and Margo to their quarters.

The buttery seats had been transformed into single beds with taut, white sheets and fluffy pillows. Blue cotton blankets lay neatly folded at the ends.

Kaylee's eyes teared up. It wasn't the main chamber, but it was just as glorious. The stained sheets and smelly mattress were vanquished into her past. She hated to admit it, but perhaps Newell was right when he said that she'd have a better life in Greece. Why fight it? Her former life with her parents, friends, and Jimmy no longer existed.

She and Margo slid into their beds.

Kaylee tucked the sheet and blanket up to her chin, forming a protective cocoon.

"Good night," Margo said.

Kaylee purposely hesitated.

She rolled over with her back to Margo, and then mumbled,

"'Night."

She'd never utter the word "good" to anyone ever again.

38

Joanna stretched on the couch. The sunlight poking through the window blinds danced on her face. She'd slept more deeply than she ever had before.

What kind of bed would Lou Ann have for her? Actually, it didn't matter because today she'd leave Miami for good. No more looking over her shoulder. She was almost home free. She'd only have to withstand a few more hours.

She heard doggy nails clipping against the tiled ceramic floor.

Isabelle was awake too.

Joanna flipped back the blanket and pushed off the couch.

Joanna bent down and petted Isabelle, who reward her with sweet doggy kisses.

Isabelle was the best friend she ever had. She was loyal and best of all, nonjudgmental. She had no idea who Joanna really was, and didn't care.

Lou Ann appeared in the living room's doorway. "She's really taken to you."

Joanna hugged Isabelle. "The feeling is mutual."

Joanna looked at the empty recliner.

"Where's Harry?"

"Harry left to get us breakfast. After we eat, we'll have to get ready for the funeral. I found one of your mom's black dresses. It has a belt so it should fit you."

"Uh…okay. What about Isabelle?"

"She'll be fine here while we're gone."

Lou Ann turned and walked away.

She blew it! A few tears or a sad face would have been more

appropriate. Instead, she fussed over Isabelle. She needed to be more careful.

Joanna petted Isabelle.

"I wish I was staying behind, too."

Isabelle widened her doggy eyes.

"But I can't."

Isabelle whined softly.

"It's all right. I'll be back soon. Then we can ride home together."

Isabelle barked.

Joanna hugged the dog.

"I love you, too."

"Breakfast is here!" Harry called.

Isabelle rushed out of the living room.

Joanna giggled.

Traitor.

Joanna pattered barefoot into the kitchen and glanced at the clock.

She still wasn't used to seeing a clock.

"Ten o'clock already?"

"Yep" Harry said. He set a two paper bags on the kitchen table. "I guess this is what's called brunch."

Joanna sat at the table in shorts and a T, and Lou Ann and Harry were still in their jeans.

Lou Ann grabbed paper plates and plastic silverware from a cupboard.

"This way there won't be any dishes to wash after the funeral service so we can leave right after."

Joanna looked at Lou Ann's pained face.

Lou Ann would never see her brother again.

Joanna had only seen Kaylee's parents in photos. Suddenly they were people—dead people. She should respect them and focus less on herself.

Harry doled out yogurt, blueberries, and ham and cheese-filled croissants from one bag, and two coffees and an orange juice from the other.

"Something for everybody. Let's eat," he said.

Joanna stared at the yogurt. She once tried yogurt and spit it out. She couldn't risk a repeat, not today. The blueberries were okay, but the ham and cheese croissant was a definite. The orange juice was a bonus.

Joanna watched Lou Ann and Harry sip their coffees.

She'd keep secret about the time she once bolted into a coffee shop and grabbed someone's covered coffee left behind on the table. She'd been so thirsty and hungry. She grabbed the coffee, a half-eaten donut, and the tip, and hightailed out of there, running as fast as she could, outrunning the angry waitress chasing after her. She ducked behind a dumpster and drank the last bit of cold coffee, and then crammed the donut in her mouth. She hadn't had coffee or donuts ever since.

Joanna finished her blueberries and her croissant sandwich, and left not a drop of orange juice, and then waited for Lou Ann and Harry to finish their brunch. She liked that word, "brunch". It sounded so sophisticated.

Lou Ann collected the empty plates and cups and tossed them in a garbage bag.

"You go get ready," Harry said to Lou Ann. "I'll empty the fridge and take out the garbage."

"Thank you."

Then Lou Ann walked away.

Harry looked at Joanna.

"How are you holding up?" he asked her.

Joanna shrugged.

"We'll get through today. Why don't you also go get ready?"

"Okay."

Joanna stood and began to walk away. But she paused and turned to watch Harry clean up everything.

He was a good guy. Lou Ann was lucky to have him.

Joanna cinched the belt over the black dress before she got into the back seat. It was still roomy, but not hopeless. She'd hide behind a hat she found on the back shelf of Kaylee's closet. If she kept her head down like a sorrowful daughter, she might be able to pass as Kaylee to whoever showed up at the funeral, including that nosy neighbor.

Lou Ann and Harry exited out the front door and Lou Ann locked it.

Harry looked strange in his black suit and tie. She liked him better in his jeans. And black definitely wasn't Lou Ann's color. It only made her look paler and older.

She had no idea what Harry did for a living. Even weirder, she didn't know what Lou Ann did for a living either. Things happened so quickly, occupations had never been discussed. All she knew was that they lived separately in Clearwater, and that Lou Ann was Kaylee's only remaining relative.

Joanna shifted in the back seat and buckled the seat belt.

She'd never been to a funeral and had no clue how to act. So she'd follow Lou Ann and Harry and do what they did.

She curled her toes in her sandals.

What if she saw them in their caskets? What did dead people look like? She prayed it wouldn't come to that.

Harry opened the car door for Lou Ann and then rounded the car to land in the driver's seat.

Lou Ann turned to look at Joanna.

"I'm glad the dress fit," she said, and then turned back around.

Is the whole day going to be this awkward?

Joanna decided that the best response was to keep her mouth shut.

Harry started the engine and reversed out of the driveway.

Joanna wrung her hands.

Kaylee should be in this back seat, not her.

No one uttered a word on the drive to the funeral home.

Every turn signal echoed in the car.

The final click-click brought them into a funeral home parking area designated for immediate family only.

Joanna was now part of that family.

She waited for Lou Ann and Harry to get out of the car first. She didn't want to stand there all awkward in a black dress that belonged to the dead woman inside. Did Lou Ann feel the same way? Maybe that's why she was extra quiet. Maybe she couldn't wait to peel this dress off as much as Joanna wanted to. All this was too weird.

A man in a stiffer suit than Harry's approached the car and opened Lou Ann's door before Harry could do the honors.

He was almost bald, and what hair remained was plastered to the back of his head in a half-circle of silver.

The funeral business suited this guy.

Lou Ann spun her legs out of the seat and reached up for the funeral man's outstretched hand.

"How are you, Lou Ann?"

She knows this man?

"I'm so sorry this is happening to you," he continued.

"You were there for my mom and dad, and now Lyle."

Lou Ann's words trailed off.

Not only had her brother died, but her mother and father too? But Kaylee would have known that. She'd better be careful and not out herself by asking about what happened to them. Still it was sad, no matter what way you looked at it.

The funeral man opened Joanna's door.

"This is Lyle and Melinda's daughter, Kaylee, who, thank God, survived the car wreck. She'll be staying with me."

"She's grown into a young lady. Last time I saw her she couldn't have been more than ten." He helped Joanna out of the car. "You probably don't remember me. I certainly look a bit different. You can call me John."

Joanna nodded.

Lou Ann introduced Harry to John.

"Nice to meet you, in spite of these circumstances," John said.

"Likewise," Harry replied.

"I'll escort all of you first so you can have private time with Lyle and Melinda. When you're ready, I'll bring in the others attending today's service. At the conclusion, they'll leave first, and you'll follow the hearse in the procession to the cemetery as we discussed."

"I remember, John. Thank you."

"I'll take care of everything. You and Kaylee take care of yourselves."

"I'll see to that, too," Harry said.

With a somber stride they followed John inside Marshall Funeral Home.

When John opened the funeral door Joanna anticipated the sour smell of death to hit her smack in the face. Instead, floral scents surrounded her. It was as if she'd stepped into a garden rather than a temporary home for the dead.

Joanna followed Lou Ann and Harry into the funeral home's sanctuary where a bronze coffin and a white one stood deep in the silent room. Sprays of flowers cascaded from the caskets' thankfully closed lids, and even more floral arrangements surrounded them.

A lot of people loved them.

Joanna followed Lou Ann and Harry to the front row of the sanctuary and sat with them.

"Kaylee, I think you should go first," Lou Ann said.

Joanna sucked a deep breath. What was she going to say? No?

"All right," Joanna said.

She rose and walked over to the caskets.

She glanced back to see if Lou Ann and Harry were observing her, but instead they were talking quietly with each other.

She'd be quick enough, while seemingly sorrowful at the same time.

Joanna stood in between Lyle and Melinda's caskets and rested her hands on each one. Her heartbeat quickened and her chest squeezed against her ribs. She pressed her fingers against the caskets. Her surprising connection to them caught her off guard. After all, they'd shared the same crashed vehicle. Her captors thought she was dead when they tossed her in with Lyle and Melinda. But she survived. They didn't.

You don't know me, she said silently. *And I don't know you. But we were together for a brief moment. I'm sorry I'm not your daughter. I don't how or where she is, or if she's still alive. I'm sure she wandered off in shock. No one knows where she is. And I'm so sorry for that. But in a morose way, I wish you were my real parents. Forgive me.*

Joanna released her grip on Lyle and Melinda's caskets and gently tapped them.

By the way, Melinda, I hope you don't mind that I'm wearing one of your dresses. Wasn't my idea, but I don't own anything black.

Rest in peace, both of you.

Joanna walked away from them and sat back in her place.

"Your turn," she said to Lou Ann.

Lou Ann pushed up from her seat. Her knees melted beneath her, and she grabbed the back of her seat to steady herself.

Harry bolted up to help her.

She waved him off.

"I'm all right," she lied.

The brother who ran by her bicycle after everyone else had failed, frustrated that she was incapable of balancing on two wheels and fly, the same brother who was brave enough to teach her to drive, was now the brother sealed forever in a coffin.

Lou Ann took one step and then another until she was next to Lyle.

She collapsed onto his casket.

"I never meant to hurt you," she cried. "I would give anything to have another day with you so I can say I'm sorry. It's too late now, and you're gone. But I want you to know that. I'll take good care of Kaylee, and I won't have to remind her what a great dad you were to her. I love you."

Lou Ann turned to Melinda's casket.

"You're the sweetest person I ever met. I know Lyle and I tested your patience, and I know that you somehow managed to be loyal to him without disparaging me. I'll always love you for that. I'm sure Kaylee will grow up to be just like you."

Lou Ann dabbed her eyes with her finger and returned to her seat.

"Harry, can you tell John we're ready?"

"Sure."

The sanctuary filled with people paying their respects to Lyle and Melinda.

Joanna managed to keep her head down under her hat and remain silent so no one would notice that she was an imposter.

Every seat was soon taken, especially the one next to her.

"I'm so sorry, Kaylee," the guy next to her said.

He eased his hand on top of hers.

Joanna froze.

Who the hell is this?

And then she pieced it together.

It must be Jimmy, Kaylee's boyfriend. Shit!

Joanna glanced sideways from beneath her hat.

Yep. He looked just like the photo on Kaylee's dresser.

Now what?

Lyle and Melinda's pastor approached the podium.

Great! Another person who could out her.

But Jimmy posed the greatest risk.

While the pastor eulogized Lyle and Melinda, Jimmy's resting hand turned into a handhold.

Worse, Lou Ann peeked past Harry at her and Jimmy.

At least she knew his name, but that was all.

After the service concluded, Joanna would pat his hand and slip away with Lou Ann and Harry to the car for the cemetery procession.

Oh, no! He might be going to the cemetery too.

Dumping Jimmy wasn't going to be easy.

When the pastor concluded the service, Joanna grasped Harry's hand. She patted Jimmy's hand like she'd planned and leaned closer to Harry.

"Are you okay?" he asked.

"Yes," she answered quickly. "It's time to go," she added.

Lou Ann nodded.

John Marshall approached and saved her.

"Come with me," John said.

Joanna fell in behind Lou Ann and Harry while following John out of the funeral home…thankfully leaving Jimmy behind.

Harry idled the car while funeral personnel loaded Lyle's casket into a black limousine and Melinda's casket into a silver one along with their flower arrangements.

He turned to look at Lou Ann's stoic face. It had gone paler since they first arrived at the funeral home. Even her lips had lost their color.

Lou Ann stared straight ahead while watching Lyle's casket slide into its place. Melinda's casket was already positioned.

Harry remained silent. There wasn't anything anyone could say that would ease her pain. And more than enough people had already expressed their condolences.

Then he looked at Kaylee through the rearview mirror. Although she sat with her hands folded in her lap, her eyes spun wildly from window to window.

"Kaylee," he gently called. "Do you need to get out and get some air?"

"No! No."

"I'll go with you," he offered.

"I just need to sit."

"Leave her be, Harry."

Harry took a deep breath. "Okay."

John gestured for Harry to proceed, and then climbed in the silver limousine.

Ladies first, he thought.

And he had two ladies who required his attention.

Harry parked behind the limousines carrying Lyle's and Melinda's flower-laden caskets and assisted Lou Ann and Kaylee out of the car. Rows and rows of headstones popping up from manicured green grass surrounded Lou Ann. Scores of people had died since she buried her mom and dad. But it would be at least a month before the headstones she chose for Lyle and Melinda's gravesites could be erected. It would just be a mound of dirt today.

Lou Ann focused on the standard deep green canopy covering the vaults waiting for Lyle and Melinda's permanent repose. Same canopy. Different family bodies. She detested the color green.

Harry positioned himself between her and Kaylee and took their hands.

"Ready?" he asked.

"Yes," Lou Ann answered.

Kaylee remained silent as Lou Ann had anticipated. She hadn't said a word since they left the funeral home.

Lou Ann wouldn't rush her, because she was still processing Lyle and Melinda's catastrophic deaths. Kaylee would have to process her parents' deaths for the rest of her life, along with guilt because of having survived. There wasn't a fix for that.

More cars carrying mourners arrived while they approached the canopy.

John supervised the caskets being lowered above the vaults.

Lou Ann tugged at Harry's hand.

"You and Kaylee take your seats. I need to do something."

Harry let go of her hand without questions. He knew where she was going.

Lou Ann backed away from the green canopy and walked to her mother and father's headstones.

She squatted between them.

"I'm sorry I haven't been here in a while, but you're in my heart every day. I know you know about Lyle and Melinda, and that you'll take care of them."

Lou Ann swiped the tears off her cheeks.

"Kaylee is with me, and I'll take good care of her. She's had a rough time, but she'll pull through like a Jasinski."

Then Lou Ann hugged her parents' headstones.

"I have to go now."

Joanna sat in the folded chair under the canopy. The front row of seats gave her a firsthand look at the deep cement hole beneath the caskets.

She winced. She was never going to die.

Lou Ann returned, sat next to Joanna, and rested her hand on Joanna's knee.

She did the same thing in the hospital.

It was Lou Ann's way of calming her, and for the most part it worked.

She meant well.

Lou Ann correctly sensed that Joanna wasn't a touchy-feely kind of person. But that was slowly changing and it was okay.

Oddly, she'd responded to Harry more easily than Lou Ann at first. Now they were pretty equal, with Lou Ann gaining a slight advantage. She needed comfort more than Harry. Seeking solace was what Lou

Ann and she had in common. And Lou Ann needed extra solace today. So Joanna faked that she needed it too.

More mourners arrived.

Joanna grumbled under her hat as Jimmy approached.

"Are you all right?" Lou Ann asked.

"I'm uncomfortable."

Outright panic was more like it.

"I'm uncomfortable too."

Jimmy sat directly behind her.

Joanna craned her neck.

She'd seen the same woman with Jimmy at the funeral home.

Everyone stood when the pastor arrived.

"Please be seated," he said.

The cemetery chairs randomly creaked as the mourners sat.

The pastor highlighted snippets from his eulogy and added a few more sentences about grief. He kept it short and then he blessed the caskets.

Then came this decorative pail filled with dirt.

What the heck…

Lou Ann and Harry went first, and each grabbed a handful of the dirt and tossed some on Lyle's casket and then Melinda's.

Okay.

Joanna dug her hand into the pail and extracted a gob of dirt and repeated what Lou Ann and Harry did.

That's what the pastor meant when he said, "Ashes to ashes, and dust to dust."

Funeral rituals were totally bizarre.

Jimmy tossed his dirt and caught up with her.

"Kaylee," he said.

When she didn't respond, he lifted the brim of her hat, exposing her face.

His eyes widened and he leaned back a bit.

She couldn't avoid him anymore. Time for damage control.

"Hi, Jimmy," Joanna said.

"Ummm. Hi."

"I'm sorry I didn't talk to you earlier."

"That's all right. I get it."

He looked into her eyes. Luckily they were blue like Kaylee's. Although she and Kaylee had the same blonde hair, Joanna's was longer and a bit stringier.

"Everyone thought you were dead, but I refused to believe it. And uh...here you are."

"I don't remember parts because I was in the hospital for a long time. You know...the crash and all."

"Yeah. Must have been horrible, but not as horrible as no longer having your parents."

Joanna adjusted her hat.

"I'm going to go live with my aunt for now."

"Oh."

"Yeah."

Jimmy took both her hands.

"I miss you."

"Me too, but I have to leave."

Jimmy leaned in closer and pressed his lips toward hers but stopped short of a kiss.

Saved by hesitancy.

"Yeah. I gotta go too. Take care."

That's it? Kaylee's boyfriend is lame.

She was overjoyed that he'd signed off, but also his rejection stung a bit in a weird way. Oh, well. At least that and the funeral were over.

She'd be in Clearwater by tonight.

Lou Ann shook hands with friends of Lyle and Melinda's she'd never met before. Peg Foster, the only neighbor she'd briefly met and sans dog, approached her.

"What a poignant service. My condolences once gain," Peg said.

Lou Ann nodded. "Thank you for coming."

She peeked past Peg's head to find Kaylee hovering near the car.

Another woman approached her.

"Hello. I'm Audrey Braxton. You don't know me, but my son Jimmy spent a lot of time at Lyle and Melinda's. He and Kaylee have dated since their freshman year in high school. We were all shattered to hear about Lyle and Melinda, and Jimmy was inconsolable when he thought Kaylee had died too. But then we were overjoyed to hear she'd survived and was in a hospital in Naples. We purposely and with great difficulty stayed away until Kaylee recovered. I'm not sure how to say this..."

"Go on. It's all right."

"Well, Jimmy came to me real confused. He said Kaylee wasn't herself. It's like he didn't recognize her. I reassured him that yes, she may look and act different, but she's been through a lot. The accident must have had such an impact that I'm sure Kaylee not only suffered physical injury, but emotional ones too. I told him to be patient with her. I understand she's leaving with you to Clearwater. Umm, perhaps in time they could get together, but only if Kaylee agrees and is ready to see him again. I mean those two were meant to be together."

"I think that could happen in time. I feel for Jimmy."

"And I feel for Kaylee."

"Would you mind exchanging texts to update each other?" Lou Ann asked.

"That would be great."

Lou Ann and Audrey entered their contacts in their cells.

"Have a safe drive to Clearwater."

"Thank you, Audrey."

Lou Ann watched Kaylee pace alongside the car.

Most of the mourners left, but a few lingered behind, hugging and talking among themselves. Not that they were malicious, but to be fair, Lou Ann left Miami years ago.

Lou Ann shot them an awkward wave, and they responded in kind.

"Are you ready to leave?" Harry asked. "I'm not rushing you."

"I know. Kaylee can't leave fast enough."

"I noticed. I think she needed to be alone. The whole day's been overwhelming."

"I agree. Go to her and both of you get in the car. I'm going to thank John and then I'll be right there."

"Okay."

Lou Ann and John met halfway between the car and the gravesite.

"Thank you for everything, John."

"You're welcome. We'll take care of the rest of it."

At least she and Kaylee would be spared the interment.

"I'll let you know when the headstones are ready to be set. Drive safely."

"I will."

Lou Ann looked back at her brother's casket for the last time, and then at Harry and Kaylee waiting for her in the car.

"Goodbye Lyle. Goodbye Melinda," she whispered.

A cool breeze swept across her cheek.

"I love you, too, Lyle."

39

Margo's watch alarm buzzed annoyingly in Kaylee's ear. She winced and dove deeper under her covers.

But Margo's roaring yawn penetrated past the covers.

She must've mentally shut down after the incident with Newell and his lipstick-crazed girlfriend. Thankfully, she didn't dream anything, or at least couldn't remember if she did. They say everyone dreams, but she quit dreaming weeks ago. Her mind no longer processed dreams, only nightmares. And if she screamed out last night, no one comforted her.

Margo poked Kaylee in the back through the blanket.

"Wake up! We'll be late for a quick breakfast before we land."

"Land?"

"Yes. What do you think a jet does? Hover perpetually in one place?"

If only that could be possible.

"What time is it?" Kaylee asked while still under the covers.

"It's noon in Greece. We'll land in two hours."

It took her a minute to calculate the time change.

In addition to everything from Newell to icky Adam, jet lag wreaked its own havoc.

"Kaylee! Get out of bed right now and get dressed," Margo ordered.

"Yeah, yeah," Kaylee muttered.

Margo ripped Kaylee's covers off, tossed Kaylee's clothes on top of her, and stomped away.

Kaylee curled up while in her bra and panties.

Once Margo was gone, she put on the same pants and blouse that she wore when they boarded Demetrios's jet.

Because he was waiting for his order—her.

The only way out of this jet was in Greece.

Jumping out was not an option.

She sauntered into the dining cabin where Newell, Sophia, and Margo were already seated.

"Look who's here?!" Newell commented with a smug smile.

Kaylee refused to take his bait and sat next to Margo. Soon she wouldn't be seeing any of their rotten faces, except for Sophia's naive, chipper face.

"Good morning, Joanna!" Sophia sing-songed.

"Morning," she muttered, her head down, keeping her internal promise to never use the word "good" again.

The same waiter in the same uniform placed a bowl of fruit on the table and a freshly baked loaf of bread with a plate of butter squares. He then filled everyone's coffee cups, including hers.

She'd get used to coffee since it was what everyone else drank, including her parents. A covert half smile crept to her face when she remembered how her dad used to whistle while whipping up the best breakfasts. Her mom had dominion over dinners, and lunches were always a toss-up.

What would Demetrios have for breakfast? He probably never saw a kitchen in his life.

Kaylee dropped a few pieces of assorted fruit on her plate and took a piece of bread and a pat of butter. That should hold her over until they shoved her into an accommodation in Greece. As Adam, his nephew, pointed out during last night's melee, Demetrios had ordered his minions to make sure she was always comfortable.

Newell had superseded his orders, and Kaylee couldn't wait to tattle on him.

Adam joined them for the abbreviated breakfast, and grinned at Kaylee, who refused an in-kind response.

"I hope everyone slept well," he said, still gazing at Kaylee.

Sophia leaned against Newell. "I had a fabulous night," she cooed.

Newell winked at her.

Ick!

Adam wolfed down his breakfast and stood.

"You'll have to excuse me. See you all in Athens."

Michael, the captain, joined them briefly to announce that the flight would land right on time. Then he loaded a plate to go and disappeared back to his controls.

Gerald scooted his chair back and helped Sophia from her seat. Praise be, he ignored Kaylee. But he rounded the table and, no doubt purposely, whispered loud enough in Margo's ear for Kaylee to hear, "Keep her in line."

Margo nodded, aware that Kaylee made note of Gerald's command.

"Come with me. Let's get you ready."

Kaylee followed Margo into one of the jet's marbled-tiled bathrooms. The on-board bathroom she used last night was equally ornate, but a bit smaller.

Margo fished a makeup bag out of her purse.

"Face me."

Kaylee looked into Margo's cool blue eyes. Margo studied her like an artist studies her canvas.

First Margo applied a light layer foundation on Kaylee's face, then brushed a frosted bronze eyeshadow from her palette onto Kaylee's eyelids.

"Look up," she ordered.

She combed black mascara onto her eyelashes without poking the wand in her eyes.

Margo assessed her work.

"Hmmm."

She chose a peach blush and swiped Kaylee's cheek with it.

"Good. You can look in the mirror."

Kaylee inched to the vanity and glanced into the mirror. Then she looked closer at her reflection. Margo could be a vengeful bitch, but she didn't do her wrong. Margo transformed her face into a dewy, mature look, unlike Sophia's cheap, in-your-face makeup that she probably slapped on every morning while half asleep.

Margo put her makeup kit back in her bag.

"Let's return to our seats and buckle up for landing. And remember, when we get to customs and beyond, you are Joanna Stemple."

Margo and Kaylee sat back in their oversized white leather seats and buckled in for the imminent landing.

"What is your name?" Margo asked.

"Joanna Stemple."

Michael announced that they'd landed in Athens.

Kaylee wouldn't have known it without his announcement.

Her heart pounded in her ears.

What's going to happen now?

Gerald and Sophia joined them.

"I have your passports," Gerald said.

He passed them out.

"Here you go, *Joanna Stemple.*"

Kaylee took the fake passport. Her life would now become just as fake.

Margo and Kaylee unbuckled their seat belts, and Kaylee stood and hesitated, unsure of her place in line to deplane.

Gerald went first and then Sophia. Margo prodded Kaylee to follow Sophia, leaving Margo in the tail position.

In single file they walked down the jet's blue-carpeted stairs. A mustached man with an olive complexion and wearing a navy suit and tie greeted them.

"Passports, please," he said.

Kaylee looked inside her passport. It wasn't her photo or her real name.

Would the customs agent pull her aside and jail her for using a fake passport to get into Greece?

Kaylee started to sweat.

Be cool.

They'd do shit to get her out of a foreign prison. She'd rot there the rest of her life. Maybe Demetrios would decide not to bother with her and order some other girl who was less trouble.

The customs agent led them to a separate building and handed the passports to another man in a navy suit who waited behind a booth.

The man examined Gerald's and then Sophia's passports, stamped them, and waved them through.

"Next," he called.

Kaylee stepped forward and presented Joanna Stemple's passport.

The agent looked at the passport and then at Kaylee, and then at the passport again.

Margo tapped her toe, while Gerald hovered on the other side of the booth.

The agent stared at Kaylee.

He'd picked her out.

Kaylee looked him straight in his eyes while struggling to take deep, even breaths.

The agent banged her passport with his stamp and handed Joanna's passport to her.

"Welcome to Greece," he said in a matter-of-fact tone rather than a truly welcoming one.

Kaylee quickly joined Newell and Sophia before the agent changed his mind.

The agent merely glanced at Margo's passport and stamped it as if he had already tired of waving the American group through.

Then they were identified again and reunited with their inspected luggage.

A man in a crisp white shirt with gleaming gold cufflinks and tailored dark blue jeans strode towards them in his leather loafers while waving.

He halted in front of them and spread his arms out. "Welcome to Greece!"

Gerald's eyes went big. "Demetrios?"

"One and the same my friend!" he responded in a jolly voice.

Kaylee stepped behind her luggage.

This was the man who'd paid for her?

His wavy yet freshly cut brown hair had strands of silver woven through it, but his body was that of a man who spent a generous amount of time at the gym.

His gaze met hers, and he walked straight over to her to offer his ring-laden hand.

Kaylee slowly raised hers to meet his.

Demetrios bent over and gently kissed the back of her hand.

"Joanna, I'm so happy to meet you."

Kaylee glanced over at Newell, who nervously shifted his weight. Sophia stood with her mouth wide open, and Margo pursed her lips.

No matter what happened after this, the looks on their faces were priceless!

"Weren't you and I going to meet first?" Gerald asked.

"Oh, yes. We'll still meet as planned tomorrow…maybe the day after. I just couldn't wait any longer to meet Joanna. Oh, so beautiful! I'll take her right away. I've wired you what we agreed upon."

Newell nodded. He just couldn't let go of her.

Good. Ha! Kaylee finally said the word. Even if it was in her head, it still counted.

Demetrios snapped his fingers, and four men came out of nowhere. Three of them grabbed Newell's, Sophia's, and Margo's bags. The fourth man picked up Kaylee's suitcase.

Then Demetrios beckoned for Kaylee to join him.

"My limousine is waiting outside for us," he said.

The top of Kaylee's head barely reached Demetrios's shoulders, and she tilted her head back in order to study him.

He tossed down a pleasant smile, then turned his attention to Newell.

"Dr. Newell, I have a limousine waiting for you, Sophia, and Margo. Your chauffeur will take you to your accommodations, which I am positive you will find more than satisfactory."

Newell simply nodded.

Demetrios had him by the balls! What a beautiful thing to watch!

"Shall we? he asked Kaylee.

"Yes."

She'd keep her replies short until she was better acquainted with him. So far, though, he'd respected her boundaries.

Gerald, Sophia, and Margo fell in behind them like stepchildren.

Kaylee walked, still with a slight limp, next to Demetrios while maintaining more than an arm's length from him with an abundance of caution. He owned her now, and she had no clue what to expect from him. But his brown eyes were warm, and the opposite of Newell's steel blues.

Sophia's spiked high heels clip-clopped behind her.

And where Sophia was, so was Newell, along with Margo tagging along behind them.

She could practically peel their eyes off the back of her head.

When they reached the two limos idling outside of the Customs building, Demetrios's men loaded Newell, Sophia, and Margo's bags in one of the limos, and the chauffeur opened the rear door for them.

None of them deserved that limo.

But, most important, she'd never have to spend the night with any of them anymore.

Kaylee couldn't resist giving them a queen's wave as their limo moved away.

But underneath her glee, was the grim realization that she was now left alone with Demetrios.

40

Joanna settled in the back seat of the car. The only difference was the moving U-Haul trailer attached to it. They left it behind for the funeral, but that was over, and the trailer only emphasized the finality.

Isabelle licked her hand.

Isabelle was just as happy as she was to leave Miami.

She hugged her new best friend while Lou Ann and Harry locked up the pink house. She prayed Lou Ann didn't live in a pink house, but she was 99 percent sure she didn't. It didn't suit her, and definitely wouldn't suit Harry. But in six hours she'd find out the color of her new house.

Lou Ann took her place in the front seat and Harry behind the wheel.

Thank God she had ditched Melinda's black dress, trading it for jeans and a T, just like Lou Ann. Harry had peeled off his suit too, and changed into his traveling clothes. They all looked more human now.

Joanna tapped the wide-brimmed hat next to her on the seat. The black dress was a big no, but Kaylee's hat was a keeper.

"Here we go," Harry said.

The trailer's wheels thumped and the trailer wobbled through the neighborhood until all the speed bumps were cleared.

When they finally reached the multi-lane of Alligator Alley, the trailer settled in for a smoother ride and so did Joanna. Isabelle curled up next to her and doggy snored, and soon after Lou Ann's snores began to drown out Isabelle's. Thank God Harry wasn't snoring. Joanna's head bobbed a few times, until her heavy head swayed on her neck and then finally lolled back.

Joanna smacked her lips and blinked her eyes open to find the orange sun dipping into the rainbow sunset that hovered over the calm bay. The view grew even more stunning at the peak of the bridge.

"Where are we?" she asked.

"Sarasota," Lou Ann answered.

Isabelle pressed her nose against the window while she too enjoyed the sunset.

Somewhere along the way both Isabelle and Lou Ann woke before she did.

"How long was I out?"

"About four hours," Harry answered.

"Damn."

"It was a long day for everyone," Lou Ann said. "I even conked out for a while there."

"We know!" Joanna and Harry said at the same time.

"What's that supposed to mean?"

"Nothing, Lou Ann."

Joanna caught Harry smiling in the rearview mirror.

She grinned and settled back, enjoying Lou Ann and Harry's banter.

Living with Lou Ann and, fingers crossed, Harry, would at least be entertaining. Maybe even fun.

The trailer swayed and once again bumped along, except they were no longer in Miami, but in Clearwater—her new home.

Harry made a wide swing into a driveway.

Joanna widened her eyes and her stomach clenched.

The police got here before she did.

They were looking for her!

Joanna unsnapped her seat belt and ducked to the floor.

"Kaylee. What's going on?" Lou Ann called.

"Why are the police here?"

Harry turned to Lou Ann. "You didn't tell her, did you?"

"Neither did you."

Joanna trembled behind Harry's seat.

"What's happening?"

Lou Ann got out of the car and into the back seat, squatting on the floor.

"That's my vehicle. Actually, it belongs to the Pinellas County Sheriff's Department where I'm a deputy sheriff. With everything that happened, I completely forgot to tell you, and I'm very sorry. It just wasn't important at the time. You were."

Joanna's first thought was to slap her, but she didn't—she couldn't.

"Honest, I didn't do it on purpose."

Harry got out of the car and opened the back seat door on the other side.

"Kaylee, she's telling the truth. It's time for me to tell you the truth, too. I work for the FBI. I'm a what's called a Special Agent. So you see, you're very well protected. We'll make sure nothing bad happens to you. You've had enough terrible things for a lifetime. I'm sorry, Kaylee. Will you come out of the car now?"

Joanna slowly rose.

Harry held out his hand and she took it.

Isabelle bolted past them.

"Someone's in a hurry," Harry chortled.

When he helped her out the car, Joanna stared at the white house with lemon yellow shutters—and thank goodness it wasn't pink! A palm tree stood tall at the front left of the house, just like the one at Brad's house. But this house was hers.

Everything was going to be all right.

She was safe.

Harry walked Joanna to the front door of her new home, and his former one. He waited with her and Isabelle until Lou Ann could fetch her purse from the front seat of the car.

What was it with women and purses? They were like mobile suitcases.

Although he shouldn't complain. After all, Lou Ann carried his stuff too.

Lou Ann jogged to the front door with keys clanging on the keyring in her hand and her purse handles bouncing wildly on her shoulder.

"I got the keys!"

Lou Ann stuck the house key in the front door and unlocked it.

"Come on in," she announced, presumably to Kaylee, but Harry took up the invitation too, and followed Lou Ann, Kaylee, and Isabelle inside.

The last one inside, Harry closed the door while Lou Ann disengaged the alarm system.

He peeked at the combination while she punched it in.

She hadn't changed it.

That gave him a sliver of hope.

Joanna stared at the living room without taking a step forward.

Lou Ann gestured for Kaylee to go ahead.

"It's all right. You're not a guest here."

Harry scanned the living room.

She hadn't rearranged that either. The sofa was right where he put it when they moved in.

Kaylee inched forward like an Alice in Wonderland. It would take her time to adjust to her new surroundings, but that was Lou Ann's role and, unfortunately, not his.

"Would you like a drink?" Lou Ann asked.

"Sure," Harry answered,

He knew she was talking to Kaylee, but he couldn't resist.

Lou Ann rolled her eyes.

He actually liked when she did that. He still enjoyed playfully getting under her skin.

Harry followed Lou Ann and Kaylee into the kitchen.

Kaylee inspected the kitchen. "Your house is so big!"

Yeah, it was roomy.

He missed roomy. His apartment was anything but.

While Isabelle lapped at her water bowl, Lou Ann opened a cupboard and took out three glasses.

Same cupboard. Same glasses.

It was as if he never left. Picking up where he left off might not happen, but he could wish.

Lou Ann went to the fridge, took out a pitcher of lemonade, and filled their glasses.

Kaylee began sipping hers, but then gulped it down. She set the empty glass on the table.

"More?" Lou Ann asked.

"Yes, please," Kaylee replied.

Lou Ann refilled Kaylee's glass.

Harry chugged his lemonade and tapped his empty glass on the table.

"Pitcher's right there."

Yeah, it was. Just like the good old days.

After they all three finished their second helpings of lemonade, Lou Ann stood. "I need to let Isabelle out in the backyard"

"You have a backyard?!"

"Yes. But it's not as big as the one you have in Miami."

"Right. Right."

Lou Ann glanced at Harry.

"Kaylee, why don't go hang out in the backyard with Isabelle?

Kaylee perked up.

"Absolutely. Come on, Isabelle. Let's go."

Lou Ann opened the sliding glass doors at the far side of the kitchen and let the two of them out.

Then she shut the doors and returned to Harry while he sat at the kitchen table, the set they'd picked out together, and the same set he let her have. It wouldn't fit in his apartment anyway. He bought a two-seater one, with one chair perpetually empty, since he couldn't find any that only sat one person.

He shrugged.

"I don't think there's anything behind that. You and I know all about victims of trauma and how they block out even the seemingly simple things in their past that aren't simple to them.

"You're right."

Wow. He hadn't heard those words from Lou Ann in like…forever.

"Why don't you guys take it easy while I unload the trailer? I need to drop it off tonight."

"Tonight?"

"Yeah."

Lou Ann frowned.

What ever happened to those magic words?

Not so easy to come. Very easy to go.

"I'll help you."

"No. It's okay."

"Yes," Lou Ann insisted.

Harry surrendered. It was easier.

"All right."

Kaylee and Isabelle returned to the kitchen.

"She did her business," Kaylee announced proudly.

"Great. I'll pooper scoop that in the morning. Harry and I are going to unload the trailer."

Kaylee raised her hand. "I'll help."

"Okay. With all three of us, we'll get it done faster."

"That's right. Because the trailer *has* to go back tonight," Lou Ann retorted.

Same Lou Ann. Different day.

Harry unlocked the trailer door and lifted it up. He went in the small space inside and began handing the lighter boxes out to Lou Ann and Kaylee, who took turns stashing the belongings inside. Then

Harry used the dolly to finish unloading the heavy boxes.

"That's a wrap," he announced, and secured the trailer's door.

Then he went back in the house to make sure the boxes weren't in Lou Ann's or Kaylee's way.

Lou Ann returned from the hallway where their bedroom was, now hers alone, carrying a blanket and a pillow.

Were those for him after he returned the trailer?

"Are you sure you don't want to sleep in the bed, and let me take the couch?"

"No, Aunt Lou Ann. "I'll be fine here. I actually prefer it."

"All right, then. We'll shop for a bedroom set for you. I'll clean out the den tomorrow so you'll have your own room."

Kaylee plopped down on the living room couch.

"Cool." Kaylee waved to Harry. "Good night, Harry."

"Good night, Kaylee."

Harry walked over to Lou Ann and gave her a quick peck on her cheek "Good night."

"Good night to you, too, Harry. And thank you for everything."

"No problem. I'm here if you need me. Just call."

"Okay," Lou Ann said softly.

"Good night, Isabelle," Harry called.

Isabelle let out an abbreviated growl.

Same dog. Different day.

"Isabelle!" Lou Ann chided her.

"It's okay. At least we're making progress."

"Yes, we are," Lou Ann said.

He'd hoped there was a double meaning to that, but sometimes hope was only for fools.

May he not be a fool.

After dropping off the U-Haul trailer, Harry pulled into his reserved space in the apartment parking garage.

Reserved for one.

He had two parking spaces allotted to him. But after months of one left empty, he let the young woman next door use it for her friends or whomever. He never had company, so he could care less. No sense in leaving a good parking spot unused.

Harry sat in the car for a few minutes just breathing in Lou Ann and Kaylee's scents—and yes—even Isabelle's.

Darn dog.

Maybe he'd get fish since they weren't picky. Plus, they were self-sufficient, requiring only fish food and a clean tank. Totally manageable.

He sighed and got out of his car and locked it.

With his keys in hand, he walked to the elevator and pressed the fifth floor. As a bonus, he had a terrace view of the bay, but he spent next to no time admiring the bright blue waterfront. It wasn't worth admiring it alone, and when he had the time, which was almost never, he'd have a beer and watch sports. He wondered why he requested the view. He guessed he had big hopes of sharing the picturesque terrace, but perhaps he was a fool.

Harry opened his tiny, overpriced apartment and tossed his key in a bowl set on a tiny table in a tiny foyer.

He disengaged the alarm system using the same code as the one at the house, except backwards.

Then he went to the tiny kitchen and opened the full fridge that looked completely out of place and took out a bottle of beer. Why would a guy need countertop space? He didn't cook. He lived on takeout or ready meals. It was wasteful to toss out food when his assignments kept him away for weeks, and sometimes months.

Lou Ann had a love/hate relationship with his unpredictable schedule. She'd brood when he was there and then brood when he wasn't. She was on rotating shifts anyway. They just couldn't get it together.

Then the beginning of the split. Men flirt, but that wasn't an excuse. It didn't help that Gail, his colleague, came on to him. However, he was responsible for setting up that vibe even though nothing intimate happened between them. Yeah, they shared a hotel room in Madrid…a very hopping city. He slept on the sofa and Gail took the bed. But she did answer his cell when he was in the shower. It was Lou Ann. And bam! Never mess with a pissed-off woman who had a firearm equal to yours. But it was the bar incident that nailed his and Lou Ann's fragile relationship shut.

He brought the beer into his living room, lay down on the sofa, picked up the remote, and flipped to a soccer game.

And, like Kaylee, he chose the sofa over his lonely bed.

41

Demetrios's chauffeur opened the door to the limo's massive back seat, and Demetrios gestured for Kaylee to enter first, then he slid in after her.

Wow. Her whole soccer team could fit in there. Despite the immense limo's back seat, Demetrios scooted closer to her.

Kaylee inched away.

The limo pulled out and drove smoothly through what Kaylee had to assume were downtown streets.

Demetrios beckoned Kaylee closer and then pulled down a bar to reveal a glass bottle with a gold bow around its neck resting in a silver bucket of ice and two crystal goblets. He uncorked the bottle and a plume of white sprayed across the roof of the back seat.

Kaylee popped open her eyes, but Demetrios roared with laughter. He filled the two goblets and handed her one.

"Let's toast to the first day of many to come."

Kaylee once had champagne during a friend of her parents' wedding. She only took a sip and the bubbles tickled her nose enough to make her sneeze. But apparently Demetrios didn't care about a mess in the leather back seat of his limo.

Kaylee lifted her glass and Demetrios clinked his with hers.

She sipped the champagne, surprised that it wasn't the overly bubbly kind. It was actually refreshing.

Kaylee finished the drink, but when Demetrios went to refill her flute, she placed her hand over her glass just like Margo did on the jet. She was not about to risk getting drunk with a stranger—a male stranger.

"Okay," Demetrios said. "You don't have to be afraid me."

Kaylee nodded and set her empty champagne flute in its place on the portable bar.

Demetrios pressed a button and the shade rolled down from the window, just like on the jet.

Kaylee opened her mouth.

Tall buildings interspersed with blue-tiled church domes passed by her window.

"Those are Greek Orthodox churches. We'll go sometime."

He was religious?

Demetrios pointed to the window.

"Look, Joanna. That is the Aegean Sea."

The water was as blue as the church domes.

Athens was a city of fantasy!

"You like?" Demetrios asked.

"Yes, I like!"

"Very good, my little angel. I will show you the whole city—no small feat."

Kaylee smiled for the first time in months, amazed that her face remembered how.

Soon the limo began to serpentine from one Ekalis cobbled road to another until the chauffeur stopped in front of a spiked black iron gate.

"I have Mr. Sakalis and Lady Joanna," the chauffeur said into the intercom.

The gates opened and the limo proceeded down a tree-lined road.

"This is all mine," Demetrios boasted, "and for you to enjoy."

Where the trees ended, deep green manicured shrubs began.

Then came the flower-lined fountains spurting sparkling cascades of water. The statue of a cherub sat in one and a nude woman was in the middle of another one.

The limo continued on the road until it smoothly entered a circular, red-brick drive.

And then she saw it—Demetrios's Mediterranean red tile roof palace that stretched almost to infinity.

"Welcome to your new home...well, one of them," Demetrios proudly announced.

Holy moly!

The chauffeur exited and opened the door on Kaylee's side.

"Miss." He offered his hand and Kaylee took it.

Within the minute, an older woman in a black dress with a white apron scurried to Kaylee's side. Her gray hair was knotted in a bun so tight it stretched away any wrinkles on her unwelcoming face. She stood at attention in her black ballet flats and scrutinized Kaylee with her cold blue eyes. The woman made her think of a much older version of Margo.

"This is Vasiliki. She will show you to your bedroom and will get you whatever you need," Demetrios said. "I'll see you later."

Demetrios took off in another direction and disappeared, leaving her with the cranky old woman and the chauffeur.

Another man, much younger than the sour woman, and also outfitted in a black and white uniform, took out the suitcase that Newell had provided her.

The chauffeur returned to the limo and drove away.

Vasiliki said something in Greek and walked away. Kaylee didn't understand a word she said, but followed her anyway while the man with the suitcase trailed behind them.

The woman and the man directly behind her said nothing more.

They walked in silence up to a set of stone stairs. When they reached the portico, two golden statues of lions flanked her.

The front double doors with gold lion knockers opened, and another man in the same black and white uniform greeted her in Greek. Kaylee only understood her new name, Joanna.

Vasiliki shoved past the greeting butler while Kaylee politely nodded to him and he bowed his head in return. The man with her suitcase dutifully shuffled along behind them.

The front doors slammed shut.

Kaylee shuddered at the familiar sound of entrapment.

Vasiliki stared at her. Kaylee drew a deep, calming breath and smiled back at the woman, who didn't move her lips an inch in response.

Vasiliki turned and continued marching forward while Kaylee hurried to keep up with her. She glanced back at the man with her suitcase and saw he'd fallen behind. He probably knew where he was headed and was also probably relieved to put distance between him and Vasiliki. Kaylee didn't blame him. If only she could as well.

When she saw Demetrios later, she'd respectfully request another attendant. But for the present she was stuck with the sourpuss.

The woman climbed a wide marble staircase to the third level without so much as breathing fast.

She must have a wooden heart.

Kaylee ascended the staircase without a bump in her heartbeat, even with her improving, but still present limp. Her strong ballet muscles carried her with pride.

The man climbed along behind them.

Kaylee continued following Vasiliki down a long hallway until they reached the last room.

The old woman fished a key out of her apron pocket and unlocked the door, standing to the side to let Kaylee pass her into the room.

Kaylee's jaw dropped.

This is her bedroom?

Her brain whirled, trying to take it all in.

The bedroom was easily the size of her whole Miami house. How could this be possible?

The man with her suitcase finally made it to the massive bedroom and set it in a corner.

A larger-than-a-California king bed took center stage in the mega-bedroom, right under a massive skylight. Crystal chandeliers hung over two alcoves flanking the huge bed. One had a provincial-style dressing table, and the other framed two side-by-side dressers that matched the dressing table. Gold-framed paintings hung on every wall, and two doors lay opposite the bed.

Vasiliki opened the first door, revealing a bathroom that could belong to a princess. Kaylee opened the polished glass doors to find a massive shower with dual gold faucets and shower-heads with a marble bench waiting at one end.

A panel with multiple keys was next to the shower entrance, and Kaylee figured it would take her days to figure out all the different settings.

She closed the shower doors carefully and turned to the double-sink marble vanity. She could fit an entire department store makeup counter in the stacked drawers. A mirror spanned the entire length of the vanity.

The belle of the palatial bathroom was a huge oval bathtub that she could swim laps in, equipped with tons of soothing jets.

Kaylee's footsteps echoed while she strode out of the fantasy bathroom. She couldn't wait to see what lay behind door number two.

The butler opened the door.

Holy moly!

Kaylee's mind boggled. She'd need a maps app on her cell to find her way around in that walk-in closet! Shoes of every sort lined one wall, and tiers upon tiers of gold rods on the opposite wall held dresses, skirts, blouses, and pants, and even evening gowns.

She went straight to a dresser on the center wall and began opening drawer after drawer, finding silk bras and matching panties of every color.

Amazingly, all the shoes and attire, right down to lingerie, appeared to fit her perfectly. Newell must have given Demetrios her measurements. The clothes Newell provided paled in comparison to what Demetrios had prepared for her. Just how much did he pay for her and all this wardrobe? It was incalculable to her. But she was here now, and Newell wasn't!

Kaylee maneuvered her way out of the closet to find Vasiliki standing there with the same constipated face. How could anyone be so crabby in a place like this?

Vasiliki muttered something in Greek and left the bedroom that Kaylee could swear must have dropped from heaven.

The man who brought her suitcase remained.

She didn't think she needed to tip him since it was Demetrios's mansion and not a hotel.

"Take rest," he said with a thick Greek accent.

"You speak English?"

"Yes. Ladydee Joanna. I speak some. Welcome."

"Thank you, ummm?"

The man nodded and pointed to his chest. "Peter."

"Peter," Kaylee repeated.

Peter wagged his finger. "Vasiliki, she also understand English. You no let her toy with you, okay?"

Kaylee smiled at Peter, and he grinned back.

"Okay."

"I come back, get you for dinner with Mr. Sakalis."

"Okay."

"Okay," Peter repeated.

He turned and left the bedroom.

Kaylee smiled.

She'd just made her first friend in Greece.

Kaylee flopped back on the huge bed. Then she rolled around on it, giggling. She couldn't fall out of this bed if she tried! She settled on her back in the middle and peered at the piercing blue sky. Not a single cloud floated into the frame. She hated to admit it, but the affluent northern suburb of Ekalis was more picturesque than Miami. It just didn't have her parents in it. But they were no longer in Miami either.

No one back there knew she was alive. She'd move on here with Demetrios, who she could tell was kind and sweet, and already doted on her. He might have paid for her, but thanks to that asshole Newell, both she and Demetrios benefited from the transaction. Regardless of how she got here, she was here to stay, even if she had to change her identity. It was a small price for her to pay.

Kaylee turned her head, noticing the terrace for the first time.

She scooted...and then scooted some more, until she reached the end of the bed and catapulted out of it, then raced to the glass doors beyond the dressing table and flung them open, stepping out onto the gated terrace. She breezed past the lounge chairs and white iron table and chairs and went directly to the railing and gasped at the panoramic view extending from the mountains, to the churches, to the brilliant blue sea in the distance. She'd wake up to this every day! How lucky was she!

She stretched, enjoying the summer breeze. College was a million miles away. But this was a different kind of education.

Kaylee drew in a cleansing breath. The time change from Miami to Greece began to wreak havoc with her body. Since they'd arrived early afternoon local time, she'd take Peter's advice and rest before dinner.

She went back inside, closed the terrace doors, and with a running start, jumped into the massive bed.

Whoo-hoo!

Kaylee curled up with a puffy pillow and closed her eyes.

Joanna stretched out on the sofa. Not only had the sunrise poked her awake, but so did the smell of sizzling bacon.

She used to collect dollars and coins while selling roses on US 1 in Miami. She pilfered the roses from people's gardens while they were at work and then turned a pretty profit. It worked well, until the cops spotted her. But she was too fast for them, and she knew how to hide under the Metrorail shrubs. Plus, she always timed it for when the cops were at the end of their shift. No cop wanted to be stuck staying late to deal with paperwork. They just wanted to get home. She'd sell the roses for about thirty minutes and skedaddle before the next, fresh shift could nab her.

Then she'd trot off to a pancake house, where she rewarded her efforts with two strips of bacon and a short stack. Damn well worth it.

But this morning she didn't have to bust her ass selling roses, because this bacon breakfast was free!

Lou Ann came into the living room.

"Good morning, Kaylee. Breakfast is ready."

Joanna tossed off the blanket and jumped off the couch.

"Yeah, I smelled it!"

"Come and get it."

Joanna hurried into the kitchen, where Lou Ann had set a plateful of bacon and scrambled eggs on her plate, along with a tall glass of ice-cold orange juice.

"This is awesome! Thank you Aunt Lou Ann."

"You're welcome. Eat up before your eggs and bacon get cold."

She wasn't about to tell Lou Ann about the countless times she was grateful to have cold eggs and soggy bacon. Nor was she going to tell her about the slop Margo served her—when she was given anything at all.

Joanna hesitated, her fork the air, while reliving her sordid past.

"Is this breakfast okay? Or maybe you want something else?" Lou Ann asked.

Joanna shook her head. "No, this is wonderful. Thank you."

She dug her fork into her breakfast.

Lou Ann ate her breakfast and sipped her coffee while Joanna scarfed hers down.

"I ordered a bedroom set for you online since you need a bed instead of a couch. They'll deliver it today."

"Thanks. I can't wait to see it!"

She'd never had a bedroom set, much less a real bed.

A bed and a family—this was a dream come true.

42

Harry's cell rang. Still half asleep, he rolled off the couch and hit the floor.

Shit!

He patted the end table and picked up one of his cells.

"Hello. Hello."

Nobody answered.

A phone rang again.

Crap! He picked up the wrong cell.

Harry tossed his personal cell on the carpet and picked up his work one.

"Baxter, here," he said, trying to sound fully awake.

"Yes," he replied. "I'll make the flight."

Harry ended the call.

He'd just left Miami.

Except this time he was flying instead of driving.

Harry got up from the floor and walked the fifteen paces into the kitchen.

He'd brew coffee while he took a shower.

But first he'd make a quick call to Brad.

"Jarett," Brad answered.

"Hey, it's Harry.

"Haven't seen you in, like, forever."

"Yep. I believe we've been put on the same case."

"Just like the good old days."

"See you in Miami."

"See you then."

Harry was toddling toward the shower when his cell rang with Lou

Ann's ring tone.

He massaged his head and then realized he hadn't been briefed yet about the case in Miami, so he couldn't divulge anything.

He returned to his personal cell.

"Good morning," Harry greeted Lou Ann.

"Good morning. I hate to bug you this early."

"Bug away."

"I ordered a same-day bedroom set for Kaylee, and it'll be here this afternoon. I'll offer you dinner if you help us set up the room."

"Hmmm. I'd like to help you and Kaylee, but I can't because I have a case. Just got the call this morning."

"Oh, I see. We'll manage."

"I feel bad."

"Don't. Stay safe. Talk to you whenever. Bye."

Before he could say goodbye, Lou Ann ended the call.

"Shit! First she kicks me. Then she kicks me out. Here we go again," he muttered.

Harry finally got in the shower and made it a quick one.

He tossed underwear an extra pair of socks in his bag, along with his badge since displaying it would attract unwanted attention at the airport and on the plane. Next, he put on his standard suit and tie. That should be good for a couple of days. He'd buy whatever he needed if this case went overtime.

Since the field office gave him two hours' notice for him to catch his flight, he'd drink the coffee in the car while he crawled along with the traffic to the airport.

Harry stuck his gun in the holster hidden under his jacket, shoved his wallet with his credentials in his pants pocket, grabbed his covered coffee, and hightailed out the door.

He'd have to get pet fish another day.

"It looks like it's just us today," Lou Ann said to Kaylee.

"We can do it together," Kaylee assured her.

"Yes, we can."

Lou Ann removed the breakfast dishes, and the front doorbell rang while she was loading the dishwasher.

Isabelle barked.

Lou Ann looked out the living room window to see a delivery truck parked on the side of the road.

"That was fast."

Lou Ann walked out the front door, keeping still-barking Isabelle from bolting out to accost the strangers who invaded her home.

"Shhh, Isabelle. Back inside."

Isabelle retreated while the workers unloaded Kaylee's bedroom furniture piece by piece.

"Where do you want it, lady?"

That's Sheriff to you.

"Follow me."

She hadn't gotten a chance to clean out the den.

Lou Ann pointed to the living room. "Just set it all right here," she told the worker.

"Okay. If that's what you want."

"That's what I want."

"Hey!" one of the workers called to the others. "She wants it in here."

The workers shoved the queen-size mattress and box spring through the front door and pushed through the dresser. Another worker brought in the rest of the bed-frame's pieces.

"Sign here," the worker said.

Lou Ann scribbled her signature on the delivery invoice. The man handed Lou Ann her copy, and then stood there.

"Just a second."

Lou Ann picked up her purse, fished out her wallet, and tipped him with what she had left over from the Naples to Miami to Clearwater trip.

"Thanks, lady. Have a good one."

"Yeah, you too."

Lou Ann turned to Kaylee who was eyeing her new furniture.

"We have a lot of work ahead of us," Lou Ann said.

Kaylee bounced up and down. "Let's get started!"

"Okay. Follow me if you dare."

"I dare!"

Lou Ann and Kaylee tackled the den, now known as Kaylee's bedroom.

Harry had stacked Kaylee's boxes in the corner, so all they needed to move were the black and white plaid chair Harry left behind, a desk, and a bookshelf.

"That chair is cool."

"Harry thought it was too."

Lou Ann hated that chair. Maybe she'd move it into the garage with some of his other stuff that he couldn't fit in his apartment.

"Can I keep it in here?" Kaylee asked.

Lou Ann scanned the den.

"Okay"

They'd make it fit.

"How about the bookshelf and desk too?"

"So we're not moving anything out? Are you sure you want to be crammed in here?"

"Yeah."

Lou Ann shrugged. "Okay."

Less work for her.

Two sandwiches and two iced teas later, Lou Ann and Kaylee stood in the doorway of her new bedroom while admiring their work. They bumped fists.

Kaylee was right. It all fit—even the hideous black and white checked chair…which actually didn't look so bad after all. Whatever made Kaylee happy.

Kaylee took a running leap onto her new bed.

"Whoopee!"

Lou Ann smiled while watching her niece flourish in her new surroundings.

She recognized that the bedroom set was a distraction from Kaylee's deep scars, but a temporary "whoopee" was exactly what Kaylee needed.

Isabelle joined Lou Ann.

"So, you like it?"

Isabelle wagged her tail.

"I'm glad you approve."

"Kaylee, why don't you take a break and go outside to play with Isabelle?"

Kaylee popped up off the bed.

"Sure! Come on, girl."

Kaylee and Isabelle took off toward the sliding kitchen doors to the backyard.

Lou Ann peeked out of Kaylee's bedroom window and watched Kaylee and Isabelle romp in the summer's thick blades of grass. Kaylee tossed Isabelle's favorite orange tennis ball and Isabelle happily retrieved the ball over and over again. Isabelle really took to Kaylee. Weird how she never warmed up to Harry.

Harry. What was his case about? She knew he couldn't tell her—

much like she didn't bring home her days and nights.

Lou Ann set her musings aside and stared at the boxes stacked in the corner.

While Kaylee played with Isabelle, she'd unload the boxes and set the items on the bed for Kaylee to sort through. That way Lou Ann could get rid of the boxes cluttering the room.

Lou Ann pushed Kaylee's first three cardboard boxes aside, but looked more closely at the two remaining boxes—boxes with "Joanna" written on the top of them in the same black marker. Lou Ann examined the boxes again.

Who the heck was Joanna?

She stopped unloading the boxes and lay on the floor.

Lou Ann's brain hurt and her stomach twisted while all the pieces suddenly snapped together—the way she bolted out of the diner, her unfamiliarity of her own home in Miami, the nosy neighbor's suspicious looks, her inability to recognize family photos and milestone events, her muted response to her parents' funerals, and then Jimmy's reaction and his mother's concern about Kaylee.

They did find her in the car with Lyle and Melinda. Lou Ann worked overtime in her head to reassure herself that was true. How could it be otherwise?

But they never identified her at the accident. Why would they?

Lou Ann returned to the window and stared at Kaylee.

She needed an explanation.

Lou Ann went into the kitchen.

Her mouth went dry and her legs grew heavy.

Lou Ann swallowed in spite of her dry mouth and cleared her throat.

She slid the glass door open.

"Kaylee," she called. "Come inside."

Kaylee and Isabelle bounded inside.

Isabelle panted and Kaylees' cheeks were sweaty and pink.

"Yes, Aunt Lou Ann. What's up?"

"Who's Joanna?"

The color from Kaylee's face drained and Isabelle cocked her head.

Lou Ann waited for the answer she didn't want to hear.

Kaylee dropped to her knees in the soft green grass and lowered her head. She pressed her hands to her forehead.

"Me," she cried.

Lou Ann collapsed to the floor and sobbed.

* * *

Joanna stood, sniffling, and swiped the hot tears from her cheeks.

"Are you going to arrest me?"

Lou Ann took a cleansing breath, and stood to face her.

"No," Lou Ann said.

"Why not?"

"Because…"

"I'll get my things and leave."

She'd betrayed Lou Ann and Harry, except he wasn't here to take the blow. But she just stabbed the woman who had taken her in as her long-lost niece in the heart.

Joanna lowered her head and eased past Lou Ann…who should slap her because she deserved that and more.

She looked into Lou Ann's strained eyes, and she offered her cheek.

"Go ahead."

Lou Ann raised her hand and Joanna breathed in and out while she braced for the hit. But there was no wind-up and no stinging smack. Instead, Lou Ann grabbed her hand and pulled her into the kitchen and embraced her. Their bodies rocked while they cried together.

Lou Ann kissed the top of Joanna's head.

"Don't leave. Come sit. You promise to tell me everything?"

Joanna sniffled. "Yes."

"Let's go."

Joanna sat a careful distance away from Lou Ann on the living room sofa.

"I don't know where to start."

"Start anywhere."

"I have no idea how I ended up in that car wreck. When I came to in the hospital in Naples, that's what they told me. They kept calling me Kaylee and telling me my parents were dead. I honestly didn't remember any of that happening, so this part is true. I blocked out every horrid thing that happened to me. But little by little, I began to remember what I desperately wanted to forget. By then Mr. Jarett had visited me, and then he got a hold of you. I was told you were my aunt, and that's where I would end up…with you."

Lou Ann kept shaking her head.

"I know this is really confusing for you, because it was for me."

"Go on."

"While I was in the hospital, I had flashes of me being shoved into a trunk, naked. I remember I couldn't move and could barely breathe.

My skin was on fire, and my sweaty hair clung to my face."

"The car stopped, but I couldn't keep my eyes open. I remember Newell carrying me, and he must have dumped me in the car to get rid of me. They thought I was dead, and at some point I think I really was."

"Hey, hold on. Back up. Who are Newell and 'they'?"

Joanna's legs began to shake, and then she couldn't stop her whole body from trembling. Suddenly she couldn't breathe.

"We need to get you to the emergency room."

Joanna waved her hands in the air and blurted, "No!"

"Okay. Okay."

Lou Ann hurried into the kitchen and returned with a paper bag, handing it to Joanna.

"Breathe slowly in and out into this bag."

Joanna followed Lou Ann's instructions.

It worked. Her breathing eased and her trembling faded.

Finally Joanna was breathing well enough to set down the paper bag.

"Better?"

"Yes."

Joanna stuttered a breath and continued.

"Dr. Newell, Otto, and Margo kept me locked in a room. They told me I was sick, so I needed to stay there. But it wasn't a hospital room, and I wasn't sick, but sick things happened to me there."

"Where's there?"

"Some house in or near Miami. I know that because the Dr. Newell talked about how he had to go to his office. And then I remembered that I felt really bad when I got my periods so I read in a newspaper ad that he treated teenage girls and women with female issues. So I called the number, and they said I qualified for free service, so I went to him. I've never been to that kind of doctor, so when he stuck his hand up in me for what seemed like an eternity, I was uncomfortable, but I thought it was normal. Then he came back in the room, shoved some clamp thing into me and some kind of rod. He told me my periods would be better now."

"Was there a nurse in the room?"

Joanna shook her head. "He did ask me where I lived, and at the time I was staying in a bunch of different shelters He said he pitied me, and told me how brave and beautiful I was. That made me feel good. Then he left the room again, and when he returned, he said he'd walk me outside to make sure I was okay. He took me out a back door, and then the next thing I remember I was waking up in a strange room with a locked door. He told me I'd passed out and he had to take me to the hospital, which turned out to be nothing more than that prison room. I trusted him."

"None of this was your fault."

Now Lou Ann couldn't catch her breath, and her face felt red hot.

"What is the name of this so-called gynecologist?"

"Dr…Gerald…Gerald Newell."

"You mentioned two others, Otto and Margo. Who are they?"

"Otto is a short, fat, bald, piece of cigar-smoking shit. I don't know how he and Dr. Newell got to know each other, but Otto slept in that house of horrors. He and his foul friends raped me nightly, sometimes up to ten times with repeaters. Even Dr. Newell took a turn, but that was early on. He did it a few more times and then he quit."

"Margo fed me and showered me in a filthy, disgusting bathroom. At first she pretended to be a nurse, but that didn't last. Then she was just Margo. Sometimes she could be nice, but then she'd turn into a bitch and slap me. She'd tie me up when Newell told her to do it. Margo couldn't stand Otto and vice versa. I could hear them screaming at each other. Newell was away a lot. He rarely slept at the house. I don't know where he lived."

Joanna took a deep breath. It was all coming out now.

"They sold me to a Greek billionaire. But that didn't happen, because 'I died." Probably got his money back."

Lou Ann's forehead wrinkled.

She doesn't believe me. If I were her, I wouldn't believe me either.

Lou Ann's brain circled tighter with Joanna's every sentence. Her panic attack was real. Joanna was a broken girl who finally busted into a million pieces, and pieces of Lou Ann were scattered among them.

By all rights she should despise Joanna. She'd dragged not only her into believing she was Kaylee, but she made a fool of Harry, too.

Harry. How would she explain all this to him?

She'd place the burden on Joanna to explain herself to Harry. He'd made every excuse for her and so had she.

Joanna sat with her head down, penitent.

Try as she might, Lou Ann couldn't hate the girl she'd come to love.

But now she needed to extract details from Joanna—details that could rip her soul apart.

Lou Ann pressed her fingers into the sofa.

"What about Kaylee?"

Lou Ann's heart clamped in her chest. She asked about the niece she didn't know.

"I've never seen her except in photos. It's eerie how much we look alike."

"You don't remember seeing her at the accident? In the car?"

"Honest, no. I searched in my head for the something that made sense, but always came back with nothing. I took the opportunity to be her to save myself from them. I panicked every day in the hospital that they'd find out I was alive, and then they'd kill me before I could betray them. Then *I* did a horrible thing. I waited for Kaylee to return to out me, but that didn't happen. As the days passed, I was too deep in the lie. And strangely, I became Kaylee. I wanted to be her. I wanted a family I only dreamed of having, and you and Harry were it."

A wave of nausea burned in the back of Lou Ann's throat.

What if those monsters who tortured Joanna had grabbed Kaylee? She said they looked alike. Oh, my God!

Lou Ann yanked Joanna up off the sofa.

"You're coming with me."

Joanna's eyes went big.

"Where?"

"To Miami, to find the monsters who did this to you!"

And to find out what really happened to her niece…the real Kaylee.

43

Brad pulled up to ground transportation at Miami International Airport and Harry hopped inside his car.

"Long time no see," Brad joked. "Fortunately, traffic was light and I made it from Naples just in time to pick you up."

Harry tossed his black bag into the back seat.

"I got a black bag just like that," Brad teased.

"And I bet it contains the same documents that are in mine."

Brad shrugged. "Who would've guessed?"

"I take it that we're off to the scene?"

"Is there somewhere else you need to be?"

"Nope. I guess the fish can wait."

"Fish?

"My future new pets."

"Hmmm. A little lonely?"

"Nah," Harry joked.

He'd call Lou Ann back the first chance he got to check how she and Kaylee were getting along.

"I hate going into the woods without bug spray," Harry said.

"Me too."

Brad pulled off the Florida turnpike and proceeded to the targeted isolated wooded area.

"Weird to have a wooded area a stone's throw from a vast metropolitan area, and not far from the airport," Harry said.

"Yeah, there was a death investigation here not long ago."

Brad continued down a gravel road, into the woods, and followed the flashing strobes.

"Looks like we've arrived at the party," Harry said.

Brad parked behind the line of vehicles and outside the yellow crime scene tape.

"Remind me why we're here," Brad said.

"I've been wondering the same, but the Miami office requested available agents to assist, and that would be me. They must be spread thin with assignments elsewhere. So let's head out and assist," Harry said.

Harry flashed this FBI badge and Brad, his sheriff's credentials, and then they and ducked under the crime scene tape.

"Hey, we've got company!"

"How you doing, Ricky?" Harry asked.

Harry had worked with Ricky in the past.

"Good," Ricky answered.

"This is Captain Brad Jarett, who's been tailing a sex trafficking ring with ties from Naples to Miami."

"Glad to see you both."

"Likewise," Brad said.

"So what we got?" Harry asked.

"Some guy with a bullet wound to the back of his head hit a tree. But the weirdest thing is his eyeball, or lack thereof."

Harry and Brad followed Ricky to the crumpled Nissan Altima.

"Perfect waste of a good car," Harry said.

"Yeah, I had one of those and loved it," Ricky said. "Miami-Dade PD ran the plate. It's registered to Dr. Gerald Newell."

"Strange. Reported stolen?" Harry asked.

"Negative," Ricky replied. "Not yet anyway."

Harry, Brad, and Ricky approached the vehicle where detectives milled about the scene.

"ME is waiting on us," Ricky said.

"Let's take a quick look before that happens," Harry said.

Harry and Brad peeked in the car.

"I see what you mean about the eyeball," Harry said.

Brad winced. "Ehh! His eyeball is just hanging there!"

A detective held up a bagged wallet. "Meet Otto Pearson, aka Otto P, apparently connected with a local sex trafficking ring that's gone international. There's a gun in the front seat.

"Let's take a closer look," Harry said.

"The car's in neutral and wouldn't be able to gather enough momentum. He didn't drive into the tree to off himself, not with that eyeball, and with that gunshot wound to his head," Harry added.

"Agree," Brad said.

Ricky and the detectives affirmatively nodded.

"Someone or someones wanted this asshole gone in a hurry, and they didn't bother to disguise the deed very well," Harry said. "And if you're in a hurry to leave the country then why bother?" Harry turned to Brad "Let's go visit Dr. Gerald Newell."

After Harry slid into Brad's car, his cell rang with Lou Ann's ring tone.

Shit! He'd planned to call her back, but she beat him to it.

"Hey, what's up? How are things going?" Harry asked.

"We're on the way to Miami."

"What?"

"I've information about a Dr. Newell, a man named Otto, and a woman named Margo, all involved in kidnapping and trafficking young girls."

"Whoa! Wait a minute. How do you know about this?"

"I can't explain right now. It's too complicated."

"I just so happen to have a dead Otto here in a car registered to Dr. Gerald Newell."

Kaylee gasped in the background.

"Is that Kaylee?"

"Yes. I need to talk to you about that too."

"I have some urgent things to do here, so I'll text you the address of the Miami Field Office. I'll meet you and Kaylee there. If you get there before me, wait. I'll give them a heads-up that you're coming, and please text or call when you get there."

"I'll do that."

Lou Ann ended the call.

What the hell?

"What's happened?" Brad asked.

"You, me, and Lou Ann are all chasing the same suspects, including dead Otto over there."

"You're fucking kidding me?!"

"I can't wrap my head around what she knows and how she got the information. We'll know more when she and Kaylee arrive."

Kaylee. What did she mean she had something to discuss with me about Kaylee?

While his mind spun on a cockeyed axis, someone knocked on Harry's car window. He looked up and found a detective mouthing something while holding up a key ring.

Harry rolled down the window.

"Found these keys stashed deep in the glovebox of the car. One's labeled 'cabin 'and the other, 'house'."

"Thanks, man."

"No problem. I've got enough paperwork to keep me busy for the next week. Share what you find?"

"Absolutely."

"By the way, we passed a cabin over in that direction." The detective pointed northwest. "Might be or might not be the one."

"We'll check it out and let you know."

"Here's my card with my contact info," the detective said.

Harry took the card and gave the detective his in return.

The detective waved to them and headed back to his car.

"Let's check this out," Harry said to Brad.

Brad nodded. "Onward."

Harry and Brad turned down a dirt path.

"There!" Harry pointed to the isolated cabin.

Brad slowed while maneuvering around tree roots, nature's speed bumps.

"Look at those holes in that brush. Someone's been here," Harry said.

"Or someone's here," Brad added.

Brad stopped the car on the ten-yard line and Harry and Brad readied their guns.

"Ready?" Brad asked.

"Always."

"I'll take the front and you go around the back," Harry said.

"Got it. Let's move."

Harry stared at the dried bloody trail that started at the base of the three rickety wood stairs and ended in a wide pool at the cabin's door, where bloody fingerprints scraped down it. He drew his gun. Someone was inside, hurt or dead.

Brad rounded to the front.

Harry silently pointed to the blood.

Brad nodded, signaling "go ahead and rescue."

A scurried tap-tap-tap fired across the cabin's roof.

Harry and Brad trained their guns to the roof.

Shit! They were being jumped!

Black claws and bared pointy teeth leapt off the roof and barreled straight at them.

"Raccoon!"

Brad fired a round and the raccoon dropped to the ground.

Brad shot another round at the injured, and probably rabid animal, ending the critter's misery.

"They know we're here now," Harry said.

Brad had to do it. He just beat him to it.

But they had an element of surprise remaining before anyone inside could escape.

Harry shot at the door's lock and kicked open the door while keeping his gun ready to fire.

The battered door groaned on its rusted hinges.

A bloodstained carpet lay rolled up against a sofa with stained foam spewing out of it as if someone had taken a knife to it in a berserk rage.

"What the hell?" Harry whispered to Brad.

Then they zoomed in on the same small, dried, bloody, footprints tracking all over the cabin.

Harry mouthed, "Woman."

Brad nodded.

Where is this woman? Where is she hiding? And who is she hiding from?

Brad pointed to the hallway and headed in that direction while Harry crept into the kitchen to find half-open drawers and wide-open cabinets, but no victim or perpetrator.

He slowly opened the cabinets under the sink. Nothing but old rusty pipes and rings of dried-up water stains stared back at him.

Harry edged along the abbreviated hallway and stepped through the open bathroom door.

The toilet seat cover had the same woman's bloody footprints, and Band-Aid strips littered the cracked linoleum floor. Harry opened the blood-smudged medicine cabinet door and took out an alcohol bottle with a yellowed label. The cap was loose.

He listened for Brad's footsteps, but Brad wasn't moving.

Shit!

Harry steadied his gun and, with nerves twitching deep in his gut, he proceeded down the hall.

He found Brad staring at the lone bedroom and moved to stand next to him.

"Fuck!"

Brad and Harry lowered their guns.

"The woman and whoever has her…or her body…are long gone," Harry said.

"Yeah, we're done here. Let's give our detective a call. But we were within in our rights to enter."

"We were, but we arrived too late. No one to rescue here. Time to look elsewhere."

Harry and Brad slumped in the car while they briefed the arriving detective and his crew.

Harry's cell phone pinged.

Lou Ann texted him that she and Kaylee had arrived.

"Lou Ann and Kaylee are here. Another reason to head to the Field Office."

"Come on, *Joanna*."

Lou Ann coaxed her out of the car.

She fought to call her Joanna instead of Kaylee. Now she'd have to prod Harry to do the same.

Joanna froze in the front seat.

"You can do it. You have to. Time's running out while you sit there. We have to nail Newell and the sleaze he runs with and find Kaylee. Don't you want justice for what they've done to you?"

Joanna unbuckled her seat belt, opened the passenger door, and got out.

Lou Ann closed her eyes and sighed.

And when she finally collected herself, she opened her eyes and held out her hand to Joanna, who accepted it.

"What happens now?" Joanna asked.

"You tell Harry everything you told me."

Joanna frowned deep, and her once-bright blue eyes turned a flat slate.

"He'll hate me."

"No. He'll be shocked as I was, but he won't hate you. He reserves his rage for those who deserve it like Newell and his filthy associates. Come on, Joanna, let's get inside out of the heat. Harry will be here soon."

They left the sizzling Miami heat and entered into the blessed cold FBI Field Office.

Lou Ann and Joanna approached the reception desk.

"We're here to meet with Agent Baxter. I believe he called earlier."

"Yes, he did," the man behind the desk replied." He stood. "I'll show you to a conference room where you can wait."

He led them to a white-walled room with a faux wood table and enough black swivel chairs to accommodate twelve. They'd only need three. Four, if Brad came.

Lou Ann and Joanna sat next to each other. Harry and maybe Brad would surely claim the seats opposite them.

The man returned with two glasses and a pitcher of water with ice cubes floating across the top. He filled their glasses.

"Sorry, this is all we have."

"No problem. This is great. Thanks."

"Agent Baxter and Captain Jarett will be here in about five minutes."

Lou Ann waved to him in acknowledgement.

She looked at Joanna.

"Take a deep breath and drink. Remember, this isn't an interrogation."

"It feels like one."

Lou Ann rested her hand on Joanna's shoulder, and then they drank their iced water.

The truth to be laid out before Harry was as stark and cold as the water.

Brad and Harry pulled into the Field Office parking lot and Brad parked next to Lou Ann's silver Honda Civic.

"Ready to go in and delve into how and what Lou Ann knows?" Brad asked.

Harry raised his hand. "Give me a second."

"Okay."

He lowered it. "All right. Let's hit it."

He and Brad entered the air-conditioned office.

Brad swiped his brow. "Hallelujah!"

"They're in the conference room," the reception worker said.

"Thanks," Harry said.

The man stood.

"I'll bring in your glasses. Pitcher of water is on the table."

"That'll feel good going down," Harry said. "It's sweltering out there. Even in the woods."

Harry and Brad entered the conference room.

Lou Ann turned around. "Hey."

"Hey," he said softly.

Kaylee didn't turn around to greet him.

Lou Ann did say they needed to talk about her.

Apparently, Kaylee backslid. They'd get her into therapy immediately. Too much had happened too soon.

Harry sat across from Kaylee and tried to meet her downcast eyes.

"Hey! What's up kiddo?"

Lou Ann had no choice but to drag her back to Miami. She wouldn't have left her there alone.

"The only one missing is Isabelle," Harry said.

"I left her with the neighbors."

"Kaylee, why don't you go with Brad and get some ice cream?"

She shouldn't be subjected to the graphic details they were about to discuss.

"I'll bring you up to speed later," Harry said to Brad.

Brad stood, but Kaylee didn't.

"Sit down, Brad. You need to hear this too."

"Do I have to tell him too?"

"Yes. He's part of the case, and he's your friend."

Harry removed his jacket and mopped his forehead with back of his hand.

Whatever this was, it was huge.

Harry stared at Lou Ann.

"What's all this about? You, me and Kaylee can talk later, but right now, I can't have her in the room."

"She's not going anywhere, and you need her in the room. Tell him, Joanna."

Harry tightened his face. "Joanna?"

"Yes, Joanna." Lou Ann confirmed.

Harry opened his mouth.

Lou Ann raised her hand.

"Uh-uh. Don't say anything. Trust me, you're going to want to listen to her. But don't interrupt her."

She lowered her hand and aimed a go-ahead gesture to Joanna.

"Tell them," Lou Ann said.

"My name is Joanna Stemple."

Brad knocked over his water.

The iced water dripped off the table and Harry let it pour onto his lap.

Nothing could distract him from what his brain stumbled to process.

Lou Ann stood. "I'll get paper towels."

"Sit down," he called to Lou Ann. "No one's leaving this room." He looked straight at the girl who'd upended his world for the second time.

"Go on, *Joanna,*" Harry prodded.

Joanna sat straight up, but Lou Ann caught her before she could bolt out of the room.

If he wasn't so invested—so taken with her—then he would have bolted out the room too.

Brad sat speechless.

"Joanna, keep going. You can't retreat now." Lou Ann looked at Harry and Brad, and then back at Joanna.

"Everyone stop!" Lou Ann cried out.

Brad removed a handkerchief from the inside of his jacket and handed it to Harry who dabbed at his lap and then the spill.

"All right," Lou Ann sounded calmer.

She nodded to Joanna. "Time's a-wastin'."

Joanna folded her hands across her chest and blurted out what had happened to her, only taking two quick breaths in between the most horrid details.

The impossible became the possible.

Joanna stood and ran to Harry and squatted next to him.

"I'm so sorry I hurt you, Harry. I swear I didn't mean to," she blubbered.

His heart felt like it was splitting in two—one for the Kaylee he thought he knew, and one for Joanna, the one he really knew.

Harry lowered his hand to Joanna's head and gently patted it.

"Lou Ann and I promised that you'd never have anything bad ever happen to you again. I'm keeping my end of the bargain, and so is Lou Ann."

Joanna and Harry stood. And in a conference room often filled with gory stories, he hugged the girl who needed it most.

Harry had requested a cleanup of the conference room while they all stepped out for a quick late lunch, and when they returned, Joanna scanned the room. The physical mess was gone, but the emotional mess still hovered.

They returned to their same seats.

Joanna set her folded hands on the conference table and leaned over to steady them.

Lou Ann, Harry, and Brad prepped her over lunch about the next step.

Harry took a photo out of the envelope in front of him.

"This is a gory photo. I want you to look past that and tell me if you recognize this person."

Joanna nodded.

He slid Joanna the photo.

"Damn! What happened to Otto? Whatever happened, he deserved it."

"Bingo! Last name?" he asked Joanna.

Joanna shook her head. "Other than Dr. Newell, I don't know Otto's or Margo's last names."

Harry pushed the next photo across the table. "Do you recognize this person?"

His cropped face stared back at her. She mashed her finger in his eye.

"Newell!" she hissed.

Joanna shoved the photo back to Harry.

"Next," Joanna said.

"That's it for now."

"Where's Margo?"

"We don't have any information about her," Harry said.

"I told you about her!"

"I know. But without a last name or other identifying factors, it may take longer. You've been a great help to us and to the many girls out there just like you."

"I'll do anything to help."

"I know you will. So for now, we're going to set you and Lou Ann up in a hotel."

"You'll be safe with me," Lou Ann said

"That's true. She could shoot the dick off of a gnat," Harry said.

Lou Ann patted her sidearm. "It's true. I've done it a couple of times."

"All you have to do is to go through this two more times, since Otto's out of the running."

44

"Gerald Newell, MD. That's the building," Harry said.

Brad pulled the car around the Kendall office and to the back of it. "Freestanding, nice location, plenty of parking."

Harry nodded. "Nothing too good for a professional pimp. "Shall we venture inside?"

He read the sign on the back door.

Staff Only Entrance

"Guess we walk around to the front."

Harry and Brad walked through the front door.

He scanned the empty patient chairs.

"Strange time of day to not have any patients."

"Better for us," Brad said.

"And for them."

A frosted glass partition slid open.

A young woman with a clean-cut bob peered at them from behind the reception area.

"May I…help you, gentlemen?"

Yeah. The suit and ties caught her attention. That, and their badges.

"Good afternoon. May we speak with Dr. Newell please?"

"Um…just one second."

The receptionist closed the glass doors.

A side door to the waiting room opened. But instead of Newell walking through it, a woman in a peach scrub top and white pants greeted them. She stood guard over the back of the office with her feet firmly planted beneath her shoulders. Her name tag read, Janice Dugan, RN.

"May I help you gentleman?"

"We'd like to speak with Dr. Newell," Harry said.

"He's not here."

"Do you know when he'll return?"

"No. Dr. Newell is away on an urgent family matter."

I bet.

Harry assessed the guarded yet quizzical look on the nurse's face. She narrowed her brown eyes at him and then over at Brad. As an agent, Harry committed people's behaviors and physical characteristics to memory. He looked past Janice's loose, free-styling bun. But she was no pushover.

Janice turned and walked away and then moved to shut the door on them.

She was covering for him.

"Wait a minute," Harry called to her. "I need your help."

Janice pushed the door halfway open.

"I'm looking for a missing girl who may have been a patient here. She may be in danger. Can you help us?"

Janice widened the door.

"Oh, my! Come on back. Let me see if I can help."

"We appreciate it ma'am," Brad said.

"I wish Dr. Newell were here."

So do we.

Harry and Brad followed Janice along a corridor and past a line of exam rooms.

She pointed to an open office.

"That's Dr. N's office."

Harry meandered inside Newell's office.

No diplomas., no certificates, not even any pictures hung from the off-white walls. His black office chair squarely abutted an empty desk. No pencils. No pens. No desk top computer. No laptop. A printer sat in ghostly silence and the trash can was empty. Didn't look like the doctor planned to return any time soon.

Harry caught up with Brad and Janice.

"This is my office," Janice said, gesturing Harry and Brad inside. "Please, have a seat."

Harry and Brad sat in the two armchairs in front of Janice's desk.

Harry looked at the computer on Janice's desk.

"Can you look up Kaylee Jasinski? That's spelled K-A-Y-L-E-E and J-A-S-I-N-S-K-I."

Janice tapped her keyboard.

"Nope."

"How about Joanna Stemple?"

"Stemple? That sounds familiar. Here she is, Joanna. I remember her. Lived in a shelter. Dr. N. took care of a lot of young ladies who had no insurance. He offered his services for free. He was that kind of doctor."

Harry and Brad looked at each other.

He was that kind of doctor for sure.

Harry craned his neck to look at Janice's computer screen.

"May I see her photo, please?"

Janice hesitated.

"I shouldn't, but if that's the girl missing, I'll print her profile. This is confidential, right?"

"Absolutely."

The printer spat out Joanna's information.

"She was last seen here four months ago," Janice said while she handed the profile to Harry.

"Can you print me a list of all the girls Dr. Newell was kind enough to see for free?"

"During the past six months to a year," Brad added. "Some of them may have known Joanna. We never reveal our source."

"Bravo," he mouthed to Brad while Janice got busy at her computer.

The printer spat out three sheets of names.

"Wow. We really did help a lot of girls."

Harry nearly choked on the word "help."

"Thank you. You've been very helpful," Harry said.

"I hope you find her."

We already did. But thanks to you, we'll find the rest, including Kaylee.

Harry stashed the printout in his briefcase.

Harry, Brad, and Janice stood.

"Are you and the receptionist the only employees?"

"Other than a cleaning crew, yes." Janice continued," I've been with Dr. N for fifteen years. Wonderful, selfless man, and a terrific boss."

Gag!

"No other nurses or assistants? You do it all by yourself?" Harry asked.

"Yes. We've managed. But we're short-staffed since Cassidy left."

"Cassidy?" Brad asked.

"Cassidy was Dr. N's medical assistant. She left us about a month ago. She and Dr. N. unfortunately didn't hit it off. But he was kind enough to get her a position with a family practitioner. I hear she really likes it there. Not everyone's cut out to work in a gynecologist's office."

"Yeah, I could see that," Harry said. "Who did you say Cassidy works for?"

"John Fisher. His office is in that tall building next door. At least she didn't have to travel far."

"Thank you again."

"Let me show you out," Janice offered.

"No, that's okay. But we're parked in the back lot. Can we go out this back door?"

"Sure."

Janice swiped her ID badge through the keypad and then the door buzzed open.

Harry and Brad exited and waved to Janice.

Janice waved back and retreated into the office.

The staff entrance clicked shut.

Harry shuddered. It was the first of many locks Joanna heard.

Since John Fisher's office was in the building next door to Newell's office, Harry and Brad decided to pay a visit to Cassidy, Newell's ex-medical assistant. Perhaps she didn't think Newell was such a saint.

Harry and Brad entered the building's lobby.

Dr. Fisher's office was listed on the fifth floor.

They stepped into the elevator with two women and a man.

Their eyeballs went directly to Harry's and Brad's badges and then snapped forward.

They made friends everywhere they went!

The women got off on the third floor. The man followed them to the fifth floor. He exited first and scurried away.

Harry turned to Brad.

"Did you wear deodorant today?" he joked.

"Took a shower, too. It must be you."

Harry sniffed his armpits. "Yeah, probably."

They walked down a hall until they reached Dr. Fisher's office and walked inside.

Unlike at Newell's office, patients filled every chair.

A young nurse wearing blue scrubs and her blonde hair in a neat ponytail walked out a side door and called to a patient. A woman stood and responded.

"Right this way," the nurse said, while glancing at Harry and Brad.

As earlier, they spoke with the receptionist, who did not hide behind frosted glass.

The patients watched the pair. Some peeked over the top of their magazines.

"Is Cassidy here?" Harry asked.

"Yes, just a minute."

Before the receptionist could summon her, the young nurse peered past her.

"I'm Cassidy."

"I apologize for the impromptu visit. I see that you're very busy. Can we speak with you briefly?"

"Um...yeah."

Cassidy came out the same door and gestured them inside.

Patients whispered and magazines crinkled.

She led them to an empty exam room and shut the door.

"Janice from Dr. Newell's office told us we could find you here," Harry said.

Cassidy didn't flinch. It was if she expected them to show up one day. Today was that day.

"Janice, huh? Newell's pet and enabler."

"I take it you didn't leave on good terms."

"The bastard covered his ass by getting me a position. Actually, he did me a favor, because I like it here. And Dr. Fisher is normal."

"In your view, Dr. Newell is not?" Brad asked.

"Nope."

She couldn't have been more spontaneous or more clear.

"Can you tell me what happened at Dr. Newell's office?" Harry asked.

"I was hired as a medical assistant, so my role was to accompany and help Dr. Newell during his patient exams. I soon became uncomfortable about witnessing him being inappropriate with women. He took a long time performing intimate exams, and he unnecessarily exposed and humiliated women. He was rough. I brought this up to Janice, who said the women were just nervous to have a GYN exam, and basically blew me off. I suspect Newell overheard the conversation and terminated me. He did find me a position, but that was to cover his ass."

"Did you file a complaint with the medical board?"

Cassidy lowered her head. "I'd be accused of being a disgruntled ex-employee. Janice would take his side. Plus, he frightens me with his beady eyes and his smugness. This is terrible to say, but I need this job. He could ruin my life."

"I understand."

"Are you going to arrest him?"

Harry sighed. "Unfortunately, I can't divulge our intentions."

"Okay, I understand. I have to live every day with knowing I didn't turn him in."

"You can rest assured that you've been very helpful."

"Will I have to testify?"

"I can't divulge that either," Harry said. Then he massaged his chin. "Do you remember a patient named Joanna Stemple? She was one of his waiver patients, last seen four months ago."

Cassidy shook her head. "I wasn't working there four months ago. But I do remember that on my last day, Newell spent an inordinate amount of time with a very provocative young woman. Her name was Sophia. They got off on each other. I'm so glad I'm out of there."

Sophia. Harry would look her up on the list Janice gave him. She might know where Newell was hiding.

Cassidy led Harry and Brad back to the lobby, and they left with as much fanfare as when they arrived.

"Let's head on over to the hotel. I want to check on Lou Ann and Kaylee...I mean Joanna," Harry said the minute he sat in Brad's car.

"You know Lou Ann can take care of herself, and Joanna, too."

Harry exhaled. "Yeah. I admit that it's Joanna I need to see. She hasn't a clue about how long she was held captive. I can tell her the exact date she was in Newell's office, and the same day he whisked her away. We already know the date of the accident when she was discovered. We owe her closure."

"We do."

Her bat ears told Lou Ann two different footsteps approached their room.

She knew there were ways to skirt security.

Lou Ann clutched her sidearm.

"Get down behind the bed," she whispered to Joanna, whose eyes looked spooked.

But she did as Lou Ann instructed.

Lou Ann wasn't about to take any chances with Joanna's safety, since Joanna would be target number one if they discovered she was alive.

The mattress would shield her if any shit went down.

Their breaths slid under the door.

Then came Harry's code knock.

Shit.

Lou Ann released her grip on her sidearm and opened the door to find Harry and Brad standing there.

She was right. There were two different footsteps. She still had the right stuff!

Lou Ann beckoned them inside and shut the door.

Joanna popped up from behind the bed.

Harry nodded to Lou Ann. "Bravo."

"What did you find out?" Lou Ann prodded.

"Some stuff," Harry answered.

"Stuff, huh? Enlightened me on your *stuff*.

"We paid a visit to Newell's office."

Joanna gasped.

"It's okay," Harry reassured her. "He wasn't there. His nurse said he's out of town. Not sure I believe her, given we walked in with our badges."

"Wherever he is, you're protected," Lou Ann said to Joanna.

"She's absolutely right," Harry added.

"Have a seat, Joanna. I need to talk to you," Harry said.

He shot Lou Ann a quick one-eyed wink.

Yeah, he found some stuff.

The four sat at the room's table and chairs.

Harry cleared his throat.

He always did that before he spilled out gut-wrenching details, like the kind that split open her heart. But this wasn't about him and her. This was about Joanna, whose heart was already in danger of splitting wide open.

Joanna fidgeted while waiting for Harry's information.

"I found the date you were in Newell's office. It was four months ago."

Lou Ann heard Joanna swallow and rested her hand on hers.

There was no way to protect her from the pain coming.

Joanna gripped the side of the table. She had to face the merciless monster who still inhabited her head. Harry just gave her the weapon to stab him out!

Joanna drew a calming breath and loosened her grip on the edge of the table. This was the first step toward evicting the bastard.

"Go on."

Harry raked his fingers through his hair. He didn't want to hurt Joanna, but he had to.

She had to go back to go forward. There were no detours. She wouldn't have taken them anyway.

"So the accident was two weeks ago. That makes four months and two weeks."

The timeline she struggled to grasp wasn't a struggle anymore. Her gory existence finally had a beginning and an end.

Joanna shut her eyes and rewound the nightmare. Flashes of Newell, Margo, and Otto and his cronies danced wildly in her head, taunting her.

"Get out!" she screamed.

Someone was shaking her.

"Joanna! Joanna!"

She forced her eyes open to find Lou Ann, Harry, and Brad hovering over her.

"I'm sorry," she apologized.

"No. We're sorry," they all said.

45

Harry beckoned for Lou Ann to join him in the bathroom. It was the only secluded place in the room, and at this point no one wanted to leave…yet.

Lou Ann closed the bathroom door.

Harry paced, debating the wrenching scenario.

"What do you want to talk about?" Lou Ann asked.

She crinkled her forehead and narrowed her eyes the way she used to when he came up with some cockamamie idea. But this wasn't an idea. This was a serious proposal that could easily go sideways, and he needed Lou Ann's trusted opinion.

"Spit it out, Harry. I can't stand it when you keep pacing. Joanna knows we're in here talking about her. And who takes a briefcase into a bathroom?"

Harry opened the briefcase and took out a key ring heavy with different-shaped keys. "Brad and I were already at a cabin in the woods where we discovered Otto, a cabin that Newell owns. It was rank, and more important, there was a lot of dried blood. Detectives and a crime scene unit are processing it right now." Harry jangled the keys. "These are to a house Newell also owns not far from the cabin. They were found in the glovebox in a car with Otto's body."

"I know what you're about to say," Lou Ann said. "I want to go with you and Brad. Newell maybe hiding there. But I can't leave Joanna alone."

"I'm not asking you to. I want Joanna to come with us. She can give us the information we need." Harry hesitated. "Plus, she needs to face what happened there, or it will continue to haunt her."

Harry stared at Lou Ann, waiting for an answer.

From the look on her "You're out of your mind" face, he'd have to go it alone.

"All right," she said.

Harry squinted at her.

"Yes. You heard right."

Damn. How does she do that?

Harry and Brad pulled off the gravel road and onto the paved driveway of the single-story white house with black shutters. It looked like any other Florida home, except for its out of the way location. Newell definitely didn't want any neighbors. But anyone who would happen to drive by it would think the same thing and continue driving.

It wasn't as deep in the woods as the cabin and one could see the turnpike in the distance. It it had all the earmarks of someone who wanted to be alone. But Harry suspected he wasn't. Joanna said Otto lived there, but Newell and Margo didn't. He'd look up other properties Newell owned, but for now this one awaited their inspection.

There was no car in the driveway except theirs, but he couldn't vouch for what was in the back of the house.

Tall reeds of grass peppered the uncut lawn and swayed in the periodic breeze.

Harry called Lou Ann's cell.

"Stay with an easy out."

"I hear you. See anything?"

"So far quiet."

"You know what to do with Joanna should things escalate?"

Of course she did. It was more for his edification.

"Yes," she said.

The minute Harry stepped out the car, his eyes went straight to a camera mounted on the white, paint-cracked front wood fascia.

He and Brad halted.

The camera stood silent. He doubted it was operational.

"I'll take the back this time," Harry said.

While Brad stood guard at the front door, Harry rounded the house to block the exit in case Newell decided to bolt out the back, if he was even inside. It suddenly occurred to him that the house could be a decoy or truly abandoned because by now they would've rooted him out. But it wasn't safe to assume that yet. He'd finish his rounds and join Brad, who hadn't yelled or fired his gun.

Weeds hidden in the tall grass yanked at his ankles.

He kicked his feet loose, only to have a brown lizard skitter across his shoe.

"Ehh!" Although he lived in Florida, he hated those critters.

He kicked the lizard aside and continued his run.

Harry maneuvered around stale tire tracks at the back of the house.

Whoever was there was long gone.

He joined Brad who looked disappointed.

Too bad Newell hadn't made an appearance. Harry would have enjoyed the takedown for Joanna and for the sake of so many others Newell betrayed in the worst possible way.

After Harry gave Lou Ann the "all clear," she pulled up in the drive and parked next to Brad's vehicle.

Joanna's eyes were trained dead front.

Harry walked over to Joanna's window and waited until she was ready to roll it down.

"He's not here," Harry said to Joanna.

"I didn't think he would be," she replied.

"Do you want to go back to the hotel?" Lou Ann asked.

"It wouldn't be a sign of weakness," Harry added.

"No, I want to go in."

Joanna opened the car door and took a deep breath. She didn't recognize the strange house. She was only here because Harry told her Newell owned it. It was too ordinary to be the house where she'd miraculously survived. After being rendered unconscious she woke up in a windowless room where her life dwindled every day. She'd never seen the outside. She was carried out in the same condition. She couldn't vouch that this was the place.

She stood between Lou Ann and Brad feet away from the front door while Harry rummaged in his car. He finally returned with a big, fat keyring.

Joanna straightened, batting away the cold shudder threatening to creep up her spine. Why would a house have so many keys? There were way too many on that ring.

"Ready?" Harry asked her.

"Yes."

Harry walked ahead of Joanna, Lou Ann, and Brad.

They stopped at the front door.

Joanna stared at the four locks on a front door as black as the shutters.

Her heartbeat thudded loud in her ears and her knees slackened.

Click-click-click-click echoed in her brain.

Joanna backed away.

Harry turned with the keyring in his hand.

"Joanna," he called.

"We'll go back to the hotel," Lou Ann said.

Joanna halted. This was it. This was the house of horror. If she walked away, Newell would win again. But she could fight back this time.

Joanna strode forward to the front door.

"Open it," she said to Harry.

One by one, Harry clicked open the four locks—the very locks Newell, Otto, and Margo engaged so they could come and go freely while she languished in the prison especially designed for her and how many countless others.

Joanna pressed her arms to her sides so no one could hold her hand. She had to do this alone.

The stench smacked her in the face.

Joanna clapped her hand over her mouth and nose, and Lou Ann, Harry, and Brad winced at the smell of rotted meat.

"I don't know what that is," Joanna said behind her hand.

Her prison room had a stale odor, and even when Margo opened her door, all Joanna smelled was Otto's cigars, but she hadn't smelled anything this rancid.

Lou Ann grabbed Joanna by the shoulders and pushed her away, but not soon enough for her to see the bloodstained green couch and the blood-spattered wall.

Joanna shook her head.

"Were you ever in this room?" Lou Ann asked.

"No. I wasn't allowed. I only saw it when I got a chance to peek through the door when Newell or Margo entered—mostly Margo when she brought me food or scraps, because I wasn't allowed in the kitchen either."

Joanna froze in front of the closed door of her former cell.

She pointed at it. "I nearly died in there."

"But you didn't," Lou Ann said softly.

"They don't know that. I'm dead to them."

"We'll keep them thinking that—except for Otto of course," Harry said.

"You can open the door now," Joanna said.

Harry put one of the keys in the door, but it opened, unlocked.

"The door was never left unlocked," Joanna said.

Otherwise she would've tried to escape.

That door groaned on its hinges while Harry pushed it open.

Joanna walked into the room, still having no idea how she once got there and how she left.

She widened her eyes.

It was the same room, with same nasty floor and stained ceiling tiles, but pieces of the bed's headboard were strewn about the room, and the ropes jumbled in with the headboard pieces, lay in contrast to the yellowed sheets tucked tight against the mattress. Margo used the same folds when she made the bed.

Someone had rebelled! And Otto was shot!

The house must have been abandoned pretty quickly.

Where the hell were Newell and Margo?

Lou Ann, Harry, and Brad stood speechless in the face of the room's depravity.

"Something bad went down here after I left. Whoever was here got out."

"Kaylee?" Lou Ann whispered.

Bam! It all clicked in Joanna's head.

They could've been twins.

Could Newell have switched a dead girl for a live one?

Joanna bolted out of the room and out the front door, where she leaned over the jungle of bushes and vomited.

Lou Ann, Harry, and Brad rushed out the door. Lou Ann held Joanna's hair back while she threw up breakfast and lunch.

Joanna wiped her mouth with the back of her hand.

"They're in Greece."

"Greece?" they all echoed.

"I was sold to someone they called 'The Greek'."

"You don't know his name?" Lou Ann asked, her voice urgent.

Joanna shook her head. "No. Honest."

Lou Ann pressed her palm to her forehead.

"I'm sorry," she apologized.

"Where in Greece?!" Harry pressed.

"I don't know," Joanna wailed.

46

Gerald stomped around the huge living room, one of twenty rooms in the mansion Demetrios prepared for their arrival.

He picked up a pillow from one of the many on the sofas and threw it across room, grazing the marble statue of a nude woman with her arms resting across her breasts.

"I should never have trusted that bitch Kaylee and that fat-assed Greek. They both played me!"

"Stop it!" Margo yelled.

He raced toward her with his teeth gritted so hard that the grind crackled like sandpaper in his ears.

No one ever ordered him to stop anything! Not even Margo!

On his way to spar with Margo, he passed Sophia, who huddled deep in a blue silk-upholstered chair.

Sophia knew her place. Although Margo was his associate, she was a woman—a woman who had coddled Kaylee, who by all rights should be right here with him instead of with Demetrios.

He and Demetrios had agreed upon a meeting regarding Kaylee's transfer to him. There was more bargaining to be done. Now that meeting was on hold, and Demetrios supposedly wired him money before they finished the final contract. He deserved more! He could've had more! He was the one who'd picked her up. Groomed her! And this is the disrespect he got?

Gerald raised his curled fingers to Margo's neck, but her glare stopped him from throttling her.

He fisted his hands and lowered them, and then turned and walked away.

God! He was so pissed!

He snapped his fingers at Sophia.

"Let's go!"

Sophia rounded her shoulders.

"Where?" she asked.

"Where we can be alone."

Shit! He'd frightened her. It was all fucking Demetrios's fault.

Gerald softened his tone.

"I apologize to you and Margo. My actions were uncalled for. I'm stressed, and I'm tired. Jet lag always makes me irritable."

He took Sophia's hand and kissed it.

"Come. Make me calm the way you always do."

On his way to the bedroom with Sophia, he paused in front of Margo and offered his hand.

"No hard feelings?" he asked her.

Margo shot him a smile and shook his hand.

"None," she said.

"Good."

He tickled Sophia's rounded bottom and she giggled.

Her ass was like succulent peaches.

Mmmm. And man, was he hungry!

Kaylee startled awake to find Vasiliki hovering over her with a silver sequined gown hanging off her arm.

Shit! Vasiliki didn't knock. At least she didn't hear it. But even though she'd only known Vasiliki for less than a day, she doubted the old woman ever announced herself.

Vasiliki placed the gown at the bottom of the bed.

"For deener," she said and left the room.

Dinner? Where at? Demetrios's mansion had more rooms than a five-star hotel.

Kaylee went into the marble bathroom to freshen up.

Margo's surprisingly light touch on the jet lingered.

Kaylee opened drawer after drawer to discover high end makeup that her friends would have given anything to have.

She applied a pressed powder perk-up, an extra coat of mascara, and a swipe of blush.

Demetrios fawned over her about her natural look. She'd keep it that way, and it made her more comfortable in an uncomfortable atmosphere where she was still finding her way—like where dinner was being served.

Kaylee slipped into the silver gown.

Oh my! Are these diamond-encrusted straps?!

Kaylee turned her back toward the mirror, reached over her shoulder, and zipped up the gown before someone knocked on the door.

What did Vasiliki want now?

Kaylee opened the door to find Peter.

"I'm here to escort you, Lady Joanna, to dinner with Mr. Sakalis," Peter said, while offering his hand.

Kaylee took his hand.

"Thank you."

"You are most welcome."

Kaylee reminded herself to respond to the name Joanna, whoever she was…if she was.

Peter walked her down three flights of a wide, marble spiral staircase that led into a dining room that could seat twenty-five. It was the kind of massive room that would return an echo.

Demetrios stood at the far end of the table.

How many people were showing up for this dinner?

"Good evening, Joanna. Aren't you a vision of loveliness?"

Kaylee scanned the long dining room table, confused about where to sit. But then Demetrios beckoned her to sit next to him.

He pulled out her chair and eased her closer to the table. Then he assumed his position at the head of the table.

No one else filled the empty dining room chairs.

Tonight's dinner was just for the two of them.

Servers dashed in and out.

Kaylee never tasted lamb, but the combination of spiced potatoes and olives surrounding the oven-roasted lamb lingered juicy in her mouth with every careful bite. Already a converted Greek, she could eat this meal over and over again!

A server topped off her wine glass. That she was seventeen didn't matter and neither Margo, nor her parents were here to object. Forget Margo, but out of respect to her parents, she'd sip it slowly and politely refuse to imbibe any more than a glassful.

However, she freely enjoyed the baklava for dessert.

She'd been dropped into paradise!

Sophia's giggles turned into groans and winces. She'd more than welcomed a pre-dinner romp with Gerald, but he hadn't pounded into her like this before. A little roughness was fine. She'd easily get into that, especially with Gerald, but this time she had cringed her toes into the mattress not out of erotic pleasure, but of pain.

Thankfully, Gerald finished with her quick and sweaty.

He vaulted out of their grand bed.

"I'm going to freshen up before dinner. You should do the same."

Sophia pulled the covers to her chin. She'd had plenty of fun, meaningless sex. But she'd hoped more from Gerald. She'd fallen for him, and she swore he felt the same.

But then he changed.

While Gerald washed away her scent, Sophia's mind swirled until it halted.

Initially distracted with Gerald's tantrum earlier, she'd breezed past what he said to Margo about Joanna and Demetrios. But why did he call her Kaylee?

The acid from her roiling stomach shot to the back of her throat. Sophia sat up in the bed and hunched to quell the burn.

The girl wasn't his niece. And Joanna might not be her real name! Gerald just sold the girl to the Greek tycoon!

Sophia clasped her hand over her mouth.

What was her fate? Was she part of Gerald's business inventory?

This wasn't the vacation he'd promised her. She wasn't going home. She was his hostage in a strange country. And he had her passport!

Maria was right.

She should never have left with him.

Gerald returned, naked and wet from his shower.

"Your turn," he said.

Kaylee dabbed the last bit of baklava off her lips with a white linen napkin.

Demetrios stood. "Let's go upstairs to your room. I have a surprise waiting for you there."

Ooh! Another surprise!

Demetrios escorted Kaylee up the stairs and toward her room.

They passed Peter and Vasiliki on their way to the bedroom. Peter lowered his head, while Vasiki rushed in the opposite direction—strange for Peter, but not for Vasiliki.

Once Kaylee and Demetrios arrived at her bedroom, he paused.

"I'll wait outside," he said.

How cryptic, yet fun!

Kaylee opened the door to find a deep blue, sapphire-studded bikini along with a sheer chiffon cover-up laid out on the bed. Shiny gold-colored sandals with what looked like tiny diamonds were placed perfectly parallel at the side of the bed.

Dang! The sapphires and diamonds were no doubt real. This bikini was too astronomically expensive to get wet.

Demetrios gently knocked on the door.

"Are you ready?" he called.

"Uhh. Just a minute."

"Okay."

Kaylee slipped into the luxe bikini and sandals and tossed on the cover-up. She couldn't wait to see the pool. It was probably Olympic size. Demetrios did everything big!

She opened the door and Demetrios whistled.

Kaylee anticipated that they'd reverse roles while she waited for him to dive into his swim trunks. She'd also find out where he slept. His bedroom must be at least three times the size of hers. After all, it was his mansion. But her quarters were beyond her wildest imagination.

Demetrios didn't stop along the way.

He led her through a maze of rooms and down yet another staircase before they arrived at the pool.

Cabanas surrounded the crystal blue water. The rectangular pool stretched from what seemed like a mile.

"Go ahead and enjoy a swim," he said.

"Aren't you coming in?"

"No, my dear. I'm going to relax here and enjoy watching you."

"Okay," Kaylee lied.

She adjusted her bikini.

She could easily get lost in that pool and out of his direct sight. But then she'd have been uncomfortable even if Jimmy watched her swim.

Perhaps Demetrios was uncomfortable in swim trunks. She couldn't see why, because he had a firm body.

Maybe if he saw how much fun she was having, he'd join her. A solitary swim was too weird.

Kaylee ran and jumped into the cool water. She swam to the surface and tossed back her wet hair. How awesome! The sapphire-studded bikini lit up beneath the water.

Demetrios reclined on a lounger with a cigar in his mouth.

Ooh! Kaylee shuddered in the water. Otto sucking on a stogie ripped through her brain. But Otto was a classless oaf. Demetrios smoked a cigar like a tycoon. Plus his must be of the highest quality because it didn't stink. She'd never smoked anything, but his cigar smoke smelled like burned vanilla. Not so bad. Kaylee doubted she could succeed in having Demetrios abandon tobacco, but he might listen. But that would be for another day.

Kaylee playfully splashed in Demetrios's direction. He returned her fun gesture with a teasing finger wag.

"Come on in! The water is wonderful!" she called to him.

"Another time, perhaps. But you go on. I like that you're enjoying yourself."

Still weird.

Kaylee ducked under water and swam until she had to come up for air.

She could see Demetrios at a distance, but she swore his eyes were laser-focused on her.

She had enough and breast-stroked back to him, and hoisted herself out of the pool. Kaylee shook the water off her body and hair.

Demetrios clapped. "Brava!" he called.

He rose from his recliner, grabbed a fluffy white towel, and wrapped it around her shoulders.

"Tired?" he asked.

"A little," Kaylee answered.

Between the jet lag, the filling dinner, and the swim, she was ready to call it a night.

Demetrios patted the lounger next to where he was sitting.

"Come, relax and enjoy the fresh evening air."

Kaylee wrapped the towel around her breasts and lay back on the lounger.

"See? Isn't this nice?"

Silver stars flickered in the night sky.

"Yes, it is," Kaylee said.

Demetrios snapped his fingers and a server arrived.

Where did he come from?

The pool was humongous. How would the server hear a snap? All she could figure was that the server remained behind the scenes, watching and waiting for a hand gesture.

"Bring us two glasses and a bottle of ouzo," Demetrios ordered the man.

"Yes, Mr. Sakalis."

The server scurried away.

"What is that?" Kaylee asked.

"Ouzo? It's a special liquor."

She shook her head. "I'll have sparkling water because I don't drink alcohol."

"You had wine at dinner."

"A glass, and that's more than enough for me tonight."

"Oh, you have to try this. You will like it. After all, you're now officially Greek. So you drink ouzo."

Kaylee shook her head.

"What, no? I give you the tiniest bit. A fly would drink more," he joked.

"Okay," Kaylee relented.

She could barely keep her eyes open. If she tasted the ouzo maybe he'd leave her be. Then she'd turn in. She could probably find her way back to her bedroom. Perhaps she'd bump into Peter on her way, and maybe Vasiliki, who she didn't trust. She wouldn't put it past the woman to lead her astray. Since Demetrios was in a good mood, Kaylee decided it would be the best time to bring up Vasiliki.

"Demetrios?"

"Yes? I like how you say my name."

Kaylee grinned. "I need to talk to you about Vasiliki. She doesn't like me."

"Oh, that's her way. She's like that to everyone, except me of course. I've known her and her family for years. She is a loyal, efficient, and a hard worker. Don't take it personally. You'll get used to her."

She had no other choice.

Demetrios filled her shot glass and then his.

"Cheers," he said.

Kaylee clinked her glass on his and tossed back the ouzo.

She popped her eyes open. "Wow! It tastes sort of like licorice."

"Good, huh?"

He poured her another shot glass.

Kaylee finished it in one swallow.

"Again?" Demetrios asked.

"Yeah, one more."

"You're too Greek," he teased her.

"Maybe."

Kaylee blinked to focus on Demetrios and the cabana, fighting the buzz.

"No more. I've had plenty. Goodnight, Demetrios."

She stood and swayed.

"I'll walk you to your room."

"Okay."

She'd never find her way now.

Kaylee leaned on Demetrios while he escorted her to her bedroom.

"Here you are."

"Thanks."

Kaylee found the doorknob and entered her room.

"I'll see you tomorrow," she told him and then shut the door.

Kaylee leaned on the door until the room stabilized. She shouldn't have had that third drink, but it tasted sweet and went down smoothly. She'd know better next time.

She walked slowly and a bit unsteadily into the bathroom, kicked off her sandals, and peeled off her bikini.

Kaylee stepped into the shower and alternated between the two shower heads because she needed a double dose to clear her head.

She cut the water at both sides of the shower and toweled off. Thankfully, the room quit spinning, and other than a mild headache, she was fine.

She donned the silk nightgown Vasiliki must have set out while she was in the shower. That woman must have snuck in like a ninja—an old, Greek ninja.

Kaylee slipped into the silk nightgown. She was more of a pajama girl, but that was in the past. She was now "Lady Joanna" and ladies wore nightgowns.

She plopped into bed and slid across the silk sheets. Good thing the bed was humongous, otherwise she would've slid right off.

Kaylee pulled the covers to her chin and her eyelids flickered.

Hmmm. What a day.

Kaylee rolled to her side. She thought she heard the door open, but the room lay silent. It must have been her imagination.

Too much of that ouzo.

She yawned, rolled to the other side, and closed her eyes.

The mattress shifted.

She bolted upright and screamed.

A hand clasped over her mouth.

Her heart beat wildly.

"Shhh. It's only me."

Demetrios!

He took his hand away from her mouth.

She skittered away from him.

"What are you doing here?!"

"I'm here to visit you."

"I...uh...no."

She couldn't believe this was about to happen to her. She had convinced herself that this would be different...that he was a nice man who needed a companion, not a concubine. Her eyes watered. She was wrong.

Demetrios hugged Kaylee and then stroked her hair.

"Don't be afraid."

She couldn't believe what was about to happen to her. She'd never had sex. Not even with Jimmy. She always thought Jimmy would be her first. Now Demetrios would claim her virginity.

"I can't. I can't. I've never done it. Please," Kaylee pleaded with him.

"Relax," he whispered. "I just want to talk with you."

Talk with me?

She tensed her legs together as a shield.

"It's all right," he reassured her.

Nothing would reassure her tonight. It was bound to happen. After all, he paid for her. What did she expect? She'd lie still and let it just happen.

Kaylee squeezed her eyes closed.

May it be quick.

But nothing happened.

Then he leaned over, kissed her on the head like she was a good little girl, and got up from her bed.

"Have a peaceful night in your new home, Joanna. I know you must be so tired. Goodnight, my angel. I'll see you in the morning."

Before she could say a word, Demetrios crept away in the dark.

The second the door closed, Kaylee pulled the covers over her head and huddled there, curled up and confused. And then she shuddered. It could've been Newell or Otto, who defiled her. She gagged just thinking about those monsters.

Kaylee lay there and listened to her breathing while safe beneath the cocoon of her covers. So far Demetrios had been nothing but patient and kind. But he paid for her and eventually he would completely claim her. Would he be as kind then? She hoped so.

He did say he'd see her in the morning.

And then Kaylee grinned, wondering what would be served at breakfast.

She closed her eyes.

Surely Vasiliki would wake her at the crack of dawn.

47

Lou Ann tossed her and Joanna's last-minute belongings in the small luggage she brought to Miami since they'd left Clearwater in a rush.

Her head buzzed. She couldn't call Joanna Kaylee anymore.

But her heart ached for Joanna after seeing the horror of that room where she was inhumanly imprisoned.

What if Kaylee had experienced the same depravity as Joanna in that horrifying room?

Acid burned the back of her throat. Joanna, although damaged for the rest of her days, was at least safe and alive, but her brain couldn't process whether Kaylee was even alive, and if she was, perhaps she wished she was dead.

Joanna sat hunched and silent on the side of the bed.

Lou Ann left Joanna to her own private thoughts. There wasn't anything she could say to make it all go away. Can't put a Band-Aid on a brain.

Shit! Isabelle. She had to call her neighbor and explain the prolonged dilemma of an unknown return date. All Isabelle would understand was that she wasn't there.

Lou Ann called her neighbor, grateful that she was happy to care for Isabelle, who although she moped initially, perked up while playing with the new puppy.

"Is Isabelle okay?" Joanna asked.

Joanna and Isabelle had struck an immediate bond.

"She's all right. She's playing with a puppy."

"I miss her," Joanna said. "She loved me despite who I am."

"Consider yourself chosen. Harry's still on her shit list."

In a momentary escape from darkness, Joanna giggled.

Lou Ann's off-the-cuff remark briefly lightened her own spirits too.

But then they sank to a subterranean low.

She'd have to shuttle Joanna back to Clearwater and then somehow catch up with Harry and Brad.

It was unsafe for Joanna to travel, plus, she didn't have a passport or the identification needed to obtain an emergency one.

Joanna was her responsibility.

"Let's get going. I'm going to drop you off in Clearwater. You can stay put in the house with Isabelle."

Joanna narrowed her eyes and shook her head. "No," she shot back. "I'm going with you, Harry, and Brad to Greece."

Lou Ann held up her hand.

"You can't travel abroad with us. You have no passport and no ID to get one."

"You're wrong."

Lou Ann widened her eyes. "Wrong?"

"Yes, that's what I said. Newell took a picture of me and filed for a passport for me to travel to Greece. He used someone else's birth certificate. He must have known how to change it, or knew someone who could. He's probably done that before. He told me everything was all set, except Otto and his filthy friends infected me. I heard Newell yelling at Otto before I passed out. For days I was so weak that I was sure I imagined all this. But I scraped my brain and it came to me like a horror movie you'd turn away from because it was too gory to watch. So I have a passport, but I don't know where it is."

Joanna approached to inches from Lou Ann's face.

"Besides, you need me. I'm the only one who can identify Margo. And where Margo is, so is Newell."

Lou Ann paused. Joanna provided a compelling argument.

"Let me think."

"Don't take too long," Joanna warned. "They move fast, especially if they find out someone's on to them."

"I'll talk to Harry."

But before she called him, her cell rang.

It was Harry.

"So Joanna has a passport somewhere," Harry said into his cell while Brad maneuvered the car through peak Miami traffic.

Harry was sure Lou Ann had the same nauseated inklings that Kaylee might have Joanna's passport, and that she might or might not be in Greece—if she was still alive. But he couldn't stab Lou Ann in her heart by saying it. Tragically, it was his working theory. There were more Joannas and Kaylees out there, and he swore he'd free as many as he could, and bring terrible closure to the families of those he'd discover too late.

He paused when Lou Ann asked for his opinion about whether Joanna should accompany them—if they could get an emergency passport. He would attest that issuing the emergency passport was on a life and death basis.

He agreed that since they didn't know Margo's last name, and that any search for the exact woman would prove fruitless, Joanna was the only one who could ID her.

He'd come to genuinely like Joanna, even when he thought she was Kaylee. That counted for a lot in his book. It was a risk that both he and Lou Ann had to take. They'd keep her out of harm's way the best they could, but it wasn't a guarantee, because there were no guarantees in this business.

"I need to do one more thing first, and Brad and I will meet you and Joanna at the Miami consulate."

"All right. I'll see you there."

Harry had entered Sophia Pavlis's address from Janice's list of girls Newell had seen pro-bono—the kind man that he was. He'd made a mental note that Cassidy recalled how Newell and Sophia had a mutual and inappropriate sexual interest in each other.

Uhhh.

As disgusting as it was, Sophia might know Newell's whereabouts. It was worth the stop.

They rounded past the airport and onward to the street address.

Brad parked across the street among dented cars and big-wheeled trucks from the less-than-modest row of single-story apartments.

"This is the place," Brad said.

They got out of the car and walked across the street after two cars had passed by.

Harry and Brad approached the front door and knocked on it since there wasn't a doorbell to announce themselves. No answer. Harry knocked again, a bit harder. Still no one came to the door. Maybe Sophia had spied them from the peephole and refused to answer. Or maybe she was in there with Newell.

"Can I help you?" a woman called from the sidewalk.

"We're looking for Sophia Pavlis," Harry answered.

The young woman assessed them.

"Why?" she asked.

"We'd like to speak with her about a person she might know."

"Well, she's not home."

"Do you have any idea when she'll be back?" Brad asked.

"Humph. I have no idea. She took off on a vacation to Greece with that doctor she barely knows. I told her it wasn't a good idea, but she didn't listen. But then I loaned her my luggage because she was going to go anyway."

"You say she left with a doctor three days ago?" Harry asked to confirm the details that could bust this whole thing open.

"Yeah."

"Did Sophia say where in Greece they were headed?" Harry asked.

"Athens. And she didn't say when she'd be back." The young woman eyed Harry. "You're looking for that sleazebag doctor, aren't you?"

"Not at liberty to say," Harry said. "Have you met him?"

"Liberty-biberty. Hell, no. But Sophia talked about how handsome and rich he is. It's just not right."

Harry gave the young woman his card.

"FBI, huh? Wow. He must be in deep shit."

"Give us a call when Sophia returns, or if you see a man hanging around."

"Will do, Special Agent Harold Boxer," she said after reading the card.

"By the way, I'm Maria Lopez, Sophia's friend and neighbor. I hope she's okay."

"We do too, Ms. Lopez."

Lou Ann and Joanna sat in the consulate office across from the clerk.

"What did you say the name was?" he asked.

"Joanna Stemple," Joanna replied. That's J-O-A-N-N A, Stemple, S-T-E-M-P-L-E.

Joanna leaned forward and Lou Ann noticed Joanna's knees were bouncing.

Please, no. The clerk would surely notice. Lou Ann decided she'd take Joanna to Clearwater. This wasn't going to work. And where was Harry? He'd have more pull.

The clerk eyed Joanna. "You say you lost your passport?"

"That's right," Joanna said.

"Hmmm."

The clerk pecked across his computer's keyboard. He halted and looked at Joanna and then at his computer screen, and then back at Joanna. His eyes roved to Lou Ann.

"And you are?" he asked Lou Ann.

"I am Joanna's guardian."

"Yes, I see she's seventeen years of age."

He sees what?

Joanna's knees bounced faster.

While the clerk was busy entering data into his computer, Lou Ann reached over and steadied Joanna's nervous knees with her palm.

They were about to be detained.

Now Lou Ann's knees began to quiver.

"I found it," the clerk announced.

Lou Ann's and Joanna's knees took a break.

And Lou Ann could peel her heart off the back of her throat.

"You could pick it up next week, or we can mail it."

A knock came at the door and Harry and Brad entered.

Backup had arrived!

"Sorry to interrupt, but I'm Special Agent Harold Baxter and this is Captain Brad Jarret. We have an urgent case in Greece, and we need Joanna in order to capture perpetrators involved in nefarious dealings. We request the passport on a life-and-death basis. It's urgent we leave immediately, before the perpetrators kill whoever they're holding captive and escape. Please," Harry added.

The clerk studied Harry and Brad.

Then he proceeded to type across his keyboard.

"Approved."

A silent collective sigh ricocheted among them.

Step one—to Greece. Step two—find Kaylee.

48

Kaylee's head throbbed. She shouldn't of had that wine and that ouzo.

Vasiliki entered without knocking.

Ugh. What else is new?

"You go out today," Vasiliki curtly said.

She tossed a dress and undergarments on the bed.

"You get dressed now."

Kaylee rolled over in the bed with her back to Vasiliki.

"No!"

"You get dressed now," Vasiliki repeated.

Kaylee ignored her.

"What? You sick?"

"Yes, I'm sick. Now go away. My head hurts."

But instead of leaving the bedroom, Vasiliki went into the bathroom and returned to the foot of the bed.

"Here. Aspirin. Get dressed. Mr. Sakalis wait."

Kaylee dodged under the covers, waiting to be alone.

The door shut.

Good. She was rid of the old crone.

Kaylee pulled off the covers, got out of bed, and showered off last night's mistake. She dressed and tossed down the aspirin.

Tiny red roses dotted the white sundress that was more her style than all the silk and sequins of yesterday.

At least she now had a concept of day and night.

Then a knock came at her door.

"Lady Joanna?" Peter called.

"Come in."

Peter entered, but left the door respectfully ajar.

"I am here to escort you to the main foyer where Mr. Sakalis wait for you. He want to take you out. He quite taken with you."

"Go out?"

Peter nodded. "Yes."

"But I don't speak any Greek. I don't even understand one word. I don't fit in here."

That was a half-truth. After her captivity, she feared being outdoors. She'd rather stay secure in Demetrios's mansion.

Peter must have sensed her hesitancy.

"Mr. Sakalis, he want to make better for you."

"I know."

It was a simple response. She didn't want to unearth her past to Peter.

"Oh, don't say that. You adapt. You can learn. I can teach you. Mr. Sakalis too. Even Vasiliki. You be happy here."

Kaylee shook her head. "Perhaps."

"It is your choice, Lady Joanna."

It wasn't her choice to come to Greece. But like Peter advised, she'd have to adapt. Besides, it was her chance to leave her ugly past behind.

Peter escorted her to the main foyer, where Demetrios waited for her and then left them.

"You look absolutely ravishing!"

A little over the top, but she'd take it.

"Thank you."

"I have a surprise for you. Actually, two."

Demetrios knelt at her feet and strapped a diamond bracelet around her right ankle.

The light from the diamonds bounced off the crystal chandelier above.

Demetrios rose and offered his hand.

"Come on an adventure with me.

She placed her hand in his.

His grip was warm and inviting and not the yank and tug of Newell's slimy hand/

"Now we're off to a day in Athens."

He led her out into early summer sunshine and to the gleaming black limo where the chauffeur stood at the door.

Kaylee looked up and basked in the sunshine that she craved.

"Good morning Mr. Sakalis and Lady Joanna," the chauffeur said in perfect English. It was a different chauffeur than the one who picked them up at the airport.

"Good morning, Marco."

"Traffic is light today," Marco said.

"Good. That gives us more time for enjoyment."

"Where to, Mr. Sakalis?" Marco asked.

"Athens."

"Very good, sir. It's a beautiful day."

Demetrios looked at Kaylee. "Yes, I agree."

The minute Kaylee slid into the back of the limo, the aroma of coffee seduced her nose.

She popped open her eyes. Unbelievable! A back seat breakfast bar, complete with white china coffee cups, cheese-filled pastries on matching plates, and a bowl of fresh fruit lay in front of her and Demetrios for the taking. This limo was far larger than the other one, and she'd thought that one was huge.

"This is amazing!"

"This way we can have breakfast on our way."

"On our way where?"

Demetrios raised his finger and grinned.

The chauffeur came on the speaker.

"Where in Athens, Mr. Sakalis?"

"Syntagma Square."

"Good choice."

Kaylee arched her brows. Demetrios and his surprises!

"It's a popular square with tourists and locals. Locals have protests there, but it's quiet today. We'll have nice walk through there, and then I'll take you to a large shopping area where we'll stop for lunch."

"I don't know if I'll be hungry after this breakfast."

"Trust me. You'll work up an appetite. And you will sleep well tonight."

The pendulum of her opinion of Demetrios swung high in the direction of "good guy".

Kaylee sipped her creamy coffee and bit into the cheese pastry. Her headache was gone, and her stomach happily accepted the breakfast. They'd grow from there. Maybe he'd toss the money back to Newell. She could dream.

"Stop brooding. Let's go out and have some fun," Sophia said. "It'll help you get your mind off things. It's not good to be cooped up."

"I agree with Sophia," Margo said

Gerald grumbled. "All right."

Sophia jumped up and down. "Yay!"

She could be such a fucking child. But then again, he loved fucking that child.

Demetrios was blowing him off. Now he had to blow off some steam before his *delayed* meeting with the rich bastard.

Demetrios's limousine had brought them to the mini-mansion, but had since disappeared. He refused to beg for another one, so he summoned a cab.

"Let's go, ladies!" Gerald summoned.

They're the ones who wanted to go, and here he was the only one ready.

"Cab's here!" he yelled.

Sophia and Margo hurried down the staircase.

Sophia's "just above the knee" skirt breezed around her shapely legs. Her off-the-shoulder white blouse emphasized her curves without screaming sex. She'd traded those shorty shorts for class. Those shorty shorts still got him hard, but now in private.

Margo looked in vogue in her stylish white pants and blouse, as only Margo could carry off.

Yeah, he could walk with those two.

The cabbie muttered in Greek, and when neither of them responded, he switched to his struggling English.

"Where?" he asked.

"Some square," Gerald replied.

Margo quickly answered, "Syntagma Square."

"Okay."

Marco announced that they'd arrived at Syntagma Square. The ride was so smooth that not a drop of her coffee spilled, and the cheese pastry and fruit sat satisfied in her stomach. Kaylee had no idea that the famous square was right outside her window.

Demetrios took her hand.

"Let's have a good time."

Kaylee grinned.

"Okay."

Marco opened the door and Kaylee stepped out, and then Demetrios.

The cloudless summer sky was bluer then blue, and the warm sun kissed her shoulders.

Buses, trolleys, and cabs glutted the busy street.

"It's always like this in the summer tourist season."

"I'm a tourist," Kaylee said.

"No, darling. You're with me. That disqualifies you as a tourist."

Kaylee giggled and pressed her shoulder against Demetrios's arm.

She could have screamed for help, or summoned a police officer and told them she was being held captive, but she didn't. They wouldn't believe that Mr. Demetrios Sakalis would do such a thing. And what shocked her most was that she didn't want help. At least not today.

Demetrios held her hand and walked her to the fountain in the Square.

He paused with her.

"I notice you limp a bit. Do you hurt?"

"No, it doesn't hurt anymore."

"What happened?"

Newell couldn't hurt her anymore, but she wouldn't betray him in case she ended up back in his iron grip.

"Clumsy me. I stepped on a twig and damaged it. But Dr. Newell took it out."

"He did a lousy job! I'll have my personal physician examine your foot. We'll walk slower."

"Thank you, but I'm all right." Kaylee squeezed Demetrios's hand. "Really."

"We'll take our time anyway. I want you to savor every minute."

Kaylee tilted her head up to Demetrios.

"I will."

His smile caused the corners of his eyes to crinkle. She'd made him happy, and for the first time in what seemed forever, she'd found a chunk of happiness too.

Kaylee stared at the water gushing from the fountain.

"Make a wish," Demetrios whispered in her ear.

Kaylee closed her eyes and wished only to be loved as she once was.

She opened her eyes and tugged at Demetrios's hand.

"Show me more."

"It would be my honor. Come. I take you to see the tomb of the unknown soldier. I was in the military."

Kaylee pushed closer to Demetrios so she wouldn't lose him among the crowd gathered to watch the most elaborately uniformed soldiers she'd ever seen."

"Those are called Evzones. They are ceremonial. See how they high-step while guarding the tomb?"

Kaylee watched the guards in their pleated khaki kilts with matching tights and buttoned, puff-sleeved overcoats clip-clop in time in their black pom-pom clogs. Scarlet caps with black tassels sat straight on their heads, and their faces beneath remained stoic and disengaged from the throng of onlookers.

"They're so serious," Kaylee whispered to Demetrios.

"That is their calling."

Kaylee stroked Demetrios's bulky biceps, no longer frightened touching them. Now they were the ones that protected her.

She examined the nude sculpture of the fallen soldier with his shield in hand and a helmet on his head. She and Demetrios passed several nude statues on the way to the tomb. The Greeks revered the body. Demetrios took pride in his body, as he should, while she'd spent years covering hers. Newell had humiliated her and forced her to hate her body more. But Demetrios freed her to accept hers.

After watching the guards, Kaylee and Demetrios turned to leave.

Kaylee's heart fluttered as fast as a frightened bird.

Newell, his girlfriend, and Margo congregated feet behind them.

Demetrios narrowed his eyes.

He saw them too.

What a hellish coincidence! She couldn't shake them. It looked like she never would.

Newell glared at them.

Shit! Here he comes!

Demetrios moved in front of Kaylee, protectively blocking her from Newell.

"Demetrios!" Newell called. "What a pleasant coincidence."

Newell peeked around Demetrios to spy on Kaylee, but Demetrios flexed his muscles thwarting Newell's skeevy attempt.

"Good afternoon, Dr. Newell."

Sophia and Margo remained in the background.

"Yes, good afternoon. Since we're both taking the day off, perhaps we can meet tomorrow," Newell said.

"Yes, perhaps," Demetrios responded, purposely vague. "I'll call you to set something up."

"Tomorrow?" Newell pressed.

"I'll review my schedule."

Go, Demetrios!

Demetrios unveiled Kaylee and took her hand.

"Come, let's go," he announced loud enough to prick at Newell's ears.

Sophia waved. "Hi, Joanna!" she called.

Newell backed away and grabbed Sophia's hand to stop her from approaching any closer.

He waved to Demetrios and glared at Kaylee.

"See you tomorrow," Newell called.

He meant you as in plural.

Go to hell, Newell, and stay there!

Demetrios shuttled Kaylee away from Newell.

"Forget him. Let's enjoy the rest of the day."

Kaylee and Demetrios walked about twenty-five feet before they turned around to spy on Newell.

He and his entourage had faded into the crowd.

Kaylee let Demetrios place his arm around her shoulders. After putting Newell in his grimy place, Demetrios deserved her loyalty… and, yes…affection.

He led her from Syntagma Square to a bustling, cobblestone pedestrian marketplace full of all kinds of stores. It was an outdoor mall on steroids! Musicians played in the tree-lined streets. And despite Newell's dark surprise, not a cloud dotted the pure blue sky.

Demetrios escorted Kaylee through every high-end store, but Kaylee shook her head in each one.

"You've given me so many clothes and shoes, and makeup. I'm not in need of anything except your company."

There went those eye crinkles again!

"One more store," he said.

He dragged Kaylee into a jewelry store.

"There!" Demetrios pointed to huge ruby ring. "It matches the roses on your dress."

"No, don't."

He wagged his finger at her. "You don't tell me what to do," he teased her. "I've more money than what I could do with. I can't seem to spend it all."

"That's a problem many people wished they had."

"Well, Joanna, it's true. Money can't buy everything. But today it can buy that ring."

"I want that one," Demetrios told the clerk.

He shoved a stack of bills across the jewelry counter.

"Very good, sir."

Demetrios slid the ruby ring on Kaylee's finger.

She wiggled her fingers, admiring his gift. It fit perfectly.

"See? Made just for you!" Demetrios said.

"It's beautiful. Thank you."

The sun bounced off the ring the minute they stepped outside.

"Are you hungry?" Demetrios asked.

"What? Uh…yes."

I'm happy you like the ring."

"Like it? I love it."

Demetrios held her hand while they ambled along to find a cafe.

The ruby stone gleamed more and more. But with each flash, her stomach began to flinch. Demetrios spent a wonderful day with her, and what's more he'd gifted a ring to an imposter. How could she tell him that she wasn't who he thought he had paid for?

Newell warned her to keep her identify secret. But Newell was a liar and a scumbag. She couldn't do this to Demetrios any longer. No matter the consequences, she'd tell him the truth. And then she'd go anywhere but back to Newell. She'd go to the US Embassy. Although, how would she'd explain how she got to Greece without betraying Demetrios, she didn't know.

"This looks like an appetizing place. Let's have a late lunch, shall we?"

"Hmmm."

"We don't have to eat here. We can choose somewhere else. You pick."

"No, here's fine."

"You don't have me convinced."

"Really. It's great. I choose here."

Demetrios peered down at her.

Kaylee averted her gaze.

"Okay. We'll stay here."

Demetrios pulled out Kaylee's chair and then sat opposite her.

A waiter approached.

Kaylee shrugged so Demetrios ordered for her.

"Water for you today," he teased.

"That's fine."

"I'll order us salads."

"That's fine."

"And a whale."

"That's fine."

"What's wrong with you? You just agreed to eat a whale. They don't serve that here," Demetrios chuckled.

"Moussaka," he said to the waiter and pointed to Kaylee and himself.

The waiter nodded and replied in Greek.

Kaylee's mouth went dry.

She licked her lips.

"Something's wrong," Demetrios said.

He guessed right.

Kaylee took off the ruby ring and set it on the table.

Demetrios wrinkled his forehead.

"Why are doing this?" he asked. "I don't understand."

"I can't lie to you anymore. It's not right," she blurted.

There was no going back.

"Lie about what?"

His eyes glommed onto hers.

"I'm not who you think I am."

Completely baffled, Demetrios raised his palms.

"I'm not Joanna. My name is Kaylee. Kaylee Jasinski. Newell tricked you, and he made me fool you too."

"Wait," he said, breathless.

"I don't know who Joanna is. Something must have happened to her. Newell and his henchman, Otto, picked me up on the roadside after my parents died in a car accident on the way home to Miami, where I'm from. I survived, only to be held captive. He sold you the wrong girl."

Demetrios's eyes sank, and he kept shaking his head.

"I'm sorry," she squeaked out.

Kaylee pushed back her seat. Tears spilled from her eyes. Her betrayal was unforgivable. She ran around the waiter who stood frozen while balancing their meals on a tray.

People in the cafe gasped at the scene.

She didn't care who saw her. But her chest grew heavy with guilt for what she'd done to Demetrios.

"Kaylee!" Demetrios yelled.

As fast as she ran, he outran her.

Demetrios grabbed the back of her dress, halting her in her tracks.

"Stop! Kaylee, please stop."

He called her the correct name.

"I'm not angry, but I am confused. Come back. I'll pay for the food, and we go elsewhere to talk."

He still held her by her dress.

Kaylee huffed and puffed while her face grew hotter and hotter.

"It's all right. Come with me?"

She had no choice. People were gathering around them. One yelled for Demetrios to let go of her. Another threatened to call the police.

Kaylee returned willingly with Demetrios before the police could arrive.

All eyes were on them as they returned to the cafe.

Thank God the ruby ring was still there.

"Please sit," Demetrios pleaded.

Kaylee sat. She'd caused him enough embarrassment.

The waiter set their meals and drinks on the table and without a word, he scurried away.

Kaylee and Demetrios stared at each other in silence.

Demetrios interrupted the heaviness surrounding them.

"This makes sense," he said.

What the hell was he talking about?

"When Newell described Joanna to me, I expected a blonde, sexy, virginal girl, that...I'm ashamed to admit to you...that I could enjoy in bed at my pleasure. Then you arrived. I thought you were Joanna. But somehow you were different. You were funny, kind, and smart.

"I can't bring your parents back, and I'm so sorry for everything that happened to you. I would like for you to stay with me. I have great affection for you. But if you want to return to the states, I will arrange it."

"I can't...I won't go back to Newell."

"No. You are free if you stay, and free to go back. Don't concern yourself with Newell. I will take care of him."

"Why?" Kaylee asked.

"Because when someone good comes into your life, you would do anything for that someone. And...I've grown very fond of you. I promise to care for you the way you want to be cared for."

Hot tears trickled down her cheeks. She found what she'd hoped for...someone who could love her.

"I'll stay."

Marco met them where he'd let them out. He exited the limo and opened the back doors.

"How was your afternoon, sir? Lady Joanna?"

Kaylee tossed Demetrios a questioning look.

"Fine, Marco, fine."

"Yes, it was full of surprises," Kaylee said.

"Let it be just between us for now." Demetrios whispered in her ear.

Kaylee nodded. As long Demetrios knew the truth, everyone else would know in time.

"Home, Marco."

Kaylee stretched. Between seeing Newell and unburdening herself to Demetrios, her energy sagged.

Demetrios patted her hand.

"Rest, Kaylee. You're safe."

She'd finally shed Joanna's skin.

Kaylee glanced up at Demetrios to find him gazing at her—definitely not a leer. His eyes softened. His offer for her to live with him was genuine. She had no one left but him. Aunt Lou Ann was only a tale. She didn't know the woman, and the woman wouldn't recognize her. Her life would continue in Greece with Demetrios, and she was more than fine with that and, thank God, so was he. She had a home again.

The limo swayed like a lullaby.

Demetrios shook her gently.

"Wake up. We're home."

Oh, to hear those words. Dad would say the same, but with different meaning. She was a little girl then. Now she was a young woman.

Marco came around and opened the door.

Demetrios took her hand and guided her out into the crisp summer evening. From the green carpet grass to the fountains to the sprawling mansion, all this was hers. She'd wake every morning and gaze out her window at everything Demetrios offered her. She never wanted to leave.

Peter and Vasiliki met them in the grand foyer.

Was that sort of a smile on Vasiliki's face? It was hard to tell. But Peter's grinning face was not.

"Good evening, Mr. Sakalis. Lady Joanna."

"Good evening to you too," Kaylee responded.

Keeping the secret between her and Demetrios was kind of naughty fun. She'd eventually tell Peter. Vasiliki? Nah.

"The cook has prepared a late supper," Peter said.

"Good. We'll be at the table shortly," Demetrios said.

Peter and Vasiliki hurried away.

"Have you an appetite?" Demetrios asked Kaylee.

"I do. I seem to have ruined our lunch."

"Perhaps at first. Then it all worked out, eh?"

Kaylee winked. "Eh."

Demetrios belly laughed.

"Come, let's have a feast."

They dined on seafood fresh from the Aegean.

Everything was fresh and suddenly new.

Kaylee sipped her wine, and Demetrios didn't insist on having her glass refilled. Nor did he offer her ouzo.

All was crystal clear tonight.

After the servers tidied the table, they left Kaylee and Demetrios alone.

Kaylee stood.

Should she?

Yes, she'd take the lead.

Just as Peter had told her. It was her choice.

Kaylee walked ever so slowly toward Demetrios and took his hand.

He instinctively knew, but he hesitated, giving her an out.

She'd made up her mind. She didn't want an out.

She led him up the winding staircase to her third-floor bedroom.

They paused at the door.

"I don't want you to feel obligated," Demetrios said.

"I'm not tonight. I'd like you to stay. I'm inviting you."

"Are you sure? And, yes, there's no need to rush."

"Yes, I'm sure. And there is no need to rush."

He kissed her slow, lips to lips. No tongue.

"Just checking," he said.

Kaylee opened her door and gestured to him to enter.

"Do you need a more formal invitation? Like a written one, perhaps?"

Demetrios grinned. "No. This is fine."

Kaylee began to unzip her sundress, but halfway down the zipper stuck.

"Allow me," Demetrios said.

Kaylee turned her back to him, and he gave the zipper a tug and then a slow pull.

The sundress slid to the floor, leaving Kaylee standing before him in her lacy bra and panties.

Her heart raced and her forehead broke out in a sweat.

She glanced at the bed and dodged under the covers.

Her momentary womanly confidence escaped, and the shaky-kneed girl returned.

Demetrios leaned over and kissed her on the cheek.

"Good night, Kaylee."

Demetrios moved toward the door.

"Wait!" Kaylee called.

He turned.

"Can you just stay with me?"

Demetrios nodded.

"Okay."

He returned to the bed and lay next to her.

"Go to sleep," he whispered.

Kaylee lay beneath the covers. She didn't want to shrink away. It just happened.

She stared at the ceiling and then glanced at Demetrios, who rested beside her.

She crept her hand onto his.

He waited patiently.

Kaylee scooted closer.

Demetrios breathed steadily. No huffing and puffing and grabbing.

She rested her head on his chest.

His heart beat strong but didn't hurry.

Her hand trailed down his belly and no further. That was as far as she'd ever went with Jimmy. But Demetrios was a man and not a fumbling boy. She was now the fumbling girl.

His heartbeat accelerated. She must be doing something right.

Kaylee could feel her sex moistening in preparation for loving. She must be doing something right on her own behalf, too.

Demetrios peeled off his pants and underwear.

She rolled to her back and touched his shoulder to signal that she was more than ready.

Demetrios lowered inside her, inch by inch.

There was no burn. He was artful and most important, considerate.

They moved in tandem.

This was what it really felt like—an easy pleasure and no pain.

He held off until the waves were undeniable and finished with pulsations that elated her. No cringe followed.

He lay next to her, different.

Kaylee snuggled against his sweaty warmth, and her eyelids fluttered until she finally surrendered to sleep.

49

Joanna scanned the rows of airplane seats, her palms sweaty. Her heartbeat throbbed in her chest. She'd never been on an airplane. Before traveling in Lou Ann's or Harry's cars, hitchhiking was her sole mode of travel. After the drama of the passport, she thought she'd calm down, but inching along a narrow aisle caused her stomach to flip, and they hadn't taken off yet.

Lou Ann placed her hands on Joanna's shoulders and guided her along.

"Two more rows," she said from behind.

"Would you like the window seat?" Lou Ann asked her.

Joanna shook her head. No way did she want to see how high the plane flew. The plane's small rectangular windows couldn't compare with wide car and truck windows where she could look out and watch the trees and other vehicles go by. The thought of a bird's-eye view made her more than queasy.

She'd been informed that Harry and Brad required aisle seats.

Joanna sucked a deep breath. Lou Ann needed and should sit next to Harry, because Joanna was the only one not carrying a weapon.

"I changed my mind. I'll take the window seat," Joanna said.

"Okay."

Joanna slid toward the window and sat. Lou Ann sat next to her, and Harry and Brad sat in the aisle seats across from each other.

"I can't swim," Joanna spontaneously said.

Water frightened her. She'd never had even one swimming lesson. She'd only waded ankle-deep in a small creek as a kid. Any other body of water, she'd sink like a stone.

"Air travel is pretty safe," Lou Ann reassured Joanna. "We're not going to crash into the water."

Lou Ann handed her a wrapped stick of gum.

"This will help during take off."

"Thanks."

Flight attendants roamed the aisle, side to side, while checking the passengers' seat belt compliance.

Joanna fastened her seat belt. It was the same as the seat belt in a car, except for the lack of a shoulder harness.

Joanna pointed to her lap belt.

Lou Ann smiled. "It's fine. I'm right here."

"Just don't hold my hand. I'm not a baby."

"Okay."

She was only acting like one.

She'd been tortured and resurrected from the dead. And here she was, frightened to fly on a plane. Insane!

Her brain rounded to Newell and Margo, the last two left to take down. Otto had already gone to hell, where he belonged. Joanna gritted her teeth. She wished the same for those two. If only she had a weapon. Maybe she'd borrow Harry's, or Brad's, or Aunt Lou Ann's. Newell and Margo would soon find out she had come after them with her own army.

The plane rumbled just the way Lou Ann said, and Joanna was an astronaut, pinned to the back of her chair.

Joanna closed her eyes.

The momentary discomfort more than compensated for the bounties on Newell's and Margo's heads.

The plane settled in the clouds.

Harry leaned over Lou Ann and peeked at Joanna, who was gazing out the window. She'd conquered her fear of flying. So much had happened since he'd been called to help investigate Otto's death, and his link to a sex trafficking ring out of Miami and their connections in Greece. Otto had been a known prick, but how the hell did a gynecologist get involved? He shuddered to think of all the women and girls that monster touched in the most heinous way.

Joanna already had a rough life, but thanks to that prick Newell, it became catastrophic.

What must be going through her head on the way to Greece?

Harry opened his briefcase and removed the folder containing photographs of wealthy Greek men. Perhaps Joanna had overheard the

Greek man's name who paid for her.

He nudged Lou Ann.

"Can I trade places with you briefly? I need to show some photos of Greek men to her."

Lou Ann nodded, and she and Harry switched places.

Harry tapped Joanna on the shoulder.

"Harry!"

"Yeah, I switched places with Lou Ann for a bit. We left Miami in such a rush that I didn't have time to sit with you and have you look at some photos I have."

"Photos? What kind of photos?"

Her voice went up an octave.

"It's all right. You're safe. But I need to see if you can identify the Greek."

"I only knew him as the Greek."

"Okay. Just look at the photos. It might stir a memory. Perhaps Newell, Margo, or even Otto may have slipped up and said his name. It's worth a try. Will you help me?"

"I don't think I can help, but let me see them."

Harry slid one photo after another over to Joanna's tray and observed her for an eye twitch or a lingering study.

She hesitated at one, which he marked, and then watched her further.

Joanna shuffled through the remaining ones and stopped at the last. Was she stopping at that one because it was the last one, or because she'd reacted to it?

Joanna stared at the photo.

"Sak....sak...Something sak."

There was only one S-A-K in the file—Demetrios Sakalis.

Harry tapped into his security laptop.

Demetrios Sakalis resided among other wealthy Greeks in Ekalis.

A lead!

50

Kaylee stretched naked under the covers. The musky scent mixed with his aftershave permeated the sheets. She breathed in their night together and grinned.

She rolled over to touch him, but her hand dented an empty pillow.

Why? Did she misunderstand his intentions?

Kaylee bolted upright to find Demetrios standing next to her bed, dressed.

"Good morning, my sweet. I didn't want to wake you." Before she could interrupt, he continued, "I need to attend to an urgent matter. I'll see you at breakfast."

He paused. He must have noticed her dejected face. She was a good dancer, but a lousy actress.

"Oh, no. It's not you. I'm not leaving you to leave, trust me. I'll explain it all to you later."

Demetrios hurried out the bedroom and closed the door.

For someone who wasn't leaving her, he just left.

Kaylee pouted, but rose, and went to take a long, luxurious shower. By the time she was finished and dressed, hopefully Demetrios would have finished taking care of his emergency, and then she'd make him keep his promise to divulge the reason he scurried away.

Kaylee rushed through her morning preparations. For every minute that passed, her restlessness grew tenfold. What was he hiding from her?

Kaylee slipped into a fuchsia tank dress and stepped into a pair bejeweled thong sandals. With her hair still damp, she trotted down the spiral staircase that led to the dining room. She'd committed a mini-map of the mansion to memory, and in time she'd expand her pathways. She accelerated her footsteps to reach her final destination—at the breakfast table with Demetrios.

She hadn't sat yet when Demetrios entered the room through another mysterious door. Where did that door lead to? She'd find out later. More important, she needed to know what urgent situation kept him from her this morning.

"Ah, I'm on time," Demetrios said with a grin.

Why is he smiling? Why is he so happy?

"I'm on time, too, to discover why you rushed away. You promised to tell me." Kaylee propped her hands to her hips. "So, tell me," she demanded.

"I actually like that you're blunt."

Kaylee fiddled with the ruby ring on her finger.

"Okay. Sit. I'll tell you over breakfast."

Servers rushed in to serve fried eggs and potatoes, coffee, and orange juice.

She thought they'd never leave.

"Well?"

Demetrios picked up his fork and knife.

"Well…I stopped the wired payment to Newell. You're a free woman."

Kaylee's silver cutlery clanged on the porcelain plate.

She opened her mouth, but the words stuck to her tongue.

"Shall we eat now?"

"Uh…yes."

Her heart throbbed against dress.

Demetrios rested his chin between his thumb and index finger and grinned.

"Yes, I'm excited, too!"

Newell slammed his coffee cup down on the table. Ceramic shards exploded in every direction, and after splashing on his shirt front, the puddle of coffee snaked to the table's edge and then dripped like a leaky faucet to the floor.

"Fuck!" he screamed.

Sophia rushed to his side.

"What's the matter with you?"

Gerald raised his hand, and Sophia quickly—and wisely— ducked.

"Move!" he yelled at her.

"Are you losing your mind?" Margo called.

"Yes! Fucking Demetrios just put a hold on the wired payment. He's fucked me over again!"

Sophia collected the shards and sopped up the spilled coffee.

"We should have servants do this! But no!"

His face was on fire and his neck pulsed.

"I got it," Sophia soothed. "I don't mind. And this house is gorgeous."

Gerald snorted. "Gorgeous? It's a shack!"

"Get ahold of yourself, Gerald," Margo said. "It's probably an error. Did you ever consider that he thought he paid too little and a larger sum is coming? After all, Kaylee is more refined than Joanna could ever be, and maybe he was so pleasantly surprised that he'd shell out a lot more."

Gerald glared at Margo. "What is this? Fucking Disney? You went soft on her. I'm going over there and repossess her!"

Sophia's eyes went wide.

"Did you really think she was my niece?"

"Who's Kathy? I thought her name was Joanna."

"It's Kaylee! Not Kathy! God! I don't have time to explain this to you. As soon as I get Kaylee, we're going back to Miami."

"How?" Sophia asked.

"A regular fucking airplane. Is-that-all-right-with-you?"

"It's fine," Sophia said. "We should all go home."

Demetrios was going to fuck him over with the fantasy clinic, too.

"Yes, we'll go home once I get Kaylee back!"

51

Lou Ann wiggled in her seat. Their business class seats not only offered plenty of leg room, but also blessed reclining space. Harry, Brad, and she had taken turns resting during the twelve-hour flight. One never knew whether someone would accost them and snatch away their firearms.

Lou Ann roused Joanna, who'd nodded off for the past few hours.

"Huh?" Joanna mumbled.

"We're arriving in Athens."

Joanna stirred and her eyes popped alert.

They were all on high alert now.

The captain announced their arrival in Athens.

The plane jiggled and rumbled until it smoothed to a taxi.

Lou Ann looked at Joanna, who had a death grip on her seat's armrests.

Screw the gum. It was too late, and they'd be the first to be escorted off the aircraft and then to a specially designated area for them at customs.

Fatigued passengers tossed them evil eyes while the flight attend held the passengers back to give them priority exit.

"We're not very popular," Joanna said.

"They're not about to risk their lives," Lou Ann whispered.

Joanna's shoulders quivered.

This wasn't going to go down well.

Sandwiched between Lou Ann and Harry, Joanna inched along the plane's aisle to the exit. Once she stepped out of the protection of the plane, she'd have to follow to the letter all of Lou Ann's and Harry's instructions to not only survive, but to arrest Newell and Margo.

The horrified looks on their faces when they saw she was alive would be worth the risk.

Harry, Lou Ann, and Brad had provided the documents regarding their business in Greece to the customs authorities, who cleared them.

Joanna stood alone on the other side of customs.

Her heart smacked in her chest.

They're not going to let me through. I'll be stranded in a foreign country alone. What if they arrest me?

The customs agent let her through.

She'd made it to Greece, but, thank God, not in the way she was originally to arrive.

She'd seen the photo of the presumed Greek. He didn't look like a monster, but neither did Newell—at first.

Harry and Lou Ann rushed her along behind Brad toward the sign, "Ground Transportation" printed in a weird alphabet with English below it.

She knew where their firearms were hidden, and if necessary, they could take down anyone blocking their trek if necessary. She'd be counting on that during their whole time in Greece.

A black car with tinted windows approached.

What will Kaylee look like? Will she remember me? Will she forgive me for fading out of her life?

Harry scanned the surroundings while he pushed Joanna and then let her into the car and then Harry and Brad jumped inside.

Soon they'd be dropped off at the outskirts of Ekalis and creep into position around Sakalis's mansion. It could end as a fruitless mission.

But Sakalis wasn't their intended target. Newell and Margo were. And the ultimate mission was to find and free Kaylee and all the others Newell trafficked. If Newell got a whiff of their arrival, he'd whisk Kaylee to another location. A lump lodged in the back of LouAnn's throat. They might never find Kaylee. That was an ugly fact.

Kaylee kissed Demetrios after breakfast.

"It's such a lovely morning. Let's go for a walk around the grounds," she said.

Demetrios frowned, looking distracted.

"You go, my angel. I need to stay here and finish business. I'll join you in a bit."

His face relaxed.

"Peter!" he called.

Peter immediately responded to Demetrios's summons.

"Yes?"

"Please take Lady Joanna for a walk through the rear gardens."

He gestured for Peter to come closer and whispered something in Greek to him.

Peter nodded.

Kaylee bounced her stare from Demetrios to Peter and back to Demetrios.

"What's going on? No offense, Peter, but I can stroll by myself. I promise not to venture far."

"I know you'll not stray far, but for now I want Peter by your side. I'll join you soon."

Peter took her hand. "Come, Lady Joanna. Let's go."

Kaylee went willingly with Peter, but her brain circled. She trusted Peter. He was her friend. But why couldn't she take a leisurely stroll by herself?

Peter led her beyond the pool and into a summer thick garden.

She halted and stared at the bulge at Peter's back. He had a pistol!

"Why do you have that!"

"For your protection."

"Why?!"

"Some people with cameras were seen coming up the road. Tourists. But you never know. And..."

Peter hesitated. It wasn't about the tourists.

Someone else had tripped the security system.

"Newell," Kaylee gasped.

"Demetrios is handling the situation. He only wants you stay far away and hidden among the gardens with me until the man is gone."

"Why is he here?!" Kaylee insisted.

"I do not know. But I have my orders to protect you."

Peter's walkie talkie squealed, and an urgent Greek voice came across it.

Peter grabbed Kaylee's hand and dragged her with him under a bush.

They'd made it to within yards of Sakalis's mansion.

Lou Ann peered through her binoculars and recognized Newell's face.

"Shit! It's Newell in that car," she hissed.

She signaled to Harry and Brad, who were ditching the fake cameras into roadside shrubbery.

She pointed to the car slowing while it approached the front gate.

Lou Ann handed Joanna the binoculars.

"Is that other person Margo?" she whispered to Joanna.

Joanna peered into the binoculars.

"Yes," she rasped.

"Who's the other woman in the car?" Lou Ann asked.

"I don't know. I've never seen her before."

Harry and Brad remained crouched while they duck-walked and back to Lou Ann and Joanna.

Lou Ann handed Harry the binoculars.

Harry peered through them.

"That's Newell and Sophia Pavlis. I don't know who the other woman is."

Joanna identified her as Margo.

"Got'em!" Harry whispered. "Lou, take the back. Brad and I will take the front. Joanna, go down the road and stay there. That's an order."

Lou Ann shoved Joanna back.

"Go!" she ordered.

Lou Ann watched Joanna until she was out of sight and then proceeded to the rear of the property.

The gates buzzed open, and Newell drove through them while Harry and Brad rolled past the gates before they clicked shut.

Harry and Brad hit the ground and lay in the thick grass watching Newell's car circle the fountains and continue on without stopping, as though he hadn't even noticed them.

Harry and Brad parted in different directions.

They'd wait there and rush to surround Newell and Margo when they eventually got out of the car.

Lou Ann sprinted along the side of the spiked black iron fence. If she'd not been recently deemed fit for her sheriff's position, she would've collapsed not even halfway to the rear of the massive property.

She filled her lungs in between her strides and slowly exhaled to fill them again.

She jogged in place while assessing the best place to climb over and onto Sakalis's property.

The property was massive and she estimated it would take Harry and Brad about a mile to approach the front entrance, all while undercover.

Meanwhile she'd make better time on her own.

Lou Ann marked the spot between two trees that would help conceal her jump onto the grounds.

She took a running start and leaped.

Ow! Shit!

The top of iron fence dug mercilessly into her palms. She pushed past the pain and pulled herself up to where she could swing a leg over. Then another leg.

Lou Ann toppled to the grassy ground.

She rolled to a stance and froze. No footsteps. No dogs. No guns cocked.

Lou Ann crouched and quietly proceeded, following a garden path.

A crunching came from under a bush, and then a girl ran toward her.

Lou Ann targeted the girl. Her heart pounded in her ears.

It's her!

"Kaylee!" Lou Ann called, and ran with her gun toward her niece.

"Kaylee!" she called again.

A man leaped from the bush, blindsiding her, and fired at her.

Her thigh burned. He'd grazed her leg from a distance.

Lou Ann limped. Her eyes went straight to his hand and saw he had a pistol. She trained her gun at him and returned fire.

The man toppled to the ground.

She'd hit him.

Kaylee ran back to the man.

"Fucking, Margo! I'm going to kill you!"

What?

Kaylee grabbed the pistol from the man and aimed it at Lou Ann.

Shit! She thinks I'm Margo!

"Stop, Kaylee! I'm Lou Ann, your aunt!"

"You've hurt my friend!" Kaylee screamed at the woman who claimed she was her long-lost aunt. What the hell was she doing in Greece?

Shit! She'd somehow tracked her here. But she couldn't waste a second to find out. She wasn't going anywhere but to Demetrios. Newell and Margo had surely arrived.

She didn't care that Demetrios told her he'd take care of them. She had her own way of taking care of them! They weren't going to leave alive. She'd take them out for good this time, like she did Otto!

But first she needed to attend to Peter.

She knelt at Peter's side.

"Don't step any closer!" she hissed at the woman—whom she didn't believe was her aunt.

"Peter! Peter! Talk to me!"

Fuck!

Blood dripped from Peter's shoulder.

Peter winced. "I'm all right. Run, Kaylee! Run."

"Kaylee?"

"I know. Demetrios told me. Run before Newell gets you."

"I'm not afraid of Newell."

"Kaylee, I'm here to arrest Newell," Lou Ann said.

"You'll have to arrest him dead."

"No. He can lead us to others like you and Joanna."

Joanna? Where the fuck was she?

Joanna may have temporarily ruined her life, but in the end she'd done her a grand favor.

The woman slowly approached.

"Let me help him."

"You've done enough!" Kaylee snapped.

"It's okay, Lady Kaylee. The woman isn't an enemy. I shot first. I hurt her too."

Kaylee's mind flashed red alert.

She ripped the strap off of her dress and used it as a tourniquet to stem the blood spurting from Peter's wound. The fuchsia strap turned bright red.

"We need to make a bigger tourniquet," the woman said. "If you allow me closer, I can help. And then we need to get to Newell."

"Okay," Kaylee said.

She would do anything for Peter.

The woman ripped off her jacket and used the sleeve to reinforce Peter's injured shoulder.

"That should hold him until we can get help," Lou Ann said.

The woman looked at Peter.

"I'm so sorry."

"You had the right. I shot at you. I thought you were someone else."

"That's seems to be the theme here," the woman said.

Kaylee assessed Peter's wound. The bleeding had stemmed.

"Go," Peter said. "I'll be all right here. Kaylee, take my pistol. Protect yourself. Newell is up to no good."

Kaylee knelt at Peter's side. "I'll be back for you! I promise!"

"I know you will."

Kaylee waved Peter's pistol in the air.

"Let's go!"

"Do you know how to use that?" the woman asked.

"No, but I'm a quick study. I killed Otto, and I have no qualms about taking out Newell and Margo."

Kaylee glanced at the woman who, now she thought of it, looked strangely like her father.

"Put your eyeballs back in your head! I've survived this far without you!" Kaylee snapped.

"Yes, you have," her "so called" aunt replied.

Joanna paced along the road. Goose bumps popped out all over her arms and shoulders.

Something was wrong. Harry and Lou Ann had been gone too long.

What if they were trapped inside that mansion…with Newell?

She'd go after them.

She wasn't about to let anything happen to them. They were her family.

Joanna sprinted up hill to the mansion's gate.

No one was going to open that gate for her. She'd have to jump over that iron fence.

She'd jumped higher fences before. Those spikes on the top were nothing compared to barbs she'd hurdled. Her back had the scars to show for it.

Joanna rounded to the side and spotted a tree in the perfect position.

She climbed the tree and leaped onto a thick branch. Then, hand over hand, she maneuvered to the end of the branch. She'd almost made it to the end when it popped and snapped.

Joanna swung her legs forward, arched her back, and sailed into the air, seemingly in slow motion. Her heart flailed in her chest. She winced, ready to fall short and land on those spikes. But she landed on her back on the other side of the fence. The force knocked the wind out of her, and she gasped and gasped for air to fill her lungs until she finally was able to breathe.

She looked up at split branch. She made it just in time. It was an omen.

Joanna inhaled and ran along close to the fence, hoping upon hope that she'd evaded security video.

Rustling coming from a distance stopped her in her tracks. She flopped onto her belly and crawled under a manicured bush.

She held her breath and waited to be discovered.

Joanna's eyes popped wide open.

Lou Ann and a girl who looked just like her ran across the grounds and headed toward the mansion, and they had guns!

52

"Wait in the car!" Newell growled at Margo and Sophia.

He grabbed his briefcase and slammed the rental car door because his Mercedes was on some fucking ship…that is if it ever left Miami. He wouldn't lower himself to take a taxi to Demetrios's mansion.

He wasn't leaving without the money Demetrios owed him, or without that bitch, Kaylee.

He rued the day he picked her up off the roadside.

She'd been nothing but trouble.

He'd sell her cheap. She deserved it!

Gerald stomped up the five wide rounded marble stairs to the white double front doors and raised his fist to pound on them, but the doors opened before he had the seething pleasure.

A man in a black and white suit blocked Gerald's entrance.

Gerald gripped the handles of his briefcase and glared at the butler.

"I'm here to see Demetrios Sakalis."

"One moment, please."

Gerald shoved the butler.

"No! Not one moment. Now!"

"You may go, Stavros," Demetrios said while he stood straight-shouldered in the grand foyer.

"Ah, Dr. Newell. I didn't expect you today, but please come in."

The pitter-patter of high heels on marble came from behind Gerald.

He pressed his lips tight and grew hotter beneath his skin.

Shit! Sophia!

"Who is this lovely lady? Demetrios asked, with a satisfied grin on his face.

"This is my lady, Sophia," Gerald said.

He might as well show her off since he couldn't get rid of her at this point.

"I told you to wait for me, *dear*."

Sophia offered her hand to Demetrios.

"I couldn't contain myself. I simply had to take a peek at the mansion from the inside."

Demetrios kissed the back of Sophia's hand, which made her giggle.

He'd deal with her later. And after he was through punishing Sophia, he would further deal with Margo, who apparently couldn't control anyone. He'd ditch Margo in Miami the way he ditched Otto.

Demetrios clapped and Stavros reappeared.

"Please take Lady Sophia to the sitting room while Dr. Newell and I discuss business." Demetrios tossed Sophia a smile. "I'll give you a tour after our meeting."

"That will be wonderful," Sophia gushed.

"Follow me into my office, Dr. Newell."

Gerald inhaled as deeply as he exhaled while he tailed Demetrios.

Demetrios closed the mahogany doors to the office, sealing Gerald and himself inside.

"Please, have a seat."

Gerald and Demetrios's eyes met and clashed.

"I prefer to stand," Gerald said.

"As you wish."

Demetrios widened his stance.

"You may speak freely here, Dr. Newell."

"I'll come straight to the point. You cancelled the wired money due me, and you've also cancelled our meeting regarding Joanna. I find that dishonest and disrespectful. I demand full payment, and furthermore, I demand Joanna's return."

Demetrios burst out laughing.

"Dishonest? You, my friend, are the dishonest one. You didn't bring me Joanna. Thank God, you brought me Kaylee. Which brings me to the second point. I have great affection for Kaylee as she has for me. That is why I cancelled the wire. I am more than delighted that Kaylee will stay with me permanently in a committed relationship."

Demetrios paced. "But I'll tell you what I'm going to do. I'll pay you half the amount for your trouble and fly you and your associate, Margo, and your paramour Sophia, in grand style back to Miami."

"Oh, no! You owe me the full amount, plus Kaylee, and plus reimbursement for the clinic, which I now know is a scam."

"It wasn't a scam. The clinic exists, and the remodeling continues. But given the level of distrust that has unfortunately developed between us, I can no longer have you as a physician there. You may return to your lucrative practice."

"And finally, the third point. You will never touch—or torture—Kaylee ever again." Demetrios glared at Gerald. "She limps to this day. Not to mention the psychological scars you inflicted upon her."

"Limps? Kaylee seemed to have left out how she stabbed an associate of mine's eyeball, cracked Margo over the head, and nearly killed me. You have no idea who you've professed your affection for. She's a killer."

"Get out!" Demetrios bellowed as he stomped toward the office doors..

Gerald flipped open his briefcase and grabbed his gun.

"Backstabber!" Gerald yelled as he shot Demetrios in back.

"Shot fired!" Lou Ann called.

Lou Ann's adrenaline masked the pain in her thigh, but she struggled to keep pace with Kaylee, who continued sprinting toward the mansion.

Was it Harry? God, please no!

Kaylee leapt over stairs while Lou Ann skipped them two at a time.

Kaylee yelled, "Yah!"

It was her war cry.

Kaylee focused her eyes straight on the back entrance and bolted through it.

May it be Newell!

Lou Ann tailed close behind her, her erratic breathing swirling in Kaylee's ears.

She'd finish Newell off!

No one was going to stop her!

She didn't care if she had to go prison for the rest of her life. It would be well worth it—and then some.

Kaylee panted while she maneuvered through the mansion's maze.

She'd targeted the grand foyer because that's where Newell would enter.

She'd intercept him there.

Kaylee ran into the main foyer.

Her heart ripped in two.

Demetrios lay bloody and motionless on his stomach, sprawled between his office doorway and the foyer, blood seeping through the back of his shirt.

Newell pointed his gun at her.

"Kaylee, we meet again."

"You fuck!" Kaylee screamed.

She squeezed Peter's pistol's trigger over and over again, and her bullets mixed in with the hail of gunfire.

Gerald managed to fire two shots that hit the chandelier above while he crumpled to the ground in a bloody, riddled mess.

Harry grabbed Lou Ann and Kaylee and pulled them to the corner of the grand foyer before jumping over them while Brad leaped over Sophia, who still hadn't stopped screaming.

The chandelier crashed to the marble floor, pelting them with a rain of crystals.

Dead silence followed.

"Is everyone all right?" Harry called.

Kaylee shoved Harry off her and ran over the cracked crystals to where Demetrios lay.

"Demetrios! Demetrios!" she cried.

She collapsed on top of him, sobbing.

"Kaylee, my sweet angel," he rasped between agonized breaths. "I-love-you.-All-that-I have-is-yours."

Kaylee kissed his lips and clutched his hand. And then he drew his last breath.

Holy shit! Something badder then bad had gone down.

She was getting the fuck out of here.

No way was Gerald getting out of there.

She'd waited long enough.

She'd go back to the house, get her passport, get the hell out of Greece, and go it alone now that Otto and surely Gerald were out of her way.

Screw Sophia. She wasn't the one who brought her along. The slut could find her own way back. It wasn't Margo's problem.

Margo had her hand on the back door handle when a fist smashed the window, and—crap upon crap—that fist belonged to Joanna, who snorted like a mad bull through the cracked glass.

Un-fucking- believable!

How's that possible?

Newell and Otto had dumped her body and returned with that hellion, Kaylee.

Before Margo could lock her door, Joanna ripped it open and dragged Margo out of the car by her hair.

For a dead girl, she had the strength of five men.

Joanna pinned her to the grass.

"Guess who?" she hissed in Margo's face. "Now it's your turn to be dead."

The first blow to her cheek knocked her teeth loose in her mouth.

Stars flickered in front of her eyes.

Harry escorted Lou Ann and Brad, and Sophia out of the mansion's doors.

He'd left Kaylee to remain with Demetrios.

"Fuck! Joanna!"

Shit! She'd killed Margo.

Harry ran to Joanna and pulled her off of Margo.

"What did you do?"

"I did what was coming to her."

Harry leaned over the battered woman—who was still breathing.

"Brad!" he yelled.

Brad left Sophia to Lou Ann and raced over to Harry and Joanna.

"Oh, fuck!"

"Yeah, that's what I said."

Harry and Brad stared at each other.

They'd dealt with worse. It was defensible, given what the woman had done to so many girls before Joanna and Kaylee.

A butler stumbled out of the mansion carrying a blanket.

With his eyes wide with shock, he handed the blanket to Harry, who covered Margo while sirens blared closer.

53

Shit! They left Peter in the garden.

Lou Ann had no idea how to get to that garden.

"Sir! Sir! Peter's in the garden injured. I need to get back to him," she called to the butler.

"Yes. I take you there.'

"Sophia, stay with Sheriff Jarett. I'll be right back."

Sophia stared straight ahead and didn't respond.

"Go," Brad said. "I'll take care of her until the ambulances and police arrive."

Lou Ann nodded and followed the butler to the rear garden.

Peter lay under a bush.

"Is it over?" he asked.

Lou Ann squatted next to him.

"Yes."

"Mr. Sakalis?"

Lou Ann shook her head. "I'm so sorry."

"Oh, noooo," Peter cried. "I go to him. I need to see him. Uh…uh. Lady Kaylee?"

"She survived."

"Thanks, God." Peter struggled to his feet, saying, "I can walk."

Lou Ann, Peter, and the butler arrived on the front lawn of the mansion to find the police and rescue crews had arrived.

Kaylee walked alongside the stretcher carrying Demetrios's body.

"Lady Kaylee!" Peter called.

She opened her arms and he ran into them.

Lou Ann wiped away her tears while she watched Kaylee and Peter's sorrowful embrace.

Kaylee kissed Demetrios's blue lips and Peter embraced him.

"Vasiliki!" Kaylee called.

The elderly woman wept and huddled with Kaylee and Peter.

Lou Ann didn't know Kaylee, but it hurt to know despite all the tragedy and torture she must have endured, she'd finally found someone who truly loved her, only to loose him under tragic circumstances.

No matter what the future held for Lou Ann and Kaylee and Joanna, she couldn't fix what happened to them.

No one could.

54

Kaylee hugged Peter, Vasiliki, and Stavros.

All the servants lined the front lawn of Demetrios's mansion, which she'd inherited. That's why he went into his office on that day before breakfast. He'd willed his mansion to her.

His nephew Adam would surely contest the will, so she'd wait until the court and lawyers finalized everything.

But she would return. Greece was her home. Not Miami. She'd sell that house, and had no intention of living in Clearwater with an aunt she no longer craved to know.

Lou Ann, Harry the Special Agent, and Joanna, her unwitting alter ego, waited for her in the car.

"Goodbye my family," she called.

"Peter, Vasiliki, please take care of everyone in my absence."

"We will, Lady Kaylee. This is not goodbye. It is until we see each other again."

Kaylee blew them a kiss.

"Until then."

Lou Ann and Harry buckled their seat belts.

"Do you think it was a good idea to put them next to each other? It's a long flight home and they haven't said one word to each other so far."

"Yes, I think it's the right thing. They share a horror that we can never understand. They'll connect, but it will take time. They've both been badly traumatized."

"Kaylee doesn't acknowledge me. I've failed her twice."

"No you didn't. You freed her."

"Did I? I freed Joanna. But I've only recaptured Kaylee."

Harry squeezed her hand.

"I'll be there the whole way with you, Joanna, and Kaylee."

Lou Ann rested her head on Harry's shoulder.

"I'd like that. I need that." Then she whispered, "I need you."

Harry pulled Lou Ann's chin up and kissed her.

"I love you, too."

The jet rumbled until it settled high in the blue sky.

"Do you feel sorry for her?" Kaylee asked.

"Shhh. Don't say it so loud," Joanna said. "Sophia's only two seats away. And yes, I feel for her. Newell lied to her. You and I know he could be very charismatic. She trusted him as we once did. But he's dead and rotting in hell."

"I agree. She's a lost soul," Kaylee said.

Kaylee twisted the ruby ring on her finger.

"Did you love him? Mr. Sakalis, I mean?" Joanna asked.

"Yes, it was quick, and furious, and heaven rolled into one. Newell betrayed him, but I confessed to him who I really was just as you confessed your true identity to Lou Ann and Harry."

"I'm glad they found you so I can move on now."

"What? You're not going anywhere. You have a family now."

"So do you."

Kaylee shook her head.

"I lost one family to find another."

Kaylee kissed the ruby stone and pressed her ring finger to her heart.

She gazed out the plane's window at the only home she'd ever know.

THE END

www.ingramcontent.com/pod-product-compliance
Lightning Source LLC
Chambersburg PA
CBHW030420310726
48979CB00009B/1545/J

* 9 7 9 8 2 1 8 0 4 5 3 8 8 *